THE LONE WOLF

Burt Wulff, after two years i _____ Vietnam, had been entitled to something nice for his trouble, so they had made him a narco. A New York City narcotics cop, with the freedom and the plainclothes and the graft money... but something had happened to this Wulff overseas: he had gone crazy. He had become a man of integrity. Eventually he tried to bust an informant, and they knew they would have to do something about this wild man...

When Wulff saw his fiancée OD'd out on the floor, he thought that he might go mad on the spot but quite strangely he did not. Wulff went straight home and discarded everything except his gun and a spare. They were hardly the equipment he would need but they were a beginning. By mid-summer, he had the beginnings of an operation in his mind. The rest he would have to play by ear. Wulff hit the streets to kill a lot of people.

First strike, the drug network in New York... and then San Francisco. He is beyond forgiveness or vengeance now. He is the Lone Wolf.

"Far far ahead of his time in both subject matter and style... Fans of Richard Stark, Andrew Vachss or Donald Goines should dive in without hesitation."
—Robert C. Giordano

THE LONE WOLF #1:
NIGHT RAIDER

....

THE LONE WOLF #2:
BAY PROWLER

....

by Barry N. Malzberg

**STARK
HOUSE**

Stark House Press • Eureka California

NIGHT RAIDER / BAY PROWLER

Published by Stark House Press
1315 H Street
Eureka, CA 95501, USA
griffinskye3@sbcglobal.net
www.starkhousepress.com

ISBN-13: 978-1-951473-60-0

Book design by Mark Shepard, shepgraphics.com
Cover design by Jeff Vorzimmer, ¡caliente!design, Austin, Texas

First Stark House Press Edition: March 2022

Prologue: The Passage of the Light

By Barry N. Malzberg

By the beginning of the 1970's, that decade of systematic disintegration it seemed clear that the country was insane, going insane, was enacting what had once been a subterranean madness, take your pick at the windows, call it what you will, the signs were everywhere. To Mailer the definitive descent (or ascent if you were an advocate of the psychiatrist Thomas Szasz) began or at least became definitive in the wardrobe of a Dallas police station. It was there, on November 24, 1963, that Jack Ruby entered unmolested that bastion of law and order, entered without having been checked in any way (he was a common visitor there, the cops liked him), brandished a pistol and killed Lee Harvey Oswald. Oswald had been in the process of being escorted that Sunday, two days after the assassination of the President, to either an indictment or a psychiatric evaluation or perhaps both, this was never quite clear to the majority of observers who undisciplined swarmed about or into the station and he called out to them "I didn't do it, I'm the patsy here," a close enough version of a disputed cry just before Ruby shot him dead. The escort of law became an emergency crew dragging the dying Oswald to the same hospital where JFK had been taken and there he exited gracelessly into a paragon history of myth, confusion, deceit, lies, connivance, suspicion, effectuation unparalleled in the history of the nation. Synchronically, the television image shifted to the simultaneous catafalque of the Capitol lobby in which the corpse of the President was about to lie in State.

That was meant to be the big, the certain, the encompassing ceremony on this Sunday, all decked with flowers, portentous observation by commentators, the colors of the nation in black and white prepared to drift through the proper dignity to proper tragedy. But Ruby had turned into a clown act, he was the one clown in the overstuffed car who tumbled into the arena, ready to shoot and kill. The necessary celebrity of State death had become in a single bullet's placement an absurdity of indecipherable meaning. It was with Ruby's bullet that all of the hidden life and obsession of the Union seemed to be given finality. Vigilantism had conquered vigilantism and turned it into a purposelessness which the damaged nation would be contending limitlessly. Surely it would drive Mailer mad; the ultimate journalist he was attuned to the moment. Surely it would drive all of us ostensibly at or near the age of reason to refraction of a clown's purposeful escort to hell. As the cops were taking Oswald toward the law's own fearful judgment, Ruby had made them and all of us part of a squirreling canvas of Bosch characters, stampeding toward a light they could no longer see.

The nation had gone mad but part of its genius lay deep in a resourcefulness which had blasted through rocks and stone and created the Trail of Tears, the nation had gone mad but the genius of that resourcefulness had always been its ability to capitalize and Oswald's history, judgment, motive, purpose, provenance became the Great American Mystery suppling in its location in that genre the Great American Novel. It lay like a whale, like Ballard's Drowned Giant, on the beach of history, belched by the waters of circumstance and through all the ensuing decades the madness became both referendum and exploit, to be observed and utilized in a thousand ways. Some of them were obvious at once... this apostasy had occurred in a *police station*. Some would be obvious later... JFK became a free-floating icon, his fate and despair a paradigm for the Trail of Tears. And some would not be obvious, not even unto this moment, fifty-eight years after the clown car burst open. Almost all of the principals and observers are gone, those who remain had elected to tell their tales long ago or had refused them. All that we had now was consequence and that was a terrible burden to place upon a nation that was yet to struggle with a true history.

Not to generalize or to exacerbate the madness but it was into this maelstrom that the first novels of Don Pendelton's *Executioner* were dropped like guppies into a racing stream. In the land of consequence, those guppies were less explanation than metaphor. Mack Bolan would avenge us. Mack Bolan would bring toward the ugliness of corruption and the hysteria of the clown car some true realization. *Executioner* was born and sent upon the land. On the racks of fifty thousand book and candy stores, came the true, no longer unwritten history of the country's long and madly sacrosanct traipse through hell.

January 2022
New Jersey

Some Notes on the Lone Wolf

By Barry N. Malzberg

Don Pendleton's Executioner series started as a one-shot idea at Pinnacle Books in 1969. By 1972 George Ernsberger, my editor at Berkley, called it "the phenomenon of the age." Eventually Pendleton wrote 70 of the books himself and the series continues today ghosted by other writers. Mack Bolan's continuing *War Against the Mafia* (the working title of that first book) had sold wildly from the outset and less than three years later, when Pendleton and Scott Meredith had threatened to take the series from a grim and obdurate Pinnacle, New American Library had offered $250,000 for the next four books in the series. Pendleton stayed at Pinnacle—the publisher faced a lawsuit for misappropriated royalties and essentially had to match the NAL offer to hold on—but the level established by the properties could not fail to have inflamed every mass market paperback publisher in New York.

A few imitative series had been launched by Pinnacle itself—most notably The Butcher whose premise and protagonist were a close if even more sadomasochistic version of Pendleton's Mack Bolan. It was Bolan who had gone out alone to avenge his family incinerated in a Mafia war while Bolan was fighting Commies in Southeast Asia. Dell Books launched The Inquisitor, a series of books on the redemptive odyssey of Simon Quinn (by a then-unknown William Martin Smith, who under a somewhat different name was to become famous in the next decade), Pocket Books and Avon began series the provenance of which is at the moment unrecollected and Ernsberger at Berkley, under some pressure from his publisher, Stephen Conlan, was ready to start his own series.

What he needed in January 1973 was someone who could produce 10 books within less than a year and although my credentials as a Pendleton-imitator were certainly questionable (they were in fact nonexistent), there was no question but that Ernsberger had found one of the few writers close at hand who clearly could produce at that frenetic level. In 1972 I had written nine novels, in 1971 a dozen, in 1970 fourteen; ten books that quickly were not an overwhelming assignment. What he wanted was a series about a law enforcement guy, say maybe an ex-New York City cop, thrown off the force for one or another perceived disgrace, who would declare war upon the drug trade. The cop could be a military veteran with (like Bolan) a good command of ordnance; it wouldn't hurt if he had a black sidekick either still on or just off the force so that they could get some *Defiant Ones* byplay going in those pre-Eddie Murphy days, and the violence was to be hyped up to Executioner level as the protagonist, after an initial festive in New York, took his mission throughout the States and maybe overseas. Ten novels, $27,500 total advance with (it is this which caught my total attention) 25% of it payable upon signature of the contract. Only a brief outline would be necessary and the tenth book was due to be delivered on or before 10/1/73.

I had never read a Pendleton novel in my life.

Hey, no problem; $6750 for a five-page outline at a time when I perceived my nascent career to be in a recession-induced collapse cleaved away scruple and, for that matter, terror. I read Executioner #7, which struck me as pretty bad, mechanical, and lifeless (like most debased category fiction it depended upon the automatic responses upon the reader, did not create characters and an ambiance of its own), wrote the usual promise-them-a-partridge-in-a-pear-tree outline, signed the contracts and began the series on 1/16/73. The third of the novels was delivered on 2/14/73.

Incontestably I could have delivered the entire series by May (the early plan was for Berkley to bring out the first three novels at once, then publish one a month thereafter) but George Ernsberger asked me to stop after *Boston Avenger* and wait for further word. There was a problem, it seemed. In the first place, I had given my protagonist, Wulff Conlan, a name uncomfortably close to that of the publisher whose name at the time I had not even known, and in the second place Conlan's victims, unlike Mack Bolan's, were real people with real viewpoints who seemed to undergo real pain when they were killed which was quite frequently. Would this kind of stuff—real pain as opposed to cartoon death that is to say—go in the mass market? Berkley dithered about this while I sulked, wrote a novelization (never published) of Lindsay Anderson's *O Lucky Man!* for Warner Books, and waited around to accept an award for a science fiction novel, which award caused me much difficulty, you bet, in the years to come. (See the letter column of the 2/74 *Analog* for any further information you want on this.)

Eventually, Ernsberger called—during dinnertime, in fact, on 3/16/73—to say that I could go ahead with the series and would I please change the name of the protagonist? Grumbling, fearing that I might never get back to the center of those novels, I started again and in fact did deliver the tenth book on 10/1/73 after all. (The first three were published in that month.) As is so often the case with imitative series, sales steadily declined from volume #1 which did get close to 70,000) but held above unprofitability through all of those ten, and I was allowed two sequels in 1974 and then two more in conclusion (at a cut advance). I insisted upon killing off Wulff in #14 against the argument of Ernsberger's assistant, Dale Copps, who reminded me of Professor Moriarty.

I signed off on #14: *Philadelphia Blowup* in 1/75. That means that I am now at a greater distance from these novels than many readers of this anthology are from their birthdates ... and for that reason my opinion of the series is not necessarily any more valid than would be the opinion of Erika Cornell on her essays in ballet class in the mid-seventies.

The purpose and development of these novels would, in any case, be clear to anyone, even the author. It is evident to me now as it was then that Mack Bolan was insane and Pendleton's novels were a rationalization of vigilantism; it was my intent, then, to show what the real (as opposed to the mass market) enactment of madness and vigilantism might be if death were perceived as something beyond catharsis or an escape route for the bad guys. As the series went on and on and as I became more secure with the voicing and with my apparent ability to circumvent surface and not get fired, Wulff became crazier and crazier. By #13 he was driving crosscountry and killing anyone on suspicion of drug dealing; by #14: *Philadelphia Blowup*, he was staggering from bar to bar in the City of Brotherly Love and killing everyone because they obviously had to be drug dealers. Finally gunned down for the public safety by his one-time black sidekick, Wulff died far less bloodily than many of his victims while managing a bequest of about $50,000 to his overweight creator. The novels sold overseas intermittently—Denmark stayed around through all 14; the other Scandinavian countries bailed out earlier; the gentle Germans found it all too bloody and sadistic and after editing down the first 10 novels quit on an open-ended contract, paid off and shut it down. I haven't seen anything financially from these since 1979 but entries in various mystery reference sources and the invitation to discuss the series in this anthology suggest that it might have found a particle of an audience. (My real pride in this series, beyond its ambition and sheer, perverse looniness is that I was able to run it through the entirety of its original contract and manage four sequels as well; no Executioner imitator other than those published by Pinnacle went past four or five volumes.) The vicious Rockefeller drug laws ("drug dealers get life imprisonment") were being debated and eventually rammed through the New York State legislature at the time I was writing through the midpoint of the series. It was a propinquity of event which led to some of the more profoundly angry passages in these novels and imputed a certain timelessness as well. (The laws were horseshit and we are still living with their existence and terrible consequence.) Calling a crazy a crazy, no matter how anguished may have been the aspect of the series which was the most admired but for me the work lives in the pure rage of some of the epigraphic statements, notably Kenyatta's. Writing these brought me close to some apprehension of how Malcolm, how H. Rap Brown, how the Soledad Brothers might have felt and how right they were: The Lone Wolf was my own raised fist to a purity and a past already obliterated as they were written, rolled over by the tanks and battery of Bolan's ordnance. (Operating under Bolan's pseudonym: "U.S. Government.") Bolan killed to kill: I think Wulff killed to be free. It all works out the same, of course.

THE LONE WOLF # 1: NIGHT RAIDER

by Barry N. Malzberg

Writing as Mike Barry

Your hooves have stamped at the black margin of the woods
Even where hideous green parrots call and swing.
My works are all stamped down into that sultry mud.
I knew that horesplay; knew it for a murderous thing.
—William Butler Yeats

Nobody cares. America is one monstrous vein and it's being filled with poison. The best and the worst are being murdered by drugs and everyone, even the murdered, profit because it's part of the system.

But I'm going to break it. I'm the last man who cares and I'm going to smash them. Their lives will be smashed the way that they have smashed millions. And I'll get joy from it and laugh or I won't even start.
—Burt Wulff

This novel is dedicated, with understanding, to those very few dedicated law-enforcement officers who, if their efforts had prevailed, would have made Burt Wulff's mission unnecessary.

PROLOGUE

Wulff, after two years in the army, most of it in Vietnam, had been entitled to something nice for his trouble, or so the department felt on his discharge, so they had made him a narco. A New York City narcotics cop which was a pretty good detail anyway you looked at it, what with the freedom and the plainclothes and the graft money, but something had happened to this Wulff overseas it seemed: he had gone crazy. He had become a man of integrity. He didn't like sucking around the piss-ass informants, most of whom he figured would be better off at the bottom of the river and he didn't want any of the graft.

Eventually he tried to bust an informant which was the one thing you never did on the narco squad and they knew they would have to do something about this wild man. Getting the informant back on the street was easy enough but Wulff was just the kind of guy who might make things really hot, follow him back on the streets and bust him again or worse. He might try going the newspaper route too. So what they did was to put him back on precinct duty in a radio car. Just for a couple of weeks, until they figured what else to do with him.

They never had a chance. Wulff's first night out in the radio car, riding shotgun next to a tight-lipped black named David Williams who seemed to know all about his background and in a private way found it very funny … his first night out an anonymous tip came into the precinct that there was a girl OD'd out on the top floor of an old brownstone. The caller suggested that Burt Wulff himself might be the one who would like to take the call and then, laughing away, hung up. The tip passed up one level and was sent on to Wulff's radio car which, as it turned out, was the closest to 93rd Street and West End Avenue where the girl was supposed to be.

Wulff had a girl. Her name was Marie Calvante and they were going to be married. He had last seen her forty-eight hours before this, before all the trouble had started, and he certainly never expected to see her the next time the way they found her. He was supposed to see her the next day. It was all set up. They would make love in her little apartment over in Queens and then talk about the wedding some more. She wanted one; he just wanted to elope. He found her lying on the floor of room 53 in this brownstone. A long time ago it had been a mansion. Horses had been tethered by the trees.

Wulff saw his fiancée OD'd out on the floor. He thought that he might go mad on the spot but quite strangely he did not. He was very calm as he checked her pulse, checked gross signs, closed the wide, staring eyes that had swept over him so gently in the night. Only then did he turn to Williams who had followed him at a measured space up the four flights and who was now looking at him impassively. The blacks saw everything but it did not seem to register. "They killed her," Wulff said.

"Who killed her?"

"The filthy drug-pushing sons of bitches," Wulff said. He stood, walked away from the body, went to the window. "They wanted to get at me," he said, "they're getting to me."

"How can you be so sure?" Williams said, already turning to leave the room. The thing to do was to get the meat wagon. He liked Wulff all right as much as he knew of him but holding his hand wasn't going to help. Besides, he did not know exactly what Wulff was talking about.

"I'm sure," Wulff said. "There are things you can be sure of."

Very slowly, he took off his badge and tossed it through the window; two hundred feet below it hit the sidewalk with a deadly *ping!* which would have killed anyone there. "I'm going to kill them," he said, "I'm going to kill some people."

"Take it easy man."

"I'm going to kill a *lot* of people," Wulff said. He was very calm. "Go down and get the wagon."

"All right," Williams said. He shrugged and went through the door. Wulff was alone in the room with what had been his girl.

He turned toward the corpse. "They'll pay," he said very quietly, "I swear they'll pay for this."

Then—no time now or ever for weeping—he went out of the room and followed Williams downstairs. At the patrol car he did not stop, however, but kept on walking east, toward Broadway. Six feet four inches, two hundred and fifty pounds of combat veteran in full street gear, moving briskly toward the place where the sun would rise. People scattered.

Wulff went straight home and discarded everything except his gun and a spare. They were hardly the equipment he would need but they were a beginning. He did not bother calling in his resignation. They would get the idea on that soon enough. Let the personnel department worry about it. They could keep their fucking pension monies.

By dawn he had cleared out of his apartment completely. He found another place and rested for a few weeks while he put all the pieces together in his mind. There was no one to explain himself to because except for Marie there had not been anyone for many years. Finally, by mid-summer, he thought that he had the beginnings of an operation in his mind. The rest he would have to play by ear.

Wulff hit the streets to kill a lot of people.

I

So you start at the beginning. Nothing else ever worked. There is always, somewhere, a beginning ...

Ric Davis parked the Eldorado at the intersection of 137th and Madison, easing it into an open space near the curb, shoving the lever to *P* but leaving the engine at idle, an old, old habit which stayed with you no matter where you went. Unless you were leaving that car for a period of time you kept the keys in the slot and the engine running and preferably enough open space in front of you to get it out fast into traffic without wrenching the wheel. He held the wheel now loosely, easily, looking at the northeast corner and then at his watch. Twelve minutes until rendezvous. Early again, time to kill.

Well, so be it. Better early than late, that was how the Ricker thought and promptness in any business was an asset. Davis manipulated the wheel slightly, admiring the power of the car, its consistency, the faint, purring sounds of the idle at the heart of the hood, just a little throb under his ass to tell him that the car was alive. No, you couldn't beat Cadillacs, particularly the Eldorado. It was true that they fell to shit inside of three years and it was also true that a Mercedes as a performance car had it all over even a new Eldorado but, and what the hell, a Cadillac was a Cadillac. No getting away from it; better to swing with the tide. Who wanted a shitbox Mercedes when for less than ten you could pick up something like this?

Davis smiled to himself, waved a gloved hand at the windshield acknowledging someone that he knew, but the guy on the corner, returning the wave, kept his distance: that was right and fine, it proved that Davis had established the approach-level just right, and raced the engine gently. He had had the car for four months now, had put over twelve thousand miles on the rack but, still, getting into it each time was like the first. He guessed that in many ways he was still a kid, mooning over his first Cadillac. All right, so be it. Lots of kids had to settle for a '59 Fleetwood with scars and horns. Ric Davis had an Eldorado. He patted the wheel again, put a hand into his inside pocket, touched the envelope, reassuringly solid against him. In place. *Rikky-tik.* He dropped the car between reverse and low, feeling the imperceptible rise of the shift, then dropped it into neutral again, turned on the radio very low hoping that he might catch the Four Tops. He loved the Four Tops. Years in the darkness but now bigger and better than ever just like Ric Davis.

No Four Tops but instead something from the fifties on NBC, the Shirelles or maybe it was the Four Seasons, singing close, pushing the theme alone. Davis tapped the wheel in rhythm, put the volume on a little higher, sang along under his breath. Attracting no attention. Just grooving along. Shit, if he wasn't at 137th Street and Madison Avenue he would take the top down and look at the sky but here it would just make him conspicuous and anyway, what the hell was there to look at? This wasn't a good looking place and no getting around it. *Someday in the country*, Davis murmured. A man opened the door to his right and came in. Slammed the door behind him, sat knee to knee with the Rikker. *On the Rikker's seat covers; his ass covering the seat covers, his wide hands tooling across the leather-crafted dashboard.*

"Hello Davis," the man said quietly, "been a long time."

Davis gave him a cautious sidelong glance, then took the man in from tip to stern. Big, heavy, healthy mother fucker this one, six feet four or so, two hundred and fifty pounds or even a little more but no fat on him anywhere, the kind of frame that seemed built for violence. Clear, undistinguished face except for the one thing that Davis saw and which made him lurch inside; the clear, luminescent almost mad penetration of light coming from those eyes. He had never seen eyes like that before. The man leaned toward him, cleared his throat. "I said it's been a long time, Davis," he said. "Hasn't it now?"

"I don't know what you're talking about," Davis said carefully. Gently he pumped the accelerator again, listened to the contained whine of the motor. "I want you to get the fuck out of my car."

"In time," the man said softly. He patted Davis's hand, gently. "What you doing up here at 137th and Madison, Davis?" he said, "this isn't your territory as I recall. You're a downtown man."

Gently Davis felt around his pockets. No revolver of course; he would have to be all kinds of fool to come to a routine drop of this sort heeled. But there was always a chance that he had slipped a knife into his inner coat pocket: sometimes he did and other times he didn't, all depending upon his mood and he never thought about it after he left the apartment. One little glint of the knife would be enough; a little trickling slash up the elbow and this bugger with the big face and the weight would be on his knees screaming, piling out of the car. No. No knife. Well, maybe that was all for the best after all. He hated the idea of violence. Violence was for another part of the Rikker's life, years ago. Now he was a changed man.

"I do want you to get the fuck out of my car," he said to the man, grasping his wrist and putting a thumb delicately on a pressure point. "I want you to get out of here right now." Shit. It was his fault. Why had he left the right door unlocked? It was almost like fate in a way, leaving it open so that this big clown could dodge in and start to throw weight on him. "I said, get out of this car."

The big clown did something with his wrist, reversed the pressure point and Davis felt a searing pain beginning at the joint, flaring upward then past the elbow and into his neck. Too late he knew that he was in trouble, had taken this too lightly from the beginning. He gasped. His eyes bulged. "Look at me," the big clown said, *"look at me Davis you son of a bitch and tell me you don't remember."*

Davis, through a haze of pain, lifted his head, turned, looked at the man. The staring intensity of the eyes, the cold, dead set of the mouth. He looked into the eyes and then he remembered.

"Let go of me," he gasped, "you're hurting." His foot, in agony, prodded the accelerator, the Eldorado screamed. The big clown put his arm across Davis's chest, seized the keys, and killed the engine.

"What are you doing here, Davis?"

"Man, I don't even know what you're talking about." Incredibly, he felt tears in his eyes. The Rikker, crying. He hadn't cried since he was eight or maybe some time before that. He knew at eight that he would never cry again. But he had never felt pain like this before.

"You're killing me," he found himself screaming like a child, "let me go, you're killing me!" He groaned, arched against the seat, flapped like a bird in the man's grasp.

"Little pain won't kill you Davis," the man said, "trouble is that you have a low threshold," but slowly the pressure was eased on him, eased only to a point where he could speak and see through the pain. The son of a bitch. *The son of a bitch.*

"Get out of my car," he said helplessly, "I don't know what you're doing but you get out of my car, you hear—"

A little more pressure on the wrist like a dark reminder of what had just passed, a mere flick and Davis quieted again. Tears flowed down his cheeks like thick droplets of mud.

"When is the meet, Davis?" the big man said. "Tell me when, now."

Clumps of people on the comer were definitely observing this. They *knew* that something was going on, *had* to know. Why didn't they come any closer? Why weren't they helping a man who was being taken over like this, by a white man, in daylight? This could not happen. *Would you?* Davis asked himself reasonably through the pain, *on a hundred and thirty-seventh street and Madison Avenue would you mind anyone's business?* "I don't know anything," he said sullenly. "I don't know what you're talking about."

"You just came to this elegant neighborhood to give your friends a look at the new car, right?"

"Listen friend," Davis said, risking a look at the man, "if you've got any questions, you can just take me downtown with you and *ask* them. You think you can book me in on what you got, you do that. I'm not answering a goddamned thing here."

"You fool," the man said with a thin, mad smile, "you really don't understand, do you? I'm not taking you downtown. I'm not running you through a booking, Davis. This is man to man now, just the two of us here. When is the meet?"

"I don't know," Davis said and then he felt another thrill of pain, more exquisite and terrible than anything so far, like the pain of a tooth extraction but much deeper and moving in waves across his solar plexus. The son of a bitch had hit him directly in the gut, one-finger. He doubled, fighting for air.

"Come on," the big man said, "you can talk. When? Now? Soon?"

"I don't know," Davis said, tears streaming again and the man waved the finger in front of his face. "Five minutes," he said, "maybe less than that, I don't know. I can't get to my watch. For God's sake, I haven't done anything! Leave me alone!"

"I'm not the law," the man said quietly, "so I can't leave you alone." He snaked a hand into Davis's jacket pocket, prodded around in there as if he owned it, and came out with the envelope, running thumb and forefinger over it. "Money this time," he said, "that means a pickup. I would have bet on delivery. You're still small time, Davis. You're still a little, little man. You're in distribution not supply and you'd probably stay there all your life."

He threw the envelope over into the back seat with a gesture of controlled violence and poked Davis in the neck. "Point him out to me you son of a bitch," he said, "show me which one is your man."

"He's not there yet," Davis said frantically, babbling a little, shifting his legs to the recess between seat and door, "I swear to you he's not there."

"He's late then."

"No he's not late. He just ain't there."

"Finger him," the big man said, squeezing the neck-bones slightly. Davis felt his eyeballs pop, reflexively. "Finger him for me Davis."

"Man, this is crazy," Davis said, "man you are crazy. I never knew any narco that acted like this. You can't get away with this kind of stuff. They'll have your ass downtown—"

"I'm not a narco," the man said quietly, "didn't I tell you that before, Davis? You're not dealing with the cops now. This is just man on man. No more policies and procedures, friend. Point him out to me. *Finger him.*"

"Now, Jesus man," Davis said frantically because he could see his contact stroll out of a shapeless Buick parked near the intersection, one you'd never notice in a million years, and take up space on the corner, the clumps scattering just a little to give him room. If there was one thing about these people, they knew where the power was, just on instinct they would stay clear. His contact looked at his watch, began to pace in even, loping circles. Davis didn't even know his name. It was much better if you could keep things at that level because names meant identities meant backgrounds meant human beings and at that point you simply couldn't conduct your business any more but then again if he knew the cat's name he could have screamed a warning, something of some sort, the words didn't matter, just to get him off the street.

Something passed down Ric Davis like a cool, grey intake of air. For a moment he thought that the big clown had squeezed him again but then he realized that it was only the shock of insight: the Rikker's new way of looking at the situation. He wouldn't warn this cat even if he did know his name. Even if he knew something about him. In this business it was strictly one man against the other and he owed this one nothing. He owed nobody anything except the Rikker and that meant getting out of this anyway he could. He looked at the big clown who regarded him with absolute calm, his eyes full and expectant. For one crazy moment Davis felt that he could get near the man, could touch him, could explain to him somehow that he had the Rikker all wrong and that the Rikker, like the clown himself, was only trying to get a job done, only trying to make out, but that feeling passed away and he pressed back into the cushions shuddering, his eyes locked to the tall, spindly black man pacing the corner in crazy little circles, head bobbing, arms moving loosely within his coat. A bad business: his contact looked like: a user. He had never noticed that before. "Good," the man next to him said, "I'm glad Davis because this makes things much easier now for all of us. Move the car."

"What?"

"Start the car and move it," the man said almost pleasantly. "Let's close in on this guy and make ourselves a pickup."

"Listen," Davis said, "I don't know who you are or what you're trying to do but I can't go along with this anymore. This is my car, my business, you can't—"

"Don't you know who I am?" the man said. He leaned close to Davis, let Davis get a good look at him, the full frame, closed face, curiously penetrating eyes and from those eyes then came a shaft of power which Davis felt only as pain. Oh man, he had never seen anybody like this in his life. There were narcos and other narcos but this was something else entirely.

He shrugged, slowly because his body was stiff and also to show the man that he would make no sudden gestures. Fuck it. He wasn't going to fight with this clown; he knew now that it would only get him killed. Whatever was going on now was beyond the Rikker's control and nothing to do but go with it and hope that he came out at the other end. *Small fish*, he thought, turning the key and bringing the Eldorado over, *they're always going to go after the small fish like the Rikker; the Rikker is going to take the heat on this one.* Professional risk. He had known that from the beginning. Black men on the street level were fools if they didn't understand. Slowly he poked the car across 137th Street, holding the wheel tight. "Okay," the passenger said, "give him a little horn."

Davis gave him a little horn, two light blasts from the Eldorado's fuck-you horn. Nothing like a Cadillac horn. They brought the spindly man's face around, whipping fast, spotting Davis and then the white man beside him. The spindly man poised on the corner like a dancer before a leap, seeming to decide whether to dodge back to the Buick, stand fast or move over. Davis could see the calculation moving across his face like little animals. The big man raised a hand in casual greeting and motioned for Davis to stop the Eldorado. He did with a little whisk of power brakes. The spindly man who must have been thinking about the money, came over slowly and looked into the window. The big clown used the power switch to roll it down, leaned out.

"Come on in," he said, "there are a couple things we have to talk over."

The spindly man gave Davis an inquiring look. *Fuck this*, Davis thought, *I don't owe him nothing. He'd do the same to me anytime and that's the truth.* "Yeah," he said, "we've got to discuss something about arrangements." The big man seemed to smile. He opened the door, stepped out lightly, pivoted to push down the front seat and motioned the spindly man inside, then joined him in the back, wedging him in there tightly, yanking down the front seat fast, pulling the door closed all in one graceful motion.

"Just drive," he said to Davis, "just take this machine and drive. Head over to the Harlem River and head upstate and keep it very quiet because my new friend and I want to have a long talk back here. Make like a chauffeur, Davis."

"Now what the shit is *this?*" the spindly man said in a high, piercing voice. In the rear view, Davis could see him raise his arms to hug himself, surround himself with his own joints, sinking back into the seat, his eyes wide and stuporous. Definitely a user after all.

"We'll talk it over," the big clown said.
Davis just drove.

II

Sure he knew what was going on. Hadn't he been a narco? But it wasn't even as if you had to be a narco to get the score: all that you had to be was a reader of the newspapers, an average American who was able to see what was going on around him and how it all related back to one central fact: everybody was getting a piece of it. The enforcers were only another arm of the operation.

Sure he knew this: he knew that the police narcotics room downtown was nothing more than another stash for the stuff, he knew that the quiet men who came in their Cadillacs from Teaneck or Rego Park or Scarsdale to do their official business in the city before going back to the wife and kids at five like every other commuter, these quiet men were as deep into it as the police who wandered in and out of the stash room twelve hours a day; he knew that everything in the city had broken down to the point where drugs were the secret of control; he who sold the drugs administered the territory. He knew all of this and a good deal more; Wulff could have worked it out and made a pretty good thesis out of it or even a newspaper story. They would have loved it in the newspaper offices. Every six months or so, just to keep circulation staggering along in the few newspapers left they would have an expose of the drug scene and some firm recommendations for how the situation must be reformed. They would love an article by an ex-narco. He might even have parlayed it into television appearances: he could have shown up late at night on a panel with a prostitute disguised as an actress, a famous author and maybe a juggler or two to give his insights into the drug business. The juggler would have nodded solemnly, the actress would have asked him well then why didn't the law *do* something? Three hundred and twenty dollars standard fee. That would be wonderful. That was a career to look forward to.

Wulff had other ideas. He had a much better idea. It was founded in what he wanted to think of as reality. He would start from the beginning. He would start as if he knew nothing about the drug trade which in a sense was almost true and would begin from the origins. He would, he decided, take a dealer and working out from that dealer like tracing the sick flowers spreading from a poisoned tree, he would follow it all the way up. Or down.

He figured that if he could approach the problem in just that way, taking it from the very top as it were, he would be handling the matter in the most direct and efficient manner. The other way was the one that had never worked; collaring the dealers say and putting them away laughing for thirty days or then again using the breaks on narco duty to bitch about the politicians and businessmen, hidden behind their gates and walls, who were really making the thing go while the narcos were concentrating on picking up the insect droppings. That wouldn't do any more.

No. You had to be patient and thorough and start in on this thing as if it made sense. Because it *did* make sense, that was the point: it was the weak man's excuse that nothing could be done because it was all too mindless, murderous, cancerous, ingrown. It was not. It was none of that. It was simply that no one had ever approached it practically and patiently, from the very top, with all the time in the world, all the hatred in the world, all the dedication...

At 145th Street and the Harlem River Drive his chauffeur did something a little stupid; tried to run the car off the road, either to simply ditch it and make a run for freedom or worse yet to contrive some kind of accident which would leave Wulff shaken and the driver in pretty good shape. And the hell to the spindly man, the other passenger, who looked at him wide-eyed and began to sob like a child when Wulff put a little pressure on. Without quite giving information yet. Give them time. The driver took the Eldorado toward an emergency area between an opening in the gate, playing the brake and accelerator alternately with moderate skill, the big car booming and shaking, then diving into the cobblestones on two wheels, shaking. Wulff reached an arm around the driver's neck, put moderate pressure on the jugular. Davis flopped against him, hopelessly trying to move sideways.

"Cut it out," Wulff said.

Davis made frantic gestures with his hands, indicating that wind was cut off. The man was suffocating against him. Murmurs like those of an infant pulsed in his neck. Wulff felt the suffering. He loosened the pressure slightly.

"I told you to drive," he said.

Davis fell against the door, writhing. The spindly man thought he saw an opening, lurched toward the front seat. Wulff put an elbow into the man's stomach, slammed him back. Now the two of them were gasping and choking. He looked at the scene with distaste. If he didn't control himself he would have them vomiting all over him and the car. Pleasant in a way to see their agony but he didn't want to be soiled. The spindly one was a user too; he had to remember that. Low tolerance level for pain. He could bop around street corners, he could crawl around in his

Buick and threaten, but pushed to the wall there was nothing there.
Muscle was not their specialty.

"Let's see it," he said to the spindly man. "Let's see the stuff."

"What stuff?"

Wulff felt himself abruptly becoming tired with the process of
investigation. He hit the spindly man in the stomach hard enough to
double him. Sympathetically in the front seat, Davis moaned, gagged.
"Give me the shit," Wulff said.

"I don't have no shit on me. I don't know what you talking—"

Almost tiredly, Wulff hit the man in the stomach again. Saliva flew out
of him as if from a tube; he felt droplets on his forehead. Casually he
slammed the man across the cheek, knocked him to the seat. "Inside
pocket?" he said. "Outside pocket? In the groin, up the ass? Give me the
shit or I'll take you apart piece by piece to make it."

"Christ," Davis said, hunched over the wheel, "give it to him. *He's not
kidding around.*"

"Good advice," Wulff said, "I'm not kidding around."

The spindly man collapsed over the seat. His breathing was shallow,
uneven. There was even less to the man than he had thought. Davis
didn't look too good either. Here he was, in an Eldorado pulled over on
the Harlem River Drive with two dying punks to the front and right of
him, traffic lofting by at a good and true fifty-five miles an hour, but
sooner or later some patrol car was going to get curious about a stranded
Eldorado and pull over. That would not be good. That was definitely not
going to help anyone. Despite his long association with the New York
City Police Department, Wulff wanted as little to do with it right now
as the two fish in the car. "Okay," he said and prodded the spindly man,
snaked a hand inside his clothing, feeling the frailty of the man, the
thudding, uneven heartbeat. "Let's get it."

An envelope fell into his hand as if it had been evacuated from the
man's body. He felt the weight, the shape of it, his fingers met
somewhere near the middle and he felt a sensation of crumbling.
Delicately he took it all the way against him, shielded it, opened the flat
cautiously and looked through.

Saw the white sands of death.

"Give me the money, Davis," he said.

"I'll give you the money," Davis said. He was still racing the engine in
neutral, desperately, nervously, as if the sounds of the car itself could
somehow save him. "Man, I'll give you the money. I don't give a shit
about this." He handed Wulff an envelope. "You lucky I'm not heeled,"
he said with a last flare of defiance, "I come out on this heeled, you are
dead—"

Wulff hit him in the face. "I'm dead," he said, "I'm dead already, you understand that?" Davis fell across the dashboard, unconscious. Wulff reached forward, grasped the ignition key and turned off the engine, carefully, quickly taking in the traffic pattern on the Drive. No signs of interest yet, no patrol cars perched above on the cliffs taking note of the Eldorado but his business here was almost done. To stay much longer would be to push his luck. Although it had been a pleasure socializing with Davis and his friend; this is the kind of relationship he should always have had with these people. That was the social work, the police work they understood: a pressure point, a punch in the mouth. Send a memo on this to the commissioner's office. He'd love it.

"All right," he said, turning toward the spindly man. "What's your name?"

A slight line of drool came from the man's mouth as he opened it. "Jessup," he said, resistance gone. "Richard Jessup."

"Good deal, Jessup. All right. Tell me," Wulff said, showing him the heroin-filled envelope, "who gave this to you to pass on?"

The man breathed raggedly, his windpipe rattling, but he looked at Wulff with painful, level eyes. "If I tell you that I'm dead," he said. "You know that."

"You're dead already," Wulff said and almost absently hit him again. "I'm dead too, all of us are dead. The whole *fucking country is dead*. Make my life easy, Jessup. Who supplies?"

"You ain't no cop."

"That's right," Wulff said and again, matter-of-factly, hit the man. The touch of flesh rimming bone was satisfying. After a long time Wulff guessed this kind of thing could become boring but that was a long way in the future. He would not be running out of people to hit for a long time, if ever. It was good for a man to enjoy his work. "Who gave you the shit?" he said.

Jessup's eyes opened wide, stunned in pain. "I told you; I tell you that and I'm dead," he said, "a dead man. Finished."

"You're dead already, Jessup," Wulff said, "the narco stash room of the police department is just another part of the supply train. They're running the stuff out of that like little pack rats. *The whole world is into it, Jessup*: do you think anyone except you and me really gives a shit who your supplier is? Scratch a street and find the users, scratch the users and find the pushers, beat up the pushers and find a supplier, back up the line and maybe you catch a dealer. Maybe not. Set a rat to catch a rat." He hit the man again in the jaw, just above the line of the epiglottis so that speech would be conserved. "Tell me Jessup," he said, "last time."

Jessup made a hopeless butterfly's gesture toward his inner coat pocket. Wulff thought that the man might be going for a gun and waited, almost incuriously to see if he would. In his condition Jessup would barely be able to hold a gun now much less aim it. But that would give him an excuse to separate the man's arm from his body. Quick look above the highway; still no signs of patrol. Thin light traffic storming by. Davis moaned on the front seat as if in sleep. Time to move it on. Time to move it.

It was not a gun but a slip of paper that Jessup presented to him, hand trembling like that of a very old man. Wulff had aged him fifty years in this car. "Name's on this," Jessup mumbled, "I don't even know his name. Wrote it down for me once." He put the paper into Wulff's hand like a caress.

"He'd write down his name?"

"Don't ask me," Jessup said, "don't ask me how he does or what he does. He said I wanted to know his name he'd give it on a sheet of paper and I'd walk around with it. Said he didn't give a shit what I did with it. Let me go, man," he said putting his palms flat on the seat, "let me go out of here. Leave me alone. I didn't do nothing—"

Wulff looked at the sheet of paper which said *Jack Scotti.* "Where does he live?"

"Oh now shit man, I don't know where he *lives!* Nobody gonna tell you where they *live* for Christ's sake."

"Where do you meet him?"

Jessup looked out through dumb, narrowed eyes, "Oh, shit, I meet him here and I meet him there. It's just like hanging around; sometimes you bump into a guy—"

Wulff sighed and hit him again on the upper cheekbone. Jessup screamed like a child, doubled over, sobbed.

"Where do you meet him?"

"Bar," Jessup said between bright little burbles of sound, "bar in the west seventies near Amsterdam."

"Not good enough. Name of the bar. The address."

"Tell him you stupid son of a bitch," Davis said from the front, "*will you tell him?* He'll kill us."

"Half Moon Lounge," Jessup said, "on 76th between Amsterdam and Columbus, right side of the block I think as you walk to the river. Thursday. Thursdays and Sundays around three o'clock I—"

"It's Thursday today," Wulff said. "It's about one o'clock Thursday."

"Well sure it's one o'clock Thursday, I'm supposed to meet him this afternoon—"

"Pass on the money, right?"

Jessup nodded once, confined, stricken. "I'm shamed," he said, "you've shamed me. You've—"

"I've shamed you?" Wulff said, "I've shamed *you?*"

"Yes," Jessup said, he was crying. "I'm a *man.* You've made me—"

"Bullshit," Wulff said and hit the man in the mouth. Again. Soft, yielding; he felt the mouth pulp underneath. "I haven't shamed you. You were shamed long before I came around."

"Man, that's not true. I—"

"You've shamed yourself. You know what you are? You're a hyena, Jessup. You eat dead bodies and then you laugh at the moon."

A green and white patrol car, far above their level, came to a stop on the other side of the Drive, near the Eldorado. Wulff caught all of this with peripheral vision that he had learned the hard way; narrowing down the line of sight he could see two small dots that could only be police moving within that car. Looking down.

Time to go. He looked at the two shivering, trembling hulks in the car to his right and in front of him, two hulks that not an hour ago had been prancing and dancing their way down the lane of 137th Street and Madison Avenue, cool and easy, in command of the premises as of course they indeed were. How truly easy it was to reduce them to the broken, sniveling wrecks which they had become, which they deserved to be. It was the easiest thing in the world if you only took on the job directly, without intermediaries of every sort and did it right. But of course it didn't matter; the Jessups and Davises had to be multiplied by a thousand and then by a thousand again before you could get any understanding of what they had done to the city alone. And that was just New York City: it was a countryside you were thinking about and eventually a world and it was impossible, simply impossible, to pulverize them all.

Wulff looked at the two of them, moaning, retching on the seat covers of the 1971 Eldorado, full power gear, power door locks, tinted glass and sliding roof panel. He felt himself to be on the verge of an enormous decision, just the second of the decisions he would have to face in his new life but possibly the more important. The first had only been a matter of what he was going to *do* whereas this was a matter of life and death, not only for these two but for who knew how many in the future. He peered again toward the parapet and saw the patrol car still hanging there, no sign of movement inside. So they were merely observing. They had picked up something but they were not going to move in at all. That was the New York city cop for you. Wulff had been one and more than that. He did not know if he could blame them. Who was he to reckon judgement? Who was he to reckon judgement for any of them?

He reached inside his pocket and took out the caliber thirty-eight police special. His souvenir from the department and they could keep their badges, their pension. He considered it and looked at the two in the car for the last time. Then, very quietly, he cocked the pistol and pointed it, first at the one on the front seat.

"No!" Ric Davis said, "no, don't do it!" catching the glint of the gun, sensing rather than seeing the heft of the barrel as Wulff pointed it. Savaged, he nevertheless churned on the seat like a trapped animal. "Please," Davis said, "oh please man, don't do it."

Wulff put the gun against the dealer's forehead and fired. A good silencer, good control; only a dead, dull *thunk!* and a small, opening hole in Davis's forehead as he fell away from there.

He turned. Jessup was cringing on the seat in the far corner, his hands also upraised. "You can't do this!" Surprise seemed to have overtaken him even through all of the pain. The man looked quizzical. "You can't do it!"

"Yes I can," Wulff said, "you see, this is just the beginning. Leave a clean trail."

He shot the man through the heart.

Jessup died beside him on the back seat. Clean, only a little streak of blood showing outside. Wulff put the safety on, put the gun away, leaned forward to open the driver's door and pushed the seat forward moving the corpse wedged behind the wheel. He tugged Jessup's body by the ankles, the man surprisingly light in death, and eased him out of the car in little wads of clothing and blood, like a serpent, dropped the body to the pavement beside the car. Let passing traffic get a good look at that. Let the patrol car enjoy it too. Yes indeed, Wulff thought, for better or worse he might as well approach the issue as if he were on stage. That was it: he was on stage now and the theatre was the world. And despite the cops and the traffic, there was no audience at all.

He worked himself out of the car quickly, took the dead Davis by the shoulders and yanked him out of the car. The corpse fell on top of Jessup's. They held one another in death as never in life, the bodies locked together in a horrid intimacy: dealer and contact man, little spots of blood pooling around them, growing on the pavement. Wulff looked at them for an instant even as traffic seemed to slow and drift around him.

It was satisfying. There was just no doubt about this. It was a satisfying thing to see.

For the first time in weeks, Wulff permitted himself, looking at the bodies, to draw a breath unencumbered by bitterness, by dread, by loss. Then, as cars skittered around him and ever so slowly and gracefully, the patrol car abandoned its position to sweep toward a highway entrance, he got into the front of the Eldorado, closed the door, started the engine and got the hell out of that spot at eighty miles an hour, keeping the transmission locked into second for acceleration.

Cadillacs had a good reputation as road cars but the acceleration was for shit, Wulff decided. Any Plymouth, even without heavy duty shocks and the high-compression engine, could beat the hell out of them. Still, riding in this big car was just like it must be to surmount Harlem on a heroin jag: it shut out everything. *Everything.* He was a corpse riding in a big, dark, painted-white-on-the-outside coffin with red leather interior and nothing, not even the eulogists, would get near him.

Yes, Wulff decided, patting the wheel and shooting the car through a closing gap into the 155th Street exit, there was no question about it. For making a meet with a man like Jack Scotti, there was simply nothing like an Eldorado. Meet the stylish, go in style. A pity that he would have to ditch the thing before he got to St. Nicholas Avenue.

Somewhere far behind, Wulff heard the keen of a siren but it didn't bother him. He took up the power windows all the way instead. The car was virtually soundproof.

Like the place where he had sent Jessup and Davis.

Everything must have a beginning.

III

Wulff ditched the car at 125th Street and Eighth Avenue where it looked as inconspicuous as it ever would, blending right into the general scene, and took the subway downtown. Riding in the crowded car of the local, pressed hip to hip with people who looked utterly beaten, he had a brief fantasy that all of them knew who he was; that they would turn on him somewhere around 110th Street and beat him to a pulp but that fantasy went away fast when he realized that no one was paying attention. No one paid any attention to anyone else in the New York subway. It was the only way to get through; start with eyeball-to-eyeball human contact and you were dead. Human beings could not survive being locked into something like this, only machines. He got out of the subway at West 79th Street and Broadway, checked his watch, walked briskly toward the Half-Moon Lounge. Two twenty. If he had sized up his man right and Wulff guessed he had, Wulff would find him there already. The Scottis always killed time for the money.

Walking there, the pressure of the revolver coming in waves against his ribs from the inner coat pocket, Wulff found himself looking at the city for the first time in many years, really seeing it instead of just cutting through around and on the edges in the cop's way. He could see the city plain: the battered, bleak faces of the men hanging from doorways, the protective scuttle of better-dressed men and women making their way in and out of the apartment houses and brown-stones, the filth on the streets: the look, in short, of a war zone. It looked, Wulff thought, something like the way Saigon had in 1966 with an important difference: Saigon had been backed up right against it, the civilians in that town could *see* the enemy, knew exactly what they were dealing with, could see their future plain.

But that was the front lines, a healthier situation. New York was tucked back of the combat zone: the civilians here did not know what was actually doing it to them. They could see the effects upon the landscape, upon their lives, lived like hunters and hunted in this place but the enemy was far afield and there was almost no point at which they could get hold of him and break the situation through to reality.

Drugs had done it to this city. The city was a map of devastation; not only the people but the landscape was shattered. Drugs had cleaved out a neighborhood there, knocked out a shopkeeper here, broken down the fabric of the city and in some places had thrown up gleaming twenty-five story prisons where the more affluent could lock themselves away or think that they had locked themselves away from the terror. Further uptown drugs had leaped and snarled their way through the older neighborhoods of Harlem, destroyed an area for square miles, paused for a minute to throw up a bleak, filthy fortress of housing projects, then run away, the job done, taking the bridge to New Jersey, the other bridge to Riverdale, spreading the stain of roads which were the network of flight. Drugs had come into the vein of the city and had filled it with poison, then in a kind of high-pressure reversal had pulled the plunger *out* filling the phial with everything that had made the city functional and had pulled it through that network of roads to the opening spaces to the north and the west, the east and the south of the city, anywhere but the city itself, that throbbing, beaten heart which at the center lay there stripped and dying.

Oh yes: you could see it plain. The Scottis would come into the Half-Moon Lounges of this city to pick up the take as middlemen for people who wouldn't even come in this far, the Davises and Jessups would run around the bowels of the city like roaches sneaking into a hidden sugar dish but what was happening was to Wulff quite clear: the city was being worked over now by only two kinds of people: those who put the junk in, those who took the money out. Crossing Amsterdam Avenue Wulff found himself walking with his hand on his service revolver, feeling the cold barrel, repressing an impulse to pull the gun out and start shooting.

Shoot them. Start and end with the indiscriminate kill. Kill the junkies, kill the dealers, kill the dark men who sat hunched over in double-parked cars unmoving for hours. Work the city like a trapeze of the kill, moving from one level to the next, taking them out by tens and twenties and finally by the hundreds so that the city would be free again.

No. It would not work. Old people shambling by him on the sidewalk, the only people in New York City that even bothered to look around because it was an old habit, these old people looked at him with terror: a six foot four, two hundred and fifty pound, compactly built angry man storming along the pavement, gripping something inside of himself. If anyone except the old people looked would there be any concealing his intentions? Wulff slowed, released the revolver, tried to make his pace more deliberate and offhand, restricted his gaze to what lay directly ahead of him like any city dweller. Better this way. He was in for the long haul. Lose control now and he would never make it to Scotti let alone up the line from there.

It would not matter anyway. He could kill every addict, dealer, supplier, crooked politician and cop in the city and all that he would have done would have been to clean it out for twelve to twenty-four hours before the next wave moved right on in. The quiet men who lived in their castles on the rim of the city did not care. It meant nothing to them. In the morning they would lift their fingers and the next wave would come on in to pick up the corpses and start it all from the top.

Better to take it as one thread, one bright single thread of purpose and trace it all the way through. Right? Of course he was right. And being right did not make you feel any better; it did not even necessarily make you more effective but one thing it did do: it resolved a lot of conflicts.

Wulff walked into the Half-Moon Lounge, *Bar & Grille, Ladies Welcome* and felt the strange, dense coolness of the enclosure assault him. The place felt like an aquarium. It looked like an aquarium too, a strange, dense greenish cast thrown by the lights, the gaping, flat face of the bartender as he came up over the edge and looked at him.

The front room was deserted. One middle-aged woman sat at the bar, rattling ice in a glass, holding an unlit cigarette; two obscure types who might have been salesmen were deep into conversation at the other end of the pit. The television set was tuned to one of those game shows which seemed to Wulff to make sense only to the announcers or the networks. Even the contestants were having trouble. *I just don't know* a short woman was saying, beaming a bright, empty, idiot's smile into the camera, *I don't know if I should go for the double naturals or stay at rest.*

What do you think? The audience seemed divided on the proposition. Some said yes and some said no. *I don't know what to do* the woman said again. Maybe that makes two of us, Wulff thought. The bartender stood slowly, wiping a glass and looked up at the television set. "I think you really ought to go for the doubles," he said. The middle-aged woman nodded at this. "Even triples," she added. The bartender put down the wiped glass and took another, adjusting his glasses for a better look at the set. "Tough decision," he murmured.

Wulff went to the bar and stood there, shutting off the sounds of the game show. It was like drugs themselves, this stuff although, of course, it did not kill. Not directly. The bartender looked his way, ambled over slowly. The middle-aged woman gave him a more calculating look, then a visible half-shrug and turned back to the set. Such was life it would seem in the Half-Moon Lounge these days.

"Beer," Wulff said and the bartender shuffled off to the taps, got a glass, came back. In a place like this it would always be tap beer; no sense even asking a customer if he wanted a bottle. Wulff put a dollar carefully on the bar and slid it across. "Jack Scotti," he said.

The bartender gave one imperceptible twitch and then his eyes became round and full. He took a towel from waist level and began to run it over the wood. "Who's that?" he said finally.

"I'm here to see Jack Scotti."

"I don't know anything about names," the bartender said. "People come in here I serve them. Who I'm serving I don't know. Do I know your name?"

"My name is Wulff. Now you know my name."

The bartender blinked. "I still don't know any Scotti."

Wulff looked casually through the partition separating bar from lounge, the panelling cutting off all but a little tunnel-vision into the other room. "In there?" he said quietly.

The bartender twitched again. "I told you, I don't know names."

"In there," Wulff said with satisfaction. He took another dollar from his wallet, laid it carefully on the bar and held his hand on it while he locked gazes with the bartender. This was easy. If you could do the procedural stuff, if you could do a Miranda, you could certainly handle a fat, aging bartender in the Half-Moon Lounge. "I'm going in there to see a guy," he said, "I'd appreciate it being a private conversation."

"I don't care," the bartender said, looking away, down at the dollar, "I don't care about any of that stuff."

"It's a very private conversation and I don't want it to be interrupted."

"Listen, this is a public place. I can't tell you—"

"We won't be long," Wulff said gently. "Just a little bit of reminiscence and we're done." He took out yet another dollar bill, laid it on the counter. Three dollars for a glass of tap beer; now that was really a little stiff. Then again he had taken four hundred and fifty dollars out of Ric Davis's wallet, another forty out of Jessup's before he had bid them goodbye forever. In that sense the operation looked like it might at least be self-financing. "Give me another beer," he said very gently not to panic the bartender, "just one to walk in on."

The man picked up the bills, shuffled away, came back with a glass and passed it to Wulff looking haunted now. Many things seemed to be in the bartender's face and none of them involved any liking for the situation. Wulff picked up the beer, took a careful sip and carrying it before him like a shield, walked into the rear room.

A small man, neatly dressed, sad-eyed and restless sat in a booth at the end of the line, smoking a cigarette and toying with a shot glass. It was not the only shot glass on the table; scattered around him were two or three others, one of them half-filled. A man who planned ahead, Scotti obviously ordered his full ration before he got settled. It avoided traffic back and forth into the room, the kind of traffic that might draw attention to the fact that he was sitting there. Also, it kept him in one place with an unobstructed view of the only entrance which meant that Scotti was a man who covered his flanks.

Wulff walked in slowly and when he came to the table, paused. Scotti looked up at him almost wistfully and said, "What do you want?"

"I came to carry a message from a friend of yours."

"I never saw you before in my life," Scotti said, "you don't know any friends of mine."

"How do you know?"

"I came here not to be bothered," Scotti said. With an attempt at being casual he took a nail file out of his pocket and began to work on his hands but the little delaying tremble of the fingers told everything. "I've got no business with you."

"No," Wulff said, "but you've got business with Richard Jessup."

"I don't know anybody named Richard Jessup," Scotti said after an imperceptible beat, "I never heard of anyone like that in my life."

"Jessup thinks you have."

"Then you and Jessup are crazy," Scotti said. He made a move, arching his back against the wall trying to stand but the position was no good. Too careful of the line of sight, he had blocked his line of exit. Win some, lose some.

Wulff put the heel of his hand on the table and pushed it into Scotti's stomach. The little man squeezed his eyes closed with pain, took the blow near the spleen and sat in an exhaling gasp.

"You're in trouble now, friend," he said and reached inside his coat.

It was all too easy. If all of them operated like this Wulff would have the city cleaned out before Christmas but the trouble is that he was working on the lower echelons and he knew it. Close to the bottom. He leaned forward quickly like a man trying to read a paper over another's shoulder in the subway, stretched out his arm and arced toward Scotti's wrist as it emerged from the coat. The gun lurched in the air, clattered to the table destroying shot glasses and then rolled to the floor near Wulff's ankle. He kicked it away.

"You're really in trouble," Scotti said softly, "now you're really in trouble."

"You know what?" Wulff said and reached out his arm again, hit the man in the mouth, knocked Scotti gasping into the booth and then, seizing a chair, dragged it over and sat close to the little man, wedging him in, "I'm sick of guys like you telling me I'm in trouble. I'm not in trouble Scotti, you are; you're in the worst trouble of your life. The harder you punks are pushed, the closer you get into the line, the more you tell me I'm in trouble but that's just like a dog being backed into a corner when he's on a chain and his jaws are muzzled. Just whining, Scotti." He hit the man across the face. "Jessup was to come here to give you some money," he said. "Who were you to pass it on to?"

"You're crazy," the little man said, "you've got to be crazy."

Wulff hit him again. Once you got into the rhythm of it it was fun. A small plume of blood spread from Scotti's mouth, arced downward. "Come on," he said, "be reasonable."

Scotti rubbed at his chin. His eyes reflected deep pain although behind this light there was a hint of something darker. "Don't do it again," he said in a level voice. He struggled to stand, found purchase on the table, reeled to his feet, "I mean that."

"Why not?" Wulff said and flicked out his hand. This one caught Scotti on the cheekbone, the man groaned and his head slammed into the wall. He came off it looking purposeful, digging into his pants pocket. When the hand came out there was a gun in it.

"All right," he said. The gun seemed to give him calm and assurance. He even looked two inches taller. The gun must have been for him what a shot of heroin might have been for one of his contacts but then again was it that simple? Was anything that simple? "All right," Scotti said, the gun, dull metal, wavering, then focussing, on Wulff's gut. "Now I want you to answer some questions."

"Questions?" Wulff said and laughed, "the questions are all coming from my end." Carefully he estimated the distance between the two of them, calculated certain angles. Did not move. The fact was that even with the gun in his hand Scotti still looked terrified.

"Who are you?" Scotti said.

"A friend of a friend." Wulff heard subtle noises behind, turned slightly expecting to see the bartender looking through the aperture. But communications in the Half-Moon Lounge did not appear too strong. Either that or the bartender had decided that his job was to provide space, nothing else.

"No good," Scotti said. He moved slightly away from the wall, holding the gun stiffly. Wulff had the feeling that the man did not know how to use it.

"Talk," Scotti said.

"Who was the money to go to, Scotti?"

"What are you talking about?"

"Your friend was going to pass on some money to you. Who takes it then?"

"I'm asking the questions," the little man said. A little trickle of sweat appeared near his eyebrows. He raised the gun.

"Don't be ridiculous, Scotti," Wulff said, "you're not going to knock anyone down in this back room."

"Why not?" the man said. He sounded almost inquisitive. "Why shouldn't I?"

"In the first place you'd miss and in the second place if you didn't miss there would be police all over the place in about thirty seconds but in the third place," Wulff said, carefully calculating distance, "your job doesn't include handling a gun. I've got you figured strictly for a contact man and you don't even *want* to handle that gun. I'm going to do you a favor, you son of a bitch," Wulff said.

He launched himself at the man. Old arrest training, never come on them frontwards but work from the side, use angles, tackle the surprise element and never give them a clear, open target. He came under Scotti's guard, pivoting, threw a shoulder into the man's armpit, sent him back in scatters to the wall, reaching for the gun. For a sickening instant he couldn't find it, could only feel cloth and flesh squirming underneath him and in that moment Scotti could have killed him, he could feel the death closing on him in this little room ... but then everything was all right. He found the gun. It slid into his seeking hand with a jolt and he yanked, twisted, tore it free and brought it protectively against his belly.

Then he kicked the little man's legs out from under him roughly. Scotti fell unevenly, hitting chairs and floor, scattering wood, finally lay there in a clump of limbs, breathing shallowly, his forehead against an outstretched arm. He looked about as helpless as a man could get without being badly hurt.

Wulff put the gun into his jacket pocket noting that the safety had never been uncocked and looked down at the man. Two guns now. Two guns and almost five hundred dollars. If he could keep this up, he'd be half an army soon.

Sure he would be.

The bartender now was looking through the aperture, having concluded that the action was over. He stood there, wiping his hands on the towel flapping from his waist. "What's going on here?" he said without interest.

"Small discussion. Little bit of a disagreement. He thought that the Giants were at least two touchdowns better than the Jets and I didn't see the margin as more than five points. So I had to beat the shit out of him."

"Uh," the bartender said, wiping faster, "football fans, huh?"

"Not me," Wulff said. "I can't stand the game. He is."

Scotti raised himself feebly on his elbows and said to the bartender "Get out of here."

"*You* get out of here," the bartender said, "I don't know what's going on; I don't want to know what's going on but I want both of you to get the hell out of here now. I just rent space, that's all."

"You only work here you mean," Wulff said, "you have nothing to do with anything that goes on. That's a good attitude."

"Get him the fuck out of here. Or should I call the cops?"

"No," Scotti said thinly, drawing his knees up under him, "don't call the cops. It's a private dispute."

"That's right," Wulff said, yanking the man to his feet, dusting Scotti off almost paternally and pushing him against the wall, "just a little disagreement between friends."

"All right," the bartender said. He moved from the opening, gestured toward it. "Go on. Get out of here."

Scotti looked at Wulff. "Go on," he said.

"You're coming," said Wulff.

"What?"

"You're coming. The two of us are leaving together. Good friends, right?"

"Oh come on," Scotti said, sweat starting again. For a small man he certainly sweated a great deal. "Cut it out now."

"Cut it out?" Wulff asked softly, "man, you don't understand anything, do you? I haven't even begun."

He took Scotti gently by the arm and led him from the room. The bartender looked at them and then past to the littered tabletop, the spillage on the floor. He seemed to be calculating how long it would take him to clean up and whether he could get away with a superficial job. But then again, as Wulff had pointed out, he only worked there.

"Hey," the bartender said when they were already halfway down the line, the sounds of the game show piping them rapidly toward the door, "wait a minute! You forgot to pay me. That's five dollars and fifty cents on that table."

"Okay," Wulff said, halting, releasing Scotti briefly and getting out his wallet. "Let this one be on me." He took out a ten and placed it on the bar, rolled an ashtray over and sealed the ten in tight. "A pleasure to do something for a friend," he said to the middle-aged lady who gave him a hideous wink. She must have taken him for a very nice young man. "Even though I had to beat him up for stupidity," Wulff added and winked back at her.

He went back to Scotti who had not moved. The man seemed to have given up; he came so submissively against Wulff as he renewed the arrest-lock that Wulff decided that he could probably make it without any pressure. The trouble with these men was that they were all up front: they had plenty of style and mannerism but puncture it, one inch deep, and there was nothing but fear and the desperation not to be hurt. All gesture, no center. Would that it be the same way all to the top. Wulff doubted it, however. There were levels of competence in any business organization and obviously the lower echelons possessed less of it than those at the top. The boys at the top had to be very good indeed, for the organization was excellent.

"Come on," the Wolf said to the trembling man beside him, "let's get to your car and take a ride. I want to meet your friends."

"You'll regret this," Scotti said, "if you think that this is going to take you anywhere you're just crazy. You'll be killed."

"And then I'll be just like you, eh Scotti?"

The little man said nothing. They started to walk. At length Scotti pointed out a faceless Dodge Dart at a hydrant, bearing a ticket and said that this was his car. "I'll drive," Wulff said.

Scotti gave him the keys without comment.

Wulff and his new friend got into the Dart and, parking ticket still flapping, went off for a little drive in the country.

Fucking transmission slipped. Pity he couldn't have stayed with the Rikker's bigass Eldorado.

IV

Albert Marasco, sitting behind his huge desk, the paintings and shelves of ornaments on the walls gleaming in the late-afternoon sun of eastern Long Island, looked at the thick man in the sports shirt sitting in front of him and said again, "I thought I told you never to come into this house."

"I couldn't help it," the thick man said. He weighed three hundred pounds and was close to six and a half feet tall but he looked terrified. "I had a problem. I had to discuss it."

"Fuck that," Marasco said with sudden passion, fury bursting out of his careful, businessman's glaze and then he shrugged, sighed, reconstituted himself as a mild man in elegant clothing, late forties, an investment broker or at least a CPA. He took a bottle of scotch from an inner desk drawer, a paper cup from another drawer, poured himself a delicate shot and drank it down, ignoring the big man for a minute, savoring the terror he could bring upon this gorilla simply by showing disapproval. "Still," he said more gently, "a mistake is a mistake, no? All of us should be entitled to at least one mistake—"

"The shipment didn't come through," the man named Joseph Terello said, "we were at the contact point and nothing happened. It seemed to me—"

"It seems to *me*," Marasco said gently, allowing himself one more inch of scotch, watching the bigger man's eyes gleam and then become sullen as he realized that this shot too was not for him, "that this is my house, my home here Terello, and it is not a place for the conducting of business. Shipments here, shipments there; that is a legitimate concern but *not in my home.*"

"I'm sorry," Terello said, "we got frantic. That's a quarter million, maybe three hundred thousand dollars' worth of the purest—"

"*Shut up,*" Marasco said savagely and stood; then, in a controlled way let the power flow out of him. Now he was no longer a CPA or an investment broker but something in the quiet clothing that made Terello, a very big man begin to shake. "Do you think I give a shit about your problems with shipments? That's your job Terello and if you don't do it you'll be replaced, that's all. This is my home. I live here. I live here with my family and I do not bring business into my home ever. Do you understand that?"

Terello shambled to his feet, dropped his hands into his pockets, stood there, his mouth open. "Yes," he said, "I understand—"

"Then why didn't you understand before you came here?"

"I'm sorry. It was a mistake."

"Aah," Marasco said and turned from the man, looked out the window at the rolling empty carpet of green outside on which from a great distance he could see children playing, his wife moving slowly into position for another tennis volley, "you get me sick. Get the fuck out of here."

"All right."

"And don't come back. Don't try this again Terello. If you do it's going to get very bad."

"Yes. I know."

Marasco turned and faced the man. "You know?" he said, "then what are you waiting for?"

Terello clambered out of the room as if he were lifting himself from a box. Graceless at best, the big man now frantic almost fell over himself getting out of the room. Marasco watched him go and then came to the door of the huge den which Terello had not closed and pushed it shut firmly, sprung the lock. He sighed enormously and then went back to the window. But this time there was no pleasure in looking out at the lawn: his children, his wife, the peace of Islip, Long Island on a late August afternoon. Instead, against his will, he found concern beating around his mind like a bee battering the inside of his skull with small, deadly stings, retreating and striking again.

The deal had fallen through somehow. The contact had been arranged: terms, prices, even the distribution had already been worked out and figured and now somewhere along the line something had happened and the deal was gone. That was bad enough, seeing something of this size go sour, but even worse was the fact that in Marasco's life deals simply did not collapse. It was a bad omen; it meant that somewhere in the chain a malfunctioning part had been developed but the only way to find it was to trace through slowly and carefully and with the chain snapped, anyone could be an enemy. *No one could be trusted once something soured.* It was something Marasco had learned very early in his career; by the time he was sixteen and still on the streets he had known this. All the rolling lawns of Islip, all the tennis courts in the world could not take this insight from him.

He could not blame Terrello, then, for being frantic. Terello was good as far as he went but he was limited; keep him on a straight course which was what delivery was supposed to be and he was fine, occasionally even brilliant, take him out of the simple procedures though and he was lost. It would figure that he would come to Islip, right past the gates, into Marasco's den to deliver the news. If nothing else it would take the responsibility off Terello, put it on Marasco where it belonged. But he had dedicated his life or at least the most recent ten years of it to keeping his home inviolate. Whatever he did took place outside of it; the home was his shell and his palace. It might represent the fruits of his work but it was not part of it. And now Terello had violated the code, used his name and his relationship with Marasco to talk his way past the gates and into the den. That was bad. That was very bad. Something was going to have to be done about the man.

It was regrettable because Terello was as good a lieutenant as Marasco had ever had, but that was business. Business was business; life was life and the two of them damned well had to be separated. Terello had crossed the line and would now have to be taken care of.

Which decision, Marasco thought, had absolutely nothing to do with the missed delivery which was even more serious. Like it or not he was going to have to move on this and very quickly. Carefully keeping his motions deliberate, playing as always to the invisible audience that was there at all times to evaluate the career of Albert Marasco and find that it was good, he lit a cigarette with an ornate lighter and moved deliberately toward the phone. Checking calls and pretty soon, through the careful network, a meeting would have to be arranged. Unless he could find that it was a simple screwup and the stuff was waiting there for Terello after all who had gotten impatient. That was to hope for. He doubted it.

Before he could take it up, the phone rang on the intercom unit.

"Yes?" he said picking it up carefully, taking the cigarette from his mouth. "What is it?" His impulse was to be curt but it might be one of his daughters. He would not want to show his agitation to any member of his family. "What is it?"

"Jack Scotti is at the gatehouse," a voice said, "this is Paul and I've held him up."

"That wasn't a bad idea."

"He wants to come in."

"Does he?" Marasco said, "that's interesting."

"There's a guy with him."

"Who?"

"I don't know," Paul said, "I've never seen this one before."

"Have you asked him?"

"He says he's a friend of Scotti's; that he goes everywhere that Scotti goes."

"What does Scotti say?"

"He doesn't say much of anything except that he's here to see you."

"I don't like it," Marasco said and then, because showing vulnerability to employees was one of the stupidest things you could do, caught himself. "Scotti must have something else to say, doesn't he?"

"He doesn't say a thing. The other guy, the big one, is doing all the talking."

"It sounds like he's got a gun on Scotti," Marasco said.

"We took a frisk already. The guy had two guns on him. We've got them both."

"That was good work," Marasco conceded, "that was really very good."

"We try."

"Pass them in," Marasco said with sudden decision. His home already violated once this afternoon could not be further invaded by letting this second invasion through. Furthermore, with instincts that had been worked out through thirty years of trouble, he had the feeling that this might tie into the matter of the missed shipment. He didn't like it but there was no way of getting around these things; it might as well be faced now. "Keep a man on them."

"I thought we would. Terello's gone by the way."

"Give me five minutes," Marasco said and hung up.

He pushed the phone away, went to the windows and drew down all of the shades, shutting off the lawn, the children, the tennis court. He would have done this before Terello's entrance except that that man had taken him without notice. Seal off, seal off: that was the whole point, set up partitions between your life and your work and make them hold. There were men whose lives *were* their work and they would not need the partitions, maybe, but Marasco was damned if he was going to fall into that category. His work was his work, his life was his *life* and the purpose of the one was to act only as a feeder for the others. To keep the lawns lush and green, as it were.

Marasco did not think of himself as an evil man. Evil had nothing to do with it; he was in business. The business he had to do with was drugs but that was an abstraction. It could just as easily have been cars or construction. The way a man could get into trouble and Marasco had seen this too many times not to remember the lesson, was to start thinking about the nature of his work and getting emotional about it. There was nothing emotional here. He was in supply and demand. He did his work well. He was a good organizer. He arranged for certain people to get what they needed from others who could deliver. He worked out prices, arrangements, methods of payment. Drugs? Marasco felt they could as well have been Oldsmobiles he was moving on the network from Turkey to New York to Saigon to San Francisco to Malaga to Chicago to...

But the breakdown in the delivery was distressing. This kind of thing was not supposed to happen. It *never* happened if you were a good businessman and exercised the kind of control and common sense which had brought Marasco to this point. *Son of a bitch* he thought and peeked through a shade to see in the closing light a flash of his wife's buttocks as she bent over on the lawn back from her tennis game, picked up a scrap of paper and walked to a pail to dispose of it. A neat, organized woman, Jill Marasco, with the kind of bearing and walk that showed a quiet, fierce sexuality without any self-consciousness. He had done very well with this one, his third. Very well indeed...

Marasco put back the shade, turned from the window and took the seat behind his desk, elbows on the panelling, rubbing his hands softly, waiting for Scotti and the other man to come in. He warned himself to maintain a glacial reserve and calm against which they could only break and die but became aware, without really being able to control it, of a mad fluttering of his right eyelid which made him feel as if his skull was being displaced. It got to you. Let the fact be faced, after a while, no matter what you did to seal off, it would get to you. It would get to Terello who had panicked and it had gotten to Scotti who had been brought here under a gun and now it was getting, just a little, to Albert Marasco.

He wondered if it was getting to Scotti's friend.

V

It hadn't been too difficult. No reason to think that it would have been, the way that Scotti had folded up in the Half Moon Lounge, but sometimes the lack of resistance even in the seemingly tough ones surprised Wulff. Even though, as a cop in the old days who had seen them taking the collapse hundreds of time, he should have been used to it.

Anyway it had not been too difficult with Scotti; the man had crumpled like a lump beside him in the Dart, speaking only when spoken to and the one time that Wulff had raised his hand the man had quivered, cowered, wrapped himself in his own armlock and fallen back against the door. "Albert Marasco," he had said and had given an address, "I was supposed to deliver it to a guy named Albert Marasco. But not today. Tomorrow. In an office."

"I think we'll make a home visit," Wulff had said, "he'll be happy to see a quickie delivery, won't he?"

"You don't understand. Never go to Marasco's home in Islip. I'm not even supposed to know his address except that I heard it around. Don't hit me," Scotti said, his wide eyes blinking, "I can't take it. The pain

I mean, I just can't take it."

"I wouldn't waste the time," Wulff said. The West Side Highway, crosstown on 34th to the Midtown Tunnel, the Long Island Expressway. The Southern State Parkway. An easy drive even at this hour but a long one. The Marascos did indeed keep themselves way out of the picture.

"Listen," Scotti said after a long, long time. Obviously he had been thinking, "you want to do this, why don't you let me out of it? Let me out of the car."

"No."

"You don't need me," Scotti whined. "You want to see Marasco, *you* go the fuck and see him. Leave me out of it."

"I enjoy your company."

"He's going to kill you you know. You ever get past his checkpoints and into that house you're a dead man."

"Nobody understands," Wulff said levelly, "I can't get the message delivered somehow, I *am* a dead man. I was killed three months and eighteen days ago and now I'm just going through the moves. There's nothing your Marasco can do to me even if he could. Which he can't."

"That's okay. You're a dead man? That's great. But why don't you just leave me out of it?"

"Wouldn't pay," Wulff said, getting a little struggle from the engine as he cut it up to seventy-five off a curve, checked out an exit sign, "I need some company. You've got a great career, Scotti; what you've got to do is to stick with it to the end."

That finished off the conversation all the way to Islip. Scotti sat compactly against the door, rolling his fingers and looking hopelessly out the windshield. Wulff supposed that if the man had had the strength he might have tried to bolt at a tollbooth or swinging off slow at an exit ramp but all the fight had gone from Jack Scotti. He was not the efficient little man who had set up his rounds of drinks at the Half-Moon Lounge, but something very different. Resistance was gone.

A pity in a way because if Scotti had still had some fight Wulff might have killed him. Killing this type was a pleasure; he had discovered that already. It would be fun to shoot him down in a ravine somewhere and leave the body for the creeping plants. But there was no fun in shooting a corpse and Scotti was more than halfway there.

Besides, he might need Scotti to get face to face with Marasco. After that he could or couldn't handle it but a cold entry through checkpoints might be really tough. Yes, Wulff thought looking at the shaking little man, mercy had its own rewards. You could do the compassionate thing and gain from it at the same time. Maybe there was a reason to be an optimist in this world after all.

He decided that he didn't like that line of thought. He killed it. *There was no hope.* You only did what you had to do now because there was nothing else. But the Wolf was a fool if he thought he was going to win or even hold them even. There were millions of them and only one of him and like pack animals they could not care in the least how many of their number dropped as long as the individual got through. He figured right from the beginning that it was hopeless.

But in the absence of anything else you had to try. *The Wolf.* He liked that. When you got started on a new life the first thing you needed was a new identity and oh yes indeed he was getting one.

They cut off a side road at Scotti's hand-gesture and drove over bumps and ruts, past greenery and enamel dogs to the checking gate.

Scotti did the talking to the man at the gate who made a phone call and there was no trouble at all. They got right through. There was the frisk, of course, but Wulff had expected that. There was never so much luck in the world that he would be able to face scum like Albert Marasco with a gun. The realities were stiffer.

But they could be more rewarding.

VI

Marasco turned and said, "I want to know what you're doing here in my house."

Wulff shrugged carefully, measuring the man. Dapper, controlled, certainly threatening but there was something about this one too which reminded him of the Jack Scotti he had seen for the first time. "I had a few questions," Wulff said noncommittally.

"I have nothing to do with this," Scotti said. His face seemed to have turned rounder and more desperate since he had seen Marasco. It was as if the man had had to calculate who frightened him more and Marasco was still the winner by a slight edge. "He pulled a gun on me."

"Shut the fuck up," Marasco said quietly. He looked at Wulff through appraising eyes. "I want to hear anything from *you*, I'll ask."

"You want me to take him?" the guard asked. A big, healthy Anglo-Saxon type in his mid-twenties. Blond hair, blue eyes, a nice healthy snout of a rifle barrel poking from between his fingers. Well, it took all kinds. He came a step nearer Wulff. "I'll finish him off," he said, "just say the word."

"In time," Marasco said with a dismissive gesture. "Back off."

"Anything you want," the guard said sullenly. Wulff had the feeling that Marasco underpaid his help. Not necessarily dumb of him: where else did they have to go? "You talk, friend," he said to Wulff. "You tell the man anything he asks, you hear?"

"I intended to."

"I told you to lay the fuck off," Marasco said to the guard. He waved a hand, the guard backed all the way into a corner. Marasco seemed very irritated, in fact, to Wulff, he seemed about to come apart. Hazards of the business.

"He pulled a gun on me," Scotti said, "and then he beat the shit out of me. I couldn't do a thing."

"My heart bleeds," Marasco said.

"I was making a routine pickup, that's all. He pulls a gun on me and wants to know where it was going. I had to tell him! I had to tell him, didn't I? What would you have done?"

"I don't know," Marasco said softly. "It's hard to say, having never been in your position "

"Now listen—"

Marasco raised his head and looked at the guard, pointed toward Scotti. "Shoot him," he said.

"With pleasure," the guard said. He lifted the rifle and toyed with the catch.

"Now wait a minute," Scotti said, his voice breaking, "what is this? I didn't betray anything. I told him that we'd go right to you and *you'd* finish him off. I warned him—"

"Now," Marasco said quietly.

"Yes," the guard said. He grunted, cleared his throat softly, hoisted the rifle and shot Scotti in the ear.

The man spun, lurched against carpeting, rolled. The guard deposited another bullet into the man's forehead. Scotti lay still.

It was a good aseptic job. Except for the scant threads of blood, Scotti looked intact. That kind of impact wound, Wulff knew, left very little trail. You had to give the guard credit then. He was a professional.

"Now him?" the guard said, pointing to Wulff.

"Not now," Marasco said. "Wait."

"I'll wait."

"Just leave the bastard here," Marasco said, gesturing to the corpse. "It improves the decor. There's nothing I like more than a dead body in my den. It gives the place a certain aura of class."

"You want me to get it out of here?" the guard said cautiously.

"No," Marasco said, "I want you to leave it here for maybe three or four days until it starts to get ripe. Maybe my wife can come in and I'll introduce her around. Also I can talk to it in odd moments."

"I'll get it right out," the guard said. He walked toward the phone, "I mean I'll get somebody to come right away."

"No you won't," Marasco said. "You shot him. You drag him out yourself."

"Oh," the guard said softly, "you mean you want me to leave you alone—" He broke off and pointed at Wulff. "Alone with him," he finished.

"I'll take the chance," Marasco said wryly. "You'll need two hands to do some wrestling so just let me hold that rifle for you."

Looking at Wulff a little edgily, the blond passed over his rifle. Marasco took it smoothly, checked the safety, blew out a little powder and putting a knee up on the desk, balanced the rifle across it, holding it in the area of Wulff's chest.

"You do that very nicely," Wulff said, "with real skill."

"Thanks very much," said Marasco. "Are you going to get that son of a bitch out of here or should I put this thing on *you?*"

"All right," the guard said hesitantly. The situation seemed entirely beyond him. He bent over Scotti's body grunting, seized it by the heels and dragged it slowly toward him. Scotti came easily, lightly into his grasp. The guard eased back a foot, kicked the door open and took Scotti away with him. As he had gone in life so did Scotti in death: submissively. He was nothing if not cooperative. The guard slid the corpse into the hallway and closed the door with an imperceptible click.

Marasco looked at Wulff and said, "I want to know what you're after."

Wulff shrugged. "I'm a free-lance investigator," he said, "a researcher call it. I like to follow things up, trace them down to their sources."

"You're cute," Marasco said. He ran a hand over the stock of the rifle. "You don't look like a clever guy but you certainly think you are, don't you?"

"That depends," said Wulff. The feeling came upon him that in looking at Marasco he was now getting as close to the true source of the power and the enemy as he ever had but he could not give that feeling too much credence. Marasco was too edgy. His hands fluttered just a little bit. When you came right down to it, Wulff was pretty sure, this was just another Scotti after all.

"I want to know what you're doing here in my house, in my den," Marasco said. "And I want to know what I'm going to do with you."

"I can't answer the second part," Wulff said softly. "But I'll answer the first like before: I'm a kind of free-lance researcher. I like to track things down to their source and draw conclusions."

"Sure."

"Sure," Wulff agreed. "I was up at 137th Street and Madison Avenue with a guy named Ric Davis who had some money in his pocket and was waiting to pick up a shipment from a guy named Jessup. Jessup was the second link you see and Jessup told me that he got the stuff from a man named Scotti. So then I had to go and see Scotti and find out who he was supposed to pass the money that Jessup got on to. And you know what? Scotti said the man was you. Now what I want to find out is what happens to the money after it gets out of *here*. Research."

"Research," Marasco said. He shifted his position slightly, raised the rifle barrel a trace, aiming it now at Wulff's head. "Guys like you, freelance researchers can get killed you know."

"Scotti was no researcher."

"He got killed too," Marasco said quietly. "A lot of people can get killed when they start poking around into the grounds."

"All I want to know," Wulff said, "is what your wife thinks you do. Does she think you're a gentle trucking magnate? Or maybe she thinks that you're a stock investigator, a market manipulator. Or do you just tell her that it's none of her fucking business and hit her in the mouth when she asks?"

Marasco carefully took a cigar from his jacket pocket and put it, still in the wrapping, into his mouth. "I don't think I like you," he said.

"It's kind of mutual, Marasco."

"I don't like your interests or your explanations. And I don't like your fucking questions either. What happened to Jessup and Davis?"

"They had a couple of little accidents," Wulff said quietly. "Like Scotti, they started imagining that they were dead and guess what? Dreams can come true, even in this world."

"Very cute," Marasco said meditatively, chewing on the cigar. "Do you think I should kill you now?"

"You did, Marasco," Wulff said.

"What's that?"

"I died three months ago. I died on the top floor of a building on West 93rd Street. You're talking to a dead man."

Marasco's eyes blinked. "Don't get philosophical with me. You're in trouble."

"I'm in no trouble at all, Marasco. I'm *dead*. There's nothing you can do but confirm it. I'm a walking, talking, angry dead man, Marasco. The smartest thing you could do would be to put me out of commission right now."

"And why shouldn't I?" Marasco said, raising the gun slightly, "why shouldn't I do just that one simple thing?"

"You won't," Wulff said. "You have no mercy. You'll keep me in commission."

"You think so?"

"I *know* so. Men like you never work on margin, Marasco. You'll deal with anything in the world except doubt. Until you find out exactly who and what I am and what I've done you'll keep me around. That was Scotti's problem. You had squeezed him dry. No surprises left. So anytime you wanted to, you could just kill him. That was Scotti's mistake; holding nothing back."

"I don't think I like you," Marasco said, uncertainty battling hatred in his eyes, "I don't really like you at all."

"I told you, it's mutual. What else do you have to say?"

"I want to know what your game is."

"If I told you you wouldn't believe me."

"Try me," Marasco said, "come on and try me." He took the cigar from his mouth finally, stuck it like an exclamation point back into his pocket. "One thing I always was was a good listener."

"You listen but you don't believe. That's the secret of your business success. You really know what I'm going to do, Marasco?"

"I'm waiting."

"I'm going to put you out of business."

"Sure thing."

"I'm going to put you out of business and the guys on bottom and top of you. And two layers bottom and top, all the way down into the sewer and all the way up to Sands Point or Malaga or the Federal cells where the *really* big ones operate because you're still small time and I see that. You're so small time you're afraid of *me;* I'm an uncertain element. I'm going to put you and your trade out of business, Marasco and get the country back again."

Marasco sighed and holding the rifle unmoving reached into his desk drawers, began to prowl around absently with a free hand. No point in trying to jump him: too much distance. Marasco might be small time but he wasn't *that* small time. It would be a bad mistake to confuse him with Scotti or Davis or for that matter, even the guard. Different levels, subtle differences of skill all the way along the line. Marasco came out of the desk with a small, thick notebook and tossed it to the glass in front of him, kicked the door closed. "I think I know who you are," he said.

"I just told you who I was. I'm trying to simplify your life as much as possible now; you ought to be grateful."

"I really think I know. And if I do it's all in this book," Marasco said. "Everything's written down. All I have to do is to look you up."

"Be my guest."

"You used to be a cop, weren't you?" Marasco said, "you worked on the narco squad."

"For a time."

"And then you got busted off the narco squad."

"That was inevitable," Wulff said. "I took my job as seriously as you take yours. Most people on my side didn't. You weren't supposed to."

"They busted you back to patrolman and sent you out in a radio car again," Marasco said, "and then you ran into this little problem over on West 93rd Street with some girl you knew."

"Yes," Wulff said quietly, "that's right."

"It was the business about West 93rd Street that touched it off," Marasco said. "There are details you never forget. Now I know who you are, Wulff."

"You could have asked and I would have told and saved you all the trouble."

"You're mad, aren't you, Wulff?" Marasco said. "Drugs got your girl and the narco squad got your goat and now you're burning."

"I'm not burning."

"You're going to shape up the world, right? Single-handed. You knock off a little supplier and a little dealer and right away you're conquering the world. You've got the skids on the business."

"I never thought that for a moment."

"You're crazy, Wulff," Marasco said harshly. He slammed his free hand to the rifle. "You know that, don't you? You're crazy!"

"Of course I'm crazy," Wulff said, "but that doesn't mean that I'm not serious."

"Straight cops wind up in the river or on pension, Wulff."

"I'm not a cop anymore."

"Reformers wind up in the river."

"And filthy little parasites wind up in Islip with blond goons to do their shooting."

Marasco trembled all over and leaned on the rifle. For an instant Wulff thought he might have bought it. But his judgement held. Marasco wouldn't do it. If he could have done it he would have the minute the blond left the room.

People like Marasco always sent someone to do the work.

The blond came in, kicking the door closed and looked at Wulff in half-surprise, as if he did not expect to see him there. If one of the prerequisites of a safe job was to know your employer, the blond had fucked up. He did not know, still, what Marasco was. "I put him away," he said to Marasco. "In the morning—"

"I don't want to hear any more about it."

"Well sure. I only wanted—"

"I don't want to hear any more about it. That's your business, not mine!"

"Well sure," the blond said. "All right. What are we going to do with this one now?"

"That's my decision," Marasco said in a terrible voice. "When *I* decide what *I'm* going to do with him, I tell *you* and *you* do it. And that's where it ends."

"Okay," the blond said. His eyes were wide with puzzlement as well as fear. Apparently he had never seen Marasco like this before. Wulff repressed a smile. The blond might have had a better job if he had seen this. Because Marasco was losing control.

"I think I'll be going now," Wulff said offhandedly. "It's been nice talking but we've reached the end of the road, you see? I hardly think I'm in a position, unarmed, to take on the two of you."

"You're crazy, Wulff."

"Although I'd certainly try if I thought I had even a one out of four chance," Wulff said, "as it is, I may be crazy but I'm certainly not stupid. Not with a rifle held on me and your assistant as backup man. Been a pleasure, Marasco," he said, moving toward the door. "I'll just pick up my guns at the gate, all right and maybe we'll talk some other time. Don't worry about giving me an escort. I'm sure that I'll be able to find my own way and I've already put you out more than enough, don't you think?"

For an instant he thought that he actually had a chance to get away with it. The blond was unarmed and Marasco, Wulff had settled, was not going to fire that rifle. *Could* not fire that rifle. If the situation had held for just ten seconds longer he might have, crazily, walked out of Islip with all the laurels although, unfortunately, no kill. Not yet.

But the blond was more alert than his employer. He came against the door, backed it, held out his hands in a karate posture and Wulff backed off. Going into a karate chop was one thing and he didn't think the blond really knew how to handle himself, but once activity started Marasco would forget what kind of man he was and shoot in self-defense. No odds. He stopped and stayed there, hanging on his toes, his hands in position to block anything the blond threw if the man made the first move.

"Pretty good Wulff," Marasco said, "that was really nicely handled."

"Thanks."

"But what kind of *paisan* you think I am you son of a bitch? You really think I'd let you get away with this? I'm no Jack Scotti."

"That's right," Wulff said quietly, not facing the man. The blond glared at him. "Scotti didn't have an estate or a gun."

"Take the son of a bitch down," Marasco said. "Put him away for a little while and in the morning I'll play with him. I want to do a couple of things before I get tired of him."

"All right," the blond said. He reached toward Wulff and then became hesitant. Wulff could see the man thinking, however uncertainly. "I think though—"

"Wait," Marasco said with disgust and there was the sound of a receiver being taken off a hook, "I'll get some assistance on this."

"Yes," the blond said gratefully. "I think that would be best."

"Would you like ten guys or fifteen?" Marasco said. "Should I ask for double riot guns and grenades or do you think that you could make it with a little less?"

"Now I don't need all that."

"Oh fuck you," Marasco said furiously and began to talk quietly into the receiver.

Wulff almost smiled. The blond's confusion was so total, Marasco's rage so uncontrollable, Scotti's death—and this was the kicker—so final that it almost felt like a victory. They were going to put him on ice and he felt that it was a victory.

With victories like this, Wulff thought, who needs defeats?

VII

Wulff sat alone in a room in the bowels of the house. No mansion Marasco's three-story home but large enough, more than large enough to stuff away subterranean passages, little rooms like piping strung along the bottom, spaces in which a dead man could lay for a very long time. Advantages of the newly-crowned he thought. He leaned forward in the darkness, testing the dimensions of the room. It was small. It smelled. It felt like a grave.

He had to get out.

He knew that it would only be a matter of time; awe or curiosity had determined Marasco's decision to stack him on ice for a while but awe or curiosity were never qualities which could withstand the dawn. By noon tomorrow Marasco would know everything he needed to about Wulff and would have concluded that there were no penalties in eliminating him. The blond would come down and put a pistol to Wulff's belly, pull the trigger and black him out. Then again the pistol might go to his temple. Compulsively neat. That was what the blond was. If nothing else he did nice work.

In his pocket Wulff had a pack of matches and a deck of keys. Little enough to be left but then he might as well be grateful; the blond had sneered at him before he was pushed at gunpoint into the chamber and said, "We ought to strip you naked. How would that be?"

"Not good," Wulff had said, "it's cold down here."

"Going to be a lot colder for you," the blond had said with a hollow laugh but then apparently having not been given such orders by Marasco settled for pushing him into the room, closing the door and leaving him to the darkness. At seven in the evening or maybe it was eight, Wulff's time sense having been wrecked by the darkness, some cold cereal and a closed thermos filled with water had been tossed in through an opening in the door. Marasco seemed to have planned his Islip lodgings with care; this room and probably others were equipped with locked partitions. The imprisonment business must have been good, at least for those that the blond had not finished off in the reception room. Well, be that as it may, Wulff drank the water, ate the cereal without trepidation—if Marasco had decided to poison him he simply would have found a more direct way of elimination—and considered his situation.

He had gone so far. The tracing through Marasco was significant; the real dealings did not end here but they certainly seemed to begin. Marasco was only another link in the network, the network was infinite; it went on and on but here he had reached a dead stop and that in itself was meaningful. *The degree of resistance was the key to the importance of the connection*, that was an old police procedural and the police background came in handy although, of course, it would be a mistake to take that kind of thing seriously. The best, the most cautious, the most diligent kind of police work might have traced its way painfully to Marasco and there it would have quit: a laughable arraignment, five or seven years later, after all the appeals, a laughable indictment and sentencing. Marasco was just the beginning. He was on the trail, that was all.

He had to get out of here.

Wulff crouched in a corner of the room, considering the situation. The room was impermeable; he had already tried the routine methods of exit. Possibly with a revolver he might have been able to do something with the locks but the blond had not sent him down here, *por favor*, with artillery. If there was a way out of this he would have to work it out himself, more in his own head than elsewhere. It was that important to get out, Wulff had decided. He figured his expected lifespan at this moment to be slightly less than seventeen hours. Sooner or later, even police work would give you instincts worth cultivating and that was what the instincts said. Maybe twenty-four hours if he was running in great luck. Marasco would certainly have him killed before dinnertime tomorrow; judging from Marasco he ate at seven thirty or eight o'clock like all of the newly crowned. The fashionable hour, they thought. But part of making it, however cautiously, into society was to manufacture the corpses before dinner so that you could eat without excess acid. Wulff sighed, less from panic than enormous regret. His entire outlook might have been different if Marasco had not moved out to Islip. In Little Italy, people like Marasco were hardly so regularized in their habits.

Wulff reached into his inner pocket and took out the matches. Bought with a pack of cigarettes two days ago, the cigarettes appropriated by the blond with eighteen still left in that pack—concentrated tension, he had found, reduced smoking rather than raised it—but the matches had been tossed back contemptuously. *Smoke 'em* the blond had said. Eighteen left; Wulff cautiously expended one to gain light and looked for the first time at his quarters; he was living in a room six by eight, a ceiling another eight feet high, a room in short just large enough for a man six four and two hundred and fifty pounds to go crazy in if he conserved his time and luck. Asphalt of course with little interstices of glue between the bricks and the match flicked out.

He lit another. His stock was limited, this meant only sixteen left but sixteen matches, his entire riches in this place could be worth more than the four hundred and fifty dollars which the blond had also taken from him. The glue was interesting; it was a characteristic of this kind of building of course. Hasty construction for the *nouveau riche* who usually were in a great hurry to move in and claim the premises for their own meant that corners had to be cut almost anywhere you could and certainly by the time you got to the basement or the sub-basement (Wulff was not quite sure) you would get into an area where glue was forgivable; it was the quickest way to slap the bricks together and although it would hardly work in the living room, guests were not likely to come poking or prying around in the nether regions checking out the builders for an angle-job. Not that the kind of guests which the Marascos would have would know the difference, of course.

Glue was highly flammable.

Wulff allowed the fourth match from his priceless pack to burn down, shook it out quickly to avoid the sulphur fumes and thought about this for a while. It was entirely possible that a single match, touched to any of those interstices would result in instant ignition. It was possible by the same token that it would result in an explosion; the glue going up with a grateful *whoomp!* as it seized upon the first real food that it had received in all of its constricted life. The *whoomp!* could well absorb the pyromaniac, however. If the glue could contain the force of the first combustion and then merely feed the fire into the brick neatly, everything would be under control, but a builder who would use glue in the first place would not be likely to order the best with the most controlled combustion he could find. It would be something like ordering the best kind of newsprint to print an art text on.

Wulff sat in the darkness and thought about this for a time. The room was soundproof and contributed to his thinking. Somewhere in the house above him Marasco and his family were enjoying the sounds and scent of the evening: entertaining perhaps or merely sitting in relaxed positions around an airconditioner in the living room, involved in their separate tasks. Central airconditioning come to think of it; Marasco would settle only for the best. He had two daughters, Wulff had found out from Jack Scotti, eighteen and twelve, and was devoted to them to say nothing of his third wife who had once been a debutante. Marasco had really made it. Did the wife and daughters have any idea what he was doing? Wulff wondered. *Probably not*, he answered himself. In fact, after about six o'clock in the evening, there was severe doubt that Marasco himself would acknowledge what he did during the days. It all went away after hours; it did not matter. He was an enterprising businessman who had moved his family to Islip and was giving them the best of all worlds.

A partition in the thick door opened and light filtered in. In the light was filtered the face of the blond. "Hello," the blond said, "you still here?"

"Wouldn't have it any other way?"

"How do you like the accommodations?"

"I love them," Wulff said. "Why don't you come in and share them with me?"

"I'd love that," the blond said, "but I have another engagement tonight."

"A pity," Wulff said, "why don't you take me along with you? We can discuss your future plans."

The blond giggled. "Let me tell you about your future plans," he said, "tomorrow morning for openers."

"Oh?"

"At about seven o'clock tomorrow morning. We'll get you up at six, though so you can have a good breakfast. Ought to have a good breakfast on your stomach. It's a full day tomorrow."

"Is it?"

"Oh definitely," the blond said, "except that it's going to be an early day too. It ought to end at about eight for you. Eight in the morning that is."

"So the word's gone out?"

"I wouldn't say the word's gone *out*," the blond said and put a hand like a paw over the opening so that he could lean in and stare down at Wulff, "it's more like the word has gone *in*."

"Of course."

"You get a good night's sleep tonight."

"What are you going to do?" Wulff asked, "date one of the daughters?"

"Well—"

"Why don't you propose tonight? I'm sure that Marasco would love to have you in the family."

"Go fuck yourself."

"Marasco would be delighted to have you in the family circle," Wulff said, "I happen to know that he has not only a great professional respect for you but feels a personal relationship and tie as well. Like a son-in-law."

"Tomorrow morning," the blond said, "at seven o'clock. I'm looking forward to it Wulff."

"Me too."

"I'll see you then," he said and closed the partition, leaving Wulff in darkness. The odor of the glue seemed to rise now in the pitch and Wulff inhaled it, felt the tongues of odor lapping at him like the frantic beating of a dog's heart. It was a high, exhaled, dense sweetness and breathing it in Wulff thought that it was like breathing in knowledge itself. His outcome had been decided. Marasco had either found out everything he needed to know or had lost interest or both. Either way, there was no postponing decision now.

Wulff fondled the matches in both hands now and then, very deliberately, extracted one, feeling that slender reed in the darkness, poor crutch to carry him to freedom, stretching out the moment. It was no longer a question of decision. Decision had passed. He knew exactly what he was going to do.

Rather it was like holding something in place until the last moment, like leading a suspect on the street with the car, knowing that he saw the pinch coming, feeling the wings of the moment tighten until at last, the clips broke and you flew in to take him. It was just like that. There was a kind of pleasure in extending the moment even when you knew, as in a case like this, that the odds were so long that it hardly mattered.

But maybe that was the point. The chances were so slender, the situation so bad that at least, if you were lucky, you could savor the moment and the anticipation.

They might be the only thing you would have.

VIII

In the living room, Marasco excused himself from his wife and went into the adjoining room to pour himself another scotch, neat. He didn't like to have bottles in the living room, not when there was a full bar next door and besides, although he hated to admit it, he did not want Pauline to know the full extent of his drinking. It was his business. He claimed that he watered the scotches and paced himself carefully, drinking only after five in the evening; best that the woman believe it. She believed everything that he said, unthinkingly. Even though it was more like five in the morning which was his starting time.

Marasco poured himself a double shot of scotch, looking beyond him down the long passageway toward the servant's quarters through which the blond was now slowly moving, his head bowed, his hands in his pockets. He finally saw Marasco and assumed a more alert posture, nodded at him, indicated that he was taking the side exit.

"Did you tell him?" Marasco said.

The blond nodded. "I told him. You told me to, right? So of course I did."

"That's good. How did he take it?"

The blond shrugged. "How do I know how he took it? He's very cool. A very cool type."

That, Marasco thought, dismissing the blond with a nod, sending him out the short steps to the grounds, was for sure. Whatever else this Burt Wulff was or was not he was a man of almost no visible emotion. Perhaps what he had told Marasco was the truth; he indeed was a dead man, to kill him would be simply to finish the job. But that was hard to believe.

Marasco liked life too much, he found it too interesting, it meant too much for him to think that there was such a thing as a man who could toss it away as Wulff seemed willing to. He had worked hard at life, manipulated it the way a juggler worked a group of balls in the air; now at forty-eight he had everything bouncing and moving neatly in the air and he intended to keep it that way for another thirty years, twenty at least, all things being equal.

He downed half of the scotch outside the living room so that Pauline would take it to be just a short, watered one and walked in, finding her as he had left her on the couch, listening to the music that poured out of the speakers. Opera? Something like opera he guessed; at least there were voices and strings and no real tune. All of it sounded pretty much the same to Marasco. But if it gave her pleasure she could have it on all the time for all he cared and sooner or later he would stop making excuses and even go with her to one of her opera nights. Why not? Wife number three was the real stuff; he had to admit it. *Third try never fails, three on a match* and what he had here was the real item.

He sat beside her on the couch, never too closely, Pauline did not appreciate affection outside of the bedroom and even there insisted upon it only on her terms. He stretched out an arm, touched her hand, smiled and leaned his head back against the wall. It was a little boring, Marasco was willing to admit, but compared to how and where he had spent evenings years ago it suited. It suited very well.

"Who were those two men who came through the gate this afternoon?" Pauline asked absently.

Marasco shifted a little on the couch. "Which two? When?"

"When I was on the tennis court. About four o'clock."

"Oh," Marasco said, "customers."

"I never saw one of them before. The other has been around a few times but one was a stranger."

"New customer," Marasco said and winced slightly. He ran his fingers along his wife's palm. "Just business."

"Anything important?"

"No. Nothing too important."

"You know," Pauline said moving toward him slightly, "I have absolutely no idea of what you're doing. People come in and out all day, you're here and gone and I have absolutely no idea of what's going on."

"Is it important?" Marasco said, "do you really need to know what's going on?"

"No," Pauline said. Her fingers brushed against his, Marasco felt the familiar warmth, "but sometimes you can get curious, can't you?"

"Curiosity killed the cat," said Marasco with slight unease. "Didn't it?"

"I don't know," Pauline said. "Did it?"

"Once upon a time."

"I'm not a cat."

"Oh yes you are," Marasco said and moved imperceptibly closer to her. Why did he always feel with this woman that each approach was the very first? Why did each approach necessitate seduction? It was like starting from the beginning time and again which on the one hand could be very exciting—and, in his late forties, he was not one to knock excitement—but on the other hand, times like now when a man simply wanted in an uncomplicated way to get laid without preliminaries, could be very exasperating. She looked up at him, the bland, impenetrable features as if sculptured, and he put a hand to her cheek feeling the cool surfaces, feeling the slow rising excitement as he drew her against him realizing that this evening was not going to be too difficult. They would always surprise you, these women, just when you felt you had them figured out they would veer in a different direction. Marasco drew his wife against him and thoughts of the missed shipment, of Terello, of the big clown in the basement went scuttling away down a long, dark corridor.

"I smell something," Pauline said.

"What's that?"

She pushed her hands against his chest, disengaged him gently but firmly, her head raised. "Don't you?" she said, sniffing in what was even then a patrician way. "Don't you smell something?"

"Look," Marasco said, "you can't do this to me. I want—"

"I'm not putting you off," she said with irritation. "I tell you, I smell something." She stood rapidly, backpedalled. "Don't you?"

And then Marasco did smell it. Desire or at least preoccupation may have blocked his sinuses but now, attention drawn, he took in the odor that Pauline had sensed before he. It was a high, dense sweetness, behind it something blacker like the odor of combustion and in an instant, for reasons that he could not quite understand, Marasco felt himself seized by a mounting, unreasoning fear. He had never liked fire. And fire was not something which happened to you in Islip.

"You *do* smell it," she said.

"Yes," he said, standing, "I do." And indeed he did; he could not understand why he had not minutes before because once conscious of it the odor was overpowering, it lapped at him, came at him in sickening, sweetish ripples and Marasco found himself gagging. One hand on his wife he moved toward the door, the odor coming at him more and more rapidly. He could feel it beginning to straighten him up; the first tendrils of the odor reached his lungs. Marasco gagged.

"What is it Albert?" Pauline said. "What's going on here?"

"I don't know," he said, holding onto her but for comfort or protection he did not know. He leaned out the door, beginning to choke her and looked toward the rear stairs.

He could barely see them. Thin knives of smoke were coming up from below. He could feel them digging at him like spears.

"We're on fire, Albert!" Pauline screamed, "the house is on fire!"

That's ridiculous, Marasco wanted to say, *fires are something that happen in tenements on the Lower East Side; junkies are rolled and wrapped in fires all the time but nothing like that ever happens in Islip, Long Island.* He opened the door to the basement, felt the heat storming at him, groaned and by leaning all of his suddenly-panicked weight on the door managed to get it closed, turned toward his wife with streaming eyes. He began to feel the fear, then. It was like nothing he had ever before known.

"Where are the girls?" he said.

"They're both out for the evening," she said, *"you see? you don't even care where your daughters are."*

"I do," he said, "I do." Strains of opera lofted foolishly from the living room; something happened to the wiring then and one of the speakers began to rumble, a high, splitting whine that caused him to put his hands in his ears. "We've got to get out of here," he said.

"The fire department—"

"No time," Marasco said, "no time." He was panicking now for sure and in some detached corner of the mind he knew this *but he had to get out*. Fire could suffocate, it could kill; the odor was beating on him now like a bird, he could suffocate here in his own house *unless he got out*. "Let's go," he said, seizing her by a shoulder, "for God's sake, let's get out."

It was getting suddenly difficult to see in the hallway or maybe that too was the panic reaction. He reached out, touched her shoulder, brought her to him and gave her a push ahead.

"Go," he said, "get out of here."

"We can't just go, Albert. The house—"

"The hell with the house!" Marasco screamed, "I can't see!" the basement door coming open again and thick, greenish plumes of smoke right behind it; the smoke gripping him like ropes; the blanket of smoke tearing at his neck, squeezing, constricting. He tried to close the door but at that point lost all orientation whatsoever and found that he could not.

It was then that panic utterly consumed Albert Marasco. In his own house, no more than six yards from the nearest exit, the fire still only at the smoky, warning stage, plenty of time to deal with it if only he could have, Marasco lost control. In his mind was a voice and the voice was saying get out, get out, *save yourself now before it's too late, just get out* and it was this voice alone to which Marasco responded. It was the only thing that mattered, the only communication left in the world: the voice that told him *get out* and he shrieked *yes, I will, I will* and headed toward the voice, the beckoning voice that would be his salvation if only he could heed it.

The voice knew. He must trust the voice. *Get out* it said and Marasco obeyed. He forgot his wife, the exit, instructions, possibilities, sinking into the certainty that only one thing mattered and that was escape. Was it possible that the man listening to it now had not ten minutes before been sitting on a couch with his wife, listening to opera, gently trying to nudge her into sex? Impossible. Impossible. The man who was listening to the voice had no wife. Had no couch, no feelings about the opera one way or the other, certainly no interest in sex. The man responding to the voice had no estate, no business, no contact, no intricate network of supplies and appointments, rendezvous and conditions which had made him behind the guise of the respectable, one of the most significant drug traffickers on the East Coast.

The thing in the hallway was a blind, staggering animal who heard only the call for its own preservation. Listening, waving its arms, stumbling in the darkness and the tongues of smoke, the thing that had been Albert Marasco lurched one way, lurched the other, collided with the swinging door, lost its balance and fell gracelessly, screaming all the way, down the flight of stairs toward the basement.

Landing at the end of the fall, babbling, in Burt Wulff's arms.

IX

It had gone even more easily than he had thought. Wulff had known from the instant of ignition that he would have no problem in establishing a fire; it was the cheapest glue imaginable and endlessly combustible. Thank the contractor for that; he had sized up Marasco and decided to take the man over. The problem was whether Wulff in the process of creating a fire would be incinerated in the room; it would make a nice, neat, tight little coffin for a man six feet four and the walls tumbling in around him would press slabs of pain into his body for awful, wrenching instants before the last moments. Wulff knew that he was a dead man already but there were ways and ways of dying; if it were all the same to circumstance, he would just as soon die the second time without pain. Feeling the heat pressing against his body, the already rising odor of the glue he had found himself for the first time that day on the outside of panic, but then, hurling his weight over and again against the door he had burst free. Fire had weakened not only the glue it seemed but the very connections holding the house together. Hell, the way the thing was made you could probably have demolished it just by vigorously jumping up and down a few times. A man like the blond could probably have carried out the entire upstairs on his shoulders.

Wulff came out of the room quickly, seeking the stairs. That would be his only problem, working out the geometry of the bottom and getting the hell out of there but the fire provided not only heat but light, and Wulff found the stairwell immediately. The flames traced a clear, clean path out of his cubicle, swung toward the heavy boiler pumping like a heart at the far corner, then almost majestically pivoted and walked their way to the opposite wall. The whole place was going up incredibly faster than he could have hoped. When the flames hit the boiler there was going to be a hell of an explosion. Already, Wulff could smell the thin, escaping gas.

But there was margin. Enough margin. Breathing heavily, he lowered his head and charged at the stairs the way that you were trained to break into a suspect's room: no wasted motion, all activities concentrated on the front end. Taking the steps two at a time as he was it must have been those instincts which had saved him when the heavy, clawing weight of Albert Marasco had landed in his arms. Wulff swayed, felt his right foot begin to lose purchase, thought for one sick moment that he was going to carry Marasco's body below the boards and into hell but his motion had been pitched forward, all of his body weight had been veered toward going *up*.

The balance held. He dragged the man upstairs.

He could have tossed the man into the flaming basement and closed doors behind him, of course. Left him to incinerate there. But something beyond instinct caused him to hold onto Morasco, struggling to make the last four or five steps of the ascent. The man was semi-conscious, babbling, shrieking, lunging at Wulff's eyes with burnt fingers like little talons. There was no attack in it, only panic. Marasco literally did not know where he was; he did not know who was holding him. Mewling, spitting, crying, Marasco clung to Wulff, his body shaking and shifting. He was much lighter than Wulff would have thought. A little man. One hundred and thirty, one hundred and forty pounds. A hoist carry was easy.

"I've got to get out of here," Marasco whispered, "I've got to get *out*."

"You're out," Wulff said, "you're out now," and came through the door at the top. One quick glance behind; the flames were charging after them like dancers. The hall itself was beginning to incinerate, little pockmarks on the floor, black rings on the walls. The house was going to collapse *inwards* rather than out, imploding upon itself like an apple crushed in a man's hand. Oh, the builder had done his work well on this one. Wulff looked at the thing in his arms and with revulsion tossed Marasco to the floor, stood over him. Hard to see now; the smoke was whipping into his eyes. "Out," Marasco was whimpering on the floor, "I've got to get *out*."

"You'll get out," Wulff said, "oh you'll get out."

"Please," the thing said, whimpering, scrambling on the floor. It seemed to be trying to achieve a sitting posture. Wulff put a foot in the man's chest and pushed him prone. *It* prone.

"Fire," the thing babbled, "I always knew that there was going to be a fire—"

"Where is it?" Wulff said, "where's the next step, Marasco?"

"Fire. Oh my God, I'm going to die."

"Who takes it after you, Marasco?" Wulff said and kicked the thing. He inhaled smoke, looked at the little flame-dancers ringing them. Not much more time now.

He kicked the thing again.

"I want to know the next step in the detail, Marasco," he said. "It's a chain, a never-ending chain. Who's next? Who do you take it to?"

"I've got to get out," the thing mewled and tried to crawl toward a door blindly sensed. Wulff kicked it again.

"Stay put," he said.

The thing rolled on its back and looked up at Wulff, eyes glinting with tears. Recognition seemed to assault it. "Please," it said.

"Where are the others?"

"What others?"

"The others in the house. Your wife, your daughters. Your blond boyfriend."

The thing came up on its elbows. "I don't know," it said hoarsely, "don't know. Got out I guess. Got to get out too."

Wulff kicked it down to the floor, heard sirens and a gong in the distance. So someone at the gatehouse had finally turned in an alarm. Not much time now.

"You supply the junk and take the money," Wulff said, "but you're small time. Islip isn't anywhere; you live in a house built like paper. You're nothing, Marasco. Who's next? Who's next up the line?"

"Don't know. Don't know what you're talking about. Don't know—"

"Tell me or I'll leave you here, Marasco."

"No."

"I'll leave you here to suffocate. They won't even find your ashes, Marasco, they'll all be mixed into the embers of the house. Your wife won't even have something to cremate. But don't worry about it. These funeral directors do marvelous things these days."

The sirens opened up, penetrated the air, came closer. Wulff's eyes were already squeezed half-shut, he was weeping from the fumes, knew that he could not hold out much longer himself. His physical reserves were near the breaking point. Still he pressed on. There was some margin. There *had* to be some margin, enough to squeeze information out of the thing on the floor.

The thing extended its arms, looked up. "Carry me out," it said.

"What?"

"For God's sake, Wulff, I can't move. Don't let me die here."

"You're going to die here."

"No. No."

"Then tell me who it goes to next? Who's your contact point? I figure you for just a middleman, Marasco. You're the guy in the center, working on margin. Who's up or down? Who's inside and out? Tell me. Tell everything."

The thing got up on its elbows, looking at Wulff through a haze of stinking fumes. "I didn't have anything to do with your girl, Wulff," it said.

He started to shake. "Shut up," he said.

"I looked it up. I told you, I understand everything about you. That had nothing to do with us."

"Just tell me where it goes, Marasco."

"You're all wrong," the thing on the floor said. It was crying. "We didn't have anything to do with it at all. I don't know what you think happened but it wasn't us. It was something else entirely."

He hit the man. Underneath the pulp he could feel heat, beneath that the suggestion of ash. Coming up fast he kicked a shin, heard it crack under his heel. Marasco squealed.

"Who's next on line, Marasco?"

"Get me out of here."

"Who's next?"

"I'm dying, Wulff, I'm dying."

Wulff knelt over him. The man was in extremis; his eyes cold and open, the face structured in shadows of bone. He inhaled; his breath caught, he gasped, and knew then that time was running out; he had to get out of here. One last try. He put a finger in the man's belly, indented in the soft place, pushed.

Marasco must have felt that he was exploding. He coughed, screamed. "I don't know," he said, "all I do is arrange the deliveries."

"Who do you pass the funds onto?"

"I'm a freelance—"

Wulff pushed again into the soft place. Marasco vomited, fluid coming out of him like blood. "Guy named Vincent," he said, "in New York—"

"Vincent. First name or last?"

"Don't know—"

"First name or last?"

"I'm dead," Marasco said, "I'm a dead man."

"You're dead anyway. Do you want to die inside or outside?"

"Peter Vincent," Marasco said, "a townhouse in the East Eighties—"

"No good. The address."

"Can't think. Can't breathe—"

"Goodbye, Marasco. You'll never make it out of here. I'll break your legs and leave you to die."

"Six-eighteen," Marasco said, "six-eighteen East 83rd."

"Good. Better."

"I never been there. Just once."

"Well of course," Wulff said, "you wouldn't deal on a social basis.

Purely business."

He came out of his crouch, waved plumes of smoke from his eyes. Almost blinded now. The thing on the floor, inert, looked up at him. "You're not going to leave me, are you?" it asked.

"Of course I'm going to leave you."

"You can't. You can't—"

"Yes I can," Wulff said. "You watch me and see." He took off his jacket, held it against his face, stumbled that way toward the place where he remembered the door as being. He grasped for it, felt it come reassuringly into his hand, heard the groaning of the sirens coming ever nearer and as if from an even greater distance, the sounds of shouting men, pounding feet. He pulled the door open, felt the touch of wind against his face and blindly stumbled into the open abscess of grounds.

Behind him he could hear the thing on the floor whimpering; then he shut the door and he heard nothing at all. Leaving the thing sealed in its tomb now, pent up like all of the crawling things, left to the pure, cleaning fire. It should have been done a long, long time ago. Back there, locked in with all the crawling things, arcing to the brush of flame the thing was still babbling and whining away the last moments of its consciousness and that too was fine with Wulff. Marasco would be alert to the moment of his death, would be able to touch and clasp and embrace it as he would a woman. He would know what was happening to him and he would drink deeply in those last instants before consciousness, like an aberration, was snuffed out of him.

Most of his victims had not had that alertness. It was the only mercy which the thing called Marasco had ever shown to anything in his life.

Wulff, free now, staggered into the empty air, feeling consciousness return. Turning at the edge of the lawn he could see the great sheets of flame arcing into the sky, smell the deadly fumes. Figures scurried on the rim with him, charging toward the house. They ignored Wulff. Some of them wore helmets. A clang and an enormous truck, a vision from an OD's last dream rumbled near the house, trailing hoses like tentacles.

Crouched on the ground a woman hung into herself, weeping. Marasco's wife. Wulff went over to her. She did not look up. No one noticed. No one noticed anything.

"It's better this way," he said to her. He couched, clearing his lungs, looked up at the sky, down again. "Believe me, this is better."

The woman said nothing. Fire had dried up her body; the sobs were dry heaves, racking. She held her hands to her face and fell into the lawn.

"Just be glad you're free," he whispered, straightening, turning from her. "I wish that I were free."

He began to move then, rapidly, away from there. Motion pumped air into his lungs, his senses cleared, he felt himself running in command of himself. Past the abandoned gates he ran, down the dusty, rutted path, small things squirming under his feet, and toward the great highway.

As he approached the road he turned then for a last look and saw the estate ringed by fire, the flames leaping twenty or thirty feet in the air, the fire cutting out tracing patterns in the atmosphere so that what Wulff thought he saw as he stared at it was the outline of a human face leering at him from three hundred yards. Fire was the eyes, fire the ears, fire the crown of the head and in the center of the fire a line of sparks which mapped out an upturned mouth as the face that Marasco's home had become hovered high in the air and laughed.

That face his face, his face the fire: Wulff felt that he was looking into a mirror. Held in fascination and yet it was time to move on. For soon, they would be looking for him and he knew that unless he found a place in which to hide himself soon, they would finish the job. He was at the end of his physical limits.

Wulff took the gun he had seized from the thing called Marasco on the floor and hefting it, struck out in a stumbling, determined gate toward the highway. He would flag down a car. He would steal it. He would use the car to get him out of here. He did not want to kill anyone more tonight to do this but God and no one else would help the motorist who ignored the flat or who refused to yield the car easily.

He was going to play their game now. Set a wolf to catch the wolves. He would be what they were but only more of it.

X

He had no trouble. The fat man driving the Ford LTD was only too happy to give him the car and take his chances on his own hitchhiking. "For God's sake," the fat man said, little odds and ends of jewelry flapping from his exposed shirt front, "I've got a wife and children. Don't shoot me. Don't shoot me. Take the fucking thing and get out of here. The mileage stinks anyway and the goddamned carburetor float mechanism was never right. She keeps on stalling on cold idle for God's sake. Don't shoot me."

Wulff didn't shoot him. He waved the man off the road, reached into the back and flung a heavy valise after him, put the gun away inside and got the car back into gear. Maybe they only did get ten miles to the gallon and maybe the exhaust-emission devices did shut the choke down too soon on warmup but the LTD's were good machines, at least for the purpose of getting back to the city on a warm August night. Wulff put the accelerator to the floor, decided to take his chances on the Southern State going flat out. He thought he had the skills to outrun an ordinary patrol car and short of that he simply did not give a damn. There was activity back at Islip but sooner or later, probably much sooner, the blond was going to get on the job and he would bring a battalion with him. Scum like Marasco had to be avenged, not out of personal feeling—there was none—but to prove that any chinks in the armor could be sealed off instantly. Otherwise, things might collapse. The people who surrounded Marasco, top and bottom, would risk death themselves rather than letting the idea get around that there might be a way to snip through the protective net.

Wulff drove like fucking hell. There was no traffic; he picked up the telltale signs of radar approaching the Grand Central link but barrelled right on through that as well. A patrol car going the other way, sirens open, flashers like a quartet of bubble dancers might have noticed him but had other things, down the line, on its mind: possibly the soon-to-be-famous Marasco fire. Wulff found that he still had his wallet, used it to pay the toll at the interchange—without it he just would have gone on through—and took the Grand Central at a slightly more reasonable pace. Thursday morning at two or three; almost no traffic. He took the Triborough, swinging wide to dodge across three lines, drove the car off at 125th Street, cut crosstown then to get to the West Side.

125th Street was active. Even at two in the ayem on Thursday, even in still August, 125th was alive and hopping. You had to give the Marascos that much credit. They were unleashing poison into the cities at the rate the utilities were pouring smoke in, but poison could have a greenish, exciting lustre of its own and 125th Street, the central point of this dying part of the dying city was filled with activity. Pimps moved their cars in and out of curbside spaces. Little clumps of junkies talked excitedly on the corners, gesturing toward one another about their scores. These were the ones that were up. The ones that were down or heading that way were individual stragglers, stretched out along the building lines or tucked as stragglers onto the stoops of buildings on the sidestreets. A few discouraged prostitutes that hadn't gotten the word yet that the action had moved out in the path of drugs, all the way to midtown and the East Side, held themselves in doorways and looked at the scene alertly. Maybe they *had* gotten the word, come to think of it. It was simply that there was less competition on 125th Street. Of course there were no customers either. White men had not come up to this area to get laid for seven or eight years. Give King H credit for that. Even the Johns got the word eventually that this was, under no circumstances, any place to be.

Wulff revved the LTD, kept it moving crosstown. He had an appointment with Peter Vincent now and he had a pretty good idea of how that was going to develop but not now. Not now. He would have to be a fool to take on the next link in the chain in his present condition. He had not slept in thirty hours, he had killed three men, he had been imprisoned for half a day, he had survived a fire. The Peter Vincents of this world did not fall into men in his condition if they fell at all. He had to get back under cover for a few hours if for nothing else but isolation. He did not know if he would be able to sleep. Sleep was not the point. It didn't matter. It was a question of incorporating what had happened into his system so that he would be able to get to the next step.

He ditched the car finally, keys in, at St. Nicholas and 125th; went for the subway. Funny how things had gone full circle; he had started out at an intersection like this one a few hours, a lifetime, ago. Leave the keys in; give some fifteen-year-old junkie an early Christmas present. Stripped for parts the LTD might be worth five hundred to someone, sold just as it was, same plates, motor running off the street, maybe two-fifty. A hell of a lot of depreciation but that was probably closer to its real value than the five thousand the salesman had probably been suckered into paying for it, ballooning into six what with the payments spread over a period of time. He cleaned his gear out of the car, hailed a taxi, and took it downtown to the furnished room on West Side which had been his coop for three months.

Now he would turn it into an arsenal and a siting point.

"You know," the cabbie said, "I took two of them up here and I was shaking like a leaf every block of the way. I figured that they were going to pull a gun on me the first red light we had and knock me over."

"You wouldn't have been the first."

"First? I wouldn't have been the *fifteenth* this year if they blew my head off. That's what drugs have done to this town."

"You're right," Wulff agreed mildly enough, "you're absolutely right."

"And you know what? They get to the Apollo Theatre and get out nice as you please and *thank* me and lay on a two dollar tip! Two perfectly nice guys; must have been musicians."

"Not too many musicians at the Apollo these days," Wulff said.

"Yeah, yeah," the cabbie said with some excitement pounding the wheel, "maybe not, but the point I'm trying to make with this story is that they're perfectly decent guys, just like you or me but they've got me in a frame of mind all the way driving uptown that they're going to hit

me over the head and rob me blind and shoot me. That's what drugs
have done to this city. That's what the fucking things have done."

"You're right," said Wulff.

"I told my wife last week, I told her no more. No more night shift. Just
one week, two weeks more and I'm telling them they can take their cab
between eight at night and six in the morning and stuff it. That's what
I'm going to tell them. But how am I going to live? How the fuck can I
walk away from the night shift when they got ten times as many guys
trying to make a living in daylight and the only time the money's
around is at night?"

"It's rough," Wulff said.

"I keep on telling myself, my wife, one week, two weeks, I'm turning
it in. Tomorrow, the day after tomorrow I'm going to tell them no more,
I'm fucking finished. But I keep on putting it off! How am I going to
make two hundred dollars a week on day shift? I tell you, there's just
no way."

"It's a tough racket."

"But you work night shift and sooner or later you're going to get it. I've
known guys, two already that got it and six or seven others that got
robbed and were lucky to get out alive. So what to do? Tell me what the
hell I'm going to do?"

"I don't know," Wulff said as the cab stopped at the rooming house and
he gave the driver five dollars of Ric Davis's money, "I really don't know.
But let me tell you, I'm working on it."

"Sure you are. *Everybody's* working on it. The Mayor and his fucking
task force and the Governor, they're *all* working on it. The Governor's
going to give them life for possession, you like that? When I'm lying
somewhere in an alley with a bullet in my heart, it'll be nice to know
that the guy who killed me is going to get life for possession. When they
catch up with him of course."

"I'll keep you posted," Wulff said and swung lightly out of the cab,
slammed the door, waved and vaulted the eight steps into the lobby of
the rooming house. Amazing how your energy levels could stay up there,
even after all that he had been through. It must have had something
to do with the therapeutic nature of the work.

He used the key to get in, security being better in this building than
most of them around, and walked up the two flights to his cubicle, room
twenty-five, and found slumped in the bed against the wall the sleeping
figure of his ex-patrol car partner, Williams. He was in a deep sleep. He
must have been waiting for a long time.

But the kid's instincts were good. He came alert quivering the minute
Wulff walked into the room, grappling in his plain clothes for a gun and

then, as understanding wiped sleep from his eyes he grinned a slow, foolish rookie's grin and put the gun away.

"Been looking for you," Williams said.

XI

"It was pretty easy to get in," Williams said a few minutes later, drinking coffee at the table made from some instant that Wulff kept near the hotplate. "I said I was a friend of yours and just wanted to camp outside and he even used the key to let me in. Escorted me up. You've got a trusting super here, man."

"Terrific," Wulff said, looking at the rookie. But Williams was no kid. He was a black man in his early twenties of medium height, compactly built and as Wulff had had occasion to know from their one patrol together, this man was no fool. Inexperience, Williams would have said, was something for whites to worry about; blacks came out of their cribs old. This one, if he made it and Wulff supposed that he would, was going to be a murderous cop. Even now, he was probably overpowering people.

"I want to talk to you," Williams said, "because I think we can do business together."

"I figured you'd get to that. But I'm dead-tired, I've had a big day."

Wulff took the gun from his jacket then, put it carefully on the cracked dresser top. He added the two wallets, not caring what Williams's reaction would be. Nothing to conceal here. Williams was not the enemy either, he supposed, but if he wanted to be Wulff would play it that way. At length he turned back toward Williams, took off his shirt.

"You look like you've been in a fire," Williams said impassively.

"Something like that."

"Want to tell me about it?"

"Listen here," Wulff said, "you're the one who came. You got business on your mind? Say it. Otherwise, get going. I can't start fucking around now."

"Fair enough," Williams said. "Suits me." He nodded once, a grave inclination of the head. He knew where everything was. "That's good. You know that I'm the only guy in or out of headquarters or probably anywhere in the department who knows where you are now, don't you?"

"Just keep it that way."

"And now I'm an off-duty cop so *no* one knows. Lots of people looking for you, man."

"I'm sure."

"I mean, a lot of people are looking for you. They're having trouble with the equipment rosters."

"That's not my problem. We're getting nowhere, Williams."

"All right," the black said. He clasped his hands, meditated over the coffee cup. "I've been considering your problem and putting the pieces together and I think we can do business."

"Yes? How?"

"You're outside the system, I'm in it. You can work your side, I can work mine. We'll build up a pressure point."

"Get out of the system," Wulff said.

"Now what I want to get out of the system for?" Williams said, his jaw going slack, switching in mood and dialect in that frightening way which intelligent blacks had. "The system's shit-rotten but at least it's keeping a roof over my head. Without the system we'd still be picking cotton and you'd be a dead man, Wulff."

"No. Not necessarily."

"*Absolutely.* The system is shit but on the other hand it pays off. It even pays off the losers," Williams said. "Everybody gets his piece of the action and those that miss out altogether, well they're dead. Nothing wrong with being dead, is there? That's an even bet. But you're all right, Wulff. From your point of view the system sucks."

"Right," Wulff said, "I'm privileged."

"Well of course you're privileged," Williams said, picking up the cup and looking over it solemnly, the cup covering the lip-movements, "everybody your color is privileged, Wulff, the system was set up for color." He put down the cup with a crash. "But that's okay too," he said, "I'm not bitter, I'm not giving you any of that militant shit because that's another hustle. The point is that I've got a little piece of it and now it's going to work for *me* and for my wife and our nice little two-family in Queens. But I can play it two levels. You want to rip down, that's fine; I can give you a little help on that end."

"I wouldn't know about help," Wulff said. He flexed his hands, investigated the damages of the day in the battered mirror propped on the shelf over the bed. Marasco, Davis, Jessup. Dead as they were they had exacted their penalty. He looked like a man of forty. The face was dented; his body bore the markings of the fire.

Wulff took a towel and some clean underwear out of the dresser. "I can't discuss system strategy," he said, "I'm going to take a shower."

"Hold up," Williams said with that deadly grin, "I can't stay long. Midnight shift coming up. Got to look beautiful to represent the finest."

"You mean you were just leaving when I woke up the systems man."

"I'm no systems man," Williams said, "but I was waiting. Patience I've got." He looked at his watch. "My wife gets nervous about a black man walking around in uniform, you know?"

"That's touching," Wulff said. "You put that uniform on; don't blame me."

"You better believe it," Williams said. "I love that uniform; that uniform is like a sheet kids wear when they play ghost. I put that on, I'm a different man. People don't see the face, just the blue and that means that no one gets near me. Let me tell you how we can do business though, Wulff. You see, I think I can use you and God knows you can use me."

"How?"

"I'm your man in the mainstream," Williams said and gave him a deadly smile. "I'm even a man of good will, I'll help you. I *want* you to succeed, Wulff. But the way you're going at it, vigilante, you could use an invisible man in blue poking around behind the net."

"Vigilante?" Wulff said, "You're thinking about someone else here in this room. I'm retired. I'm semi-retired, I'm beating the bushes in the park for birds and someday I'll write a book about it. My fucking memoirs. Listen, I just want to take a shower and get lost if it's all the same with you. Nothing personal of course."

"Never personal between a black man and a white man," Williams said wryly. "But that's all right. I respect you, you've got your reasons for this just like the rest of us do."

"That's nice. I've won your respect and admiration."

"A vigilante has the best reasons in the world even if he has no control. The boys in the Klan, they are convinced of their righteousness Wulff and so are you."

"I'm not in any Klan."

"In a way," Williams said vaguely, standing, "in a way, but let's not get into that. I figure the girl was mixed up in this somehow," he said after a pause. "No one else knows but I figured that out on my own. You figure they got her, huh?"

"The girl is out of it," Wulff said quietly. He moved toward Williams, looked at the man in level fashion and such force must have come from him then that even Williams blinked, gave an inch. Looked downwards, back-pedalling slightly.

"I don't want you to mention the girl," Wulff said, "ever. You dig that?"

"That's all right, man," Williams said, "the girl can stay out of it. She's got nothing to do with it if you want it that way."

"That's all," Wulff said. He did not move. "I ever hear that mentioned again and I'm going to kill you, Williams. Let it go this one time."

"Yeah. Sure."

"This one time. Because you're a cop and I have nothing against you. But after the one for free, no more."

"All right," Williams said. His cool was intact but there were a few absent dribbles of sweat on his forehead, "Have it your way on the girl issue. I won't bring that up again here."

"Anyone mentions the girl gets himself killed," Wulff said. He moved away then. "I don't see anything more to say now," he said, "I'm not negotiating for ransom or a partnership and I need my rest."

"Just take it easy," Williams said, raising a hand which did not tremble at all. "I still haven't said what brought me here in the first place."

"You're not getting any closer."

"We can make it Wulff," Williams said quietly, "the in man and the out man. I think that I can give you some help."

Wulff paused for a while, looked at the empty spots of the ceiling of the room. "I don't work with anyone," he said finally.

"Yes you can."

"This is a death trip."

"I figured you'd see it that way. But you don't have to die if you don't want to. Life comes too cheap if you don't know what death is. I do."

"How do you know what I'm doing? I told you, I'm a retired man."

"Bullshit," Williams said, his voice very low. He could have been working over a suspect at this moment, toying with the meat, playing him in for the collapse. "Whatever you're up to, you're not retired."

"Prove it."

"I'm not out to hurt you baby," Williams said, "paranoia, that's supposed to be *my* game. I'm here to make myself useful to you. Man, I *love* the system; I'd be dead without it. But that doesn't mean I can't do a little prying from the outside."

"I'm not accepting any help."

"I didn't think that you'd be begging for it, that's for sure."

"So what brought you up here?"

"You know," Williams said. He moved toward the door, adjusted the table. "You know you can't do this all alone, you're going to need something along the way from someone. You're a crazy, overprivileged white if you think this thing is rigged for you."

"It's not."

"You're going to make it all the way on your own? You became a nigger the minute you quit the force. You'll *be* a nigger until they drill you full of holes."

"I'm still waiting for it," Wulff said.

"I could help you, Wulff," Williams said. "Whatever you're doing can't be all on your own. It doesn't work that way."

"Sometimes it can."

"Besides, you amuse me. I'd like to see how you feel when *you* find what it's like to go up against the system. I want to be there when it all comes clear, right at that moment. You'll see why I've learned to love it baby."

"It can be smashed."

"I've got the blue," Williams said. "I'm not like you, I'm playing it by the book. Hating it from the inside. I'm in for the big hitch, I've got a wife and the wife is going to have a kid soon. Know that? Congratulate me. We hope. But that doesn't mean that this isn't all a big game to me too. That's all it is."

"You wouldn't want to touch it."

"I'm in it too deep already. I'm in your room."

"Why," Wulff said then, pausing at the door, looking at the man, "why would you want to get involved in something like this anyway?"

"Williams? Why would he get involved?" The eyes swung in the black's head, he tipped a hand. "I think you know that," he said.

"No I don't."

"Because I want to see some shaking and some making. The roofs over my head; let's see how it is if the house comes down in sections."

"Maybe it'll all come down."

"And maybe it won't," Williams said intensely, "maybe it's a prefabricated house and I'm the man in the right room." He put out a hand. "Far enough," he said. "You think about it and let me know."

"Quit the force," Wulff said savagely, backing away from the hand, "turn in your badge and pistol and wife and fucking Queens and get yourself a furnished room in this nice section of town."

"I can't do that, Wulff," Williams said, again with that amused tint to the eyes, "I owe the system everything. But if I can see a man working around the edges like you are and it isn't flaming my territory then why not? Why not do something like that?"

"You want to make *me* a tool."

"How say that?" Williams said, "how can you say that? Now you know they've got me hooked in. I've got the mortgage and the wife. I bought their lies all the way down the line and I even have a nice college degree from Fordham too to hang on the wall, it helped me get this civil-service job. I love them. I love them so much I hate them. You want me on those terms?"

"I don't think I want you on any terms."

"You're going to need help, Wulff. You can't do it all alone, you can't even think that you could. Don't tell me that, man."

"You don't even know what I'm doing."

"No," Williams said, over this, "no I guess that you just don't understand. It's easy not to understand when you're a white man and that's all you are."

He took his hat off the bed, knocked it against a knee, put it on and walked toward the door. There weren't many around who would wear a hat like this in dead summer, let alone with that kind of style. Why did the blacks, just about all of them, have style?

"I'm through negotiating," Williams said flatly, "I've put it on the table and that's enough."

"Were these negotiations?"

"I don't know," Williams said. He grasped the knob. "I think you thought they were begging but that's your mistake. It was a simple business deal you were being offered."

"Call it a misunderstanding."

"What a hostile man," Williams said, "you are one angry son of a bitch. You even sound black."

Wulff shook his head. There was just nothing to say about that. Nothing at all. He had somehow managed to think about everything else in his life but never the so-called race issue. It had never entered one way or the other. If the blacks wanted to think of themselves as a race apart that was, as far as he was concerned, their problem. Except that it was becoming *his* problem. That was what Williams was bringing home to him now. Quickly. "Shit," he said under his breath.

"You know where to reach me," Williams said, "you've got anything to say, you need some help, you just give me a call. This is my first and my last offer, man and it's on terms of mutual respect. I'm going to stay clear."

"You lay around here for ten hours just to tell me you wanted to *help?*"

Williams smiled. "It's a little more complicated than that, Burt Wulff," he said, "because there's no such thing as help in this world." He patted his pocket where the gun was hidden. "That's what it comes down to," he said, "and that's why I'll take the system my way, because I've got the equalizer right here. Power over power and nothing else matters, not to them, not even to people like you."

He opened the door, stepped outside. "You need help from one solemn black rookie cop with good access to the files, you just give me a call," he said, "and then again if you don't need help you just don't bother. One thing is sure, Wulff wouldn't call to socialize."

"I might have once. You just don't see that, do you?"

"You might have once but now you're not in the system anymore, you don't have to look up a black man for social reasons. That's all right with me," Williams said quietly, "that suits me fine. It's all business."

"If you want it that way."

"If I can help you in your business, you give me a call."

"I don't have any business."

"Good deal," Williams said, "good deal. Have it your way and we'll sink the ship."

Slowly, solemnly he winked, balanced himself on the threshold of the room and then went out closing the door gently.

He left Wulff alone.

Slowly, carefully, Wulff put his things together and worked his way down the hall like a blind man. He went into the stinking little bathroom containing the single rusty shower outlet. The accommodations, like the system, left a good deal to be desired.

The system indeed sucked.

But so did his life. Explain *that* to Williams.

XII

Peter Vincent got news of the Marasco fire early the next morning. News simply filtered into Peter Vincent without his having much to do with getting it. It was like affairs being offered to a beautiful woman. You turned down fifty for the one that you picked up but that didn't mean that you minded the other ones. They kept you in the center of things, improved the feeling of self-worth. Vincent got this news on the phone from a contact on Wall Street who liked to call himself a stockbroker. At least the contact did have an office and a phone; there were a lot who didn't.

Peter Vincent sat surrounded by possessions and impermeable locks on the fourth floor of a townhouse. The third floor was his office space; the first two floors were supposed to be offices too but he had had them sealed off a long time ago. One staircase with blind entrances carried the visitor up to the third floor, a small, self-controlled elevator would take him up to the fourth if Peter Vincent desired. Two housemen lived off the corridors of the third floor, another lived on the fourth directly across from Peter Vincent although with his own entrance and exit. Peter Vincent valued his privacy. There was no reason why he should not. Didn't everyone want privacy? Wasn't that what man struggled for; the increasing bit of living space that was his own?

He was sealed in and he liked it that way. The call came in at ten o'clock from the man he preferred to know as Gerald. Vincent was alone on the fourth floor at the time and thought about letting one of the housemen take it downstairs before he figured the hell with it and took the button himself. It was a slow morning anyway. And there was no question that anybody who knew the number on which the light was flashing was not there to invade his privacy. Very few people knew that number. The few who had without Peter Vincent's permission and continuing approval were mostly dead.

"Marasco's dead," the voice said almost instantly. Gerald cut corners wherever he could; the man was all business. Vincent could admire that. "There was a fire there last night. The place is ruined; a four-alarmer. His wife got out but she's in the hospital. Nobody else got burned up but everything's lost."

"Everything?"

"Looks that way. The place is a total loss from what I pick up."

"Arson?" said Peter Vincent.

"Probably. Of course for the police it's an open and shut accident. They'll be happy to leave it that way on the books."

"I can imagine."

"Marasco wasn't exactly their favorite person in the Eastern District."

"No," Vincent said, holding the phone delicately against his ear with his shoulder, taking a toothpick out of his pocket and placing it in his mouth. He had given up smoking two years ago in the interest of long life and health; toothpicks helped a little although they were not the same. Nothing was the same, "I can't say that he was."

"Where does that leave us?"

"I don't know," Vincent said, "I'll have to think about it a little bit."

"Don't think too long," the voice said. It acquired just a little bit of an edge which made Vincent wince; for the first time that morning he seemed or would have seemed if there had been anyone else in the room to have lost his composure, "We respect your brain but something's got to be done fast."

"I know that," Vincent said.

"There's a shipment yesterday that fell through. We wanted to have that checked out even before this happened."

"Sure."

"Terello," the voice said, "you're going to have to get hold of him."

"I will. It's just morning now. Give me a couple of minutes to get organized."

"It's not good," Gerald said sharply. "There were two men pitched off on the Harlem River Drive yesterday too. Small time guys."

"You think that ties in with the fire?"

There was a pause; Vincent could hear the man breathing. "We think maybe," Gerald said finally, "but mostly we don't want to think. That's your job."

"That's right," said Vincent, "I'll be in touch."

"Don't wait on it," Gerald said and broke the connection.

Vincent sat, still holding the phone meditatively, placed it finally in the cradle and sat back on the chair, letting the sense of the situation build within him. Sealed in as he was from the world or at least that part of it which would have made things confusing and difficult, he was able at least most of the time to do his thinking in a vacuum. Feed in the material as input, like a computer he would come out with *modus operandi* as output. But as he sat there, Vincent could feel the first stalking unease hit him.

It didn't look right. It just did not look right. The fire at Islip was a possibility and Vincent had had to deal for a long time with the fact that Marasco was pushing his authority a bit and might have to be dealt with someday. In that sense the fire only solved a problem before it truly arose, always a satisfying thing to a man like Vincent who kept his options open. Marasco would have to be replaced and that meant work of course but what the hell; he could solve it with a couple of phone calls. The missed shipment was another problem, it was inconvenient and it could make for complication but, hell, in this business missed shipments, deliveries that fell through, were all part of overhead. They almost had to be considered as part of the basic cost of doing business. You would amortize them right in.

But the business of the two bodies on the Harlem River Drive. Small time Gerald had said. Good enough; to Gerald of course almost everyone was small time. Peter Vincent was probably called small time himself by Gerald to other people. But the bodies on the drive the same day as the arson and the shipment that had not come through—

Vincent could feel his senses prickle. His skills were limited, he knew perfectly well that in the outside world he would be lucky to be in middle-management. If that. But he had gotten this far because he had one invaluable ability and it was respected, however grudgingly, by the Geralds and the people up the line who gave Gerald the orders. Vincent had sound instincts.

Things that would not have come together for an ordinary man came together in a terrifying way for Vincent: random factors, chance puzzles, little coincidences of time and circumstance could build to him a meaning as compelling and beautiful as an artist might find when a work, finally, began to take shape. And now he had that feeling again: almost with excitement he understood at some basic level below words that the bodies on the drive and the disaster in Islip came together. Neatly and irrevocably at some level they hooked in perfectly.

He picked up the phone and by memory dialed Torello's number. "Get him there," he said to the woman who answered.

"He not home now. Who is this calling?"

"Get him to the phone."

"I told you," the woman said, "he went out a long time ago. Maybe he be back tonight maybe tomorrow morning. Who is calling?"

"This is Peter Vincent," he said, "get the son of a bitch to the phone, please." With news of the fire, Terello would be holed up in his apartment, he knew. Too cunning to expose himself but too frightened to run he would lock himself up like a rat.

"Oh," the voice said, "Peter Vincent?"

"I said who it was. Get him to the phone right now." He kept his voice level, calm, played his fingers over the desk. Show no emotion. Show no emotion ever and particularly to the lower echelons play it like a machine. If there was no *personna,* they could never touch him.

Terello came on the phone, his voice open and breaking. Peter Vincent simply did not call the Terellos of this world; the man must have been terrified. "Yes?" he said, "Mr. Vincent."

"This is Peter Vincent. What went wrong yesterday?"

"Well I don't know," Terello said after a choked pause, "I just don't know anything about it. I mean, to talk over the phone—"

"Are you trying to tell *me* how to talk?"

"No," Terello said desperately, "no. Never."

"What happened to Marasco?"

"I don't know," Terello said. He sounded bleak, stripped now of energy. "I just don't know."

"When did you last see him?"

"I was there yesterday afternoon. I left early though. I had to tell him about this thing—"

"I know about that," Vincent said shortly. "What happened?"

"I tell you, I just don't know. We were there; the stuff just wasn't. The guy supposed to be making the transfer—"

"Did you take it?"

"Are you crazy?" Terello squealed. His voice modulated instantly. "I'm sorry," he said, "I apologize, I really do. But you should know me better than that. I'd never do anything like that at all. I do my work."

"What about the two ditched on the drive?"

"I don't know what you're talking about."

"Don't you? Are you sure?"

"Honest to Christ," Terello said, "what two on the drive? What is this?"

"Two men I know were found on the Harlem River Drive yesterday afternoon, very dead."

"I don't know anything about that at all," Terello said, breathing raggedly, "this is the first I hear about it. I'm not into that kind of work at all—"

"I didn't say you were. Then the fire."

"I know about the fire. I told you, I left there in the early afternoon."

"When did you last see him?"

"About four o'clock," Terello said. "Jesus Christ, you don't think I'm messed up in this, do you? He was my *boss* for God's sake."

"So maybe you're an ambitious man."

"I'd have to be crazy to think like that. I would have been *dead,* years ago, if I thought like that. I came home about six o'clock and I was home all night. Ask my wife."

"Spouses can't testify in court," Peter Vincent said dryly, "inadmissible evidence."

"You're calling this a court?" The man was babbling now. "Listen, Mr. Vincent, I beg of you. I didn't want to see him die, I'm just sick about this. I didn't love the man, I can't lie to someone like you but I liked him and he was my boss and that was all there was to it. I wouldn't ever do anything like that, I'd get myself killed. And the two on the drive, I don't even know who they could be. I'm not into that."

"What about the shipment?"

"What about it? I was there; the stuff wasn't. You can't hang me on something like that for shit's sake! Please, give me a break, will you?"

Vincent took the phone away from his ear and regarded it for a moment. He had a vivid picture of Terello at this instant even though he had never seen the man: he would be a short, fat, balding character sitting now in a bathrobe, hunched over the phone, smoking, huge beading droplets of sweat pouring off him as his wife looked at him frantically from the bedroom door. He would be waving his wife away, trying to tell her to get the hell out of there but she would not be moving because she had no idea what was really going on and would be afraid that the man was having a heart attack. Vincent sighed. Good instincts didn't mean that you had to necessarily enjoy the pictures they painted in your mind. He brought the phone back to his ear.

"All right, Terello," he said, "you sit tight."

"You mean stay indoors?"

"That might not be a bad idea."

"I got things to do and I did hope to make the funeral—"

"Don't worry about the funeral. Going to the funeral won't do you any good and it sure as hell won't help Marasco where he's at now. You stay at the apartment and wait for word."

"How long? When will I get word?"

"I don't know," Vincent said quietly, "that depends on what I decide. It could be five minutes from now and then again you could be sitting around in your bathrobe for ten years. Take up crossword puzzles. Learn solitaire. Watch some television."

"Okay. Okay."

"Stay underground and be reachable at all times."

"Oh I will," Terello said, "I will."

"And don't you ever try to get in touch with me," Vincent said. "I have something to say, you'll hear. Otherwise you just sit because if you don't hear I've got nothing to say."

"I wouldn't even know where to reach you."

"That's good," Vincent said, "that's real, real good," and put the phone down abruptly, took the toothpick from his mouth and considered it.

He guessed that if he wanted he could project his instincts again and see Terello now; the man had barrelled the phone into his gut like a midwife might hold a baby, the cold surfaces were chilling him, the cigarette dangled from his mouth, smoke burning his eyes, he was weeping in terror. *What the hell is this?* his wife was saying, *I thought that you were in sporting goods.*

Well, that could wait. Terello was clean at least in the sense that he had had no part of this and had no information. It might be necessary to have him removed simply in the interests of keeping things neat at the end but that would depend upon other factors and strictly speaking might be avoided. There was no way to decide how to deal with Terello, however, until he understood the full picture and Vincent knew that he was a way from that, a long long way.

He sighed and threw away the toothpick. A strange, rolling constriction spread through his own gut: Peter Vincent had a feeling that he was in for it. He picked up the intercom and told the houseman that he had better bring up a pack of cigarettes right away. Also, divert all calls away from him; he was going to be tied up here for a while.

The houseman said sure. He asked Vincent if he really were going to go back to smoking after all the good work he had done to kick the habit. Vincent let him get away with it because the man was a good employee who also knew karate at the seventh level. He said that yes he was going back to smoking. He had tried smoking and that was good and he had tried quitting which was even better so now he would go back to smoking again so that he could have the satisfaction of quitting from the start.

The houseman seemed to understand this. Vincent concentrated on the phone, sharpened every singing nerve, and got down to serious work.

XIII

Wulff got up eight hours later, feeling a little better. The business from yesterday was little more than an ache in his guts; it went away when he stretched. He got out of bed, dressed, had some coffee, went outside leaving the door unlocked to pick up a paper. Let anyone come in; let them take whatever he had. This was the best way to co-exist with the rooming house. Everything that he needed he carried around in his head and jacket. The gun came in tight against his ribs.

Story in the late *Times* about the Marasco fire. The *Times* called him an executive. No one else had died. The *News* was somewhat more interesting; there were a couple of pictures in the centerfold and the *News* seemed to think of him as a mobster. Right on, *News* Wulff thought, *vox populi omnia* and went back to the rooming house, meditating.

Time to take on Peter Vincent, of course. But there was not only time, it was a question of timing; Wulff was still pacing it out. Going after Vincent would put him into a truly exposed position for the first time. Davis and Jessup were in a place where they could not talk; Marasco was there too, so far so good. The blond knew plenty of course and in due time would get the word out but it did not seem as if he would have to worry about the blond's people for a day, a couple of days anyhow. Then they might have a good deal of trouble finding him. The trace would come to the police department and then, like Marasco's black book, hit a dead stop. No one knew where he was now except Williams and Williams, Wulff was very sure, was not going to spread it around. That had been a sincere offer earlier today. He would have to think about it. He had always seen this as a solo operation, make it all the way or get dragged down alone but never involve or injure other people, but Williams was offering to go in with his eyes wide open. He would have to consider that. He would certainly give it some thought.

He walked back to the rooming house, digging the scene on West 97th which was pretty much like the scene all over town these days except for the residential East Side and parts of the business district, and those two sections were being kept clear only through a massive influx of cops and private security. As long as the business district and the one or two upper-class residential sections held out the city could avoid the appearance of total collapse but Wulff knew, the cops knew, the city knew that they were losing ground. It was only a matter of time now: two years, maybe three and the last vestiges of safety and wealth would collapse and New York City, the cities all over the country, would collapse into the pools of hell that surrounded them.

It was something to see, the West 97th Street scene; it was not even noon yet but the streets had the stuporous languor in August of a combat zone that had been passed through by two massive, if incompetent armies. On the fringes of the devastation or skipping around the middle once again were the isolated sources of energy: a resident struggling with grocery bags and terror trying to make it back to one of the high-rises before the club fell against the neck, a junkie freaked out on cheer dancing in the gutter. Oh, it was just beautiful. Wulff took the *Times* and pitched it as far as it would go, took the *News* and kicked it after. The hell with the newspapers. They were on the outside of it too; at best they could tell you what was going on. They would never tell you *why. Why* was not a newspaper game: start printing the truth and the free press would go out of business.

Wulff thought about Peter Vincent. The name, the address, the general relationship meant that this one was probably holed up in a townhouse with private security and alarm systems; there was probably the arsenal of a small army up there too. How the hell was he going to take it? There was no point in going in frontally; they would wipe him out in one burst. But security was of the type, probably, that could not be circumvented easily. Come in by air? Wulff smiled a bit wryly at that. He was not the 41st Airborne Division and Vincent was no bunch of ignorant peasants in a valley. They would eat him for breakfast.

So why bother? He had gotten three: not much but something and the Marasco knockoff would certainly be instructive to the next man who moved into Marasco's approximate place. Why not retire or at least back off a long way; why not start picking his spots from now on? It might be more effective in the long run and it would certainly be conducive to a longer life.

The hell with life, Wulff muttered, sprinting up the steps of the brownstone, *there's no such thing for me anymore* and that, more or less, seemed to be the point. There was no backing off now. He was already too far committed and more than half-dead. How long before he was tracked down? Did he really think that he could drift underground again, go back to the dreaming and careful planning of these past three months?

Bullshit. They would be coming after him in waves.

Up the stairs and into his room Wulff went, already thinking of the best way to take a reconnaissance on East 83rd Street, and as he opened the door he was hit with something that felt the size of a brick and was filled with spikes. He reeled and instinctively brought himself at bay against the wall, fighting before he even saw. So this was it. What a fool he had been to think that he had any open space at all.

The blond and his friends had been waiting for him.

At that he was lucky. The shot that he had taken ought, by rights, to have killed him, but the one who threw it was an amateur, overeager, a little scared, so anxious to get in the suckerpunch and crusher that he had not timed it properly. It was this one who now dived at Wulff, frantic to make up for the lost opportunity. Not thinking even about the gun he held which had been reversed and used as the clubbing weapon. A well put together beer-drinking type in his mid-twenties, this one, not that Wulff felt that he had the time to do extended character analysis in the middle of this.

The beer-drinker could have given him one shot, just backed off five or six paces like a quarterback dropping back fast into the pocket, and it would have all been over. But the only thing that this one seemed to understand was collision. He came at Wulff screaming, leaped at the last instant and launched himself into a shoulder tackle. Wulff, hurting bad, braced the shoulder that had been hit against the wall and came out fast with a foot, knocking the beer-drinker off balance in the air and upending him with a shriek. He fell to the floor screaming from pain and frustration and then remembered the gun, began like a child to level it with two hands, painfully.

Wulff, shoulder and all, fell on top of the man immediately. He had to bring the gun *in* he told himself, that was the way the training went anyway, bring it into the subject, the closer the better, you wanted to make him eat that gun, the gun was fine as long as it stayed wedged in close because that way he couldn't shoot except by accident; the risks were too high. He might hit you or a piece of himself. Wulff concentrated on keeping the contact, letting the blows fall off him as they would. That wasn't the important thing. The important thing was the *gun*. He ran a hand down the man's thick forearm, found the gun finally and began to grapple with it.

The man's knee flailed toward his groin. At the same time Wulff, turning in struggle, saw his old friend the blond framed suddenly against the window. Oh, the blond was a cute one; he sent his friend out to run the interference and then he came right through the line. If the interference got killed, so much the better, that way the blond could take all the credit with no one to dispute him. There was a gun in the blond's hand. He levelled it.

"I'm going to kill you, you son of a bitch," he said, "get ready for it, it's coming."

Those who announced their intentions had their doubts. Old police

rule; most would-be jumpers simply jumped, didn't stand on ledges and
building roofs for hours gathering and entertaining crowds. If you
wanted to do it, you already had done it; simple rule of life or death.
Wulff forgot about the blond for the instant. Let him consider the act
for a few instants longer while he dealt with the beer-drinker. The beer-
drinker was certainly enough of a problem. This one was without
doubts of any sort; *his* only problem was that he was stupid.

"You son of a bitch," the beer-drinker said as Wulff explored his groin
savagely, gambling on one final assault. It became a whine of pain. *"For
God's sake Mel, help me,"* the man groaned.

Too late. Wulff had the pistol. The beer-drinker went slack underneath
him, the pistol rolling free and Wulff took it, rolled and rolled himself
on the floor, ducking for the relative safety of the bed, waiting in one
partition of his mind for the bullet from the blond to come. If it ever came
it would come now; people like this, if they could hit at all, would do it
with a fleeing target. No shot. Wulff pushed the bed aside, wedged
himself in there and coming around very, very fast, shot the blond in the
throat. The blond's gun fell, he heard a burbling scream of defiance and
revulsion and the blond hit the floor.

Then he shot the beer-drinker in the knee, looking for the tendon right
behind the joint. That would incapacitate the man, turn him into a
cripple for life, on the other hand there would be so little bleeding from
this spot that the man could lie here for hours losing barely a pint of
blood. The blond wasn't going to be doing a great deal more talking
although he was bubbling and thrashing about energetically. That
meant he had to save one of them for some answers.

The beer-drinker gurgled with an agony so profound that it defied
sound of any sort and held himself rigid against the floor like a man on
a crucifix. "Shut up," Wulff said, and kicked him, "you'll live."

"Son of a bitch," the man said, "oh son of a bitch." He held himself tight
on the floor. The lightest movement of the leg, Wulff knew, would cause
the man to pass out. He remembered how it was.

Wulff got up fast and investigated the terrain. The blond dead or dying
under the window, the beer-drinker screaming deep in his throat in the
center of the room. The door itself flapping open, mindlessly, in the weak
inner ventilation of the rooming house. He stepped to the door and
looked down the hall. Absolutely no sign of activity. Usually there was
a fair amount of traffic in these halls at almost any hour; fifteen to
twenty living units on a floor full of drifters or drunkards meant plenty
of action to and from the bathroom at all times but now Wulff could have
been living in a deserted townhouse. He could have been beaten to a
pulp in here and killed—and only a certain ineptness on the part of the

attackers had prevented that—and no one would have peeked out a door.

Of course that was New York for you and not necessarily to be blamed. What did these people owe him? What did he owe them? People could not be blamed for sealing themselves away if it was the only means of survival.

He kicked the door closed and went back to the scene in the room. The blond appeared to be dead although there was so much blood surrounding the respiratory areas that it would have been difficult to check. Blood covered the blond's face, streamed around his nostrils, flowed into his ears. His neck could not be seen at all. He lay in a curiously cramped position—even in death this man could not seek grace—staring with round, open eyes at the ceiling.

It was a dismal thing to have the ceiling of Wulff's furnished room be the last thing you would see in this world but Wulff guessed the man rated it. There had always been a certain ineptness about this one, he suspected. He had selected a career with a dead man in Islip which meant right away that he had no gift for choices.

Wulff went back to the beer-drinker who had not moved. "All right," he said, "talk."

The man shook his head. Strain showed deep in his eyes; tears as well. Pain could make any of them cry. "No," he said.

"Talk," said Wulff gesturing toward the leg, "or I'll move you."

The man seemed to fold within himself in defeat, then the pain reared him up again in tension on the floor. "Nothing to say," he gasped. "Strictly free-lance. He asked for some help."

"Who did?"

"Marty. You killed him. You killed Marty."

"I hope so," Wulff said. "How long you been in the murder business?"

"No murder," the man said hoarsely. "He just said beat you up, teach you a lesson. I don't murder."

"He lied to you, didn't he? He came here to kill."

"Don't kill. Wouldn't kill."

"That wasn't nice," Wulff said, "you keep the wrong kind of company."

"You've got to get me some help," the man said, "you got to get me some *help.*"

"For what?"

"Pain. Won't walk. The *pain*—"

"You'll live," Wulff said. "Believe me, you won't find it worth it, but you'll live."

He stood from his crouch. He kicked the beer-drinker in the wounded leg. The man shrieked like a woman, his cries rose clear out of amplitude and he lay there screaming without sound, his mouth locked into an *o* of agony.

"Now you've fucked up everything," Wulff said, "you've blown my cover. I got a corpse and a half in this room. What the hell am I supposed to do? Roll over and make space for the two of you?"

The blond sobbed unexpectedly, launched a last gurgle and then, hovering to his knees, threw a last spray of blood across the room and collapsed in it unmoving. Wulff looked at it in disgust.

"You see what I mean?" he said.

The beer-drinker continued to say nothing. His only percentage, he had apparently decided, was in making no sound. Either that or he was beyond speech. Same difference. Meant nothing.

"You see," Wulff said, talking to the man now almost as if he was an old friend, going to the closet, taking down a valise, beginning quickly but absently to toss equipment into it, "I never thought I wanted to get in as deep as I have already. For three months I lived here happy as a clam, reading newspapers and taking little walks in the neighborhood. My expenses were about four dollars a day and I could have stayed here indefinitely. It was fun living underground. It sure as hell made more sense than being a cop. I was getting more accomplished and making more of a contribution to the human condition just lying around in this bed over here than I ever was as a narco."

The beer-drinker pivoted slightly, screamed, reversed to his original position. "It hurts," he muttered, "it hurts."

"Well sure it hurts," Wulff said, "everything hurts terribly. You won't be able to move that thing for months without screaming, that is if they find you in time. But the thing is that you've just complicated everything now. I've blown my cover and I've got to get out."

He closed the valise, shouldered it for weight, put it down and opening the top bureau drawer began to assemble his arsenal. "I got curious," he said. "I wanted to run down one thread, that was all. Start tracing it from beginning to end to see what I can see. Well, there's just no end to that thread, is there? Once you're in, you're really in. You should have thought about that yourself before you decided to free-lance with your late friend over there. There are no half measures."

He went to the man, knelt, moved him slightly with more little gurgles and took out the man's wallet. Identification, credentials, meant nothing, he went for the money. One hundred and eighty-five dollars; three fifties, seven fives. The hit business was definitely improving if goons like this used one eighty-five for walking-around money. He threw the wallet against the wall, folded over the money and put it away. Add it to the reserve. The operation, as far as he went, would be self-financing.

"You've fucked up my life," he said to the beer-drinker.

The beer-drinker said nothing. He appeared to have fainted.

"You drove me out of the underground," he said, "I was doing fine until you had to screw up my lodgings."

Little droplets of the blond's blood, running free, dribbled toward him. Wulff shrugged.

"All right," he said to the blood, "so I never wanted to be underground after all. I just needed a little time to think."

He turned, walked to the door, opened the door, went out. As he trudged down the hall the thought occurred to him that the blond and his friend had had absolutely nothing to do with what was happening to him now.

His course had been locked from the very moment that he opened the door of Ric Davis's Eldorado and slid in. Up until that instant there could have been reversal. He could have backed out at any time. After that one gesture, everything was sealed.

He felt as if he were in an iron pipe somewhere and the pipe was strung toward eternity. Down that pipe he would run, screaming. But before he was done, he guessed, he would take a few with him.

Wulff was not a sadistic man; he did what he had to do only because it was necessary. He took little pleasure from suffering as long as the sufferer was in no position anymore to hurt him. So at the corner of Broadway and 97th he found a public phone, the only one in a bank of them that had not been looted and wrecked, and called the police.

He told them that there was a little trouble on the third floor of the rooming house on West 97th and that they would be advised to check it out. Maybe send an ambulance while they were at it.

He told them that the cops could send regards from the Wolf.

XIV

Vincent completed his work early in the afternoon and sat back, thinking about all of it. Finally he shrugged and put in a call to Gerald. There was nothing else to do.

"What have you found out?" Gerald said when Vincent got through the network of secretaries and relief men. "Go on, there's no tap."

"Might be one at my end," Vincent said although he knew there wasn't. The thing was to try and keep Gerald a little off balance all the time. In the long rum it wouldn't help much but it was the only edge he was likely to get.

"I'll take that chance," Gerald said. "Come on."

Vincent paused. "It looks bad," he said finally, "I think it does all tie in together."

"That's what I told you."

"There are a couple more bodies."

"Oh?" Gerald said.

"One of Marasco's bodyguards and a goon got shot up over on the West Side this afternoon. The bodyguard is dead, the goon is in pretty bad shape."

"You're sure of this?"

"It's my business to be sure," Peter Vincent said. "They were found in a furnished room that had been rented a few months ago by an ex-New York cop named Wulff. Wulff left the force a little mysteriously."

"Wulff," Gerald said, "somehow the name connects."

"He used to be a narco."

"Yeah. Maybe that's it."

"It's Wulff doing it," Vincent said carefully. "It all comes together on him."

"I can see that," Gerald said.

"No sign of him of course. The cops are looking for him now but they'll never find him."

"Can we find him?" Gerald asked. That was the man; he was, if nothing else, always to the point.

"Better than the cops I think."

"Let's find him," said Gerald.

"I thought you'd say that. I'm already in motion."

"I don't know who this guy is but let's wipe him out."

"Okay," Vincent said. He paused, considered the mouthpiece for a moment. "There's only one real problem I see," he said softly.

"Yes?"

"We know who he is," said Vincent. "He left a trail clear as blood."

"Yes he did."

"But he probably knows who we are," Vincent said carefully.

Gerald thought about that for a moment. There were clicks and buzzes on the line. Vincent lit another cigarette and let Gerald think. His twenty-fifth of the day. No sinner like a failed saint, he thought and inhaled deeply anyway. With all of his security, he had never exactly considered the possibility of a long life.

"Maybe," the man said. "Just maybe. That doesn't change anything though, does it?"

"I guess not."

"That's your job, Vincent. You're the organizer. You have the connections and the instincts, right? Just get to it."

"I figured as much."

"Get to it now."

"All right," Vincent said softly.

"And keep me the fuck out of it. All I want to hear is that it's done," Gerald said and slammed down the phone.

Vincent raised his eyebrows at the crash magnified within the inner ear, winced, took the phone away and delicately put it back on the cradle. He sighed enormously. This should be an easy job and he didn't think that this Wulff, whoever he was, would pose much of a challenge but—

Why did Gerald treat him like hired help?

XV

He settled his belongings in another near-flophouse in the nineties off Second Avenue, two weeks cash in advance, and then took a walk over to cautiously investigate the premises at six-eighteen East 83rd Street. He was putting himself into an exposed position but it might take them a few more hours to catch up with him—the blond, their best squeal, was now permanently out of commission and the beer-drinker knew nothing—and he felt a sensation of haste, rising pressure. The situation was as bad or even worse than he had figured; it was a three-story, seemingly impregnable building nestled down at the end of the block, the very end, overlooking the river. To the east of the townhouse was a massive iron gate sealing it off from approach on the riverside, to the west of it was an empty lot large enough to hold a building of exactly that size. A gate was on that side too. Wulff figured that Vincent probably owned the lot too and at whatever sacrifice kept it vacant for security purposes.

It didn't look good. The townhouse itself had a sealed-in, shut down kind of look, the shades pulled, closed gates on all of the windows, the basement entrance which might have been the best idea closed off by a massive iron door. The stoop led straight up, four steps, to the most massive set of doors he had ever seen, decorated in brass with what seemed to be little portholes now closed over. So they could sight from those doors as well, although with only a four-step climb toward the doors sighting would hardly be necessary. Having the entrance low to the ground, flat to the street side was clever. A stupid man might have thought that safety lay in getting as high as possible, building up the frontage, but Vincent knew the secrets of security. Stay low and be able to control all of the terrain.

It looked very bad. Worse than he would have conceived and he had drawn no pretty pictures of this in his mind. He could of course walk up those four steps, use that ornamented knocker and ask his way in. That would be very bright. They probably worked through a succession of locks and entrances like divers coming through decompression chambers and he would be likely to be dead before he ever got to the surface on which the fish, Peter Vincent, floated. He could come in blasting, that was a bright idea; he might be able to take a guard down with him before they cut up his body for dead meat.

It did not look promising.

He thought of dropping it. Five down wasn't bad: Davis, Jessup, Marasco, Scotti, the blond. The Marasco killing was the only important one in administrative terms but it would keep them shuffling around for a while. He could just back off, be a hit-and-run man, start to burrow in from another angle. Instead of following through the thread, snap it then, find another spool elsewhere. Guerilla tactics.

No. It wouldn't work.

If you were going to do the job you had to do it *right*, trace through the strand, sever out a whole line of responsibility and succession. Chewing little bites out of the fabric here and there was like killing roaches in hand to hand combat. You could take down one or a thousand but they would always swarm in.

The thing to do was to track the roaches to the point of infestation and then blow up the breeding hole.

He put his hands into his pockets and slowly walked west on Eighty-Third Street. No one was on the block, no one seemed to notice. Quite possibly in fact probably, he had been sighted through the windows but they could not identify him by face, not just yet anyway, and for the Peter Vincents of this world it made little sense to start sniping down strangers, no matter how suspicious, on the street. This could lead to inquiries. Eminent domain, as Wulff understood it, did not from the property owner's point of view extend beyond the sidewalks into the streets. In the country that the Peter Vincents would build for us it would of course extend beyond the water's edge but they were about five or ten years yet from having that kind of country. It was getting closer but there was still a little margin left in which you could operate.

Wulff found himself possessed by an idea. He walked back to the new rooming house quickly. As the East Side was considered, generally speaking, to be one generation advanced in lustre, temper and sophistication from the West Side, so this rooming house was an improvement over the one on West 97th. He had a small bathroom in his room here. The drug traffic seemed to be contained within the rooms of the individual residents rather than spilling into the halls and the lobby. The lobby itself had a desk clerk, an ancient, incoherent man who sat on a chair behind a high place and nodded off into a stupor but he was, to be sure, a desk clerk. And this rooming house even had a public telephone in the lobby which worked. All in all, things seemed to be looking up.

He dialed into the precinct and asked to talk to Williams. Williams, it seemed was not in; he had called in sick a few hours before and would not be in for his four to midnight shift. Wulff noted with a jolt of surprise that it had been only sixteen hours since he had last seen the man; that was two murders, another lifetime ago. He took a card out of his wallet on which a long time ago he had jotted down some numbers and called Williams's home in Queens. His wife answered.

"He's sleeping," she said.

"Get him up."

"Who is this calling?"

"This is Wulff," he said after debating it for only an instant.

"Oh," she said. "*Oh.* Okay. I'm sure he won't mind getting up for you."

"Don't bet on it," he said.

The phone went down in his ear. A little later Williams, hazed with sleep, said, "Wulff, how are you doing? What's going on?"

"A lot and a little. I think I want to take you up on part of your offer."

"That's great," Williams said, "I'm sincere, that's great, but I've had no sleep except what I'm getting now for days and I don't feel like no two man army—"

"No army," Wulff said, "this is me alone. I just need some information from you."

"Go on."

"Information only you can get for me I should say. Through the department. I need some plans; a survey of a particular building."

"Oh man," Williams said, "oh man, that's murder. Documents bureau."

"I know where it is. I need the stuff right away."

"How soon? What's right away."

"Right now. Fifteen minutes ago. But I'll settle for midnight."

"That's rough," Williams said. "I was going to sleep this shift off. Maybe I could get up and hustle a little. But *documents* bureau? City survey?"

"You said you wanted to help."

"What's the address?"

"Six-eighteen East Eighty-Third Street. I want to know anything about it you can get. Piping, supply, electricity ducts, foundation, tunnelling, the whole works. And I need it fast."

"Rough," Williams said again. "I'll see what I can do though."

"When you've got it, I've got myself a new address too."

"Oh? What's that?"

Wulff gave it to him. "One more thing," he said, "maybe you could get me some riot equipment."

"Come again?"

"Grenades, launchers, machine guns. You know. The good old stuff."

"You're kidding," Williams said.

"Practically."

"You can't get that stuff. They won't even admit they *have* that stuff."

"I know that. It was just a thought."

"Man," Williams said admiringly, "I will give you this; you have ambition." He laughed dryly, all the sleep gone from his voice, and hung up.

Ambition. If there was one thing he had it was ambition. Wulff went up to his room, second floor this time, and opened the door half-expecting to be hit by a volley of shots or men, all of them bearing name tags saying *Peter Vincent* but saw nothing. Roaches of course, cracked fluorescence, small threads in the walls through which, once, fingers must have groped. But if it was not an attack all of these could be interpreted as friends.

Wulff locked the door, worked in his own chain-bolt quickly and skillfully, pulled down the shades after securing the windows and hurled himself to the bed like a low inside pitch. He slept a sleep devoid of dreams. If his timing and expectations were right it might be his last sleep for a long time; he had better take advantage of it.

Still, as dreams grabbed him, he felt nagged by guilt. The enemy never slept. The enemy worked in shifts and was always active. Sleeping was just turning over time to them.

But he was only one man.

XVI

The man known as Gerald did most of his contact work over the phone too. The phone was fast and convenient and even though the tap was probably omnipresent Gerald knew that it came down to a matter of auditing these tapes. Who listened? With five million phone taps in existence and still growing, they would need half the population of the country just to cover.

But for this one, he figured, it was best to show up in person. He did not want to take any chances at all with the passage of this kind of information. So although Gerald looked with distaste upon going out of his home or offices or car at all, much less face-to-face dealing with lower echelon personnel, he put on his jacket and met the contact downstairs in a back booth of a Wall Street luncheonette. The contact could be identified only by the white jacket he said he would be wearing. He was an information man, bland and colorless behind rimless glasses and as far as Gerald was concerned he would never see the man again so there was no need to make a further personnel inventory. If it ever became necessary to get rid of him he could do that over the phone. You simply did not have to get involved with the lower echelons.

"I got what I could," the contact man said. He slid a dossier underneath the table. Gerald took it. "It's all there, pretty much, as far as I could go."

Gerald looked at the waitress and ordered coffee. Nothing for the contact man; there was no need to feign sociability. He would never see the man again. "Sum it up quickly," he said. Gerald disliked reading. He could read perfectly well, even intricate and detailed materials, but talk was simply easier for him. If you talked you could manipulate people and get to the sense of things.

"He's an ex-narco who got himself busted off the squad," the contact man said. "The official story is that he was back-talking lieutenants and couldn't take discipline but it looks like the truth is that he was taking suspects into back rooms and beating the shit out of them. Also he wasn't turning over stash except under pressure."

"User?"

"Not at all. He didn't trust security. Didn't like the idea of turning stash over so it would go right back into the dealer's hands he said. He got a little bit noisy about it."

"Interesting," Gerald said, "sounds like a dedicated man."

"They're all dedicated at the beginning. This one looks like he played it straight all the way through, though. On the force ten years. Two years of that off, military duty, Vietnam. Volunteered."

"Volunteered for the draft? Cops are draft-exempt."

The contact man shrugged. "Dedicated," he said. "Maybe he wanted to take a look at the trade firsthand too. Who knows? Riot training, was on the TPF squad before he got into narco. Streetwork, drove a radio car, special detail; fact is that he practically did everything. Worked Harlem during the '64 riots in the front lines."

"A career man."

"Looks that way," said the contact man. He looked longingly at Gerald's coffee as the waitress put it down but said nothing, then shook his head. "Never made sergeant, though. Was on the list but somehow they kept on going around him."

"Usually do with these types," Gerald said. He stirred his coffee, put in some sugar, stirred it again, unaware of the contact man's gaze. "Sounds pretty tough," he said, "but so far he doesn't sound crazy."

"Oh?"

"Man would have to be crazy to do what he's doing," Gerald said. "Wouldn't he? Somehow, I don't see that yet."

"One other thing," the contact man said, "which might explain a little more. He had a girl. She was found OD'd in a tenement over in the West Nineties."

"That's interesting," Gerald said. He balanced the spoon delicately in his fingers, sipped the coffee. "Now that's very interesting."

"Nice Queens girl, someone named Marie Calvante. Can't get much on her; he knew her for a long time though."

"How did she get to the West Nineties?"

"That's the point. It doesn't show. She was found OD'd in a tenement over there. It might have been suicide or the girl might have been put down. You know how these things are."

"Yes," Gerald said, "I know how these things are."

"Wulff took the call."

"What's that?"

"A blind tip came into his precinct while he was in a radio car."

"Going a little too fast for me," Gerald said. Very cautiously he put down the coffee cup. "Last I heard he was a narco. Back to radio car?"

"They didn't know what the hell to do with him so they put him back on patrol in his old precinct. He was just too hot to handle."

"And he was on duty when the tip came into the precinct?"

"He took the call himself," the contact man said. "The girl was dead."

Gerald thought about it for a moment, looking at the ceiling of the luncheonette which looked oddly enough like the ceiling of his office. "That might make a man crazy," he said judiciously. "I can understand that."

"Yeah."

"How did the girl die? Was she a junkie? Or was it murder?"

"That's the thing," the contact man said. He leaned closer to Gerald, his knee brushing for a horrid instant before he retracted it, "That's a blind alley altogether. All that I can say is that nobody I can reach or that is known by anyone I can reach had anything to do with it at all. Whatever it was, it came from outside channels."

"But he thinks it came from inside."

"Obviously."

"So he's going to patch up his girl that way," Gerald said. He pushed the coffee cup away from him and succumbed to a sudden, pointless anger as he was already poised to stand. The contact man had nothing more to offer him. "It's goddamned ridiculous," Gerald said.

"What's that?"

"This guy is trying to shake the whole city loose and it doesn't even have anything to do with us. The girl probably was a junkie. How the hell she got into the nineties from Queens is something you can research but she probably OD'd herself. But he'd rather kill every dealer in the country than face that fact."

"I don't know anything about that," the contact man said cautiously, "I just deal in information, you know. I try not to think. Mind if I finish your coffee?"

"I don't give a damn what you do."

"Don't get mad at *me*," the contact man said, holding up the cup defensively, "I did the best I could. I can't tell you what you like to hear; you got plenty of guys for that. I deal in the *truth*."

"Take pride in your work, huh?"

"What's that?"

"Sincere, dedicated, highly motivated, can't be bought off for anything; you and your truth. You'd never make sergeant you know."

"I don't understand that," the man said, blowing steam off the cup, "I just don't know what you're talking about. Hey, don't forget the folder. I put it all down for you in detail. There's a lot of stuff in there I didn't even discuss; details and so on. Just gave you the high points."

"No low points?"

"What's that?"

"Any decent file should have the low points too, don't you think? High points and low points." Gerald put the dossier under his arm. He found himself struggling with an insane impulse, one he had not felt toward anyone for twenty years. It made no sense but this only rendered it the more tempting. He wanted to hit the contact man a doubling-over blow in the solar plexus and then finish him off with a right to the mouth.

"I don't understand," the contact man said, sitting over the coffee, "I just don't understand."

"Don't make me help you," Gerald said, "just don't make me help you."

He got out of the place quickly before he could give in to the impulse. It would not do him any good if he yielded. Gerald's entire life was based upon the avoidance of confrontation. Confrontations made trouble. Better to do it behind closed doors or at levels of suggestion.

He took the elevator up to the heights, went into his office, locked the door and looked over the dossier with disgust, shaking his head, biting his lips now and then. As the contact man had said, it was all there. It was all there.

Stupid son of a bitch.

What got Gerald, he decided, what was *really* infuriating him was the feeling that if they only had been able to get to this Wulff themselves at an early stage of the game and has a chance to deal with him, he might have worked out to be a hell of a useful man for them. There just wasn't much of this kind of dedication nowadays.

Forget it. Too late.

With a sigh of regret, Gerald put in the necessary call. Wulff was prey for anyone now.

But he would have made them a hell of a good man.

XVII

Williams came in less than three hours, jolting Wulff out of sleep, shaking his head but carrying a huge tube in which were rolled documents. He was a good man, there was no question about it. Either the rookie had matured enormously or Wulff was seeing strengths that he had been unable to appreciate before. "Son of a bitch," Williams said, "don't ask me to do something like that again. I'll have half of civilian review on my ass for the way I charged through there. I knocked down clerks like bowling pins." Then his face turned serious and he said "I don't know what you're planning but I want to help you."

"No good. No deal."

"I'm ready."

"I know you're ready," Wulff said, "and I believe you. But this is mine. This one I've got to do on my own."

"Why?"

"Because it has to be," he said. He did not tell Williams about the appearance of the townhouse or how impregnably Peter Vincent had sealed himself in. If Williams was half a cop he had already studied those blueprints and knew it himself. "This one is mine," he said.

"Doesn't have to be."

"Yes it does. There will be others," he said to Williams. He doubted it. His best calculation was that he was going to break himself open on Peter Vincent and end a promising career. Be that as it may. He wasn't going to drag down anyone like Williams on this kind of shot. "Lots of others," he said.

"I hope so."

"I'm in business now."

"I believe it. I believe you really are."

"But this one has got to be on my own." He realized that he had more than committed himself to Williams for future ventures. If there were future ventures. That was a spotty commitment indeed. But looking at the man, sensing not only the appeal but the strength in those eyes, he knew that he had a man he could trust if he wanted him.

"I believe you mean that," Williams said.

"I believe I do," Wulff said and put out his hand.

Williams took it and there was almost the feeling of pact in that handshake. Melodrama, posturing, made Wulff vomit but he could sense the significance of what had just happened. "I appreciate this," he said, motioning to the plans to break the moment.

"Ah bullshit," Williams said and very quickly went out of there, closing the door. So he too hated scenes.

Wulff looked over the prints. They did not make him more optimistic. There were viaducts, piping, tunnels, small chinks in the armor which Peter Vincent had constructed but none of them were significant and all were pretty well under cover themselves. It was a question of having to penetrate the defenses, virtually, in order to penetrate the defenses. The intricacy of the network surrounding the seemingly impermeable townhouse was interesting of course. The intricacies of urban life. But Wulff did not feel that he was in a position to take much comfort from this.

At length studying, tracing, calling on the reserves of some almost-forgotten army reconnaissance experience, Wulff noticed that there were exposed gas lines there. They traced themselves out of the house like snakes and wound up very near street level at the rim of that abandoned lot. That was interesting.

He bent over and became completely absorbed. It seemed impossible, no way that something like this could work and yet, be damned if it did not look like those lines could be reached by simply going for them with a shovel. They were close to the surface, they may in fact have gaped open like little mouths in the ground there, releasing their vapors to mingle with the odors of East Eighty Third Street—

Fascinating.

XVIII

Terello waited around until nine in the evening. Then he decided he couldn't stand it anymore. Hanging around the apartment, waiting for the ax to drop was impossible. He couldn't go on this way. His principles were founded upon getting out of the apartment and into the world, solving whatever problems arose with action, and he simply could not nod off in here like a junkie with the feeling that outside, people unknown to him in ways completely outside of his control, were deciding his life.

He had to see Vincent. The man simply could not do this kind of thing to him, put him under wraps for the duration. Who was Peter Vincent? His boss was Albert Marasco; he had always taken his orders from Marasco, now this Vincent was muscling in and talking as if he took it for granted that he owned Terello. He did not own Terello. No one did. Terello was no man's fucking property. Whatever happened to him now he was not going to check out with the feeling that he was owned by someone.

Terello got out of his bathrobe and pajamas and got dressed. Instantly he felt better. He was assuming some control of his life now; he was in action again. He went into the small living room where his wife was watching television, laughing a little and talking back to the screen. "You tell 'em, Merv," she said, leaning forward, elbows on knees, forehead almost against the screen, "you show them up. They may have thrown you off Channel 2, baby, but you're still number one in my heart." He literally could not stand the woman. All right, it wasn't completely her fault. If he had had a different kind of life, taken more interest in her and in being around the house, maybe she would have gotten away from the television and talked to him a little. Not let herself go to hell like this. But on the other hand that had been his choice and decision. Terello knew that it could have been no other way. He had things to do.

"I'm going out," he said.

She did not look up. "Merv," she said, "you are a wonderful creature."

"I said I'm going out," Terello said more loudly. He would have simply walked out except that he needed to leave a message. "Tell anyone who calls that I'm asleep and can't be disturbed."

She looked up, finally. "You're going out, Joe?" she said, her eyes blanked. "Are you supposed to do that?"

"Sure I'm supposed to do it."

"Weren't you supposed to stay around for a few days?" She looked guileless. "Didn't you tell me you'd be staying home for a few days?"

"Change of plans," he said, "the deal came through after all and now I have to go."

She shrugged and turned back to the television set. "Okay," she said, "but I thought you were supposed to stay at home."

"Shut up now, will you?"

"All right, Joe," she said mildly, "you don't have to scream at me."

"Anybody calls, remember, I'm fast asleep. I can't be disturbed for anything."

"What if they really want to talk to you? Should I wake you up?"

Terello felt himself convulsing with rage. "Didn't you *listen?*" he said, "I told you I'm going *out.*"

"Oh," she said, "oh, that's right, I forgot. You're going out." She paused. "But weren't you supposed to stay in for a few days, Joe?"

"The hell with it," he said and went out of the apartment. All right, maybe he should have left her a long time ago. It wasn't as if there weren't women around, all of whom would have been a hell of a lot better looking than the pig this woman had turned into in the slow twenty years they'd been married. But what was the point? He had never thought of getting out. Getting out took energy and ambition and in relation to his home life Terello had none. Just a little peace, that's all he wanted and this at least the woman gave him. Hell, she made no demands at all. The only time she showed emotion was when the television set broke down or there was one of the frequent Queens power failures. Otherwise she co-existed with life and Terello without difficulties of any sort.

Hell, she was better off than he was. Terello knew himself to be a sensitive man. Hell, he wasn't the run of the mill kind of guy who got involved in this sort of stuff. He had feelings. He suffered. He took a longer view of what was going on and he kept his eyes open. If he didn't keep his eyes open he would not have lasted so long and he certainly would not be in the trouble that he was now because they knew that when you were dealing with Joe Terello you were dealing with a shrewd kind of a son of a bitch, a guy you couldn't put things over on. Of course they'd want to keep him under wraps. Otherwise he might find out too much. He even might find out that his boss had been double-crossed and take a terrible vengeance. Everybody was afraid of Joe Terello. Damned right He was no ordinary kind of man.

He went to his garage and got the Electra 225 started. Just listening to the motor, being behind the wheel again made him feel better. There was nothing like being behind your own car, controlling your life making your own choices. The Electra was a 1964, hell, nine years old but it was still a better car and a better looking one goddammit than the newer stuff or the foreign shitboxes that some of these guys drove. With the depreciation being the way it was on all of those cars it made the most sense to get one five or six years old which had been nicely broken in and which some other guy had already taken the complete beating on. He had picked this one up for just five hundred dollars two years ago. Sure he had a little transmission trouble and the shocks had had to be replaced and the exhaust system wasn't all it should be, but where were you going to get a car like this for five hundred dollars? Hell, buying new you couldn't get the wheels off a Volkswagen plus the hood for five hundred dollars. It was all rigged, the whole thing. The only way to beat it was to buy used.

Terello drove through Rego Park on Queens Boulevard, heading toward the 59th Street Bridge. That was the best way to go this time of night; not much traffic build-up on Queens Boulevard, the street of high-rises. All right, he should have gotten out of Rego Park years ago. The area was going to hell with all the black stuff starting to move in on the edges and who wanted to live in fucking Queens anyway? He would have wanted a little house in Jersey, not too far out from the bridge but far enough so that he could have gotten some decent air but he had been so caught up in the job that there was never time to sit down and read the papers and really take the time and trouble to think out a move. Besides, without kids it didn't particularly matter whether they stayed in Rego Park or not. Who cared about the school system? And his wife would have lived anywhere at all with four walls and a television set.

Hitting the bridge he picked the Electra up to fifty. It skittered and knocked a little but fifty was a good speed for a nine-year-old car. He felt a little twinge of anticipation and fear: what would Peter Vincent say when Terello confronted him face to face? Exactly what would Peter Vincent do?

Terello did not know. Nor did he particularly care. He had never met this Vincent clown nor after this one confrontation did he expect to see him again. But he was going to make it clear to Vincent that the Joe Terellos of this world could not be put under wraps, locked away under cover like dogs in a pound.

No. No sir. He would not stand for it nor would he permit Vincent to get away with this. He had worked with Marasco in good times and bad for ten years now. Marasco was his boss; Marasco was the man who told Terello where to go and what to do and he was not taking orders from *any* clown who in the absence of Marasco thought that Joe Terello was property.

In fact, he thought, pulling the car off the bridge and taking the sweeping turn onto First Avenue at thirty miles an hour, the hell with the traffic light, in fact, he would not be surprised if Vincent was simply some kind of sharp operator himself, a guy who thought that with Marasco out of the way he might be able to wedge in a little bit on the line of succession. *He might even be trying to keep Terello from the job which was rightfully his. Terello might succeed Marasco.*

"Son of a bitch," Joe Terello said aloud. Now that he had had a chance to get behind the wheel of the Electra and really think this situation out, all of his senses had returned to him and he was beginning to understand the situation. Of course. What had happened to Marasco was unfortunate but it sure as hell had nothing to do with him; he had worked loyally and without question for ten years. Now everybody knew that it was Joe's turn to move into the position which had been vacated by Marasco. Wasn't it? That was the way it worked when a man was a loyal soldier.

Except that this Vincent had horned in from outside, some sharp guy, an operator on the fringes of the line of succession who thought that now he had a chance to take advantage of the situation by cutting a piece for himself. All that he had to do was to keep Terello out of the picture for a couple of days until he had had a chance to make his moves and that would be the end of Terello's possibilities. He wouldn't be there at the funeral, he would not have shown proper loyalty, he would be passed right over.

And there would go the ten-year, waited-for, down-the-line chance.

"Son of a *son* of a bitch," Terello said again. He burst the car up York to 82nd Street, started the long drive toward the river, went back three blocks and came up 83rd. Six-eighteen Eighty-Third Street, there it was. Did this Vincent really think that he had no understanding at all? Did he take him for such a fool? Didn't he realize that Terello had contacts, friends, moves and a brain too and that he would be able to dig out the address of this silky mother-fucker just as quickly as he wanted?

He grunted, putting on the foot brake and bringing the car to a halt across the street from six-eighteen. Illegal parking all the way up and down both sides of the block of course; trust the sons of bitches in the high-rent district to treat their streets like private property. That was all right, he wouldn't be here that long. His business might be very simply accomplished. He was going to get face to face with this clown and show him where he stood and if the clown got funny with him ... well, he would have to get a little more serious than that. This was the ten-year down-the-line chance and it was not likely to come again.

He used the trunk key to open the glove compartment of the Electra and took out the point thirty-eight. In ten years he had had to use it only four times, each for a distinct reason. He was not a violent man; he knew himself to be in fact a man of great gentleness and basic compassion who could only become violent regretfully and with much pain. But he was as tough as he was gentle, as firm as he was compassionate. Nobody was going to take his ten-year chance from him now. *Nobody.*

And he had been able to work all of this out on his own too. That certainly showed that he had far more brains than he might be generally credited with at least by the likes of Peter Vincent. They thought he was some hired man, some bully and fool, some errand boy who carried the late Albert Marasco's coat and wiped his nose for him. Little did they know that it was Terello's right, his absolute *right*, to be the next in the line of succession.

He came out of the Electra brutal and quick, ready for any kind of attack, doubling himself over and hitting the side of the car, then whirling with the gun, but the street was quiet. There was simply no sign of life whatsoever. For a moment he felt like a little bit of a fool, carrying on with a gun on a perfectly empty street but then he reminded himself that nobody ever fell behind in his work because he was cautious. Or took preparations.

Now to get the job done. He holstered the gun inside his jacket, gave the Electra a last affectionate look, started across the street. It gleamed in the streetlight. It got maybe seven miles to the gallon and had a hell of a dent in the left rear door but from this side it looked absolutely flawless. From bumper to bumper the right side of the Electra 225 was magnificent. And some day he would get the necessary body work done on the left side too.

Boy, he thought, this was some townhouse. For the first time he got a good look at six-eighteen. A massive yet somehow squatty building hulking by the river, dangling ornaments and brass. This was some security trap that Peter Vincent had gotten for himself. Maybe the guy wasn't such a small-timer after all.

Didn't matter. Terello reconnoitered, got onto curbside, paused a minute before heading for the stoop. Absolutely quiet, no light from behind the windows of six-eighteen although it was probably set up on dead shades. Sure, he had heard of something like that. They probably had him under observation. So what? They must have known that sooner or later Terello would come to settle out his side of the bargain.

A few scraps of paper wafted down the street, moving lightly in the August breeze. He felt them brush his ankles as they continued their strange journey to the river. A foghorn sounded from far to the North; something probably going under the Triborough Bridge. He vaulted the four steps of the stoop quickly, lightly, and seeing the huge knocker on the door lifted, hit. Hit that door once. Twice. Three times. Let there be no doubt in their minds but that Terello was here and that he was heading in. He felt the point thirty-eight inside his jacket and smiled at the weight of it. It was a good one. It had never failed him. There were dead men, a couple, who would testify to that.

The foghorn again. That was a big motherfucking ship or at least a loud one. Probably come to think of it it was some little tug with a big sound like a tiny woman with a big ass and mouth. The door opened and a short man with grey eyes wearing flowing robes was looking at Terello from what appeared to be some kind of vestry. Cold, impermeable, measuring eyes.

"Yes?" he said.

"I'm here to see Peter Vincent."

"Peter Vincent is not at home now, I do not think sir."

"You don't understand. My name is Joe Terello."

The eyes seemed to glint. "Ah," the man said, "perhaps there was some kind of misunderstanding in that event. Would you like to come in, Mr. Terello?"

"Maybe Mr. Vincent would like to come to the door." He was no fool. What did they think he was; a fool to walk into a blind entrance like this?

"I see," the short man said, "I may have to discuss this with Mr. Vincent of course."

"Of course."

"In the meantime, while I am discussing it, would you like to wait inside the vestry?" The short man seemed very amused. He seemed on the verge of winking. "No harm can come to you in the vestry, Mr. Terello," he said, "and we do prefer to keep the door closed."

"Do you?"

"We dislike the street traffic that might come in otherwise, with an open door," the short man said. His robes wafted in the night. He giggled.

"All right," Terello said. He stepped inside. What the hell could they do to him? He felt the gun swaying reassuringly inside his clothing. He almost touched it but decided not to. Too risky to call attention to it in that way. Better to save it for the crucial moment if it ever came.

The short man closed the door, locked it, opened the inner door which appeared to lead into a long hallway which had carpeting not only on the floor but the walls and ceiling in mottled red hue. "Wait right here, Mr. Terello," the short man said, "and I will be back quite promptly." He closed the door. Again there was the sound of a sliding lock and Terello, now free to hold onto the gun, was left in the vestry.

He stood there holding it loosely, balancing on the balls of his feet, prepared for anything. After a few moments he noticed that it seemed to be becoming a little bit hot in the vestry which well it might since, he saw, there was no ventilation. A moment after that he noticed that it was becoming much hotter in the vestry and, as a matter of fact, due to the absence of any ventilation he was having difficulty breathing. He loosened his tie, sighed, exhaled, wished that the little son of a bitch would come back already and give him the word. Wasn't he aware of the fact that he had sealed Terello in here?

Well yes, Terello realized, it was possible that the man was aware. It must have been over a hundred and twenty degrees in here now and he could not breathe, he simply and absolutely could not breathe. *They were trying to suffocate him.*

They were trying to kill Terello. It was a new thought; this Peter Vincent, whoever the hell he was would have to be *crazy.* He was serious. Terello had come over to try to have a reasonable discussion and Vincent wanted to *kill* him.

What kind of people were these? Terello did not have time to ponder the question. Panic began to gnaw at his edges; he felt as if a huge, black cloak had been dropped over his body. Swaddled within the folds of this cloak he simply could not breathe. He went for the gun, the point thirty-eight caliber that had never failed him and could not possibly fail him now. He began to shoot, methodically but desperately at the lock toward the outside. The bullets hit metal, spanged back, the second hit him on the hand, grazing bone and drawing blood. He gasped with fear and pain, dropped the revolver. He scrambled for it, his knees hitting the plain boards painfully, sending small circuits of pain wafting through him but he could not seem to find the gun. He felt as if a scarf was being tightened across his neck. He could not breathe. He literally could not breathe.

The lights began to go out. Consciousness whisked away from him the way that life had whisked itself away from his wife. Scrambling on the floor of the vestry Joe Terello knew that he was a dead man. He had been stupid, incredibly stupid, and now he would never see the light again.

And then, giving him the first and last break of a lifetime—because after giving him a glimpse of the light it killed him and sealed him to the darkness forever—the whole house blew up.

XIX

Wulff had done the best he could. The incendiaries he had given up on pretty much. Simple household devices, that was what he would need to blow up the Vincent mansion. Start getting spectacular about it though and that mansion would blow up in his face. Professional results through amateur techniques, that was the ticket.

He got the metal cutter in the hardware shop along with the instant coffee heater; the Eveready batteries came from the cigarette store right around the corner. The only other stuff he needed was in his own head. He needed patience and a good deal of discipline. The luck part of course was in a different territory.

He thought that he could bring it off. He was no explosives expert but he had fiddled around here and there in Vietnam, he knew land mines, grenades, the sense of an explosion and what constituted an ignition point. Any man who hangs around the ordnance depot out of simple curiosity for a couple of days is one step ahead of the game right there. Wulff had confidence. He had reasonable confidence in himself.

Back in the room he got to work. Most of the work would be done on the site but a dry-run was important, he had to see if he could manipulate the materials, if they would go together in the right way. It looked okay on paper but what the hell was paper? On paper the drug war was working too and there were seventy million worth of drugs, street value, safely locked away in the department property room. The metal cutter, an intricate little saw with sharp tiny teeth cut a neat swathe in the door of his medicine chest, attacked the steel door of the room itself with some efficiency. With pressure and luck he would be able to cut a swathe the size of a man's arm. The coffee heater worked fine from standard current, producing a neat, mean little glow within a minute and a half that would have turned anyone's flesh to water. He timed it from plug-in to glow, it came down to eighty-three seconds, give or take a few and it seemed to work just as well when the cord was cut, the lines exposed, and the lines worked around the batteries, but at that point you moved into unknown territory. The batteries worked fine now but heater and batteries wrapped together would have to survive a drop of something like six feet. Would the splicing hold? Well, you could only hope so.

It was interesting work, whatever else you had to say about it. He was going to try to knock over a fucking guarded townhouse with a couple of five and ten cent tools. If he brought it off the deed should live forever but then again he could not go around looking for praise or awards. He looked through the materials Williams had given him, carefully, using his fingers, tracing the gas lines, the point at which they entered the basement. It *looked* all right. Of course the plans were old and Vincent himself might have made changes in those points of entrance, not being anyone's fool. But Wulff doubted that. People who bought guards and constructed elaborate doors just didn't think of little details like gas lines.

No. No indeed. They just did not know, as Wulff did, what it was like to get behind the enemy lines. He would get behind them. Part of it was a matter of desperate efficiency—Wulff was now dealing with an enemy who was aware of him and he would have to strike before that enemy or not at all—but another part of it came from a feeling that if he did not deliver this killing punch immediately, everything that he had already done would be meaningless. Jessup, Davis, Scotti, Marasco, the blond, all of them would have died in vain. Aborted mission. He owed it to these corpses to carry out the job just as far and fast as he could.

So Wulff ran through it again, over and over again until everything was mechanical and he could do it even in the dark. Cut steel, tie in the batteries to the heater, drop the heater. It worked every time but on a softer surface. Still, how hard could the floor of Vincent's basement be? He waited for dark. He was ready to go, more or less, but nothing to do until he had darkness and that meant, in late August, waiting until at least eight o'clock to go.

He couldn't hold out. At seven-thirty he was ready to go, the hell with it. Fog and soot had rolled in from the river, the city was reeking and stinking anyway as only the city could at the end of summer, no one would be looking for him in the haze if it was still light when he began to work. Wulff tossed the materials and the prints into the empty suitcase and got out of the room carrying nothing but that and a gun. The suitcase was amazingly light. Demolition equipment fit to blow up a townhouse and it could not have weighed, all of it, more than two pounds. The gun wouldn't hurt although the way things were set up now he doubted that it would do him much good. He would either bring this thing off, in which case the gun would not be necessary, or he would fail and if that happened, the gun or even a full machine clip weren't going to make much difference. They would wipe him out. The gun was only for security because actually he was going in there unarmed.

He walked the suitcase down Lexington Avenue into the eighties and then all the way over to the river. The six-eighteen block was empty of course. No traffic on it at all, no people, no cars. Nothing. It was as if the medium-to-bigger-fish like Peter Vincent or Albert Marasco made sure that their own areas were clear of the cancer which was otherwise poisoning the country, the cancer which they had themselves created. It was a pact between the Vincents and other parties to keep it the hell out of their part of the world. Just like he had figured it before, things had long since reached the point where the enforcers were merely another part of the overall operation. They were getting their share too. For a healthy little piece of the action, they could make sure that the Vincents would live undisturbed. Virtually invisible.

He went to the building and reconnoitered briefly. Then he went to the empty lot, squatted in the place where the blues had shown him the line rested, and went to work, ripping up the soft dirt with his hands.

The line was there. He tracked it downrange to the side of the building where it fed directly into the basement.

Risky. Very risky of course, all of it was. He was up against the house now, so tight to the wall that they might not see him except by leaning through a window and peering, but how close did he want to come to Peter Vincent? But then again, Wulff told himself, even if the guards did take to scrambling around the windows which probably wasn't in their employment contracts, what would they make of a man in faded army fatigues working obscurely against the building? Who could he be? He could only be a maintenance man, someone from the gas company, checking out the lines. Of course. Men like this were invisible in New York. They were and were not there like the filthy river and the darkening sunsets. Nobody made anything of them at all.

All right. Take the chance. Up and down the block he might be noticed but no one was going to call the cops on a faceless maintenance man. The Peter Vincents and their employees, generally speaking, liked as little to do with the cops as possible. They were not going to call cops to the site unless they had something they clearly could not handle themselves. What was a maintenance man? As a general rule the Vincents were great citizens, they wanted to co-exist with the cops and you certainly did nothing if you could to offend them but you didn't call police to investigate maintenance men even if they were starting to poke around your walls. Who would try to get into a fortress? If his luck held he'd be all right, Wulff thought. Otherwise forget it. He kept his shoulders hunched, dug in the suitcase for the cutter and folded into himself. Fuck being observed. He just couldn't worry about it; he had work to do.

He began to work on the basement wall, at the point where he was sure the gas line entered. The saw made little chattering noises in the night; he held it steady. The wall was concrete which crumbled rather easily; all in all it was easier to cut this than it had been during the dry runs. Vincent had everything protected but way down below the walls were falling apart. Vincent would not think of that. It was like the cities themselves; at the bottom they were rotten.

He cut a ragged hole into the basement wall large enough to get his arm through.

He should have brought a flashlight, he realized that now. He hadn't because he was afraid of the beam but the angle of thrust would have been invisible to anyone not actually in the basement. So be it. He took his arm out and carefully, letting the little light drifting in from the west to work over his shoulder and into the hole, he peered into the basement.

He was in the meter room. Looking across he could see the meter on the wall opposite, letting go cheerful little ticking noises. The gas line that he had tracked ran about two feet off the floor, right into that meter. It was well within reaching distance.

For the first time Wulff smiled.

He took the metal cutter again, backing out to get it and at the same time a patrol car whipped around the corner, sirens dead but streamers on. It came by him fast. He thought for a moment that it was for him but the car had a downtown disaster in mind. At the intersection, finding traffic, the car cut on the siren and churned out of there, bellowing.

Nothing to worry about there.

He went to work on the gas line itself.

This was a different deal altogether and Wulff thought for a few moments that he was beyond his depth. The line was tough steel, ancient of course and rust spattered which meant that there were weak spots around the joint if you could only get into them but he was working blind, in a cramped position, bunched up against that wall and the line would not yield. The cutter worked on it for a long time without any feeling of progress, once he thought that he had dropped an inch but then again it just could have been an illusion. His arm was exhausted. This line was tough; it was not for nothing that it had been shielded like this for inside that line circulated pure death.

Then he heard a hiss.

It was a pure, high sound, a sound like the ecstatic gasps of a young girl and Wulff found himself more excited by it than he ever had been by any girl but there was no time for calculations of triumph now. He was working on a very, very short margin. The pipe snaffled and wheezed away, pouring gas into the air. Even outside, shielded by concrete, Wulff could smell it. He took his arm out slowly, letting the metal cutter drop with a *ping!* into the basement, now the meter. It would never make any difference now.

He had lost track of time he knew. He gripped the shoulder of the working arm, grunted, worked the stiffness out. His concentration had been so intense that all sense of time had fled. It could be midnight. The gas line had been a son of a bitch in the cutting; he must have been on it for hours. His arm was numb enough. He gritted his teeth with the pain of returning circulation, inhaled raggedly, felt wisps of gas clot his lungs. The basement was filling up fast now.

Now for the heater. He went back for it.

And as he stood over the suitcase yards downrange he dived, held shuddering to the ground as a big cornering car came fast, hit the brakes and then, headlights fading, lay inert across the street. A door thunked and a man came out of the car and looking only casually to either side sprinted up the four steps and hit the knocker of six-eighteen.

Shit, Wulff said, *shit.*

The man took no notice of Wulff at all which was to be expected but how could he not notice the gas? It was already beginning to fill the air with those fine fibers of odor and surely, although the wind was carrying it this way, it would only be a matter of time until the occupants of the house smelled it as well. Lying pinned to the ground in the low-crawl combat position, Wulff had a sudden insight staring at the man: this had nothing to do with him. Peter Vincent had a visitor, that was all. Atrocious bad luck but at least impersonal. He raised his head barely off the ground and squinting through the darkness examined the man. He could not do anything further until he was inside the house, that was for sure. Short heavy frame on this one, thick features glinting with excitement in the pale light. He was armed. He kept on fondling the inside of his jacket.

It sure was taking Vincent a hell of a long time to answer. The man waited and waited, hit the knocker again. The sound of his curses drifted across the lot. Wulff could not get the words but the sense was all there: Peter Vincent was a dirty son of a bitch. Yes he was. He could agree with the guest on that one point.

Wulff stayed on the ground, hoping that the man would be let in. If he wasn't, then Vincent was probably not at home and this was going to complicate matters. Did he really want to do this if the house was unoccupied by the rat? It had never even occurred to him. Shit, again.

The door opened. A thin streak of light poured into the street. There was muffled dialogue at the door. Could they smell the gas? Apparently not. After a time the visitor went inside holding himself rather stiffly. Wulff felt his bowels tighten a little. The door closed.

He was alone again on East Eighty-Third Street. Nobody had noticed him at all.

He picked the heater off the ground, fumbled in the darkness to make sure that the battery connections were tight and then having done that, loosened them. He didn't want the thing going off until he had time to get away.

Well, then. Add one more to the equation within the house he thought. From the length of time it had taken that door to be opened and from the way the man at the door had been holding onto his concealed gun, this was an unexpected visit for Peter Vincent. And not a social one for the visitor. Probably it had something to do with Marasco's death: one of Marasco's lieutenants, probably, resolved to assert his influence with Vincent as quickly as possible. A stupid man Wulff suspected: any man who thought that he could call upon Peter Vincent unexpectedly with nothing but a revolver for security had not analyzed the situation properly.

Fuck it. That was Vincent's problem. Wulff picked up the heater and the batteries two-handed and went back to the basement

It would be easier this time. No delicate work, just suture in the power source, toss it and run. He felt, standing there, however, a strange reluctance. Even up until this moment he supposed he could still have gotten out of this. Gas was in the air, choking him, still he could get out of it. The boys surrounding Vincent, Vincent himself, now knew who Wulff was and after a while would come after him but there was margin, decent margin: he had days at least until things got really close again and there was a chance that they might not come after him at all. *They were going to smell that gas soon.* Essentially the Marascos and the Vincents believed in de-complicating things. They had gotten where they were by making as little trouble as possible. Hell, there was a good chance that if Wulff didn't go looking for them they would return the compliment. Even. Everything evened out.

Fuck it. He fumbled with the batteries and heater, made the splices, his eyes streaming from the odors. It was too late to get out of it. He could slide underground again but the man that he had become wouldn't stand for it. It might be hopeless, in fact it *was* hopeless. What could one man do against the seas of poison being craftily allowed to stream through outlets into all the spaces of the country? Would it make any difference whatsoever? What could Burt Wulff do?

Except get himself killed. He finished the splices, gasping in the reeking air. Being killed was all right though. He had died in a furnished room on West 93rd a few months ago and since then, thank you very much, he had really got it on. There was, in fact, less pain in being dead than alive. The thing about getting himself killed was in itself pointless.

But he could take a lot of people down.

He smiled at this finally. He had been deluding himself, all the way up to this moment. There were no more lies now. There were no furnished rooms in his future in this city, there was no more underground. Like it or not, Wulff was committed. In the chain of circumstances the first action implied the last.

The moment that he had stepped into the Rikker's Eldorado it had all been sealed, right up to this moment.

If nothing else they were going to know that the Wolf was around.

He held the batteries-and-heater in his hand, just a little instant coffee heater, forty-nine cents with cord, and he tossed it through the hole into the basement which was filling rapidly with gas.

And then he ran like hell.

A minute, minute and a half until that heater attained radiance. If it did. If it hadn't all come apart on the floor. A minute and a half was enough. Longer than that and he knew he would have failed.

He ran through the gas fumes through the lot like a wild beast, looking for ground. At the far edge of the lot he hurled himself to the Earth, doubled himself over in the protective position and then, rolling once and putting his face to ground, he waited.

He had done everything that he could do. Nothing more. It either would or would not work, his forty-nine cent incendiary kit and then he would see where he went from there.

He had faith. He had faith.

He should have. Six-eighteen East Eighty-Third Street blew up like china on a stove.

XX

Walls flew outward. It was like being under flak except that flak never made this kind of noise. The noise was intense, unbearable, the high whining squeal of ignition followed by a seemingly endless pulsating roar as piece by piece the house went down. Dust rose and fell, hit him with such force that it felt like pebbles. And even behind closed eyes Wulff could see the flash that made it day.

He could not wait too long. He counted off ten seconds, twenty, thirty, when the barrage eased, then stopped, he was already on his feet, running, staggering toward the remains of the house. Six-eighteen looked like the cartoon house that had been huffed and puffed and blown to death by the big bad wolf. Some of it hung in dangling pieces from itself. Other parts were scattered streetside. The parked Buick Electra was covered by debris and on fire.

But otherwise there was not much fire at all. A controlled explosion, it had done its job on detonation, not explosion. Limping, staggering, Wulff held his face against the heat and walked into the wreckage. How long did he have? As isolated as the residents of East eighty-third Street might be, they could not ignore this one. The entire block had shaken although the damage had been restricted to six-eighteen. Right into the feeder cables. Maybe he had five minutes to get out of here. At the first sound of a siren he would have to run. He gasped, choked, inhaled gases, weeping. He tripped over a body, that of the short, fat man who had been at the door. This one had been killed instantly, probably by impact. Hurled against something. He moved through foundation matter, little crackling pimples of flame. What had been the first floor was a parody of itself; grotesquely enough it looked like a living room that might have been imagined by a drunk. Another body here, this one twitching and talking to itself in a wedge between two chairs. Broken arm, scars through the forehead. Vaguely oriental cast.

Not Peter Vincent. Wulff took out his revolver and without bothering to consider it, shot the houseman in the head. He probed deeper through the wreckage.

What had been the stairs dangled and twirled in the winds. Some of the supporting beams had held however, there was still a definable upstairs. With no access. Something hit him in the back. Wulff whirled, saw another oriental scrambling feebly to rise and deliver another kick. The attempted death-blow must have unbalanced him. He still had the revolver. He shot this one too. The oriental fell, flapping his arms like wings. Ascending toward death.

He looked toward the street. Inside, he was yet outside. The ventilated home. A new concept in urban design. The fire was out now except for small mean crackles and flickers in isolated areas. Hopefully it would stay out. Of course if one of those gas lines got open again and added a swift breath of fuel to the situation….

Wulff stumbled against a wall. He tripped, fell on his hands and knees, shaking his head. More had been taken out of him than he wanted to conceive. He found himself looking into the eyes of a man.

The man was standing at the second level of the house, poised over a parapet. He was a slender man who ten minutes ago might have been thought of as elegantly dressed. Now his clothing hung in stripes and filaments. Black marks were all over his body. His eyes were round and desperate. He held a revolver, pointed it at Wulff and fired.

Wulff dodged. The bullet went past him, buried itself in ash. The man fired again. This one tore through a sleeve. Another bullet passed above his head. His luck was holding but he was pushing it. He went for his own revolver, toppling sideways.

He got his hand on the revolver, hitting the floor, just as the man deposited another shot next to him. Wulff rolled in the ash, feeling splinters of decomposed wood and metal digging themselves into him. No matter. He came out of it fast in a crouch and shot the man.

The man screamed and dropped his revolver. The hit had been in the hand. Perfect. A rose of blood appeared on the man's hand as he staggered and wept. Wulff levelled the revolver for another shot, watched instead as the man leaned over the parapet, burst through and fell heavily to ground level, landing on his hands and knees. He gasped, tried to get to his feet, flopped, laid still.

Wulff got over to him fast. Breezes darted through the wreckage bringing tears to his eyes. He seized the man by the throat, pulled him half-erect. He looked into Peter Vincent's eyes.

"Who's next?" he said in a perfectly level voice.

The man's eyes bulged. He hung like a pendulum in Wulff's eyes. His tongue went over his lips, retracted. *In extremis.* But this had been the man from whom Albert Marasco took orders.

"Who's next?" he said again.

"What—" the man said and paused, gasped, tried to find breath. The fire must have seared his lungs. "What—?"

"You're part of a chain, Vincent. You're just another link in a long, long connecting chain. Who's the next one? Who do you take your orders from?"

Vincent fainted in his grasp. That was easily taken care of. He hit the man in the mouth, skittering him sideways. Released him. Vincent fell into ashes, weeping.

"What have you done?" he said, face to the floor, "what have you done?"

"I've blown up your fucking palace, Vincent, and that's just the beginning."

"You killed Marasco," the man said, "you killed the others."

"That's right."

"You're crazy. You've got to be crazy."

Wulff heard sirens rising in the distance. Not much time now. Not much time at all. He kicked the man in the ribs. Vincent let out a strangled cry, fainted again. Wulff revived him with another kick.

"Who do you talk to?" he said, "where do your orders come from? Who's the next man on the list?"

"I'm dying."

"Everybody's dying. You're killing them all, Vincent. Come on," Wulff said, "I don't have much time."

He knelt next to the man, seized his throat, took out his revolver and levelled it. "One last time," he said, "tell me where the orders come from."

Intelligence seemed to flare in the man's eyes for the first time. "I'm dead anyway," he said.

"That's right."

"Why tell you anything?"

Sirens were closer. Wulff, in the fading gases, could smell the river now. The explosion was over. The scavengers, the enforcers were about to come.

"Because you can die peacefully or painfully, Vincent," Wulff said and put the gun to the man's forehead. "I can take you out quickly and cleanly or I can just skewer little holes in you and leave you to the police.

They'll get you out. They'll put you in a ward somewhere and after five years of suffering you'll be ready to stand trial."

The man looked at him. "Gerald," he said, "I talk to a man named Gerald."

"Where?"

Vincent told him, struggling with the syllables. Wulff held the revolver steady.

"You never see the stuff do you, Vincent?" he said. "You just deal over the phone. It's all outside of you isn't it? You never have to look at what you've done."

"I'm dying."

"Yes you are. You certainly are dying. Everybody you ever touched is dying, Vincent. But you never had to look at the death, did you? It was all something going on uptown. You sealed yourself off in your townhouse and called it the world."

He yanked the man from the floor, forced him to a standing posture. "Look," he said, "look at what you've done."

He propelled the man forward, showed the man the street, the splinters, the demolition, the ruins of what had once been his home, of what had once been a fortress. "That's what you've done, Vincent," Wulff said, "do you understand that?"

"I don't understand—"

"This is what you've turned New York into. Don't you understand?" Wulff said then with a terrible, sweet, slow patience as he held his revolver. "Don't you understand, Vincent, that the inside of a junkie's head looks just like this does now?"

He saw comprehension or thought he saw comprehension growing in the man but Wulff was just not interested. He was not interested.

He pointed the revolver at Vincent and held the trigger. "I'm going to give you more peace than you ever volunteered for anyone, a better end than you've wished on a thousand demolished souls," he said.

And shot the man in the head.

Vincent dropped before him with an exhaling sigh, almost as of relief to finally take leave of life. Looking at the dead man in the growing fury of the sirens Wulff felt a twinge of envy: Vincent at least was out of it. Wherever they went, however they had been taken, the dead, at least, had been granted release.

Which he had not yet been and which he knew now he would never bring upon himself. For death was either for the sick or the weak; it was not for him.

No ease for Burt Wulff.

He picked his way through the broken spaces of Peter Vincent's house, stumbling through the ash. The beacons were close now, the sirens upon him, all up and down the block people had come to windows and open spaces to look upon his work but he felt that he just might be able to make it out of there undiscovered. The proper way was to the river and then picking his way along that blind back up a cross-street.

He breathed raggedly, unevenly, tears and gases mingling in his lungs but he was breathing.

And he was walking.

The great siege, he knew now, had begun.

EPILOGUE

The man dressed like a stockbroker came quickly into the midday crowds, an attaché case swinging, headed north toward Broad Street. Briskly he stepped from the curb, dodging without thought the heavy traffic, separating himself from the bodies around him, opening himself up for space to move freely. His eyes instinctively measured the traffic, the crowds, the amount of space given him, like any New Yorker's they saw without seeing. The man opened up to full stride as he crossed the street and began to speed toward his destination. He was already a little late. It was an important meeting, dealing as it would in part with the allocation of Peter Vincent's domain.

The bullet caught him behind the ear, spun him on the pavement and dropped him in his tracks. The contact had been so precise, the impact so shattering and yet bloodless that it appeared as if he had merely been stricken by a cerebral hemorrhage. The man lay there, his case dangling at his side, his sightless eyes looking up toward the great buildings he would never see again. People eddied around him, being careful not to touch. It was certainly best in New York not to get involved with cases like these if you could help it.

A tall man with hollow, pained eyes came from the crowd and knelt quickly beside the fallen man. He appeared to be a friend or a doctor, quickly checking him out for gross signs of damage. The tall man nodded once and took his hand away from the other's wrist. Then he reached over and took the attaché case and standing, moved off quickly into the crowd. All of this had taken no more than thirty seconds.

The fallen man lay there for fifteen more minutes while the crowds swarmed around. At length a patrol car came, prodding itself haltingly through the traffic and two cops came out. They checked him, shook their heads, put in the call. Then they started to go through his pockets for identification.

There was no identification of any sort. The man with the bullet in his head had no papers, no credentials. A wallet empty except for two one hundred dollar bills and five singles fluttered open on the pavement.

The cops looked at one another and then shrugged. It was possible. A lot of these Wall Street types recently, because of all the security problems on the street, all of the pickpockets, had taken to carrying their identification papers in their attaché cases which they could hold onto, see with them at all times. Someone had probably snatched the attaché case and run with it. It didn't matter. The cops would find out who he was and if they never did it wasn't their problem anyway. The problem was the sniper in the district and that made their palms sweat a little as they waited for the wagon and reinforcements to come so that they could at least get some coverage....

But the sniper was already heading uptown holding the attaché case. In due course he would open it up, get a look. He couldn't wait.

The contents of the case would tell him where he would be heading next....

THE LONE WOLF #2: BAY PROWLER

by Barry N. Malzberg

Writing as Mike Barry

Men have died
And worms have eaten them—
But not for love.
　　　　　　　—Shakespeare

Junk is eating this country up alive. Junk has
destroyed the cities, poisoned the landscape, killed
half a generation.

But it's an ill wind that blows nobody some good. I'm
going to take on junk: I'm going to kill some people and
I'm going to have some fun.
　　　　　　　—Burt Wulff

For Juice, Sessie, Ritta . . .

*Documents stolen from the attaché case were extremely specific and
precise, and all parties in the San Francisco area are warned that they
may be on Wulff's "list".*

This memorandum is to be shredded immediately upon completion of
reading and is not to be reproduced.

Details of the bounty on Wulff will be transmitted separately.
END OF REPORT.

I

He went first to a furnished apartment in the Oakland Hills. Every quest must start somewhere. This seemed as good a place as any to begin. Before he was done, if he lived, he would hit them all ...

Wulff took the stairs two at a time and smashed open the door in the instinctive entry kick. He dodged to the side, revolver ready. If they were going to hit him they would do it right away but he would not even give them one clear shot.

After a while, hearing nothing, he turned the corner cautiously. There was a girl lying on the floor in the center of the room.

She was about nineteen, he guessed, maybe twenty, one of that new breed of girls who had come out on both coasts in the mid nineteen-sixties and were now, through the force of television, throughout the country. Long, straight blonde hair, high cheekbones, no makeup, simple sweater and pants which did not so much cover as frame the body. She was breathing in shallow, ragged gasps through her mouth; there were small white spots at the corners. Her knees were arched to the ceiling, her eyes open. For a moment he thought she was stuporous but then one of the eyes fluttered and she turned her head slightly. "Help me," she said, "help me."

Memories fluttered through Wulff's mind like birds. He remembered another girl, another floor, another furnished room and for the moment the two combined: what he had seen, where he was now. He felt bile rising within him and thought that he might vomit. With an effort he rammed the bile down, brought himself into focus. He remembered that he was in this room because the attaché case of the man he had killed contained documents indicating it was a pickup and delivery center. This room. That was why he was here. It had nothing to do with the girl. He had not expected the girl to be here.

"You've got to help me," she said again. Her breathing was poor. Her hand tried to gain purchase on the floor, fell back. She shook her head.

Wulff knelt over her. Faint discoloration in the pupils, shallow respiration, seeming dehydrogenation of the lips. He took her hand, clamped her wrist and pushed his own hand up to her elbow, peeling the sweater back. No apparent needle marks, which meant little of course; these girls with straight hair could shoot it, they could sniff it, they could induct it in other ways as well.

She seemed to be smiling up at him. "You think I'm a junkie?"

"I don't think anything."

"I'm not a junkie," she said.

"Get up," he said, checking her pulse. No flutter, steady at sixty-eight, gross signs appeared normal. Distension of the pupils, however—that dryness of the lips. "Get off the floor."

"It's speed," she said with a giggle. Her face was flat; she was still looking up at the lights. "You've got to measure it out. I guess I measured it out wrong."

"Stand," he said.

"First you get the rush," she said, "and then you get this nice easy sweeping feeling just like riding a carpet and then you get the crash, but if you know what you're doing you don't have to crash at all. You just have to time it out right. But I guessed I timed it wrong and I don't feel so good." Her voice broke. Abruptly she looked much younger. "I feel sick," she said.

"I bet you do," said Wulff. He had turned his attention from the girl finally, was doing a quick check-out of the rooms. Disorder, clutter, cheap furniture strewn about, unmade beds glimpsed through the half-open door to the next room but no indication of big doings here. If this was a transfer-point they brought the stuff in from outside. All right. Gerald's book had given him plenty of names, even an address or two, although the addresses could only be of lower-echelon people. All right. That was good enough; you had to start somewhere. He had started at the bottom in New York as well and wound up with an attaché case. Also, more than a few people who knew his name.

"Help me," the girl said again. Her voice was thin, strained. "I want to get up."

He put a hand under her elbow, tugged, shoved. She came to a seated position, wiping the sweat from her forehead, her face tensed into a cracked smile. She might have been a little older than he had thought at first but no more than twenty-four. He could feel the rhythm of the blood under her wrist. "It hurts," she said, "it really hurts."

"Come on," he said roughly, "stand now." He wanted no involvement with this girl, much less talking her through the downside of a speed-jag. She moved her legs as if aware of their presence for the first time, leaned harder on him, then came to a standing position. He felt the fullness of her weight upon him. A big girl this one. Basically, she was probably quite healthy. Most of them were very healthy right up to their twenty-fifth birthday or so; that was why they were able to carry on so far. Of course, after that point, it was all downhill.

"I have to get out of here," she said. Her eyes, purposeful while she was on the floor, had become vague again. "Don't you understand, I have to get going."

"You don't live here, then."

"What are you, crazy? *Nobody* lives here," the girl said, "at least nobody I'd ever want to get involved with." On her feet she seemed to have become hostile. She did not feel as bad then as she had on the floor. "Who are you, anyway?"

"That's a long story."

"What are you *doing* here? You're not a cop, are you?"

"No," Wulff said, "I'm not a cop."

"Let me out of here," she said abruptly, wrenching herself free from the hold. Wulff let her go. Enough of this. The girl took a couple of halting steps toward the door and barreled inwards, clutching her stomach.

"I feel sick," she said, "I really feel sick." She gasped, got to a wall, leaned against it, still clutched in. "You've got to help me," she said in the tone she had when he entered the room.

This was tremendous. This was everything that Wulff could have hoped for. Come to San Francisco to track the drug network further, go to a contact point which looks promising and find yourself with a sick girl. All that he had was a rental car, a street map, and a very rudimentary knowledge indeed. He didn't even know where the hospitals were, come to think of it. And if he showed up with a girl in this condition, he was going to be asked a lot of questions.

He looked at her with disgust. Instinct told him to get the hell out of here because the situation could only become more ugly and complicated. But instinct was one thing, compassion another. He could not help himself. He responded to the girl. She was another victim too. All of them were victims. And she reminded him, however vaguely, of another girl with straight hair, dark hair this had been, lying quietly on the panels of flooring on the top floor of a rooming house ....

"All right," Wulff said quietly, "let's take you to a hospital."

"*Hospital?* Are you out of your mind?"

"You've got to get to a hospital," Wulff said. "You're in shock. You probably need detoxification—"

The girl was shaking with little gurgles of laughter that roiled within her. Her breathing became uneven again. "You've got to be out of your *mind,*" she said. "Do you think that I could just walk into a hospital—"

"Then you can stay here and die for all I'm concerned," Wulff said quietly. He looked at her; held the gaze. "I don't care," he said, "you're nothing to me. The way you look to me now, you could hold out all of two days, possibly three before going into a coma. Plenty of time. What's your hurry?"

She looked back at him and it was as if for the first time understanding pierced those eyes. It was no longer this girl that was looking at him but rather the girl that she might have been two, three years ago before all of this started. Something intricate and trapped wheeled in her eyes. She weaved, reached out a hand. "It's hopeless," she said. "I'm too far gone."

"Maybe."

"It's too late, don't you understand that? Leave me alone. Just leave me alone!"

"I want to help you," Wulff said. He could not believe what he was saying. Ten minutes into this room, one hour into San Francisco and he was already talking commitment. In his three months underground in New York, no one, nothing had touched him. Was it the air out here? Was there indeed something in the climate which created the life-style? Madness he thought; he could not afford commitment.

"All right," she said, holding that reaching posture. "I don't know who you are but I'll go with you." Her body quivered, her breasts moved loosely under the sweater. "I don't know who you are but I believe you want to help."

He moved forward to take her—and a door opened and a man came into the room.

He had not even heard the approach. Maybe the sound-proofing in this place was pretty good, as it better be for a contact-point, maybe he had just been so caught up with the girl, against his will, that normal caution had deserted him. Either way, a bad practice. He was making mistakes already. You had to keep the terrain under observation at all times and you had to control all of the space you could see. Combat knowledge. Too late now.

The man had a beard, was wearing a sweater with a chain emblem dangling, tight pants, a rather distracted expression. Much older than the girl although he was trying to cultivate an appearance which would let him pass for twenty-five. Nonsense, Wulff thought, appraising him. This bastard was forty, forty-two. But everything about this culture was style, wasn't it? And from a distance he could pass. Perhaps.

The man looked at Wulff quietly and then reached for something in his pocket. A gun, Wulff realized, just an instant too late to be able to do anything. The man had a pistol, a point forty-five Wulff guessed. He held it on him.

The girl screamed, lightly, and tried to dodge behind Wulff. The man waved her off, she staggered, crossed to another part of the room. He waved the pistol; she held position. He flicked the gun at her as if she were a piece of furniture he had now located in the proper position and turned toward Wulff.

"What is this?" he said. "Who the hell are you?"

Flat voice, penetrating eyes. Yes, Wulff decided, the pistol was not for effect. This man could kill him. He held his ground.

"He's trying to help me, John," the girl said. "He came up here to help. I'm sick. I tell you—"

"Shut up," the man said absently. The gun was held tight on Wulff's stomach. "I want to know who the hell you are and what you're doing here and I want to know it now."

No way to get to his own gun. Any man who could handle a pistol this offhandedly, this expertly, could certainly drop him in place before he could even get his hand on the point thirty-eight. He looked at the man called John and without working it through at a conscious level came to an instant decision: yes, this man could kill. He had killed before and he could do it again as easily as this girl could float off into another amphetamine haze. Killing meant nothing to him.

It might be San Francisco but Wulff felt right at home. In a way it was almost comforting. The landscape might change but he would be going up against the same types time and again. He had beaten them in New York. He guessed—if he got by this one—he could in San Francisco. Medallions or sport coats they were all the same.

"I said I wanted to know who the hell you are," the man said.

"Please—" the girl said.

"Shut up, Tamara. Just stand against the wall and be nice. This is between me and my new friend here. You'd better talk, my friend. This is breaking and entering for openers."

"I'm a freelance writer," Wulff said. Say anything, just keep talking and keep the man distracted. "I go here and there trying to report on events in various parts of the country. This month I'm doing music. I understand there's a big festival here and I was directed to come here—" Tamara, he thought, while he was going through this. That was an interesting name. He would go twelve to five that she had been born Betty or Helen, though. Something like that. Those were the ones, once they hit this culture, who needed more than the average to feel exotic.

"Don't give me that shit," the man said. For someone wearing a medallion showing the emblem of peace, he had a rather rough approach. "I want to know who the hell you are."

"Is this your apartment?"

"Please John," the girl said weakly before the man could answer, "please leave him alone. He was going to take me to the hospital. I tell you I'm sick—"

"You freaked out bitch," the man said softly. "I think you've fucked up just one time too many. You shut up or I'll knock you down too."

"Who is he?" Wulff said, turning to the girl, "who is this man."

"He's—"

"Shut up, Tamara," the man said, but saying it wheeled his attention over to the girl and it was at that point, that brief flickering instant when the man's eyes were one way and the gun the other that Wulff moved.

He moved quickly, diving to the floor even as he was reaching for his own gun, scrambling for balance on the floor. The girl screamed but that was all right, almost a plus factor since while it wheeled John's attention back to Wulff it also shook up his sense of timing; the gun was already firing but the girl had driven him off balance and he was firing to the place where Wulff had *been* rather than toward the new position on the floor. Even so, it was much closer than Wulff had wanted it to be. The man had good instincts; he was a shooter. Even off balance, the girl's screams rippling higher and higher in the room, he drove the first bullet only inches above Wulff's right ear, put the second into the floor where his kneecap had just been, and all the time Wulff was fumbling, fumbling for his gun which had gotten jammed inside his clothing.

Stupidity. It was the kind of thing which happened to people who were long dead, but he had somehow gotten the butt of the damned thing going head over heels from the barrel and it had caught on the cloth. For one sickening instant Wulff thought that he was not going to get the gun out at all. He was going to die pumped full of holes on this floor not two hours after he had hit San Francisco, and what the hell would be made of *that*. Should have stayed in New York, Wulff, at least you knew the territory.

But the girl's screaming helped a lot. Speed made you overreact, brought events on top of you and then *froze* them so that they seemed to be happening over and again at a terrific slow motion. The girl must have felt herself to be inside death, watching what was developing in front of her; the crash-end of the amphetamines had not blunted but sharpened her perceptions so that rolling over her in waves came pain and fear and she reacted against them, squealing and screaming hysterically. But at last, even as the third bullet came just a few inches off his middle, Wulff was able to get the damned gun out and rolling and he pointed it where he thought John would go when he tried to jump, and fired. Once, then twice, the recoil, small from the point thirty-eight, enough in his position to knock him into the wall. The sound of John's body falling was covered by the sound of his own impact as he collapsed into the wall, and then slowly he turned, came to one knee, looked in front of him. John was lying on the floor, his pistol two or three feet away, flung then as he had taken the shot. His face already seemed frozen into the rictus of death. John had been living death for so long that when it came at last it swaddled him under it as if he had been dead a hundred years.

The girl was still screaming.

Out of control, on the verge of breaking open. Wulff came to his feet, put the gun away breathing heavily, and went over to her. He held her against the wall, palm to stomach, not hard but enough to apply an even, testing pressure pinning her, and then he slapped her across the face very hard three times. It was the only way.

She stopped, caved in on herself, put her hands to her face. "You killed him," she said, looking at the corpse. "You killed him."

"Let's get out of here," Wulff said.

"You killed him and I'm a witness." She began to laugh, ricocheting little spasms making her breasts jump again. Her face was dead white; underneath the panels Wulff could sense the animals crawling. "Are you going to kill me too?"

"I don't know," he said.

"Why don't you just kill me too? You came up here to kill me, didn't you?"

"No."

"You're crazy," she said. "You're crazy, you killed him. You killed John. *Nobody* can kill John. He told us once that he was already eight hundred and fifty years old and that he was going to live forever." Laughter split her open, she fell against him. "What am I going to do *now?*" she said.

"I don't know."

"Where am I going to get all the pretties? Where?"

"We'll talk about it," Wulff said. He put an arm around her, wrenched her off her feet. Hoist-carry. It was going to be literally the only way he would ever get her down those stairs. She launched herself against him with the force of a small child, then collapsed.

"I don't have anything anymore," she said. "I can't fight. Go on. Kill me fast."

"Let's go," he said, kicking open the door. He half-expected to see people waiting for him on the landing, but no. No one. John was a loner. He got the girl down the steps. Speed had wasted her; for all her height she was maybe one ten, maybe just a hundred pounds. There was nothing there. He could feel water sliding underneath her skin. That was all she was: a reservoir for water and for jolts of energy that had eaten her away.

"I'm glad you killed him," she said, starting to laugh again, "I'm glad, I'm glad."

"I'm not."

"You did the right thing. You must be the avenger, that's who you must be. I had a dream about the avenger," she said as he carried her. "I used to have this dream that the avenger was going to come, he would be ten feet tall and he would save me from all these people and what they were doing to me, and I really believed in the avenger. Tamara's avenger, I used to call him, and it was my secret, but do you know something I realized only a little while ago? Do you want me to tell you? There's no such thing as an avenger at all, because he couldn't do it to anyone. He would have to do it to *me*. To Tamara. Because all along it was just me, you see. I was the one doing it to my*self.* There was no one else."

"All right," Wulff said, "all right." One more flight down. Lucky if he could make it. If anyone came into the building now he was dead. The only way out would be to use the girl as a shield and fall, fall atop her those last stairs, hoping that she would take the attack. But he doubted that he could do it. "Come on," he said. He readjusted the carry, staggered through the darkness and grease odors through that last flight.

"So I gave up," Tamara said. "I knew there wasn't any avenger—don't you see?—that I was the avenger and I was dead, but then just when I had completely lost hope you came along. You killed John. But what am I going to do without John? I can't cope, Avenger, I just can't cope."

"All right," Wulff said. He kicked open the door, carried her through the reeking vestibule and onto the street. Not much traffic here, no pedestrians at all; nobody was on the streets out here unless enclosed by a vehicle. A bus passed them on the other side of the street, the few passengers facing this way looking at them without curiosity. Street scene. Wholly unremarkable. Tall men and straight-haired girls came out of places like these in hoist-carries all the time. Live and let live.

"Can you walk?"

"I can't walk," she said, "I can't even breathe." The air hit her; she started to laugh again. She ran a hand through her hair, fell against him. "Hello Avenger," she said.

"Don't be ridiculous." He put a hand under her armpit, felt her small breast with the back of his finger, rooted her to her feet. There was no sex in it whatsoever. He felt no desire; desire was something that, along with many other things, had been purged out of him a good long time ago. What he did feel, and the sensation was strange, was a kind of distant protectiveness. He liked the girl.

The air seemed to take hold of her, she steadied, began to walk with only slight assistance. "Hey Avenger," she said, "there are going to be a lot of people looking for you now. There seems to be a dead body up there. Have you thought of that?"

"I've thought of it," Wulff said grimly. Down the winding block he could see his rented Ford parked exactly where he had left it. False credentials to make the forms, but who cared about that? America was a credentials society; lousy or true the only point was to have the proper papers in your wallet.

"You know," she said, a little distant sea-wind bringing sudden color to her cheeks, "you've done everybody a *favor,* Avenger, but a lot of people aren't going to be thinking that way. Have you thought of what you're going to do?"

"Briefly."

"The avenger would only think briefly," Tamara said. "Is this your car?" she said as he brought them to a halt. "Oh, it's beautiful. Somehow I had you figured for a Sedan de Ville or maybe a Cougar, but the avenger in a Galaxie 500! That's wonderful." She giggled again, reeled, fell against a door. "Johnny was a wonderful, wonderful person," she said, "and I'm so glad he's dead that I could spit."

He opened the door from the driver's side, propelled her through. "Get in there."

"Are you going to kill me too, Avenger? Are you going to take me for, what do they call it, a ride? I'm the only witness to the murder you know. But I promise you," she said from the seat, wrapping a knee under her and looking at him almost seductively, "I won't tell a soul. You see, you've made my day. You've just made all my dreams come true."

"That's fine," Wulff said. He eased her over, got behind the wheel, and slammed the door. Put the keys into the ignition and held the wheel. "We've got to get you to a hospital," he said.

"I don't want to go to a hospital."

"I'll just drop you off," he said, "I'll trust you not to say anything, and even if you do what difference does it make?" He was thinking aloud, an old habit garnered from working in partnerships. "You don't know who I am and then again too many people know exactly who I am."

"Of course I know who you are," the girl said, "you're the avenger. I created you out of my dreams and you're not going to take me to any hospitals because I've already had the detoxification unit scene and like who needs it? All I need to do is to get some food, crash for a couple of days and I'll be fine again."

Wulff started the motor. "Ready to take off you mean."

"Oh no," she said, clasping her hands, "why I wouldn't think of it. I wouldn't possibly go back on speed or anything else again. I've learned, you see. I've had a profound shock which has changed my personality completely and has made me regret my wasted life. Drugs, Avenger? Nothing. Not even an aspirin from now on, I swear."

He put the car into gear, began to move it slowly. "Besides," she said, "if I went to a hospital they'd only have me back on the street in a couple of hours. You don't think they'd move someone like me out of the emergency room now, do you?"

"Where do you live?" Wulff said, poking the car up a hill. All of San Francisco was hills, it seemed. Hills and mist, that deep-hanging grey fire which on even the brightest days clung to the nostrils but was in a way, somehow, not unsatisfying. He came to a major intersection, pointed the car north. What he was going to need was quarters outside of the central city. He needed a little space opened up, anyway, between him and the quarry—that is, until he made his run at them....

"Nowhere in particular," the girl named Tamara said. "What I mean to say is that I live in a lot of places but don't like to call them home except that anywhere they hang my hat is home if you know what I mean." The air had brought her to life again; she seemed a little manic now. One way or the other, it would take forty-eight hours to clean the girl out, even to see what kind of person she might be under all the junk that she had been pouring into her system. If there was a system left. There probably was. All of these people were strong and healthy right up until the day they fell apart, and Tamara's time had, apparently, not yet come. "Where I was I'm not going back," she said more quietly. "That's for sure."

"Was that why I found you up there this morning?"

"Something like that, Avenger," she said. She tilted her face upward at him; looking at her sidelong he could see that she once might have been very pretty. In fact still was, in and out of the haze of sickness. "You not only shoot the bad guys to kill, you think," she said, "you think really good. I think you'd better take me with you. I'd like to move in with you, Avenger."

"You're crazy."

"Not as crazy as you think," she said. "I won't be any trouble, believe me. I can cook, clean, keep house, make conversation or shut up as the mood hits you. I can even make fairly intelligent conversation because the fact is that I had two years of college at State." She belched, covered her mouth. "English major. I learned a lot about Chaucer at State, would you believe that? And I learned about a lot of other things too. Oh, don't worry about me," she said as Wulff gazed at her quickly again before he overtook a bus, leapt ahead of it and shot the car into a freeway entrance headed north, opening the Galaxie up immediately to sixty, old prowl car technique. "Don't you worry about me, Avenger, I'm not making an illicit gesture or anything like that at all. In the first place I *know* that the avenger isn't interested in sex, he's too pure and fine to get involved with it at all, and in the second place I don't have anything there at all." She looked at him bleakly, her eyes suddenly cold and empty. "There's nothing like that," she said. "It all went away a long time ago. No, we can live together in a purely platonic relationship. You're not going to let me go," she said, her voice suddenly becoming panicked. That was a characteristic of the drug, the moods shifted violently, there was no emotional rudder at all. "Please, don't let me go, they'll just throw me out of the hospital because I'm not sick enough to stay. That's happened before and if I go back where I was I'm finished."

"You have nowhere to go?"

"No," she said. She slid against the seat, the pressure on her shoulders seemingly brightening her again. "No, I guess that I'm what you'd call one of those liberated bitches. Here, there, everywhere and nowhere." Her head rolled and her eyes closed suddenly. He swerved the car, almost panicky himself until he noticed that her breath had become deep, even, regular. The girl was asleep. That was all.

He continued to drive. There was nothing else to do. Sausalito would be all right; he could pick himself up some kind of furnished quarters in Sausalito. A motel was no good at all. It wasn't a matter of money— there had been plenty of money in that attaché case, cash and certified checks, his prey had carried his escape hatch with him at all times— but of a relatively exposed position. Motels were on freeways, they were at cloverleafs, they were wide open and exposed to the major traffic arteries and were at all of the points of convergence. In a furnished room on the other hand, off on a sidestreet, he might be able to buy a little time before they would close in.

Not much of course, but maybe two or three days. Wulff did not think he would need much more than that. All in all he had planned his San Francisco expedition to take no more than a week. Longer than that would be diminishing returns; they would surely get him. No, if he was going to be able to accomplish what he was out to accomplish, a week would be plenty of time. If he did not get them in a week, the odds are he would never get them. He would be dead....

Wulff drove. The wind, battering his face through the open window of the Galaxie, felt good. It enabled him—that and the fatigue drifting through him—to momentarily avoid his biggest problem. The problem was not the dealer who lay back there dead. He was cancelled out and all leads would come to Wulff anyway. No, the problem lay beside him. He glanced at it through peripheral vision and then away. He simply did not know what to do.

In its sleep the problem reached out a hand and touched Wulff delicately on the hip. He felt the pressure, as gentle as it was, all the way through him. It was not a sexual thing at all. It was much more complicated and ominous than that....

"Oh please, Avenger," the problem said, "do not desert me in my hour of need," its eyelids fluttering, its mouth smiling in semi-sleep. And Wulff drove and drove through the gathering mists of San Francisco, feeling all of his fibers come to the slow realization that it looked as if he had himself a roommate.

He just couldn't dump her. If he did it would negate everything that he was trying to do.

His war was for the victims.

II

On a hill twenty miles south of this in the living room of a house framed by glass that looked out upon clear area for almost five miles, a short, heavy man sat alone at a desk crumpling a sheet of paper savagely before he threw it into the wastebasket beside him. He cursed in a dialect which no one had heard him use for a decade and looked out upon the sea, taking for the first time little pleasure in the view. All of a sudden Savero felt very exposed. It was not a view, godammit, he was a target.

Who were they anyway? Who did these New York men think they were, to dump a memo like this on him and then just get out of the way? Did they think he was a fool? Did they think that their Wulff, this lunatic who *they* had failed to cancel was no longer their responsibility just because he was three thousand miles away? The hell they did. They just did not care. As long as Wulff was off their turf, they didn't give a shit, that was all. They could even write a taunting memo like this which said between every leering line, *go fuck yourself friend.*

"Well fuck you, you sons of bitches," he said to the empty room and went for the phone. Nicholas Savero did not have to put up with this kind of shit. Nicholas Savero had not struggled for all these years to earn a house on a hilltop and then be told by a bunch of *schmucks* from New York that some raving lunatic had landed in his territory and it was Savero's job to get rid of him. If there was one thing that he had learned in all these years, and he guessed he had learned several things, it was that you protected your territory for all it was worth but *you did not dump your problems outside of it.* What you had to settle on your own you settled. That way you expected the same of others within their territories.

And now the code had been broken.

Well fuck that, Savero thought again and put through a long-distance call to New York. The call switched through grids and wires, operators and circuitry, was bounced from a receptionist to another line, shifted over to a connecting link, radiated through the miracle of modern communications through a routing grid which took it sixty miles from there, and finally Savero got his party. "Hello Cippini," he said without preamble when the man got on, "this is Savero out in San Francisco and I got your fucking statement this morning."

"Now take it easy," the man named Cippini said. He had a low, pleasantly modulated voice; he was a good public relations man. That was all he was. Behind him there were other people who sent out memos over Cippini's signature, and those people, Savero knew, he would never be able to get hold of, but this was at least some satisfaction. Get the man who signed it anyway. "This is all a little more complicated than you might think—"

"It's a fuck a hell of a lot more complicated!" Savero screamed and then thought of the slight heart irregularity his doctor had noticed at the last visit, nothing serious the doctor had said, but nevertheless watch it. He tried to watch it. "What the hell kind of lunatic are you dumping into my city?" he said more quietly.

"We're not dumping anyone," Cippini said. "We've had a lot of problems here. The man got away—"

"I know the man got away! I goddam well see that he got away and I want to know how he got away and what the fuck I'm supposed to do about it!"

"That's not going to do anybody any good," Cippini said pleasantly. "We're all sorry about this, but we've got specialists working on it, specialists who are on their way to the coast at this hour, as a matter of fact, and I'm sure that we'll have the problem solved. We're all in this together, Savero, and believe me, they understand that well."

"Do they understand this?" Savero said. "He already killed one of my distributors!"

There was a dead, flat pause at the other end, then Cippini said quietly, "You know, there's the question of a tap—"

"Don't give me any tap bullshit! I take care of my own territory and you take care of yours! If there's any tap, it's at your end, asshole. Did you hear me? They killed one of my best men, that fucking ex-cop madman of yours."

"That's impossible," Cippini said haltingly. "We've traced his moves and he didn't even leave New York until late yesterday. He can't have been over there for more than half a day at the most and we've got to assume that he would go to ground—"

"He went to ground all right. He put a hole in my man's stomach! I protect my men, do you understand that? I don't know what kind of shit you're playing with in the East, but here when I work with a man, when I send him out, I'm with that man all the way. I don't just hide myself and take the money and let them get filled with holes. They hurt my men, they hurt me, you understand that?"

"Are you sure it's the same man?" Cippini said. His voice, filtered through the continental wire sounded almost unctuous. "Surely there's no definite evidence; it could be anybody. Don't tell me that there aren't certain risks—"

"My man lived," Severo said flatly. "John lived. He was hurt bad and he was dying when we found him but he bled to death, he wasn't shocked to death, and he was able to talk. He told us who did it and it was your guy. What do you think of that?"

"We told you he was dangerous—"

"Yes, you told us he was dangerous!" Severo said, his voice rising to a shout again. "That's a big godamned help, isn't it? You drop a bomb on us and tell us there might be fallout. Who the fuck you think you guys are anyway?"

"There's no need to shout," Cippini said. "This isn't getting us anywhere."

"You bet your ass it isn't getting us anywhere!" Severo said. He grasped the edge of the desk to still his shaking free hand, noted how the circulation was cut off almost immediately, the knuckles turning pure white. Only forty-eight but the circulatory system was starting to break down. How long did he have? With this madman at large in his territory, how long did he have anyway? Severo felt the distant prod of what he would have known twenty years ago to be outright fear; now he could not deal with it, had to give it a different name, called it rage instead. "I want this guy out of here," he said. "I want him taken clear. Do you understand that?"

"We're doing everything we can—"

"This guy is your responsibility! You dropped me a loaded gun and told me to pull the release! He's not mine, he's yours!"

"We know that," Cippini said soothingly, "and believe me, we'll have this situation resolved sooner than you think. In the meantime, normal precautions—"

"Now you listen to me," Severo said. He had the feeling of coming down several feet, now he was talking to Cippini at ground-level, man to man, addressing him through bleak panels of empty space, "because I'm not going to say this again. This is my territory and I've spent a lifetime building it up. I've made it good and I've made it tight and the way I've done this is to make sure that there are no problems. Now if any more of my men are hurt by this lunatic I'm going to hold you personally responsible. Do you hear that?"

Cippini seemed to sigh. "I hear it."

"I'm going to go out and take care of this guy with my own men in my own way," Severo said, "and fuck your specialists. But if it turns out that it has to be me who has to solve the problem that *you* gave me, then that's worth remembering, isn't it? That's something which I'd have to keep in mind in the future, wouldn't it? Because if you're not giving me cooperation, then exactly what the hell is the point of any of this, eh?"

"All right," Cippini said. His breathing was rapid; through three thousand miles of circuitry, Severo could deduce the rasp as it passed over what were undoubtedly uneven teeth. Wonders of technology. "I think I've heard enough, Severo."

"You'll hear more."

"I hope not."

"He was one of my best men."

"That's not my affair," said Cippini, "it's not my affair who your man was and now if you don't mind I've got other things to do."

The clang of the receiver was a dull, hurtful thump in Severo's ear. Severo put down his own end, swearing at the New York son of a bitch. That was the way all of them were; it was typical of everything about the operation right down the line. They thought they were superior, they still felt that the East Coast was top flight, and that the people like Severo could only, eternally, be the second string and they did not know, these New York bastards, that they were finished. They had been finished for a long time. They could not even run their own operation; now they were starting to spread their problems out in ripples.

It was only a matter of time, Severo knew, until it would be necessary to go in there and reorganize. It was still a while away; they held a stranglehold over the formal organization and the East Coast roots in the network of the system were deep, and sunk through thirty years— but the time was coming when they would have to be settled because *they were no longer the system.* That was all there was to it. The whole thing was falling apart on them and they still could not, would not admit it.

When people will not face the truth it is sometimes necessary to ram it down their throats.

Severo looked out the window toward the hills. Once this view had given him pleasure; soon enough he was sure it would give him that pleasure again, but now for the first time it communicated only unease. The hanging mist, the tracks of the freeways pressed down into the distant hills as if they had been laid in there with mesh, only reminded him of something that through twenty years he thought he had forgotten: that he was in a highly exposed position. Not that he had ever looked at it this way until this moment—but anyone who really wanted to go out to get him probably could.

He turned from the window with a shudder. Not to think of it. He pressed a buzzer on his desk and instantly his secretary responded. She might be too brightly blonde, and she was certainly dumb, but that one thing gave him pleasure and had for the years he had carried her: she responded to his calls instantly. On a worse basis than that he would have kept her going.

"Send him in," he said into the intercom and closed off the buzzer.

He hooked his thumbs into his belt line, strode around the room ignoring the window. The man who had been waiting outside for three hours came in, as noncommittal and obsequious as if he had been kept waiting for three minutes. That was professionalism. Severo had to admire this. Just like his secretary, the man knew what counted. If nothing else he had surrounded himself with good people. Pity that New York had not done the same.

"All right," he said to the man who carried a luger pistol in his belt, used a rifle anytime he could get away with it, drove a car armored and weaponed like a late 1960's tank. A walking arsenal this one. "It's all settled."

"That's good," the man said. His name was James Trotto and he was both competent and ambitious although the ambition had always been subsumed, for Severo anyway, in the respect that breeds absolute trust. "Anytime then?"

"I want you to get that son of a bitch," Severo said. "I want you to hit him just as fast and hard as you can."

"I intend to."

"I want him dead, do you hear that? If he's as dumb as he is crazy, he's probably left a trail a mile deep and I want you to track him and get him. Do you hear me?"

"Yes sir," James Trotto said. "Yes, Mr. Severo."

"And I want you to come back here and tell me that he's dead."

"Yes sir."

"Go on," Nicholas Severo said, "what are we waiting for? Go out and do it now."

"All right," Trotto said. He inclined his flat bald head gracefully. If he felt any confusion or doubt it was held completely in check. A professional. Just like Severo. He was a professional. What had been built here was a sound, professional organization, and no New York lunatic was ever going to fuck him up.

"I even think I know where to look," Trotto said, and saying no more quickly left the room.

After the initial surge of trust and confidence was displaced yet again by the unfamiliar—like a heart attack, in the first onset always known—Severo was left with a taste of fear.

III

San Francisco was a beautiful city. It was built over the San Andreas Fault of course, and someday, probably within the next ten years, was going to fall into the sea. But it was still a beautiful city and Wulff could appreciate it. It had the best climate in the country even counting the rain, which was good for the jungle animal from which man had evolved. It had hills and beaches and views and wealth, the best landscape in the country, and vaulted straight into the ocean and that clear escape from America for which Americans had always yearned. It had good sex, good bars, good colleges, good restaurants and, barring the San Andreas Fault, almost every natural advantage which men could seek or want. But Wulff could not enjoy it. Not even for a moment.

He had not come to San Francisco for relaxation; now, in the town for no more than four hours, he could feel the old tension and terror beginning to leak from his gut into all the other places. Of course he was scared. He had been scared all his life and he would go on being scared; it was a myth that people like him did not feel fear. Of course they felt fear. It was the fear which kept them going, drove them forward, saved them time after time from accidents which would have finished off courageous men because it was the fear which kept you on the move.

He felt it now. Looking over the two large furnished rooms with kitchen he had hastily rented, looking at Tamara who had collapsed into one of the single beds and was now, finally, in a deep, wistful sleep, he could feel the little hedges and outcroppings of the fear. Here in San Francisco he was perhaps coming closer to the enemy than he ever had before. San Francisco was a transfer point; lying on the ocean, nearest point of access in the country to the major supply routes, everything probably passed through here before heading east and south. San Francisco then was the major node; it was the vein into which the poison was introduced and it spilled it all through the body of the country.

Looking out the window Wulff could see through the mist the familiar wreckage and devastation, the signs of what junk had done to the country. It could only be junk that was doing it. The organized, massive drug trade was the only new element since the beginning of the 1960's, and as the one wild card in the deck, Wulff thought, it had changed everything. It was not his country any more. Like a burned-out tenement it was *no one's* country; it existed only for the looters and the vermin.

There were a few people shambling on the streets, there to the south were the grey buildings which signified the downtown district. There again in the distance he could see the bridge, gateway to the West, he guessed they had called it, but he did not know if the mist through which he stared was climate or drugs; probably it was a little bit of both. The factories had spilled the poisons into the air, that was true, but there was a deeper poison running on the surface and underground, infesting every crevice of life, and that was what had put the stink up. Pollution and industry were only the excuses they had given for what had happened to the country. What had really happened to the country was more obvious and irrevocable than that.

He looked at the bed where Tamara was sleeping. That was one sign of what was going on. Multiply it by millions, Wulff thought, and you could begin to see what had happened. Part of a whole generation, maybe all of it had been permanently removed from the line of succession because of what the manipulators at the far end were doing. In Harlem it was heroin, in the college and bohemian scene it was speed and hash, scattered all through this was pot, clouds of it, the easiest and most insidious drug of all because it set them up for the harder stuff. Pot was to heroin, Wulff knew, like that first ceremonial beer the neighborhood bartender used to give you when you were eighteen was to hard gin. It established the mood, it opened you up, it got you going. Once you could accept pot you found the next steps easy; you were just trading in a mild high for a series of shorter but more thrilling ones. At the end it was all the same. He looked at the sleeping girl. She came from a culture where pot was handed around the way beer had been drunk in Wulff's living room a long time ago. She could not understand. None of them could understand. That was the key.

Enough of this. He could feel the restlessness edging within him. What he needed to do was to get out and begin to smash, hit San Francisco the way that he had hit New York, but he felt an undertow of reluctance. Gerald's papers had already yielded one bad item, the distribution point in the Oakland Hills. Did he dare to trust it for another? The first place he had hit had turned up a sick girl and a dealer who had tried to kill him; now this girl was in his room and the dealer lay dead. One hour in town, one corpse. Wulff had nothing against killing, killing was necessary if you were going to get anything done against these people— just the price of the operation, so to speak, kill or be killed—but it was time to retract, be cautious if only for a few hours, until he had figured out a game plan. A lot of people were going to be out looking for him, he knew. Half of them would be from the East, the remainder would be local talent. They would be coming at him in waves.

Well, he had not expected to live a long life, anyhow. Most of his life had been given away in a furnished room on West 93rd Street in Manhattan; he had not been kidding when he had told the New York people time and again that they could not scare him or buy him off because they were already dealing with a dead man. Wulff was dead. He walked and talked, breathed and thought, functioned and conceived but something was gone, gone for good. Could a dead man be killed? Not really, he supposed.

Nevertheless, he felt the fear.

He opened the attaché case and looked through it idly. San Francisco was on top because, according to these notes anyway, there was some kind of massive shipment expected in here within the next few days, a million dollars, a million and a half of heroin, the notations had not been specific. The man named Gerald who looked like a stockbroker and had worked on a high floor in the Wall Street district had never been specific, not even to himself. All that had been clear was that something big was moving in here, that it was expected around early September, and Wulff had figured that it might be a good idea for him to be here as well, because a big shipment keyed up everyone, brought them into focus and alignment the way a strategically placed lump of sugar could draw the roaches, skittering, from tabletops and basins to start lapping away. The Oakland Hills address, noted by Gerald as a transfer-point, had seemed to be a very good place to start: his mistake. Maybe he should have started off instead with a man named Nicholas Severo who, according to what he deduced, was one of the keys to the transfer. An address in Sausalito, twenty miles north. He was obviously one of the most important men in this section; he seemed to be the one arranging and controlling this deal. He should have gone, he guessed, right to Severo.

But Severo, any top man, was going to be difficult to hit and he had thought that it would be better to ease his way up the line, starting with an actual reconnoitering of the proposed transfer point. He was pretty sure that that *was* the proposed transfer point. Oh well. Live and learn.

He heard a car door slam in the street and instinctively was on his feet, stuffing the materials back into the case, going to the window to check it out. There were sounds and sounds; long years of training, of being on patrol in Vietnam, and then New York City again had taught him how to discriminate at some subliminal level between the meaningless noises and those which had significance. Now, immediately, Wulff was at screaming alert.

A Fleetwood had parked across the street. There seemed to be a man at the wheel; small puffs of smoke from the exhaust indicated that the car was at idle. Another man came from the passenger side, checked the street up and down, and then walked toward the rented Galaxie which was parked three car-lengths behind the Fleetwood. The scout looked at the Galaxie intently, then kneeled to check the license plates. He stood abruptly, went back to the Fleetwood, poked his head in and seemed to be in conversation with the driver. Then the scout opened the door, went in, slammed it. The Fleetwood's motor was shut off then. The exhaust dribbled off.

So. So easy. They had found him.

They didn't know where *he* was, of course, not just yet, but they had located the car. The rest would be easy for them, they must be figuring. Sooner or later Wulff would come to that car and they would take care of him then. If by any chance Wulff had observed them and made sure to stay away from the car, that was all right too. They probably had a complete make on him by this time, and as soon as he came into view they would take care of him one way or the other.

If he didn't come into view, that was okay too. They would wait him out. The important thing from their point of view was probably to tie him up indefinitely; they could kill him at their leisure. Right now, so quickly, they had him bottled up like a fly in a jar.

Wulff walked from the window, looked at the sleeping girl whose sleep, he now knew, was going to be ripped apart. He took out his revolver, pondered some. Sniping at this pair would be ridiculous; sealed in that Cadillac they were invulnerable, they were not going to come out of that Cadillac two at a time. All that sniping would do would be to pinpoint his position to a couple of competent professionals, which he was sure they were. Their employer might even be happy to sacrifice one to draw fire, just to make sure that the other put Wulff away permanently. How that looked to the professionals in the front seat, of course, he did not know.

If he was ever going to get anywhere in San Francisco, he was going to have to take them frontally.

That meant going into the street, going into the line of fire, taking whatever they were willing to offer. Riskier that way but cleaner. *All right,* Wulff muttered, *let it be.* He had not come to San Francisco on a pleasure trip. And everything within him called out now for violence. It was better that way; it was like professional football players beating up members of their own team on the sidelines before kickoff just to get the feeling of contact.

He needed the feeling of contact.

"All right," he said to the sleeping girl, "Tamara, you've got to get up." He was gentler than he had thought he would be. The girl moved slowly on the sheets. She fluttered an eyelid, seemed about to move purposefully, then collapsed into sleep again.

A hand waved idly in front of her face; she seemed to be trying to put him, along with consciousness, away.

Well, why not leave her that way? Wasn't that the way that they came off the amphetamine jags? Twelve to twenty-four hours' worth of sleep and they were ready to start again, most of the hard edges of the drug cleaned out of their systems. The trick was to be able to come down into sleep in the first place; most of them, when they were as far into the drug as Tamara seemed to be, just went on and on, showing a more highly developed schizoid syndrome until nature finally pulled the plug in the form of a complete collapse, and then there they were, a lot of them poking around mental wards or striding through the streets of the cities with a strange, absent brightness in their mad eyes. But this girl had been able to crash, without the help of any additional drugs (unless she had slipped something into her mouth—Wulff just didn't know); she had been able to sleep, and when she came out of it she probably would be a good deal better. A healthy young girl this one for all the seeming dissipation: she would be able to take right off again. Yes indeed, Wulff thought, she had a considerable future to look forward to.

So why not just let her sleep? He was tempted. Whatever happened would happen outside of these rooms, and if he was clever enough, the two hit men outside would not even know from where he had emerged. The girl was probably safe here, as long as she kept under cover. Why not simply go on his way, do what we had to do? If he came back she would see him in good time and if he didn't she probably wouldn't even miss him. That was the way they were.

He couldn't do it. He admitted this to himself wryly. He was willing to face the fact: he was involved with this girl at least to the degree that he wanted to say goodbye to her, let her know that he was going. He couldn't just walk out on her with the small but real chance that he would never see her again, and with her unwarned.

Not half a day into San Francisco and he was more involved than he had been with anyone in months. Not since the day he had seen the girl named Marie Calvante in that furnished room had he been involved with anyone. He had dealings with the rookie cop, Williams, who had been on patrol with him that night and had offered to help Wulff any way he could, but Williams did not really count. If he ever got in touch with the man and he suspected that he would it would be strictly business. That was all. He would be getting in touch with Williams because he needed something out of the man. Whereas this was different. There was nothing this girl could do for him. Anything that she *could* do would lead only to disaster. If nothing else, even if all of his luck had run out, Wulff still had his instincts. His instincts told him that there was no future here at all.

Who needed a future? He had all the past that he could take. He reached out and touched her again, in the sensitive part in the small of the back. She stirred in the deep sleep, seemed to revolve to the finger-point, fluttered her eyes again. "Tamara," Wulff said, "please get up."

She rolled toward him, her eyes still closed. "I don't want to get up," she said.

"You can go back to sleep in just a minute."

"I don't want to sleep either." She pivoted on her back, opened her arms. "Do you want to hold me?" she said. "I want to hold you, Avenger."

"Not now."

"Can't I hold you, Avenger? I've wanted to hold you for so long. You can do anything to me you want." Her eyes opened then, slightly and suddenly, her mouth poised into a smile more open than he had ever seen, her breasts straining against her sweater. She was very pretty. He should have seen that all along. How had he not been able to see it? Tamara was a very attractive girl.

"Come," she said, "come here now." She put a hand against his lips. "It's all right," she said, "it's all right. I don't mind. I want you."

"No," he said, feeling the gentle pressure of her finger, and with that pressure it was like moving back into an abscess of memory he had deserted a long time ago, thin tubes of sensation opened within him and he felt the stirrings of old, grey liquids which slowly moved through him. And more insistent than all of this was a sensation of tenderness, and it was this, more than anything else, which stopped him from what he otherwise might have been tempted to do. Not the men staked out in the car, not the attaché case and its thousand horrid reasons why he had come to San Francisco—he could have dealt with any of these; he might even have been able to deal with the memory of Marie Calvante who was, after all, and he could now admit this, dead.

But he could not deal with the tenderness. Because a dead man could not, would not, must not feel tenderness and Wulff had worked himself into a territory now where the only way he could operate at all was if he calculated himself to be dead. A dead man could exact penalties but he could not be destroyed himself. A dead man knew the darkness and there was no greater darkness into which he could be dragged. Only the living felt fear, only the living would be able to calculate the odds against him and the furious quest of revenge that he had set himself upon in New York months before. He would not join them. If tenderness would vault himself into the land of the living he could not afford it.

Later on he might be able to deal with the two of them together. The ability to feel and the ability to go on and do the job that must be done. But not now. He was not ready. It was as simple as all that. It was too early.

He pressed a hand against the bed and came away from her, gently, but so quickly that she must have felt it only as a kind of ferocity. "No," he said, "no, Tamara."

She caught the force in his voice and something seemed to collapse within her. "All right," she said. "All right. See if I care, Avenger."

"I have to go now," he said. "I may be back, I may not. But I wanted to tell you that I was going."

"All right."

"You may hear some shooting and some excitement downstairs. There are two men sitting in a car waiting for me and they're going to have bad luck and find me. But nothing will happen to you if you just stay up here."

She nodded solemnly. "All right," she said.

"Stay away from the windows," he said. "Under any circumstances, don't go to the window, don't look down, don't look out, don't draw attention to yourself. If police come later, stay inside, don't get involved in the crowds and if by any chance they come up here to check you out, you're staying here alone."

"That won't last too long Avenger," she said. "The landlord saw us, we were together—"

"We can worry about that some other time," Wulff said. "Hell, that's a long way off, there may well be no police and there probably won't be any checking out of the buildings at all. I don't see why there should be. But if it gets to that point, you can always say that I helped you into the room and then took off and you have no idea at all whom I am."

"That happens to be absolutely true," she said. She twisted on the bed. "You know, if this keeps up, I'm not going to want to stay here at all. I'm going to want to come out there with you."

"That's impossible. That's absolutely impossible; that's the one thing you must not do."

She looked at him her eyes deep and penetrating. "It's bad, isn't it?" she said.

He nodded. "Yes, it's bad," he said.

"I knew it would be. Does it have to do with your killing John?"

"Maybe," he said, "probably. Everything ties together pretty quickly out here I've noticed."

"I'm glad you killed him," she said, "and I'm not afraid of you. I should have been frightened when I saw you kill him but I wasn't. I wanted to go with you. I know he would have killed you if you hadn't killed him."

"That's right."

"You're a serious man," Tamara said "you're a very serious man."

"That I am."

"All right," she said. "Will I see you again?"

"I don't know," he said. "Getting past those men is just part of it. I have to get somewhere from them."

"You don't want to get past them at all. You're going to kill them, aren't you?"

"It's possible," Wulff said. He shrugged and stood. "Anything's possible."

"I think you're a good man," she said, "I really do. I mean that. I don't even know who you are and I may never know, but you're a good man."

"All right," he said, "that does help." Strangely he meant it, it really did help. He stood by the door, reached inside his jacket in that characteristic gesture, checked the presence of the point thirty-eight. All ready. He gave the attaché case a sidelong glance, decided not to bother with it. It might give him some minimal bulletproofing if it got to that but it would also encumber him. And he did not, whatever happened, want it falling into the hands of these others.

He pointed at the case. "Take care of it," he said. "Put it under the bed or something."

"All right. I won't even look at it." She came to the side of the bed, sat with some effort, shaking her head, leaning her chin then on a hand. "I don't feel as good as I thought I did lying down," she said.

"You'll be all right. You've come back a long way."

"I don't think I'll ever be all right again."

"Well," Wulff said, "that makes two of us then, doesn't it?"

Standing by the door he looked at her for just an instant more. If he wanted he could stride over there and kiss her; he even knew that he had a hold on himself now and the kiss would mean nothing. It would just be a passionless, affectionate goodbye between two people who had known one another. But although the impulse hung like a little balloon in the air, so near that he could have reached to grasp it he let it float by. Then he punctured it. Then he nodded to her once, abruptly, almost formally, and ducked his way out the door, closing it firmly to hear the lock click.

And then, carefully blanking his mind so that he could turn into a killing machine, he went out into the street to cut his own little slice of destiny.

IV

Trotto touched the other man in the ribs from behind the wheel and said quietly, "I think he's coming out."

The other man who Trotto knew only as Ferguson grunted and without turning said, "Good. Do we hit him now or wait thirty seconds?"

That was Ferguson; a good practical man. Not much imagination but a performer all the way. Give Severo this much: he had taste in personnel, and when Trotto asked for a man Severo got him a dependable one. Nevertheless Trotto felt a little thump of unease. It wasn't *that* simple and never had been. If it was just a matter of knocking the man to the pavement and bailing out, Trotto could have done it himself. The trouble was that there was just almost no way you could teach the Fergusons that they lived in an enormously complicated world.

"We wait," Trotto said, holding the wheel loosely and reaching for the ignition. "We see where he goes."

"Why not hit him and be done with it?"

"Because you can't hit a man in broad daylight even on a sidestreet without taking risks," Trotto said irritably. "We're not here to take risks at all, just to get a job done. Besides," he added, "let's let him get a little closer in. We want to make sure that he's our man and not some poor fool who looks like him."

"I don't know," Ferguson said unhappily fondling the gun which was exposed at his hip, "Back in the East we used to hit them in broad daylight on streets which had ten times the traffic this one does. What's the difference? If you got a good silencer and you know how to get away through local traffic it's better just to do the job, not sweat it."

"That's the difference between here and your East," said Trotto without humor. "Differing lifestyles, you know?"

Their man came down the street casually, showing no indication that he knew he was being cased. A big bastard, just like the reports had said. Shit, Trotto had pictures but the pictures somehow had given no indication of the *bulk* of the man. Six four, that was about all, six four wasn't so sensational in a world where your average professional basketball player went six-nine, two-seventy or so, but this guy was *massive*. It had something to do with his being constructed low to the ground so that everything seemed to compress purposefully in his center. Yet for all of that he moved quite swiftly and gracefully, his eyes alert, Trotto knew, to every indication in the scenery. Hell, he had picked up the Fleetwood and its two passengers a long time ago. Those eyes, those New York cop's eyes missed nothing at all. But the guy was good, Trotto had to admit, he could see and he could take in, but he could do all of these in a way so offhanded that you might think, if you were casual, that he didn't know what the hell he was doing.

Trotto decided that he didn't like it. He didn't like it at all. This guy, whoever the hell he was, was no clown; he had left a short brilliant trail in the East which had left them in panic and worse yet they had let him get away. They had not even cleaned up their own mess but had dumped it on Severo. And now he was walking toward them, walking right toward the Fleetwood, those casual eyes, sweeping right and left seemingly not noticing anything, their quarry was coming right toward them, just striding along and by *mother of God they were the prey:*

"Watch out!" Trotto screamed, seeing all of it in a second, lunging for his own gun, trying to alert Ferguson, "for Christ's sake watch it!" trying to do everything in one motion, fire the gun, start the car, move the car, galvanize Ferguson, protect himself, and although his reflexes and coordination were as good as they possibly could be for a man of his age, Trotto could see from some dead calm center of all of this that it was too late. It was not going to work. The second was crucial; this guy worked on seconds just as Trotto did and he had the drop on them.

There was a *spang!* which came so quickly that it was hard to coordinate it with the revolver that had appeared in the man's hand. The windshield before Ferguson opened up like a flower and Ferguson fell toward Trotto, a strange, discombobulated look on his face. "Holy shit," Ferguson said his face sprouting blood, and he collapsed against Trotto's shoulder groaning. Trotto shoved him away, wrestling for his revolver but Ferguson's collapse probably broke open what might have been his one good chance to get a shot at the bastard. Trotto could not get to his gun. It caught inside his clothing.

In the same instant he knew he was dead. *Holy* shit, he muttered, echoing Ferguson and waited for the shot that would split his brains open and kill him. In one way or the other he guessed he had been looking for that shot for twenty-six years. No guy got into this kind of business, Trotto understood in a sudden flare of insight, unless a good part of him *wanted* that shot. But he was a professional. He was no dumb hit guy like Ferguson, waiting to have his brains exploded in a final gesture of dumbness. If he had lost he could at least lose with some dignity. He drew himself up behind the wheel of the Fleetwood, no longer struggling for the gun. Let it be this way then.

All of this had taken no more than five seconds. Things speeded up incredibly under the perception of death. But then, when the carpet of death had been yanked from under him and to his surprise Trotto saw that he was still alive, everything slowed down. Now it was as if time was a chain that was slowly expanding, bubbling under water. In slow motion he saw Ferguson roll to his lap, oozing blood from his mouth and roll across his knee to the floor; in slow motion he saw the little spurts and jets of blood that marked Ferguson's trail. Then the guy, holding the revolver was standing by the open driver's-side window. Stupid. Stupid again. He had had it rolled down all the time during the reconnoiter.

Couldn't he have anticipated something like this? Why hadn't he rolled it up? *Stupid,* Trotto thought, stupid.

The guy held the gun to Trotto's head. No one was watching. A couple of college kids far down the block were squatting in an alleyway passing one another a joint. The anticipation of death had made Trotto far-sighted. He felt the gun tickle his temple. "Are you going to cooperate?" the big guy said. The gun was cold and steady. Trotto could feel it, wedging a point all the way toward his brains.

"Yes," he said. What else was there to say? When you came right up against it you followed the orders of the man with the gun if you wanted to live. Ten minutes ago Trotto would not have believed it but yes, he wanted to live very badly. Twenty-six years old. Severo or no Severo, he wanted to go on living. Outside of this world Severo was not going to protect him. "Yes, I'll cooperate."

"Reach in your pocket," the man said, "reach inside carefully and hand me your gun, barrel first. Try anything funny and your brains will be in that pocket along with the gun. You hear me?"

"This guy is dead," Trotto said, inclining his head toward Ferguson. Funny the things you found yourself saying when you were under pressure like this. Still the discovery was new. Trotto had killed a few but he had never had to sit beside a dead man. The hits had been at far range and only once in close but he had immediately left the room. The thing was, he guessed, that he just had no stomach for it.

"I know he's dead," the guy said. Wulff, that was his name, Burt Wulff. Now it all came back to Trotto. They had had information on him and everything. They had had the drop on him all the way and it should have been a routine hit, so what the hell happened? Was it possible that it wasn't New York's fault at all; that they had just gone up against a guy they couldn't handle? "Hand me the gun," the guy said quietly. "Hand it over now."

Slowly, Trotto dug inside his clothing. No time to try anything now. He wouldn't think of it. If you're a professional, you know when you're beaten, it was as simple as that. You accept challenges if they are possible but you don't break against rock. This guy was rock. He was out of Trotto's class. He was willing to admit it. The hell with it. Beaten was beaten.

He handed the gun, barrel first to the man outside. The man looked at the gun, looked at Ferguson, cracked open the gun and cleaned out the chambers. He dropped the bullets out onto the sidewalk as if they were pellets of candy.

"Now what?" Trotto said.

"I'm thinking," the guy said. He looked at Trotto intently, motioned. "Unlock the back door," he said.

Trotto twisted around slowly, opened it. The guy held the gun on him and got into the back seat. He closed the door with a solid *thunk,* locked it and seemed to lean forward pressing the barrel into Trotto's neck.

"This is no good," Trotto said. "People will see. You can't get away with this."

"Leave that to me," this Wulff said. "Don't worry about my welfare. I make out. Start driving."

"All right," Trotto said. He hit the ignition, something he should have done five minutes ago, of course. Too late, too late for all false chances. The car started with a little whine. 1971 Fleetwood, full power gear. No front seat/rear seat partition, the only option missing but otherwise the works. It didn't seemed to have stopped Ferguson from dying in it, unfortunately.

He dropped the car into drive, pulled out from the curb at a whisper. Ferguson, dead or not, was bleeding all over the front seat; the cushions, the mats, even the dashboard had little speckles of his blood. Who would have thought that there was so much blood in a dead man. "I can't drive this way," Trotto said mildly. "I just can't."

"What's wrong?" Wulff said, "there's no blood on the windshield is there?"

"You don't understand. I think I'm going to get sick."

Wulff seemed to sigh. That was all right; Trotto had been afraid that he was going to laugh. "That's all right," he said, "you'll get over it. The sick feeling passes sooner than you think and then you're just riding next to a dead man."

"Someone's going to spot us," Trotto said. "I tell you, these windows aren't one-way. Some cop is going to look in and see this corpse here and ask questions."

"I see," Wulff said slowly. "Tell me, do you think that it might be better to just stop here and dump him into traffic then? You're perfectly free to do that if you really must."

"No. No I'll skip it."

"I think that's a good decision."

"What do you want?" Trotto screamed, his control breaking spontaneously, like a rubber band pulled and pulled and finally severing into raw, painful halves, smashed back against his senses, "what the hell do you want from me?"

"I want to take a drive."

"We're *taking* a drive. If you want to kill me, *kill* me, but I can't take this."

"I'm sure you'll be able to," the man said quietly. "Everything takes some getting used to, that's all. I also want to have a talk with you."

"So talk! *Talk!*"

"I always wanted to see the Golden Gate Bridge," Wulff said. "Why don't we head there? I think that I want to go north anyway. That's the best way, isn't it?"

"It depends."

"Let's try it. And on the way we can have a conversation."

Trotto felt the nudge of the barrel against his head again. "Go on," the man said, "get to it. You're still alive aren't you? You son of a bitch."

Wulff and Trotto and a dead man hit the freeway to see what they could see.

V

The Golden Gate Bridge, Wulff decided, was much narrower than he would have thought; in the movies all you saw was this great arching span rearing high above the bay connecting the two great port cities, and the illusion was one of vaulting space, the height and hush of the cathedral—but the actuality was something else again. The lanes were impossibly narrow, oncoming traffic through the thin divider seemed about to lurch out of control at any instant and spill the Fleetwood, screaming, into the ocean; and the Fleetwood itself, no small car, seemed to hang dangerously out of its lane although he could see that Trotto, regardless of the pressure he was under, was an expert driver and was doing everything that he could to keep the big car going straight and under control.

It was just another question of illusion versus reality, he supposed; the postcard illusion of the Golden Gate Bridge versus this narrow, tormenting tangle through which the Fleetwood cut perilously. But he could give only a part of his attention to the landscape because the most important thing was to dig as much information out of Trotto as possible. The man was talking, he was talking inexhaustibly. One thing about these men: they might come on, on their own terrain, like lions all right, but they were simply kittens when they were put to pressure. He would remember that. It was one of the valuable lessons he had picked up since he left the police force where he was still willing to concede that tough guys at least were really tough. No they were not. Not really. "Nicholas Severo," Wulff said meditatively, remembering to keep the gun rigid and levelled at Trotto from the back, although he was no longer prodding the barrel against his neck. The man might faint. "I know that name."

"I'm dead," Trotto said excitedly, "don't you understand? For telling you that, I'm a dead man." Nevertheless he was an excellent driver. The car soared on. The corpse beside the driver lolled indolently, a clown's smile freezing onto the locked features. A peaceful, pastoral scene circa 1973 in the Bay State.

"Why?" Wulff said, "why does he want to get rid of me so desperately? What am I to him? What's the difference; can one man make a Nicholas Severo uncomfortable? I thought that he had an empire."

"I don't know shit about empires," Trotto said in a high voice. "I'm a freelancer, I hire out to do a little work for the guy, that's all. How do I know what he's got in mind? This son of a bitch is bleeding all over me."

"Do you deal, Trotto?"

"What? What's that?"

"I asked you if you deal. Do you hustle the stuff? Do you move the junk? Do you make connections? Are you an action man? Whatever the hell you people call it out here, I want to know if you work with the hard stuff."

Trotto's shoulders shook but he held the wheel steady. In the rear-view mirror Wulff saw the man gulp. "No," he said, "I don't mess with it."

"Not at all?"

"I told you, I don't mess with it! I've done a lot of things in my life; I'll do a lot more but I don't mess with junk. It's a personal thing, that's all."

"You really think you'll do a lot more with your life?"

"Listen," Trotto said desperately, swerving the vehicle to capture the right lane, braking to hit the first exit, "listen, I've got nothing against you. It's nothing personal at all. I went out to do a job, that's all; it was just a job and I had no part in it at all. If I knew that you were this kind of guy I never would have taken it."

"I bet," Wulff said.

"Where do you want to go?" Trotto said hesitantly. "Look, we can't go on this way. This guy is bleeding all over the seat. I tell you, there are cops patrolling all the fuck over the place here; they're going to pick us up and pull us over and then where are we going to be?"

"My problem," Wulff said. But Trotto was right. He was going to push his luck if he kept up this particular version of a death ride. The San Francisco police might not have the alertness of New York's Finest, but that was just parochial pride showing, Wulff supposed, and anyway the cops would have to be flat-out incompetent not, over some thirty miles of freeway, sooner or later, to get a look into this car. The point was that he had nothing in particular against police at all. He felt that he was working with them. Nevertheless, if the car was stopped he would have no choice but to be pitted against them and this opened up a series of choices which he did not want to consider.

He found himself thinking of Tamara for an instant and then deliberately, like moving furniture, pushed the thought away. He did not know if he would ever see her again and he did not know if this made any difference at all to him.

"Sausalito," he said to Trotto. "That's where I want to go."

"Saus—"

"I think that maybe I'd better see your boss face to face. We can work out our differences like gentlemen. Besides," Wulff said, looking at the barrel of his pistol, "there's a hell of a lot of junk moving through this vein soon and maybe Mr. Severo would know something about it, eh?"

Trotto said nothing. His shoulders trembled. He cut to an access road heading north, opened the car up again as they merged with highway traffic. "That's crazy," he said, "you can't go up there. You'll get yourself killed."

"You care about my health, Trotto?"

"I'm just telling you'll get yourself killed."

"My problem," Wulff said, "but before we head up to Sausalito there's one other little detail which has to be settled. No don't get off into the left lane, Trotto. I want you to take the next exit and find me a nice little side road."

"In this section. This is Greater Oakland, man, there ain't nothing—"

"You're resourceful, Trotto," Wulff said sharply, "you're resourceful enough to go around killing people, you can find me a back road near here. Now shut the fuck up and just drive."

"What you going to do? You going to dump this stiff? That would be a good idea but—"

"Shut the fuck up, Trotto," Wulff said bluntly. "Just move the car."

Trotto shut up and moved the car. He found an exit lane, took the car off the freeway and rolled down a long ramp, came to an intersection piled with franchise food stands, traffic lights, large vans and women with baby carriages. "This is a populated area," he said in a whine, "for

God's sake, anyone can look in this car, can see—"

"Shove him down," Wulff said.

"What's that?" Trotto asked, the car idling in a line of traffic at the light, his shoulders hunched as he peered through the windshield. "What are you saying to me?"

"I said shove him down to the floor if he offends you," Wulff said. "You see, it's your problem, not mine."

"You want me to touch him?"

"Why not? Never seen a dead man before, Trotto?"

"Not up this close. Never like this. I—"

"Shove him down," Wulff said and touched Trotto ever so gently in the back with the pistol. The man jumped. He extended an arm, gave Ferguson's body a weak shove, then pushed harder when the corpse failed to move.

Ferguson fell to the floor in a little leap and shower of blood.

"Better," said Wulff as Trotto, shuddering, got the Fleetwood moving behind the traffic again. At the intersection he cut right, right again, they headed into a long two-lane blacktop, opposing cars hurtling toward them perilously. Wulff shifted his attention for just a moment, looked around, focused on the terrain. It looked exactly like Queens or Patchogue, Long Island. The clutter of the highway, the arrangement of the stands, the flicker of the used car lots, even the way the landscape had been carved out to fit this junk looked like any suburb he had ever seen.

The thing was that they had made all of the country the same. Differences, if there ever had been any at all had been abolished. Just as the network and their dealers had moved into the central cities throughout the land, cleaving them all into a single pattern of waste and devastation, so the developers, the used-car men, the franchisers had come into the near countryside and made it their own. On the one hand, junk was being poured into the central cities; on the other, a different kind of junk was being dropped like bird pellets into the countryside. Maybe Wulff thought wryly it wasn't a coincidence or a matter of two forces after all. Maybe the eager developers and the junk network were the same people operating out of two briefcases; from the one they pulled arrangements for shipments, from the other they grabbed another vacant lot zoned for private use, bribed a few councilmen to change that zoning and threw up another "Wonder Waffles." In both cases they were out to level the country, to make it exactly the same all over, to erase all differences from the land because if the land was all the same then one policy, one government, one program would work as well as any other and there would be no will left to fight them. Maybe you could see everything that had happened in these last twenty years as the outcome of the fact that the country, down the line, had lost all sense of its differences. You didn't want to push that theory, any theory entirely too far but it was certainly a possibility.

Trotto, retreating into himself had taken the car a long way down the blacktop. Now the country was beginning to open and Wulff could see the savaged remains of what it might have looked like nearer the intersection a few years ago. Wasted grass, ruined trees, low-hanging mist, a few discouraged houses and industrial buildings thinning out even further as they moved on. They were getting away from the built-up district after all. In a few years, maybe less than that, the developers would have gotten out this far but it still was not quite worth their while. Aside from burning out the landscape and scattering a haze of pollution through it like a child dumping sand on a beach, they just didn't have too much interest. Yet. Wulff took a couple of deep breaths and sat patiently in the back of the car. Trotto was his chauffeur and was carrying him off to an appointment. Look at it that way. Wulff knew exactly what he had to do now; it was just a matter of timing.

"What are you doing?" Trotto said nervously, as if catching this throat, "what are you going to do?"

"You'll see."

"Listen," Trotto said quickly, "I told you, I have nothing against you. I just work for a guy, that's all. I don't mean you any harm at all."

"Of course not."

"I don't!"

"I know it," Wulff said quietly. "You don't mean me any harm at all; you would have killed me back there but it would have been nothing personal at all. All right," he said, noting that the scenery had now opened up almost completely, devastated grass, brown, withered foliage, "stop this car."

"I mean it!" Trotto said, his voice bleating, "for God's sake, don't do this to me!"

"Don't do what to you?"

"Don't kill me," Trotto said. "I'm twenty-six years old; I don't want to die." He did not slow the car.

"Nobody wants to die," Wulff said. "In the whole history of the world there have been only three or four people who really wanted to die, they're the great exception, but nevertheless, everybody *does* die, don't they? It's just one of those things you've got to put up with Trotto, like turning in a car every two years and taking the depreciation. I told you to stop this thing."

The car swerved, brakes locking. Trotto seemed on the verge of trying something desperate; Wulff had to poke him once with the gun in the back as a reminder to keep his mind centered. Trotto finally braked down in a series of little swerves and buckings, the car spilling off the road and onto a rutted shoulder, little clouds of dust being kicked up by the wheels. Trotto held the wheel tightly as the car braked down and seemed to be peering through the windshield. He twitched.

"Shut off the motor," Wulff said.

Trotto cut the engine and turned to face him. "You're really going to do it, aren't you?" he said.

"I don't know what I'm going to do. Get that corpse out of the car."

"What's that?"

"I said, get Ferguson out of this car. He's staining the upholstery and I don't feel like riding around with a dead man anymore."

Trotto looked behind him nervously. "There are cars all the time—"

"There are no cars now. That's your problem, Trotto," Wulff said. "I'm just going to sit in here and look at this gun for a while. You do the housekeeping."

Slowly, reluctantly, Trotto opened the door and moved out. Wulff watched him carefully. "You won't get away with it," Trotto said.

"I expect not."

"And if I had the gun on you, Wulff—"

"But you don't," Wulff said. "You don't have a gun on me. I have the gun on *you* and that's the only relationship you understand so you just go ahead and do what you have to do Trotto."

Trotto walked around to the other side. Wulff leaned forward, unlocked the door for him. Trotto leaned in, took the corpse by the shoulders and tugged. The corpse did not move. Trotto shuddered and pulled harder.

Ferguson came free from the car like a clump of seaweed being pulled out of water.

Wulff sat and watched it. Working on the passenger side as he was, Trotto was shut off from the road. No one would be able to see what he was doing, working close into the car, not that it mattered anyway. On the road, no one stopped. This was the one basic rule of the new American road: *stop for nothing*. That was what the country had turned into; people in little air-conditioned cubicles rolling quickly, ignoring the scenery. There was no scenery. If your own car malfunctioned you were just out of luck. Maybe a cop would stop and maybe he wouldn't. Maybe a truck would come along and then again most likely it would not. The best thing to do when your car malfunctioned was to start hiking and if you were a cripple or a pregnant woman in deep labor that was just your tough luck. New rules of the road: *everyone is a stranger.* Except at the franchise food stand, of course. There, these people were your *friends* just like the dealers who always knew you at the beginning.

Trotto holding the corpse in a ballroom embrace, wandered some yards from the car, dropped Ferguson heavily on the ground. The body made just a little clump on the earth; it would look from the road like a shallow rise. Colorless, merged into the earth. All of the blood had come off it in the car.

Trotto stood there for a moment and then came back to the Fleetwood slowly, reluctantly. He seemed to be limping. He walked around to the driver's side, opened the door, started to slide in.

"No," Wulff said. "No, Trotto."

The man stopped in mid-gesture. Wedged, half-in, half-out of the car. He looked at Wulff.

"You're not going anywhere," Wulff said. Softly he opened the driver's side of the back seat, got out in one quick motion, walked up behind Trotto. Now he was covering him, belly to buttocks. "Back out of the car," he said, clearing a little ground. "Back out very slowly and don't try anything."

"No," Trotto said, "you can't do this to me."

"Try me."

"There are cars! There are people—" Confirming this, a Rambler American bounced down the hill behind, came up to and by the Fleetwood fast, children peering out the windows. It was out of sight even before Wulff could smell the exhaust.

"No one cares, Trotto," he said. "Everybody just wants to get to where they're going. They don't look at this as being real at all. It's just something you drive *through.*"

Stiffly, Trotto moved around the hood. His hands were trembling. "In broad daylight—" he said. "On a public road."

"That's life. You would have knocked me down in a street. Isn't this better? You can die in the grass."

"Don't kill me," Trotto said. "For God's sake don't kill me, Wulff."

"I've got to do it," Wulff said quietly. He let the man wander toward a little group of bushes about twenty yards downrange; instinctively Trotto must have been, like a wounded animal, seeking cover. "But I want to tell you why I'm doing it."

"Don't kill me. Don't kill me!"

"I have to," he said. "You see, the trouble is, Trotto, that you just don't care. You just did your job always, you never thought about what it meant or what was happening to people. People never meant anything to you Trotto; you never thought about them. But if you're going to be a piece of machinery then you have to pay the price of being machinery. When it malfunctions, you replace it."

He raised the gun.

"It's nothing personal," Wulff said as the man started to run, and shot him.

The man seemed to collapse into sections; little pieces of him hitting the ground unevenly, his body falling not so much in a heap as in scatters as if a bag of stones had been exploded upon the ground. No rolling, kicking, he took to the ground and he lay still, his face buried in the dust. Wulff went over and looked at him.

Medulla oblongata. Clean drill. It was a job that Trotto himself could have been proud of.

Wulff put the gun away and walked back to the Fleetwood. Three more cars like dogs, came prowling up the hill and, sniffing, went away. No one looked out of them. There was nothing to look at. The road was just a passage of time like a dream. It did not exist at all.

He got into the Fleetwood, slammed the door, locked up everything and started the motor. Trotto was right; it was a hell of a good performing, quiet automobile. The bloodstains on the mats and seat, the odor of death in the car was almost gone. The climate control was fantastic. It could clean out everything.

He put the car into gear and began to drive. He was not all that familiar with the geography but Trotto's instructions had been pretty good, particularly for a man issuing them at gunpoint. Wulff guessed that he could find his way.

He was going to see Nicholas Severo.

VI

There had been a good deal of security getting into Albert Marasco's estate in Islip, Long Island, Wulff remembered. Marasco was only a minor boss but he had a checkpoint system which would have done the Berlin Wall proud. Severo, he suspected, was a bigger operative in his territory than Marasco in New York, and he expected a lot of difficulty, but there were no checkpoints at all. Not even a booth; nothing on the outside of the high house indicating an observation point.

They did things differently here, that was for sure. A more informal, relaxed culture, that was what they said. Wulff wheeled the car down a long rutted driveway, bounced the Fleetwood toward a small parking area that had been ringed out to the rear of the house.

All the time he was hunched over the wheel, much as Trotto had been forty-five minutes before, half-expecting the whining impact against the windshield or back panel that would warn him that his safety margin had expired. One or another of Severo's stake-out men would know that the Fleetwood showing up here with only one man was sure indication that something had gone wrong. Even if he could not recognize Wulff from that distance, the fact that a man was coming back alone would have been sufficient for this theoretical point-man. He might try to blow up the car on the spot.

But there was no point man. There was no observation post. There appeared to be no security at Nicholas Severo's quarters at all. The driveway had been open to the highway, no gate closing it off, that driveway had led straight to the house, the house seemed open and accessible. Was it possible that his man felt himself so far above danger that the thought of protecting himself was absolutely foreign? Or more ominously, had Trotto, holding out to the end, given him false information and sent him to the home of some unsuspecting suburbanite?

Wulff doubted it. He thought he knew his customers pretty well by this time, and Trotto had been a man broken and squeezed open. If he was sure of anything it was that he had taken everything out of Trotto that he could before he had thrown him away. Nevertheless this situation struck him somehow as being even more ominous than being received by machine-guns. A situation he would have been prepared for in Fleetwood. He had been in a worse situation at Marasco's and gotten out of it. But this was something that he did not know quite how to tackle.

A question of differing lifestyles.

Wulff stopped the car, shut off the motor with a *tick!* and let the keys dangle as slowly he eased himself from the car. However he went out of here—if he went out of here at all—he was pretty sure that it would not be in the Fleetwood. Coming to ground he reconnoitered carefully, checked the upper levels of the house, the small, neat grounds, the three swans circling idly in the small pool of clear water on the lawn before the house, a nice touch this, and then very carefully, holding the gun, he walked toward the main entrance.

Sitting duck of course. Or sitting swan. If Severo was watching behind glass the man could finish him off with one shot. But Wulff's instincts were holding now. He had a feeling that if he were indeed being watched and if no shot had been taken by now, he was going to get into this house. Curiosity would overtake caution. Had overtaken it already. Or maybe there was some kind of bounty for his being taken alive as opposed to dead. A promotion for Severo within the ranks, from sergeant major to warrant officer, say. Who knew exactly how they worked? He would find out though.

He kept on walking. Into the enemy's lair. He was driven; had been driven from the first. Since he had seen Marie Calvante's body lying on the floor of that damned room, since he had died three and a half months ago, he had been driven by only one purpose: to keep on moving. To come into their center. To simply keep on going up the line until he confronted them in one naked, open moment. Then he would kill them. Or be killed. But he would not stop coming. They could kill him but they could not stop him. He was a machine. Machinery could not be stopped. He kept on going.

Up the stucco stairs and to the house. Large, ornate door, a bell prominently displayed. He reached for the bell. Chimes, something symphonic. They did things nicely in Northern California. No response. He hit the bell again. A new theme, not a repetition of the previous one. Good system. Highly elaborate. Severo had taste. All of these people in San Francisco had taste. They probably tied up the junk in rolled up prints of old masters for delivery. The special touch.

The door opened slowly and before him stood a short, bald man holding a cigar in one hand and a revolver in another. It was levelled directly at Wulff's heart, Wulff noticed. That was good. Whoever this man was he had some alertness after all. It was not as easy as it had looked.

"Mr. Wulff?" the man said.

Wulff said nothing. He stood and stared. For the first time since he had hit the bell he realized that he still had his own pistol in his hand and that that pistol was covering the short man. They were covering one another. The short man looked at him and something almost like amusement moved through his features, discoloring them slightly. "I said," he said, "are you Wulff?"

Wulff said nothing. What was there to say? He held his pistol and the short man held his own. They looked at one another. Dead stalemate. Both could die or neither but there was no progress from this position.

"Look" the man said quietly, "this is a draw."

"Favor the runner," Wulff said.

"What's that?"

"Never mind. It's an old expression."

"Stalemate here. I think we should talk."

"I don't think we have a damned thing to talk about, Severo."

"Oh?" the man said, his eyes widening slightly, "then what are you here for?"

"I came here to kill you."

The man exhaled flatly. "They're right," he said, "the reports are right. You're crazy."

"Maybe."

"You're crazy, Wulff; you want to take on the whole world. Don't you understand there's nothing to take on? I think that we should talk."

"There's nothing to talk about," Wulff said. "I've just killed two of your men, don't you know that? What could we have to talk about?"

Severo looked at him flatly. "I'm not surprised," he said. "I figured you would kill them. After I talked around a little and read the reports I knew that we should have sent out a fucking army."

"There's a big shipment coming through this territory very soon, I figure," Wulff said. "A couple of million dollars worth of junk. You want to talk about something? You want to help me? Tell me where it's moving in and when. That's what we can talk about."

Severo shook his head and chuckled. With his free hand he beckoned to Wulff. "Come in," he said, "come on in and we can talk about it."

"Go in there? You think I'm crazy, Severo? I may be crazy but not by half. I'm not going into your house on your terms to talk about anything."

Wulff willed himself to a further pitch of alertness, held the pistol so as to discharge it at the instant that Severo seemed to bring concentration to bear on his own gun. But he had misjudged his man; either that or Severo was operating on some level which Wulff could not yet comprehend. For the man shrugged, ducked his head and dropped the pistol abruptly to the ground. It clattered and lay by Wulff's foot.

Severo spread his hands and looked at Wulff. "All right," he said, "let's go for a little walk along the grounds."

"Why don't I just kill you now and save the little walk?"

"You're not going to kill me now, Wulff. If you were going to you would have done it ten seconds ago. You're not crazy at all, I respect you, you're a man of purpose and it doesn't suit your purpose right now to kill me. You think I might be able to tell you about that shipment."

"Will you?"

"I don't know," Severo said. "I want to see what you have in mind. Maybe I'm not so crazy about this damned business myself, maybe I'm looking for an edge of some sort. You never know. We might be of some use to each other Wulff."

"I doubt that."

"I've been looking for someone like you for a long time," Severo said. For the first time emotion seemed to infiltrate his voice. "Can't you understand that? Can't you follow what I'm saying to you? I've been looking for this for a long time, Wulff, and maybe now it's come. Now you don't want to go into the house that's all right. We can just walk around these grounds and talk. Or I'll get into your death car over there and we'll take a ride and talk."

Severo looked at him, five feet five inches of curiously concentrated authority, and Wulff felt the unreasonable respect building. It was impossible but he was dealing here with a man of force and responsibility who on some level had taken over from Wulff. It was now Severo pushing the bounds of the confrontation. "You really hate this don't you?" he said, "you hate us."

"I hate junk," Wulff said flatly. "I hate junk. I hate the people who deal in it, I hate the politicians and the businessmen locked away in safe places who make it all possible. Yes, I hate that."

"So do I," said Severo softly. "So do I."

"So what does that mean?" Wulff said. "Should I give you a fucking medal because you say you hate junk? You've lived on it all your life, Severo. It built this place with walls to keep the junkies out."

"Not all my life. Not all my life by half. I think that we ought to take that ride, Wulff." Severo kicked at the pistol, moved it further from him. "I've put myself in your hands, don't you see? I've laid myself down in front of you. Now are you going to listen to me or not?"

"I've killed two men today. I've killed three since I've been in San Francisco. Why shouldn't I kill another?"

"You can kill a lot more," Severo said quietly, "if you want to, you can kill hundreds. I *want* you to kill hundreds. But first we've got to talk. All right," he said with an abrupt gesture, a change of mood, "I'm not going to go on with this indefinitely. I'm going to go to that car and have a seat and if you don't join me in thirty seconds I'll assume that you don't want to talk and you have nothing to say and I'm going to get out of that car and go on back inside, and lock the door. So you'll have to either kill me or let me go or talk to me, Wulff, that's all there is to it."

He brushed by him quickly with the gesture of a stranger rushing to catch a train in the New York City subway and strode toward the Fleetwood. Wulff watched him for a minute and then slowly putting the pistol away, followed the little man at a moderate pace.

All right. He would admit it. The little bastard if nothing else did have the habit of command.

They certainly *did* do things differently out here, didn't they?

VII

Severo was angry. That was all it came down to; they were trying to squeeze him out, bypass him, circulate the traffic around his domain, eventually shut him out of the lucrative junk trade altogether. Why they were doing this was obscure but it seemed to have something to do with a power struggle in which he had been involved, a power struggle which he was losing. Severo's business was just like anything else corporate in America; it went through levels of influence, interlocking directorates, conglomerates, spheres of influence and so on. Severo was a good American. Now he was being undercut in a business which he had spent two decades building from the ground, a business which had given him much pride and sustenance, and he was mad. Extremely mad.

Junk had nothing to do with it at all. It could have been anything that the fat little man was involved in. Talking to him Wulff could begin to understand that. He had a lot to learn about this business, he was the first to admit it, and Severo taught him a lot. The people who dealt in junk didn't think of it as junk at all. They thought in terms of gross lots, profit, loss, inventory, turnover, round figures and even distribution. What they were buying and selling never crossed their minds, at least in any way that they would have to come to terms with it. They were poisoning the country, they were killing people, they were breaking up the old social order of America, that's what Severo and his interlocking conglomerates were doing, but they just didn't see it that way at all. They didn't see it any way. It was just a job.

So there was nothing to do with the fat little man. You might want to kill him—Wulff had not discarded the possibility—but it would be just like putting the squeeze in a junkyard on an old car. The car was in no position to understand what was being done to it. It was inanimate, insensate, it didn't realize that it didn't work. The same way with Severo. Pull the trigger and you would get elimination but you would never, *never* get understanding. You could parade his victims in front of him by the hundreds and thousands, quivering, beaten addicts, the victims of the victims following them, all of the people who the addicts had stomped and burned and mugged and stolen from and killed to keep the mainline running, but that would not make any difference to Severo either. He just would not see it. *Really?* he might say raising his eyebrows and whispering so that his gentle voice would not disturb the addict's march. *Is that so? Terrible social condition; what can I do to help? Will you take a check?*

So that was the way it was. It was no more personal to the Severos than Trotto's murder had been personal to Wulff. In that way if no other, he guessed, Nicholas and he had a great deal in common. They were out to achieve objectives and people who got between them and those goals simply had to be cleared out of the way. The trouble was that Severo, at least to date, had been a hell of a lot more successful than Wulff ever expected to be.

They drove around and around the surrounding area in the Fleetwood,

Wulff at the wheel, Severo hunched forward near him, hands outstretched, talking earnestly and inexhaustibly. If the little man took any notice of the bloodstains he made no comment; he was like a well-bred relative talking to a child with a harelip. He would not embarrass Wulff. He would not make him feel awkward about the blood in his car. They drove past estates, wooded areas, trees and glades, they drove past children playing in the streets and beautiful women in tennis shorts carrying racquets and walking their way gracefully toward the courts. They drove past used car lots and hamburger stands, Wonder Waffles and clothing discount stores and then past the estates again. It was a nice area. It was convenient to all shopping, as the real estate ads would put it, but secluded enough from the shopping that commerce did not have to infringe upon the private life-style. Just like the junk, in short. Severo was a man of taste, it would seem. He knew how and where to live.

The junk was coming into San Francisco Bay tomorrow night. It would get there by a circuitous route according to Severo. From Saigon to Peking, a little crossover at Istanbul, switch to airplane to get to Malaga, another flight then back to Peking and finally by laborious freight, weeks on the ocean, toward San Francisco. Severo did not try to explain the reasoning behind this. Wulff did not press him.

Traffic was always a complex and dangerous business and nothing which he had ever tried to understand; the point was that it *worked.* Customs was a joke, security a punch line. The country had ten million points of access. Who could cover them all?

All that mattered was that it was coming in by freighter tomorrow night, and a little piece of it was for Severo. Most of it was not; the shipment was being cut up in twenty to thirty pieces to be taken by various distributors and point men all over the country. Severo was only a twentieth or a fiftieth of the pickup. But because the delivery was being taken in his territory he had a kind of loose control over it, a loose responsibility for the connections. That was the way the business worked. In San Francisco you had to clear everything with Severo. Drive twenty miles east or five miles north and it was two other people you had to talk to. But here his control was what mattered.

They drove into Severo's driveway again just as the man had finished mapping out the specifics. Wulff had been listening for an hour, saying very little, saying nothing in fact, taking it all in and wondering if he dared trust the man. He supposed that he could. Severo by getting into the Fleetwood had absolutely put himself at Wulff's mercy. You did not put yourself under a gun and then begin to babble lies. Or did you? He could not figure these people out. He supposed that he did not have to as long as he could beat them.

"I don't like the business," Severo said as Wulff brought the car to a stop, "you hear me? I just don't like it. I didn't get started to get into it, it just came along five, six years ago, and how could I pass it up? If I didn't take it over some other guy would instead and they'd use it as a wedge to push me out. But I've been thinking it over for a long time and I don't want to mess with it anymore. It's a dirty business. You know, back before the 1960's they didn't even want to touch the stuff. Most of them had children, they could see what the stuff would do, they didn't want to get involved. But they had to get into it finally in self defense."

"Why?"

"Why? I told you why. Because they were starting to get squeezed out. Because the business just got out of hand, it was so big, there was so much money, and so many guys started to push their way in that things were starting to fall apart. Pressure built up, and they were losing so much money, so much money was going to these other sources that they were really beginning to lose hold. So they had to get back into it but there were a lot even then who didn't want to touch it and they started to get obstructed. So—"

"So the gang wars started again," Wulff said.

"Yeah," Severo said with a shrug. "I mean it wasn't quite that simple, but that's the general idea. I forgot; you were in New York through all that shit, weren't you?"

"I got around a little, yeah," Wulff said, "Just a shade. And now, I should just march in there and take it over, right? And what about you? What are you going to be doing when I'm ditching all of your plans?"

"I won't be there," Severo said. "You don't think anyone in the higher echelons appears personally, do you?"

"You have people who do the contact work."

"Something like that," Severo said. He opened the door and pushed his way out of the car. "So I'll wish you luck now," he said.

"Wait a minute."

Severo raised his eyebrows and stayed in position, half-in, half-out, hunched over. "What is it?"

"You think I'm just going to let you go? We finish our talk and I let you out of the car and you go home?"

"Those were my plans," the little man said. "You had another idea?"

"You think you're just going to walk away from this?"

"I think we understand one another, Wulff. You have nothing to gain by killing me. Look, I've put myself at your mercy as a measure of good faith. I think you can trust me."

"Why should I trust you?"

Severo held his position, looked at Wulff levelly. "Because I'm telling you the truth and because I think we can help each other."

"You're using me to work out a double-cross."

"Something like that, yes. It's much more complicated than that, though. Like the gang wars."

"I ought to kill you," Wulff said.

"Of course you ought to kill me. I know your track record, Wulff; you've been killing everyone. But what do you have to gain? Actually you're not a killer at all; you're a businessman. You're just trying to get a job done like I've been doing, and that means getting people out of your way. But I'm not in your way, you see. I'm trying to help you."

"Just let you go back into the house and call down every hit man in San Francisco to catch me near that freight tomorrow."

"If you think so. You're quite wrong, though. You know," Severo said, "I'm getting very uncomfortable standing in this position, Wulff. Now the Fleetwood is mine of course but I can see where you might find it awkward to leave it here and just take a bus on back to wherever you're staying, so you can have it to get back there. I suggest you leave it somewhere convenient and give me a call and I'll arrange for a pickup."

"You've got nerve," Wulff said, almost admiringly. "You have really got nerve. Severo, I've got to give you that."

Severo shrugged and moved away from the car, hitched his pants up in the driveway, kicked out a leg, a dancer. "You don't get into a position like mine without learning a few things," he said and started to walk toward the house.

"Stop," Wulff said.

The man poised, arched in the air almost as if expecting an impact and for just a moment Wulff could see, even from behind, the mask of this man shift and fall: Severo was terrified. Underneath all of it he had been a man on the edge of terror for two hours. Regardless, he had gone on and done what he had to do.

Severo turned slowly and looked at Wulff. Whatever happened to his face had already been subject to reassembly work in the instant after he had seen that no bullet would hit him. No little trace of what he must have looked like was on his face, there was only a hint in the eyes, closure, blood, then vanishing in the whiteness of pupil. Nevertheless, just knowing that he had opened up the man in this way was probably enough for Wulff. He understood himself now. There was no need to kill Severo after all, at least not yet. He only had to see that the man recognized the line where the killing might have been done. Severo saw it. He saw it clear.

"I had a question," Wulff said.

"Oh?"

"It's a question about you, not me."

"You're interested in me? Why that's very touching, Wulff."

"What's going to happen to you, Severo, if I break up this delivery of yours and everybody in the area begins to wonder who might have tipped me onto it? What are you going to do when every middle boss and hit man in the area starts to crawl around these trees?"

"That's a problem I'll face, Wulff. Nice of you to think of me, though."

"You really think you *can* face it? You think it's something you can deal with, you'd put your head into that kind of oven?"

"I know my business," Severo said. "I've been in my business for twenty years. How long have you been in yours, three months? Goodbye, Wulff."

He walked away. No twitch in his shoulder blades this time, no swerve of his head. The bastard knew he was safe. He had gone through the other side of the confrontation and now even if Wulff hit him it would not be the same. Severo would die in confidence.

Wulff let him go.

He let him go, nothing else to do. Obscurely he understood that, by the code he had created for himself and was now living by, if he was going to kill Severo he would have done it immediately. Or at the latest, as soon as he had pumped the man clear of information. You did not keep the butterfly on the pin, you did not draw out the moment either for your own enjoyment or for their suffering. That put you on their level. They loved death. They played with it like normal men might play with a woman.

Wulff did not. He merely used it as another technique. And by letting the moment go by he had lost the opportunity to bring it.

Severo, positions reversed, would have shot him. He was sure of it. But the positions were not reversed. Lonely, locked in, he was always going to be himself.

He watched the man walk confidently into his house, close the door and flick out the lights.

Very meditatively, Wulff started the Fleetwood and drove the hell out of there.

VIII

Severo did not stop shaking inside until he had closed and locked all the doors clear up to the study on the third floor which had chain bolts and which no one, he hoped, would ever know about. It was his fortress;

at the last moment if they ever came to get him he would meet them there. In that fortress now, bolts on, bars across the window, he sat in a chair in a great gasping explosion of breath and allowed the tension at last to ease out. He put his hands in front of his face and in the private way he allowed himself only in this room and only then once or twice a year, rationing it out, he cried.

He cried convulsively for two or three minutes and then all of the little crawling sounds and fears were gone and he was himself again. He leaned back in the chair, lit a cigarette and smiled.

He had won, though. He had walked into the valley of death all right, he had met the monster, he had worked him over like a woman or a violin and he had won. He had him exactly where he wanted him now.

They could have done the same thing to him in New York and cancelled him right out if any of them had the guts or the craft. But no, it had all come to him, Nicholas Severo, and he had done it. They called everything outside of the northeastern circle the minor leagues, did they? They would have to begin to re-evaluate their thinking.

He picked up the phone and dialed a number, got a voice which he recognized. He told the voice to call another voice to the phone, and when the second voice came on he explained quickly what had happened and what he had done and exactly where Wulff would be tomorrow night.

"I want you to hit him with everything you've got," Severo said clearly.

The voice said that he would take care of it.

IX

Heading south again, out of Sausalito, Wulff was cut off by another car and almost ditched. It all happened so fast that there was no time to evaluate, no time to even consider what was happening to him. He was going on a long stretch of pretty good highway, working the right lane pretty close to the top limit of the Fleetwood, peering through the rear view every ten seconds to make sure that his rear was staying as clear as the front. Maybe eighty-five miles an hour, which for all its tricky suspension and soft riding insulation, was all that the big car could safely handle. Sure they were road cars, the reputation was deserved. They were road cars on long, flat, empty straightaways without ruts, when held below ninety miles an hour. Any two-year-old patrol Plymouth could have left this thing for dead in a parking lot.

The Mercedes in the far lane came upon him so quickly that he did not even see the damned thing until it was alongside. It must have been going a hundred and forty, a hundred and forty-five miles an hour. That was the only explanation. Otherwise, on his ten-second sweeps of the rear he certainly would have seen it. The man beside the driver riding low, hunched over, looked at Wulff for a bleak instant as the car, decelerating, hung alongside the Fleetwood. Then he said something to the driver.

The Mercedes spun ahead and screamed across Wulff's left front fender. The idea of course was to make him brake so abruptly that the Fleetwood would rear out of control, then a quick fishtail of the Mercedes, a quick cut left, storming back then into the passing lane would finish up the job. It was an old maneuver; Wulff had done it himself on patrol quite a few times although never to kill. There you did it to bring some drunk to his senses and to a crawl but the fishtailing motion was the real killer. That you never did. You stayed in front of them and braked them down quickly, but turning your right rear into a battering ram: that was the killer.

All of this he was able to judge and calculate in a frozen fraction of a second. He knew exactly what they were trying to do; the question was whether he had the reflexes and the experience to overcome before he passed over the point of losing control. At eighty-five miles an hour in a Fleetwood that point came up very fast. He hit the brakes to the floor with all his strength, making the car scream and hurling himself against the wheel but in the next instant he released the brakes totally so that the car sprung back. He fell against the seat, holding the wheel desperately, having picked up six or seven feet of clear space behind the Mercedes. All of this had taken perhaps a half a second.

The car was trying to fishtail now, the driver reaching the accelerator to the floor to pick up the necessary power. The Mercedes itself had braked down to about fifty or sixty miles an hour to get into lane and boiling down like this in just a matter of seconds must have shaken the driver too, enough so that his only impulse was to get to the floor and get the car *out* of the sudden pocket as quickly as possible. But even as the Mercedes was looking for speed and passage to the left, Wulff was deep on the gas himself. He pulled the Fleetwood into the left lane and pedal to the floor ran up alongside the Mercedes.

He did not have half the power or suspension of the other car; it was only surprise that had gotten him this far, surprise on the part of the other driver and his own quick reaction in not slamming the brakes but *stabbing* them, meaning that the Fleetwood was still under power and in control at a time when by the Mercedes' calculations it should already have been looking for an exit hatch from the road—the fishtail would only finish the job. But that would mean nothing unless he was able to capitalize on the surprise. He tried to literally drive the accelerator through the floorboards. The Fleetwood, screaming, did the best it could. He got it in one whining explosion above its control limit, one hundred and five miles an hour.

Now he was slightly past the Mercedes, he had an impression of astonishment in the other car, the passenger his mouth open distended, almost screaming, the driver risking a quick sidelong glance of absolute shock. What the hell was the Fleetwood doing *there?* the driver wanted to know. Wulff had almost the same question but he was not going to push his luck. So far the car was handling. If it did not continue to handle he would be no worse off than he would have been otherwise.

This had taken no more than five seconds. Now he perilously worked the Cadillac forward, trying to gain a car-length on the Mercedes. He could not outrun that other car on a straightaway, couldn't come close. He was capitalizing, he hoped, only on the driver's shock. If the driver realized in the next second or two that the Mercedes was in no worse position than it had been when this began, that he could accomplish his deadly work as easily from the *right* lane as the left, and Wulff would be finished. He would not have a second chance at this.

But the driver was not thinking. For too long he had probably depended upon the wonderful resources of this car and the panic of his victims; left to his own devices he could not handle the situation. Wulff, at a hundred and ten miles an hour got his car-length. Got a little more. He could see the puffs of dust and fumes rising from under the Mercedes even as he inhaled once, tightened his lips and took the wheel hard right, got in front of the Mercedes and before he had even established himself in that lane cut it left.

He felt a shudder roll from the left rear of the Fleetwood all the way through his buttocks to his knees and then he was moving away in the left lane again, the Mercedes dropping far, far behind, in two seconds already down ten car lengths and then he saw the car wobble, begin to leave the road and start a long, long roll through the frail guardrail and out into the flatlands beyond. He braked the Cadillac down and turned, watched the car take six or seven revolutions and then, almost lazily explode. Then he was back behind the wheel: driving, driving, and the Mercedes, bit by bit, was out of sight and his life. And the driver and passenger out of theirs.

There was nothing to think. It might have been Severo, treacherous, putting these people on him. It might have been any freelancer in the area looking for a boost in the hierarchy. Or it might have been someone from New York, flown out to do his specialty.

Then again, it might be some fool who liked to go out on the parkways and kill people.

He was pretty sure he would never know. It did not matter. Wulff put it out of his mind within five minutes and just kept on rolling back toward San Francisco.

You could almost call it part of the hazards of trying to do his business.

X

Tamara was not in the apartment when he returned, but she had left him a note. AVENGER—she had written—I FEEL BETTER AND AM GOING OUT FOR A WALK. STAYED UNDERGROUND FOR TWO HOURS AS PROMISED AND CHECKED CAREFULLY BEFORE GOING OUTSIDE BUT ALL LOOKS CLEAR. WILL BE BACK LATER TONIGHT. HAVE NOWHERE ELSE TO GO YOU SEE. HOPE YOU WILL BE HERE. IF NOT TOUGH LUCK. The note was held between two coffee cups, half-filled, in the kitchen. He shook his head, almost smiled, and ditched it.

It did not matter; he might even want to see her but now all he wanted to do was sleep. There was too much in the past, too much coming up, somewhere in between the two of these Wulff had to sleep.

He had taken care of the Fleetwood half a mile from here. Putting it any nearer would have been stupid; if Severo was indeed bound on treachery, and Wulff thought he might be, then the Fleetwood would be a dead lead to him. Trotto and Ferguson had tracked him once through a car; better people, the first string, would be coming now. So the Fleetwood lay a long way from here, the keys dangling from the ignition, the license plates stripped and thrown into a sewer. If he was lucky, and Wulff thought that his luck might hold on this one, a couple of kids would hit the car and take it far down the freeways before he had even walked back to the apartment. So much for the Fleetwood then. It had been a good car, it had saved his life, despite its poor suspension and essential unresponsiveness, when he had needed it, but he was damned if he was going to get sentimental about it at this time. If the kids who came along to steal it had any sense they would strip the thing blind before they ditched it themselves.

The Galaxie was more easily taken care of; he drove it five blocks away, pulled the plates from that one as well and just left it. A stolen-car alarm would go out from the rental agency of course but he doubted if he would have to worry much about that. He had rented it on a false credit card, no supporting documents had been asked for. It was amazing in this credit society exactly what you could get away with if you could present a card, any kind of a card, with the right expiration date. And getting hold of the card through false information had been as easy as hell, too. All that you had to do, it seemed, was to send in the request in the mail and ask for it. They didn't care; like the junk merchants the credit-card companies were willing to move the stuff any way they could.

So he went to sleep. Wulff went to sleep. He secured all the doors, although not with the chainlock which would have kept Tamara out; he took off his clothes, stripped the bed and laid on it. Ghostly, her perfume and body odor stalked from the sheets to envelop him, but he discarded this. He would not be moved by the girl. If she came back, she came back. She was object, not subject....

Wulff slept. He slept in the secured room and he dreamed of junk. Junk was everywhere; it was all through the nation. The country was a huge vein and the dealers and businessmen were shooting it up. The junkies were hooked into that vein, they were deep to the center of the country, but the dealers and businessmen were not what you would call slouches either. Everybody was getting theirs. Everybody was getting theirs off the system while the junkies died and the cities wept. The system was paying everybody off in kind, the suppliers were getting one kind of return and the enforcers another, and the pimps in the administration creating jobs for themselves at ten to the minute were picking up the pieces and only the junkies were paying any kind of price. They kept the whole thing going by dying. The cities did their share by collapsing. But that only meant that you could appoint experts to study the fate of the cities so that part was all right too. Nobody was paying except people who, if you had enough money to wall yourself off from, you didn't even have to look at....

In the middle of the dream of the devastated country, Wulff was awakened into what seemed, for a moment, to be another dream. There was a girl against him and she was holding him tightly. Her clothes were off, she was naked to the bone and he could feel her skin, her hair, her breasts, take in the rising smell of her. The girl was touching his cheek with her lips and she was talking to him. Wulff struggled against the shell of the dream, trying to shatter it open so that he could clamber out, and then he found that he was not dreaming and that Tamara was against him.

"You came back," she said.

He felt her against him. He had taken off his own clothes to sleep and the pressure of her body was maddening. He could feel her then, and despite himself, could feel his own response. With it there was a kind of horror because he remembered another girl who had died in a room. "No," he said, "no."

"Quiet," she said, "it's all right."

"No. It isn't all right."

"Yes it is," she said. She moved her lips down his cheek to the panels of his neck and began to stroke him below. "Quiet," she said.

He thought of the other girl in that room of months past and the coldness started to run like fire from his belly, moving up and down, gripping him in fingers of shame. "Please," he said, "no."

"I want to," she said. "I want to, it's all right, stop it, lie back, sleep, do what you were doing," and he could not struggle against her any more. Her fingers, soft, were insistent as well. She gripped him.

The grip brought back to him feelings that he thought had perished in New York. He was a dead man. Had he not told this to all of them? He was dead and could not be killed again, yet here was this girl and she would not let him die. He battered like a bird against the wall of self. Against himself, he felt himself rising.

"Yes," she said, "yes, yes, it's all right."

"It isn't all right," he said again, "it isn't, it isn't," but in command all day he felt control slipping from him now, felt the situation heave and then like water draining, felt the initiative pass from him to her. He was struggling, but no longer with conviction; she was working on him, but no longer with doubt. He felt her breasts against him; saw them for the first time, full, pouting, contrite, the breasts of a woman, and he reached for them. He could no longer stop himself. She turned and suddenly he was inside her.

"Slowly," she said, stronger than he. "Slowly."

And so he worked on her slowly; feeling the engorgement which was at first merely a memory but then took him to the present time; so quickly the months fell away like ash and he was once again locked into present time, seeking her. Seeking this other woman. He pressed himself into her and felt himself being drawn slowly through and out the other side of her. She was wringing him dry.

"Slowly," she said again. Her eyes fluttered underneath him. He reared over her and found himself looking at her, eye to eye, as if from a great distance and he broke his rhythm, arched himself, followed her will, let her lead him. He reached his hands to her breasts and stroked them. It was at first like a foreign substance; he had not touched a woman's breasts in so long that he had forgotten the feel of them, the soft, gelatinous wobble, but then memory and the present moment intersected and he found himself at last ready to function. He leaned down, bit at her breast, felt her rhythm increase.

"Now," she said, "you can do it now. Do it, *do* it," and very expertly, carefully, began to curse to excite him. She said every foul expression that he had ever heard looking up at him through those carefully ingenuous eyes. "Come on," she said, "come *on.*"

He was there, he was almost there, he was getting close, he felt himself unbidden leaping to fall into her and then orgasm overtook him finally. Like gears finally meshing on a car that had lain abandoned for months. He poured into her, furious and gasping, and reciprocally she came back at him. He felt her muscles tense and then she was open and free, plunging, her teeth biting into his cheek. Her words broke into little empty moans and sounds and he held her shoulders tightly, rode with her.

Finally it was done.

He rolled from her, curiously contented. He had not thought that he would be; it was surprising how good he felt. With the ease was a spreading pool of guilt, because he did not think, could not have thought, that he would have been able to have a woman after being dead. Dead men did not fuck. Nevertheless he had. It was an interruption in his calculations and might change the situation. But he would not worry about that now. For a few moments in the dead-center of what was going to happen to him he would permit himself to be at peace. There was enough time to think about this later.

"That was good," she said. "That was the first time I've come in months, do you know that?"

"If you say so."

"I thought that I could never come again, but it was very easy. Maybe it's just being off speed for a day. Do you know this is the first time—"

"All right," Wulff said. Unbidden, his mind was already racing ahead. He had an appointment to keep, things were happening almost out of control. And he would need a good deal of equipment to take down to the Bay....

"I don't even know your name," she said. "I still don't know your name."

"Yes," he said, "all right." He wanted to lie with her in this bed, talk with her, tell her who he was and even, unreasonably, what he was doing, but his instincts were against it. He could feel the instincts thrashing like snakes underneath the surface.

"No time," he said. He sat on the bed. "Later."

"Later?"

"We've got to get out of here," Wulff said, "it's not safe anymore. I tell you—"

She looked at him, her mouth opening. "What's wrong?" she said, "is something going to happen now?"

"I don't know. I think so." He thought of Severo, of letting Severo go, of the Mercedes on the freeway, of men beginning to come out of the corridors now to take their shots at him, one by one and then in groups.

Open season. Open season on the wolf. "Get your clothes," he said.

She came alert against him immediately. Give her that, this girl was no fool. In fact, out of the haze of drugs, her purpose and sense of self-preservation might have been as significant as his. "All right," she said.

"Quickly," Wulff said, "quickly," filled with a desperate sense of urgency which sex had only heightened. He bolted from the bed, seized his own clothing, began to get dressed with the same fury and economy of motion with which, not five minutes before, he had possessed her. Tamara was already into her pants, pulling them up, walking awkwardly within them across the room to seize her sweater.

"What happens now?" she said.

"I don't know," Wulff said, seizing the pistol and then putting it near him on the bed as he pulled on his shirt. "Do you understand that? I just don't know."

"You're in a lot of trouble, aren't you?" she said.

"More than you think."

He heard a clattering sound on the staircase. Someone was moving up very quickly, very quietly but you couldn't trust these old rooming houses, something unsteady on the staircase, he had slipped. They were closer than he thought. No time to order himself, he lunged for the pistol—

And the door burst open.

Two men came in, holding guns, plunging on them. The accident on the staircase had probably made them decide to discard caution; they had made their presence known so they might as well make their move. They were short, heavy types. Wulff was sure he had never seen either of them before. One of them raised his gun. He aimed at Wulff and fired.

Tamara screamed. As pointless as his own ducking motion. If the man had been on target that would have been the end of it right there. But anxiety, haste, shortness of breath from the climb, any one of a number of things had thrown him off. The bullet struck into the wall above Wulff's head with terrific force. He felt the plaster sifting down on him, coating him.

He raised his gun and fired just as the other man, the one who had come in second rushed him full out. The tactic succeeded. Wulff felt himself hurtling over the shoulder, striking the floor hard, a jolting contact that almost blew the gun out of his hand. But it did not. He held onto the gun and shot the first man, the one with the poor aim, in the leg.

The man screamed and went over. Tamara screamed again, her hands rising to her face. She was trying to cover herself. Assertion had given way to panic. Wulff levelled his gun at the man who had rushed him. He had a pure, blank second to level; this man apparently had forgotten that he was holding a revolver. His rush through the door meant that he wasn't comfortable with a gun in his hand. That gave him a little time.

He shot this man in the forehead. He went down instantly, circuitry of blood sprouting from his head. For one instant he seemed to be in inexpressible pain; he seemed to be trying to say something. Too late. He died.

Wulff went back to the one on the floor. But that one had moved. Injured leg and all he had staggered to his feet and embraced Tamara. He was holding the girl tightly against him now and with an extended arm was trying to point his gun.

Wulff shot the gun out of his hand. The target was too easy to miss. It smashed against the wall and came spinning to a point underneath the window. But the man held on. He had Tamara clutched against him now in a desperate bear hug. The girl was beginning to discolor.

"Help," she said weakly. Her eyes rolled. It had all happened too quickly for her. She looked as if she was about to faint.

"Let her go," Wulff said.

"Are you crazy?" the man said in a thick, foreign-sounding voice. "She's my ticket out of here." He must have moved his leg then; he screamed in a surprised, feminine-sounding way. "You hurt me you son of a bitch," he said, "now drop your gun."

"Let the girl go. She has nothing to do with this."

"Fuck you," the man said. He clutched her more tightly. Tamara's cheeks puffed. "You son of a bitch, you killed Willie."

"Willie was going to kill me."

"You dirty bastard," the man said almost as if he were complaining. "This was supposed to be an easy job. Where did you come from?"

Wulff concentrated levelled the gun. But the man was clever; he had the girl flat and hard against him like a plank of wood. There was simply no area at which he could risk a shot. She was taller than he if not as wide. He could try to squeeze off a shot into his ribs but one anticipatory flick and the girl would take it in the heart.

"Let her breathe," Wulff said, "let her breathe or I'll shoot anyway. You're going to suffocate her."

Understanding seemed to penetrate the man's eyes. Subtly he relaxed his grip on Tamara. He felt the rasping intake of her breath more than he heard it and color seemed to return. She was crying.

"I'm going to take this girl out of here," the man said, "her and me down the stairs."

"With that leg? Are you kidding? You take one step and it'll go out from under."

"You shot me in the *leg*," the man said. Like the issue of Willie's death, it seemed that he was rediscovering it. The only reason that Wulff was here was because both of these men were profoundly stupid. Couldn't Severo find better personnel than this? Or were they free-lancers, looking for a bounty? Everybody was going to come at him now.

"You need help," Wulff said calmly. He felt edges retract, felt suddenly in control. The worst that could happen was that all of them in this room were going to die. It was too bad that Tamara was part of it but this had been her decision. "That's a fast-flowing wound. You could bleed to death."

In confirmation, the man looked down at his leg. The blood was coming out of a vein in the calf like milk being wrenched from a container; staining rivulets of it already flowing into the panels of the floor. "You son of a bitch," he said.

"Please help me," Tamara said, breath back in her. She sounded as she had the first time he had seen her; in that other damned room. "He's hurting me. He's—"

"I'm trying," Wulff said quietly. "I'm doing what I can. You have to stay calm."

"Your cunt," the man said, his face twisting. "Tell your cunt to stay calm."

"Quiet," Wulff said. He felt a shroud of detachment settling over him. He had literally nothing to lose. Tamara was dead, the man was dead, all of them were gone anyway. Anything that happened was a benefit.

"I'm going to walk this cunt over to the stairs," the man said, "and I'm going to take her downstairs and into a car and you're going to let us go. She's going to be wrapped around me all the time, just like she was wrapped around you."

"I can't be hurt anymore," Tamara said, "I just can't be hurt; I've had too much."

"Do what he says, Tamara."

"You're going to let him take me out of here?"

"We're in a bad position. I have no choice."

"You can't do this to me. You can't."

"Yes he can," the man said. He began to lead her with difficulty toward the door, stumbling. "He's going to go along with me because he has nothing else."

"That's right," Wulff said soothingly. He allowed the gun to fall, let the man's eyes follow it, "I have no choice."

"We're going to get into that car and drive away," the man said, "if you try anything I'll kill you." He extended an arm behind him, pulled the door open, the maw of the hallway seeming to leap toward them, "and then I'll figure out what to do with you."

"I thought you cared," she said. "I thought you cared for me."

"He doesn't care for anyone, cunt. He doesn't even care for himself. All he wants to do is to get out of this alive. You shot Willie. You shot him down. You're going to pay for this."

The man backed Tamara into the frame of the door. Wulff let the pistol hang by his side. He felt the weight of it dragging him clear up into the neck muscles. The girl's eyes were open, desperate. She was right. She had not been lying to him. She had been hurt too much; she could not take any more. And the odds were that she would never get in or out of that car alive.

"Come on, cunt," the man said. He increased the pressure; Wulff could see the blackening start in Tamara's face again. He was cutting down her wind. Her physical reserves were almost exhausted; he saw her begin to slide toward unconsciousness again. No. Do not warn him.

He stepped her into the door, retreated toward the hall. The man was in even worse shape than Wulff had figured; the leg bleeding more freely now with the slight motion, his balance precarious. He would probably never make it down those steps, not carrying the girl. He would stumble, pitch and fall before he ever got to the street. What would the difference be, however? The fall could kill Tamara as easily as a gunshot. The odds were only slightly improved.

Her face convulsed, mouth fell open. Her eyes seemed to hang from her head. She collapsed in the man's arm, unconscious, slumped forward slightly.

The weight pulled him off balance. That and the leg were too much, he could not handle the alteration. He stumbled, shifted a leg, grabbed for purchase on the floor. Tamara's leg locked behind him.

He swayed. She slid forward exposing an open area of his chest.

It was enough. Wulff raised the revolver and fired.

The man died slowly. First he weaved like a dancer in front of him. Tamara, his partner fell away, fell away, hitting the rug in a heap. The man clutched at his chest as if stricken by heartburn. He began to babble.

Wulff did not have the patience to watch him die slowly. He fired the gun again and hit the man in the forehead. Powder spilled from the gun. He smelled kerosene at the center of the report.

The man groaned, made a watery sound, flipped backward over the staircase. He fell straight down, a plummet. Wulff heard him hit on the next landing, bounce and begin to roll.

He left the stairs as he had mounted them, then, off-balance, scattering.

He knelt over Tamara. There was no sound within the rooming house. There never was when anything like this happened. Rooming houses were for the kind of people who had long since adapted to their lives, if they had adapted at all, by denying anything outside of them. They were people who had found surviving difficult, either because they could not come to terms with the world at all or because the coming to terms had hurt them terribly at sometime in the past and now they simply wanted no part of it.

Either way, Wulff guessed, he could set off a bomb in his rooms and as long as it failed to bring down the quarters of the various roomers, they would stay inside.

He knelt over the girl. Once again her respiration was smoothing out. She was coming around. Healthy, vigorous, for all the abuse that this body had taken, she would get it started again. Wulff at that moment felt all of his thirty-two years. Thirty-two was not so much older than twenty-three, not really, but it was at another stage of life altogether. He just could not take what he used to, what these children were routinely taking now. Maybe it was a kind of evolution. The drug culture was breeding, by elimination, a frame which before it ran out altogether could hold up almost anything. He could never have taken, even in his twenties, what this girl had. He knew that.

She stirred, opened her eyes. Alertness, intelligence returned. "He's gone?" she said.

He nodded. "He's dead," he said, "he's somewhere down on the next landing or the one below that and he's dead."

"Too much death," she said, shaking her head. "There's too much death."

"We've got to get out of here," Wulff said. "There's a dead man in those rooms too. We can't stay now. We have to leave."

"Why?" she whispered, "why—"

"I can't explain," he said, kneeling by her. "There's just no time. There's no time at all."

"Everybody wants to kill you," she said, "why does everybody want to kill you?"

"Because I'm dangerous," he said, "because I'm digging in closer to them than anyone has for a long time." No time to talk now. He took her thin wrist, prodded her, rose. She came to her feet and fell against him heavily, licking her dry lips. She reached out toward the wall weakly, then balanced herself.

"I can't take much more of this," she said.

"I know," said Wulff. "We're getting out of here. Is there someplace you can go now?"

She looked at him. "What do you mean?"

"Someplace safe you can stay. I don't mean another crash pad and I don't mean back wherever you've been. Do you have a family? Do you have parents?"

Her eyes narrowed, seemed to calculate. "I did," she said, "it was a long time ago."

"How long?"

"Six months. Six, seven months."

"You've got to go back," Wulff said. He pulled her into the room. The corpse lay there in a solemn pile, unblinking. She gasped and covered her face, then slowly drew her hands down, past her cheeks and held them on her chest.

"I can look at it," she said. "I've seen death before."

"I don't want you to see any more now. You've got to go back home."

She shook her head. "I want to come with you."

"You can't."

"Why?" she said.

"Because you see what's happening. This is the way it's going to be from now on, right through to the end of my life. You can't stay. The next time we won't be so lucky. It's happened twice already."

"Why don't you stop?" she said. "Whatever you're doing, can't you stop it, can't you get out of it before it's too late?"

He felt her touch against him and the touch made him think about that, if only for an instant. "No," he said then, "I can't."

"You're the avenger, you mean."

"I don't know what I am," Wulff said. He left her standing there, went to the closet, took down his one suitcase, reached again, seized the attaché case. "It doesn't matter what I am either just as long as I don't take you all the way down with me."

"You saved my life twice."

"I only saved your life because I put you in situations where I almost got you killed," he said grimly. "It can't go on this way. I think your gratitude is misdirected."

She looked at him. Beneath the wall he could see feeling in her eyes. "You're really serious, aren't you?" she said. "Whatever you're doing, you won't stop."

"No, I won't."

"You *can't* stop, is that it?"

He nodded once. "Something like that," he said. "Come on, this isn't going to last here. We aren't safe here anymore. We never were."

She stepped over the corpse delicately, however, went to the window and looked out. This was a girl who could adjust to anything. "I won't forget this room," she said, "I won't forget you."

"All right."

"Will I see you again?"

He looked at her, paused. "If I get out of this, maybe," he said, "maybe you'll see me again. But I won't be out of it for a long time."

"Being the avenger is a full time job, isn't it?"

His voice sounded strange to him. "It isn't a job," he said. "It's a pleasure."

"That too," she said, "I knew that."

"Will you go back to your parents?"

"I never thought I would. They'll ask me questions. They'll ask a lot of questions. They're not people who can just accept—"

"So tell them. Tell them what they want to know. You've got to be safe for a while."

"And tell them about you?"

"If you want. It doesn't make any difference at all."

He hoisted the suitcase, the attaché bag. "Let's get out of here," he said then.

She turned from the window, stepped back over the dead man and took his arm. "This is ridiculous," she said, "this is the most ridiculous thing I've ever lived. There's a dead man in this room and another one downstairs and ten minutes ago they were going to kill us and now I'm going to walk out of here as if it doesn't matter. Did you ever hear of anything like that in your life?"

He said, "Of course it doesn't make any difference. It doesn't make any difference to them so it can't to me. You just have to go on."

"But can people really live that way?"

"I can," he said. He led her to the door, they walked through. In the hallway she dropped his arm so that they could go down the stairs single file.

The man he had shot twice lay still at the second landing. His hand, clenched in death, was holding his shirtfront, pulling it straight up. His face looked much younger than Wulff had seen it before and seemed to be utterly at peace. For some of them, death indeed was a release.

He stepped over the body. The girl followed him. It was very quiet in the rooming house. No one was looking out at all. As long as events did not infringe upon their lives, these tenants could take anything. It was like the war or the drug business. *Business as usual, just don't touch me.*

He went outside. He had expected, ten minutes ago, never to see the light again but the sight of day did not impress him. Day and night, the landscape, it was just a background against which you carried out the acts of your life. Would the man named Willie have noticed the daylight streaming over Wulff's shoulder as he shot him?

Tamara came beside him. The street was very quiet. A car which probably had been the one in which the men had come was parked crosswise, front tires nestling against a telephone pole, over the curb. They had not expected to be very long, obviously. An old Plymouth, dented in on both sides. Probably bounty-hunters after all. Regular operatives would have driven a better car.

"I'm going to put you in a taxi," he said, "and get you out of here as quickly as possible. That's the best way."

"You'll find very few taxis around here," she said and then one turned the corner, coming up fast. Wulff waved at it, half-expecting that it was carrying someone who would again take a shot at him. But it was empty. The driver brought it to a halt, leaned out, a young bright-eyed man with a beard. All through the country it was a new breed of taxi-driver. The middle-aged men without hope were being phased out.

"I'd come with you," she said, "you know that."

"I know that."

"If you really wanted me to I'd come with you through it all. But you don't want me, do you?"

"No," he said.

"You don't want anyone."

"I want someone," Wulff said, "but she died sometime back and that was the end of that."

She moved toward the taxi. "Did I remind you of her?" she said.

"In a way."

"I thought so." She opened the door, then stopped. "Do you want to know where my parents live?" she said, "so you can get in touch with me when this is all over?"

"It will never be over."

"Do you want to know?"

"Yes," he said.

She told him. It was just numerals on an avenue in a suburb; it had no significance to him. But he knew he would remember it. "All right," he said. He reached into his pocket, took out his wallet. "Let me give you some money," he said.

"I don't want money."

"Don't be foolish; you can't even pay the taxi."

"I hate to break this up," the driver said, "but if it's all the same to you, I've got to make a living too." Wulff had sentimentalized him; once he began talking he sounded exactly like the middle-aged men.

"Here," Wulff said. He took out two hundred dollars and put it in her palm. It was all New York money anyway. Compliments of the great Northeast to the culture of Love. Tamara looked at it wonderingly.

"You make me feel cheap," she said, holding the bills, "that's all."

"No need," said Wulff, "you're not cheap at all."

"Oh no?" she said with a bitter smile, "you should only know what you don't know."

"You made me feel alive again," he said. He pushed her into the cab before the driver could make another protest. Then, on an impulse he would not try to understand or guide he leaned down and kissed her. He felt the cool surfaces of her forehead underneath his lips, touched her cheek once tentatively, moved away.

"I'll be in touch," he said. She ducked inside the cab. He slammed the door and the cab, steaming out little ropes of exhaust, moved away from there.

He stood there and watched her go. Sentiment had nothing to do with it, although he knew that if he gave into the feeling that was all there, moist liquid rolling inside him, he would never get out of the vat if once he opened the tap. No, this time it was not sentiment. He looked after her with wonder.

She had been with him for no more than a day. In that time she had seen him kill one man, watched him leave the room to kill two more, lived through a nearly-successful attempt on her life to see him kill yet another two. She had made love to him, pumped him dry, taken everything that had happened and at the end it was she who had comforted *him*.

She was one remarkable, tough broad and that was all there was to it.

And she had gone through all of this on the down-end of a speed cycle.

Too much. Too much. Wulff watched the taxi out of sight and then very slowly, checking his rear and sides, he trudged down the sidewalk after her. Where she could ride he could, for the moment, only walk. He took off his hat to her. Also his badge—if he still had a badge that is—and about thirty-two years of knowledge.

Remarkable. She was absolutely remarkable. She beat him cold.

He wondered if he would ever see her again.

XI

Severo felt the nervousness hit him again. He had felt pretty good behind the two locked doors making his calls and better yet when he had called in the reinforcements. Now he had the place absolutely locked up tight. This clown Wulff had almost gotten through to him because Severo had not taken the proper precautions, but that was mere sloppiness. It would not happen again. Now he had the situation absolutely under control. There was a cordon of the finest, toughest men anyone could command ringing the place and if anyone even thought of penetrating those defenses he was out of his mind. This Wulff had knocked over a steel townhouse in Manhattan, that was the story on him anyhow, but just let him try it here. Just let him try it. They would take his grenades and his incendiary devices and give them back, all of them, right up his ass.

But the nervousness was there. It was a little roaring fire in his belly which was being stoked, gradually but incessantly by little scraps of information. First was the word that he had somehow broken out, with the girl no less, of the miserable rooming house where he had been holed up. Then impossibly, he had not only gotten away from the Mercedes, which had figured since he had obviously gotten back to the room, but he had knocked the car off the road and had killed two men. And then there was the growing knowledge—and this was the worst of all because it had been building up in the back of his mind from all the other pieces—that he had given Wulff the right data on the shipment tomorrow night. Time and place, chapter and verse.

That had been his mistake. He should have concocted something else for the guy just as he had concocted the whole story of running out on the business. But how was he to think, once he talked his way out of this spot, that Wulff would be able to get away? If the guy was gullible enough to have fallen for that piece of shit song and dance which Severo had made up for him, then he was surely so dumb that they should have been able to have taken him out with one shot in a matter of hours.

Yet there was the guy now out of contact and by all rights he might well show up tomorrow night.

What it came down to, Severo admitted sourly, pacing the grounds restlessly outside, was that he had cracked. Severo had cracked. Under stress, the pressure and tension and knowledge that he was in the toughest spot of his life and that this guy Burt Wulff could actually, genuinely kill him, he had failed to invent details but instead had blurted out the whole story. It gave little credit to him, that was all. Severo, who thought that he was impermeable and knew all the moves, had buckled under the knife.

If something went wrong tomorrow night there was going to be all hell to pay. So far he had handled this right, he thought. It was all his own show and they were letting him call the shots on it since it was in his territory, but if the guy actually got through and fucked the deal up tomorrow, Severo was going to be in far more trouble than a lot of people above might think he was worth. There would be only one way, consequently, to deal with him then.

Severo didn't even want to think about it.

He jumped as he saw a large Cadillac come up the drive, heading toward him at least ten miles an hour faster than it had any business doing on his property, and then as the car swerved and slowed, he forced himself to relax. The men surrounding the place were absolutely trustworthy. They would let absolutely nothing through unless it had been checked out. Cursing himself for breaking open for the second time that day—but the first time in the study, crying, with all the doors closed could not count because no one could ever see him there—Severo strode toward the Cadillac, a car he had never seen before.

A tall man wearing dark glasses got out of the car on the driver's side. He was travelling alone. He took one step as if checking the ground and then waited, allowing Severo to come up to him.

Severo scuttled up to the tall man, aware as almost never before of his awkwardness, and stood there. The tall man who was wearing a heavy overcoat despite the comparative warmth. He looked at him, both hands in pockets, with seeming impassiveness.

"Yes?" Severo said, furious with himself again. This was his ground, his house, his terrain. What was he doing running up to this guy like a butler?

He should, by all rights, have been in the house, waiting for the guy to come to *him*. He was not himself. Godammit, he was falling apart and it all traced itself back to this Wulff. He was going to have to kill the son of a bitch himself to get any peace. All right. All right then. If that was the only way, he would do it.

"Severo?" the tall man said.

"Yes."

"Severo, you've done a piss-poor, fucked-up job."

"It's my job and I'll handle it my way," he said. "Who the hell are you—"

"You're no fucking good, Severo. You're smalltime. You're out here on the Bay because you're minor league, do you understand that?"

"I don't know what you're talking about," he said, although with a thrill of terror he realized that he knew exactly what the man was talking about. "You let me handle this my way all the way through to the end, and then tell me if you have any complaints." It did not sound like defiance. It sounded like the whining of a small boy.

"If you go on handling this your way, Severo, we'll all be six feet underground," the tall man said. He held himself lightly alert, hands still deep in pockets and Severo realized then exactly what he was doing and what was going to happen to him. But it was unfair. It was profoundly unfair. They had never even given him a chance.

"Get out of here," he said. "How the hell did you get through anyway? There's a roadblock—"

"You stupid fuck," the man said and he sounded almost pitying, "after all you've managed to do so far, do you really think we'd let you seal yourself up here with your own men? Who the hell do you think is out there?"

Severo turned to run but he could not. His frame was locked, body frozen. He had never been any good at this kind of thing anyway. He could talk his way out of a tight spot and he could put the screws on others but when it came down to a matter of body, he could not function. That was one of the reasons he had lived to seal himself in; why he did his business over the telephone.

He saw everything. He saw the dark man lift the gun out of his pocket, take careful aim and fire. For one instant Severo's heart and hands fluttered desperately, but almost instantly he relaxed. He was dead. He knew he was dead.

He began to realize how a woman must feel when she is about to be raped and realizes that there is nothing, absolutely nothing she can do to stop it. *Lay yourself back honey and just enjoy.* Death was coming out of the gun and he realized that he had wanted it, had always wanted it; it was one of the reasons why he had ordered so many others killed. Bringing to them what he had so terribly wanted for himself. The Golden Rule.

The man shot him in the heart and Severo staggered backward two steps and fell, a little flower or insect opening up in his chest, burrowing, burrowing away.

The dark man looked down upon him from a great height with an expression which Severo knew because it had been on his own face so very many times.

His last thought was that he hadn't really been lying to Wulff; when you came right down to it he hadn't been lying at all. He had always wanted to get out of the junk business.

Although not quite this way.

XII

Another hour, another room. Wulff wondered if this was what dealing with the junk business came down to: you lived in one miserable cell of a furnished room after another, the insides as interchangeable as the rage which was still beating away in his skull. One thing was sure: the merchants, the suppliers, the quiet men who stood at the top and away from all of this, *they* did not live in furnished rooms. They lived on estates or high floors or in sealed-up townhouses. Sometime, he decided, they should get down to the level of the enforcers or users and see what it was like to look at life from ground-level.

Then again, a lot of them had probably been there and were dedicating their lives to seeing as little of that reality as possible.

He got a little further into the downtown district, took a room there paying a week's rent in advance and went to cover there. There was nothing to do, really, until tomorrow night. Staying outside could only undercut his position; he was quite convinced now that it was open season on Wulff and that everyone, everyone who had the price of a rifle was on the trail. The two back there had been bounty hunters; the streets would be crawling with them. Which only indicated one thing, of course. A lot of people were getting desperate.

Still, there was one thing which he had to do and he decided to get it over with. Telephone facilities were not a specialty of this house so he made his long-distance phone call from an odorous little booth in a candy shop downstairs. The owner looked at him nervously through the open glass of the booth, a scuttling, nervous little man, probably a refugee—wasn't everyone in California?—from Brooklyn. From the traffic in the store and the way the owner kept on peering at him, Wulff decided that there was probably a small, not flourishing, numbers business being run out of this hole. All right. So what? What would a candy store be without a numbers operation? Nine-tenths of them would not be able to stay in operation for a week.

He called person-to-person collect. His party couldn't afford it either but it was less of a hassle than to wrestle with coins. Williams's wife got on and the operator got him through to Williams. Easier this way. He didn't have to talk to the woman. She was a nice woman, he supposed, but she could hardly have enjoyed her husband's involvement with Wulff.

David Williams had been the other patrolman in the car the night they took the call on Marie Calvante. He had come up the stairs after Wulff had not come out and for a minute had stood with Wulff, looking at the body, saying nothing. He must have known what had happened although Wulff had never discussed it with him.

He had thought that the black rookie patrolman was immature, naive, not really able to understand and deal with the reality which Wulff had recognized, but he guessed he had been wrong about that one at least. Williams had come to him in New York to offer his help with Wulff's war; the man had on his own figured out why Wulff had left the force and what he planned to do next. *I've got to stay inside the system,* Williams had said, *but that doesn't make it real and it doesn't mean that you're not doing it a better way. I can help you though. Let me help you.*

Williams had been sincere and he had meant business. Wulff had turned down the offer then, mostly because what he was doing was single-track, would have to keep on that way if he were to have any success at all, but Williams had nevertheless helped him at a crucial time by using the police department resources to dig up a detailed city survey on Peter Vincent's townhouse. He had used the plans to go in through the gas lines and destroy that townhouse, had pulled Peter Vincent out of the wreckage and before he killed him, gotten the information which had taken him to San Francisco. So Williams had helped. He had really helped. Maybe the man had a point: if you were going to go at it vigilante style it was always a good idea to have someone inside the system.

Williams got on the phone and in his high-pitched voice said hello. Wulff was running in luck for the first time since he had hit the Bay; the man could well have been on duty. Hours were irregular; there was no way as Wulff remembered well, to calculate even a week ahead which shift you'd be on. It led to a nice, ordered, regular, relaxed home-life is what it did, he thought bitterly, which was one of the reasons, until he had met a girl named Marie Calvante, he had thought that he would not marry until he retired.

"It's me," Wulff said.

"I figured it was you. I didn't think anyone else would be calling long-distance person to person. Man, where are you? What have you been up to? You took New York by storm and then you left."

"Oh? What happened?"

"You blew up that townhouse, didn't you?" Williams seemed to giggle. "Man, I could get into some trouble if I was associated with *that* one. There are rumors that you have singlehandedly cut the traffic in half here."

"That's good."

"You're shaking up a lot of people, but you are playing some dangerous game."

"I never expected anything else."

"Where are you now?" Williams asked.

He had to trust the man. There had to be at least one person around who you could trust; also he needed help. He risked a cautious glance through the glass of the booth, observed that traffic in the candy store had suddenly become very brisk. Three juveniles had come in and were conversing sullenly with the proprietor, hands in pockets. It occurred to him that wedged in the booth as he was he was an inviting, open target: he would have to watch this. "I'm in San Francisco," he said.

"Beautiful San Francisco. So then what?"

"I need some help," Wulff said, "some information."

"I'd love to oblige but I can't fly out to San Francisco just tonight. If I had known—"

"It's all right," Wulff said. "I told you in New York, this is a singlehanded operation at least for a while. I don't want to involve you or see you get hurt. Not now, anyway. Maybe later—"

"Cut that," Williams said. "Tell me what you want."

"I want to buy some explosives," Wulff said, "and I didn't think that the thing to do was to go into the Yellow Pages. I want you to find out particulars for me."

Williams on the continental line laughed. "You are *seized* by that idea," he said. "Don't tell me you are planning to do in San Francisco what you did here?"

"Something like that," Wulff said cautiously. The juveniles had now ringed the proprietor whose glasses glittered faintly in the reflecting light. They seemed to be pushing him while at the same time talking in low intense voices. Good Lord, had he walked into the middle of a robbery or worse? Any second they were going to notice him in this booth and then what?

"I just don't know," Williams was saying. "You want a legitimate source of supply?"

"Yeah, if possible. But I'll take it any way I can," Wulff said. "That's up to you."

"And where am I supposed to get this information?"

"A New York cop can get hold of anything," Wulff said, which in a way was the truth. He thought quickly of his days on the narcotics squad. Yes indeed, there was nothing you couldn't get hold of if you were willing.

"Well, I'll see what I can see," Williams said sounding doubtful. "Where am I supposed to reach you on this?"

"You're not," Wulff said. "I'll phone you back." The scene outside had taken a completely ominous turn. The proprietor had sunk completely out of eye-level and two of the youths were leaning over him. The third was watching the front and back in a quick reconnaissance and as he did his eyes fell across the booth and Wulff.

"I'll call you back in two hours," Wulff said rapidly and hung up. He put a finger on the handle, poised against the door then, looking at the kid.

The kid had already turned and was quickly telling the others what he had seen. Wulff hesitated for only an instant before pulling the handle into the booth. There was a bad moment, bringing the door against him as he was, when he was wedged *into* the booth and exit would have been impossible but he got past that point and came out quickly, reaching for his gun.

The kids appeared to have no weapons. It was an intimidation kind of thing. They were going in barehanded, which meant on the one hand that they were clever because carrying made it armed robbery right away, but they were stupid in that they were not prepared for emergencies. Wulff had the gun out and levelled on the nearest one even before they could complete the turn. The circle broke open and he could see the proprietor lying on the floor, a small, fine spider of blood coming from his bald scalp.

"Let's get out of here!" one of them said and the three of them went for the door. The gun, as always, had made the balance; if they had not seen the gun they probably would have jumped him. In his condition they would have had a good chance too. He held the gun as they ran for the door, debating for a long, agonized instant and then he let them go. They thudded into the street. He wanted to shoot them, in fact he wanted to kill, but it was just not worth it. It would get him involved at a level that now, with much greater stuff on the line, he could not afford to take.

He knelt over the old man on the floor quickly, checked him out. The man had little apparent damage, no skull fracture, and even as Wulff prodded him gently he regained consciousness. He looked up at Wulff with dread leaking from the pores of the old seamed face.

"Don't," he said, "please don't—"

"It's all right. You're all right."

"Take anything. Take everything. Just don't hit me again."

Too complicated. He could stay knelt there and explain to the old man that he was his rescuer, not an assailant, but what was the point? The old man would survive this one; in two days or two months the three kids or another group would come in hunting again, but nothing to be done about that. Once you were knocked over you were meat on the rack. Wulff stood. The old man saw the gun dangling from his hand and began to whimper. He rolled on the floor, hands crossed in front of his face.

"Please," he said, "don't shoot. I'm seventy-three years old; I'm going to die soon anyway. It's not as if I'll live a long life—"

Wonderful. Wulff turned and ran from the store. In San Francisco as in New York, junk had changed everything: this old man felt that he was going into the combat zone every morning when he unlocked his candy store. Nothing was being held in place any more. Everything was falling apart. He bolted into the street. A small crowd had already gathered; as they saw him then, the gun still unconsciously in his hand, the urgency in his gestures, they scattered, screaming. He raced through them. In the distance he heard a siren.

The old man, apparently not injured seriously at all, had gotten to his feet and was at the door. "Stop him!" He shouted, "stop him, *stop him!*" Thirty seconds ago he had begged for mercy, gotten it, now he wanted Wulff arrested. That was gratitude for you.

Nothing to do. He turned and ran. Disgust filled him with every intake of breath. It was not enough to have every clown, bounty hunter and hit man in the area crawling after him. That was not satisfying enough. He needed, it seemed, more attention yet. Now he would have the cops too. Because he had happened to make a phone call from the right place.

Never say that he would lead a lonely existence. *Shit,* Wulff thought. He ran. He turned a corner, putting the gun away in full stride. The siren was closer but approaching from the other direction.

Scream of tires and that patrol car had braked. In the distance he heard another siren, different direction. Then another. People on the street looked at him with curiosity. He forced himself to return to a normal pace, turned another corner, moved out of there.

More sirens. Every cop in town was going to get in on this one. The Severos, it seemed, could carry on their lives without harassment, but when you got down to the really important stuff like a candy store being knocked off, the cops were out in force. They would take all credit for averting the robbery.

Police work was always very good at mopping-up after the deed had been done. The police might not prevent crime but they sure as hell could catalogue it. Wulff, at normal stride, walked the five blocks back to his new rooming house cursing. There was no question about it; events were running at a flood. He wondered if he was still, in the last analysis, being a cop: attracting and creating crimes rather than eliminating them.

XIII

Forty miles north of there eight men sat at a table, some of them with hands clasped, listening to a ninth at the head who was talking. The speaker was almost indistinguishable in appearance from the others, yet he was listened to with the kind of attention which bespoke power. Some of the men at the table, in fact, found it impossible to confront him at eye level but instead like nervous students stared at their fingers or the floor intermittently.

"This thing has been completely fucked up," the man whose name was Anthony said. *Anthony, never Tony and leave my last name out of this altogether.* "I don't like it."

He paused; the men shifted, looked at one another uncomfortably. "Can anyone explain this?" Anthony said.

There was another long, thick pause after which one of the men at the end of the table finally said, "It was just something that kind of got out of hand. We weren't really warned—"

"What do you mean you weren't warned?" Anthony said in a deadly voice, "there was a memo put out on this man which all of you in this room received."

"He came so fast," the man who had spoken said unhappily, "it just happened so fast—"

"This is intolerable," Anthony said quietly. "This man should not have lasted here for half an hour. He's managed to stay around for a lot longer than that. And now he knows far more than he ever ought to."

"Severo," a small man nearer the head of the table whispered, "Severo."

"Severo has been taken care of," Anthony said. "Nicholas Severo will not trouble us anymore, and in due course arrangements for the succession will be made. In the meantime however, the late Severo turned over enough information to our friend Wulff to put us in real trouble. Now I'm not here to talk, I'm here to listen. We've got a shipment moving in here tonight that might be worth more than a million dollars and which we've worked on for months." He paused and looked at them one by one along the table. "Do we call it off?" he said.

No one answered. Men mumbled, licked their lips, shuffled feet. They might have been a group of junior copywriters being questioned by a vice president on the failure of a campaign. If Anthony was there to listen, not to talk, they found it hard to believe.

Anthony rubbed his palms together and just for a moment the rage came through the blank surfaces of his cheeks. "There's a question on this table," he said, "and I want it answered. Do we call off this shipment?"

The man who had spoken first said, "No, I don't think we should." He seemed to shudder with the audacity of this and turned from Anthony.

"That's good," Anthony said, "at last we have an answer. We have a respondent, an answerer. Why shouldn't we call it off? A million dollar shipment in which five hundred men and half a year have been tied up and which we could lose if we don't take it tonight. Tell me why we should go ahead."

The man realized, finally, that Anthony was waiting for him to say something. "Because we'll have everything covered," he said unhappily. "We'll have it ringed with a hundred men if necessary, full arsenal, everything. He may know where it is and what's happening, but he just won't be able to get by. There's no way he can get by. If he shows up there we'll kill him."

"Ah," Anthony said, "that's fine. You'll kill him."

"Well, he can't stop things from going through," the man said defensively, spreading his hands. "How the hell is he going to stop us? If he exposes himself he'll be a sitting duck. I tell you, this thing is going to be ringed."

"Don't you think he'll know that?" Anthony said quietly.

The man jerked in his chair, shook his head. Being the speaker had definitely been the wrong idea, he seemed to realize; it had given Anthony a target. The other seven looked straight ahead, seemed quite glad that the speaker had taken them at least momentarily off the hook. Any one of the hundreds of people who lived and died by these eight men would have been surprised to see them now. Terror seemed to ooze from the close, dense spaces of the room.

"I suppose he'll figure that out," the man said.

"So we've got a lunatic at large," Anthony said. "This guy has killed at least ten men, some of them important. He's starting to hit us the way he did New York."

The speaker seemed to decide that in for a dollar was the same as in for a dime at this point. "I think he'll show," he said.

"You do?"

"Yes I do. I think that he'll try to take it over. He's gone too far to stop now. He's serious about this business of his, that much we know. He won't be stopped by thinking about the security."

"A dedicated man," Anthony said dryly.

"That's right. We don't know much about him yet, but I think we know that."

Anthony shook his own head and stood. He looked down the table, a slow, hot light coming from his eyes, and the men seemed to quiver and shrink further yet. The one who had spoken became interested in his hands, looked at them with seeming fascination.

"All right," he said, "we'll go through with it. But you're being held personally responsible. All of you in this room."

No one said anything. Anthony put his palms flatly on the table, leaned forward.

"Things in the Bay area have been fucked around for a long time," he said. "We let you get away with a lot of things mostly because we're interested in cool and quiet, and you had us convinced that if anything out of order came along you could handle it."

He paused. "But you can't handle it," he said. "This is the first crisis and all of you lose. When you came up against it you couldn't handle it."

He moved toward the door. "So you're making it necessary for us to consider a whole new series of arrangements," he said, "which we probably should have done a long time ago. But first you've got one more chance. We're letting you handle this one. That shipment goes *through* and that man is taken care of tonight—both of those conditions—and we'll forget about this. Any fucking up," he said flatly, looking at each, one by one in the eye until the men shook like flowers and folded under, "and you'll all end up like Severo."

Anthony opened the door and walked out, not closing it. The eight men sat there for a while not looking at one another, each slumped in some personal meditation.

Then, one by one and quietly, they got up and left until the room was now empty, only the sound and shape of Anthony's words still hanging, like poisoned vapors, in the air.

XIV

Wulff picked up the stuff in mid-afternoon at an obscure little shop downtown. Williams for all his doubts had fantastic leads. From the front it looked like of all things a bookshop, but inside it was pure infantry barracks; and what the old man had in the back was fantastic. He had never seen anything quite like it.

Williams had said that all he could say was it seemed that the San Francisco police used this place to build up their private arsenal. Trade was not restricted to police of course; the fact was that anyone with the price and manners could probably get into a place like this one and do business. Here was one establishment, in short, where the enforcers and the enforced could mingle, cheek by jowl, for exactly the same purposes.

The line between the two, of course, was getting thinner all the time.

Wulff knew that this was an increasing phenomenon in the cities; the cops were loading up. They wanted more than the regulation equipment which the cities were issuing them. Walking around the inner cities all day was enough to convince you that a pistol would never be enough. They wanted full riot gear, they wanted a battery of devices, they wanted mace and tear gas and even deadlier stuff, and they wanted to have access to them at all times. These cops' basements might well look like the back room of this store, in miniature of course.

It was just not enough for them, the regulation gear. How could it be? The cops wanted more, they were arming up. You had to figure that being a cop meant that a lot of people would get your home address sooner or later; most of them would stay away because even in this war there was a code which said that you left a man's family out of it—but the old codes were breaking down. There was a new breed coming in at the edges which invented their own code or more likely had none at all. They would do absolutely anything to get their share of the power.

So the country, underground, was turning into an arsenal. It might not take the fabled enemy attack at San Francisco to blow this city up, much less the famous earthquake that was supposed to be due at any time at all, next year by the latest. Most likely when the city went up it would be the enforcers, those sworn to protect it from attack who would do the blowing. Imagined attack and then the over-reaction. The basements would empty and the blood would be running fresh and free in the streets.

Wulff hoped very much to be out of town when it happened, but he doubted it. His quest, inevitably, would carry him deep to the heart of the inner cities. That was where the vein terminated, the cities were the carotid of the junk business. It began in little fields in Turkey or Malaga where indolent farmers stroked the ground and stared in emptiness at the sun; it moved then to little ships and planes over great surfaces of water—but always, always like corpuscles tumbling toward the site of an infection, it would have to come into the cities.

The old man gave him everything that he asked for and made suggestions as well. Williams had obviously alerted him; otherwise Wulff wouldn't have even gotten into the shop, not with that perpetual CLOSED sign banging against the doors. Wulff took grenades, he took tear gas, he took a machine gun and two more pistols. He loaded up like a small platoon.

The owner stood aside and let him take what he wanted. He knew his customers; he did not get between them and their purchases. His eyes were reserved, calm, blank; he did not know what the materiel would

be used for and he did not care. Probably he was half a fanatic himself.
You had to believe very deeply in this stuff to get into the business. A
lot of it was for love.

Wulff paid him twelve hundred dollars in cash. He still had the New
York money but the twelve hundred stripped him down pretty well. He
knew that he was going to have to go and raise some soon. The one
problem he couldn't face in the life he had now given himself was lack
of financing. Stupid that he hadn't stripped the bodies of the men he had
killed. Stupid that he hadn't frisked Severo down; the little man was the
kind who carried twenty or thirty grand on him around the waist, just
to convince himself that he was real, that he was alive. But the habit
of being a cop stayed with you at least a little while; it was hard to realize
that just as the bounty-hunters were closing in on him, so he too must
take bounty off his victims.

But then again he had seen plenty of cops strip corpses before the
wagon came. For a man on street detail, it could be a pickup of ten
percent on his yearly salary. Not steady, nothing to depend on, but like
eating on the arm, it was a fringe benefit, every little thing helped.

"Got a car?" the owner said as Wulff stood over the stuff, considering
it.

"Yeah," he said. He had jumped the wires on a beat-up Continental a
few blocks away, driven it cautiously over here and parked in front of
the store. Stealing cars was a tricky business, but he needed something
with the trunk capacity of the Continental to carry the stuff, and
maybe the owner would not even miss it.

The owner shrugged, looked at him. "Big job to transport," he said.

"It beats working for a living."

"I guess so." There was an unhealthy pause. Wulff realized that the
man was not going to offer him any help transporting. Well, why the hell
should he? He sold the stuff; he didn't offer pickup and delivery service.

"All right," Wulff said and opened his suitcase. He was able to fit most
of the incendiaries in there, but the machine gun, the extra clips would
just have to go into the open air, no way about it. "You can keep an eye
out when I take this stuff into the street though."

The owner laughed. He was a younger man than Wulff had at first
thought, maybe only in his forties, but the steel-rimmed glasses, the
thinning grey hair gave an impression of senescence. Maybe he had gone
into the arsenal business because it gave him a feeling of recaptured
youth. Who the hell cared? Why worry about it? "Don't sweat it," the man
said. "You don't think that anyone's going to bother one of my customers,
do you?"

"I don't know."

"Everybody knows about this store. The police aren't going to touch any man coming out."

Wulff guessed so. That stood to reason; the policeman would wind up, likely, questioning another cop and you never knew when positions might be reversed. Of course he might also be questioning a criminal, someone buying for the purpose of perpetrating a felony and so on, but you couldn't make an omelet without breaking eggs and if you wanted access to a store like this, you could tolerate the other customers. This, Wulff was thinking, in the modern jungle of the cities, was as close as you could get to a true neutral zone. Here, everyone declared truce, if only because it was a refueling stop. He was probably as safe here, he decided, as he had been anywhere since he got off the plane, in what seemed to have been another stage of life altogether.

"All right," he said. He hoisted the suitcase awkwardly, stumbled to the door of the shop and checking the street quickly, staggered to the Continental, pulled open the trunk which he had left unlocked and tossed the suitcase inside, then went back for the rest of the stuff. The owner looked at him impassively, hands on hips.

"Big doings, eh?" he said.

"Not exactly, no."

"You got enough stuff there to clean out a brigade."

"I wasn't thinking somehow of taking out a brigade."

The man shrugged as Wulff struggled with the machine gun and clips. "It's none of my business what you do with them," he said.

"I didn't figure it was."

"I just sell the stuff, that's all."

"One thing," Wulff said, pausing at the door, balancing things uncomfortably. "I'm just curious. Has anybody come in here to make a buy and then turned the merchandise on you when you asked them to pay?"

The owner smiled, a big but somehow impassive grin. It was the most animation he had ever seen on the man. "Oh yes," he said, "that's happened. Once. Once or twice it has happened."

"What did you do then?"

The grin broke open into laughter. "That was all taken care of," the owner said.

He closed the door in Wulff's face.

Reconnoitering the street again he went to the Continental, put the rest of the stuff in and closed the back, breathing hard. His first idea had not been a very good one, he decided. He was just going to use the Continental to transport the stuff back to his quarters, empty it out, then leave it back on the street, as close as possible to the point where he had stolen it. But he had not taken into account the weight and heft of the stuff he would be carrying. His best bet then would be to leave it in the car for keeps and drive it down to the Bay tonight, which meant that there was going to be one pissed-off owner of a beaten up, mud-grey Lincoln Continental walking round.

Then again, the owner might be pleased as hell. The book value of this thing was probably twice as much as it was worth. The transmission was gone, the front end suspension completely shot, the car had an alarming wobble at any range over thirty miles an hour. All in all, he supposed, a certain inexperience was showing.

If he was going to go into automobile theft among his other activities, he sure as hell could have stolen something in better shape than this bomb, Wulff supposed.

He got into the car and started the engine. The car came to life reluctantly, he drove it out of there and toward the outskirts of town, back to his room. Just getting out of the inner city made him feel better. San Francisco downtown looked the same as Chicago, as New York, as all of the metropolitan areas he had seen. Past the bright scatter of office buildings, the center business district, there was the grim, grey clutter of the streets where only the victims could live. It looked like Munich must have in 1946, a bombed-out war zone in which everything worthwhile had been stripped by the enemy or smashed up by the occupants in sheer frustration. Garbage sifted in those streets; throughout was an air of total hopelessness and acceptance. In these streets, even in daylight, people either walked quickly looking to neither side or sat aimlessly on crates, leaned against building frontage.

Oh yes, the cities were finished. Wulff could not doubt it. In his ten years in New York, minus two for a little reconnoitering in Saigon, he could see the total devastation of that city. It had gone from a city perilously on the edge of defeat to one which was untenable for all but those shielded from it in that decade. The illness was strongest and most visible in New York because it was the largest of the cities, but New York was only a taste of everyone's future. The same thing was happening throughout the country. Detroit was already finished. There were midwestern cities which had been literally walled off by factories and expressways; no one went into them outside of these protected zones.

And then there was San Francisco, which by all indications would eat itself up long before the earthquake got it. At the rate this inner city was going, the earthquake would have only the rats and staggering, post-human forms to work on if it did not get down to business almost immediately.

Let the earthquake come, Wulff thought, if this is all that we can put up against it. It would be better by far to have the cleansing fire of nature's devastation than this, if this was the best that men could do. Nature, even at its most mindless, brought a more purifying form of destruction than man could.

He drove back to his lodgings, hearing the armaments rattling in the trunk, the Continental shifting uneasily in the roadway when he tried to compensate for the swerving. Outside of the rooming house a car was parked, two men seated in the front. Wulff saw them immediately, slowed the car, tensed himself to alertness as he headed for a parking space across the street. It was impossible to live in a constant state of crisis and yet—

And yet the men started firing before Wulff had even stopped the car.

The first bullet fired hastily hit the windshield, the second cracked into the driver's door in an explosion of glass. Wulff forgot about anything except seeking cover. He dived toward the floorboards of the car, hitting his chin a terrific crack on the dashboard, opening up his palms to ward off some of the impact. The car, still rolling, hit a parked car and cracked halfway through it, stopping with a terrific jolt. Wedged tightly in front of the passenger's seat, Wulff weathered the impact.

The men were still firing. Bullets hit the car like snow. He could feel glass sifting down around him. Then there was the sound of a door slamming, voices shouting to one another. They were taking no chances. They were coming to get him.

He rolled, twisted, got his gun out. These assassins did not care, obviously, who was on the street, they were going to get this job done quickly at any risks. That made them probably working under orders and it also made them desperate. The driver's door yanked open. From his angle he got no more than an impression of a body standing there, grey cloth, an extended thing that was a hand with a pistol.

Off-balance Wulff fired into the center of the greyness. The thing in the door fell away and he found himself looking at another man right behind it, this man also holding a gun. As he faced Wulff's pistol his round face broke into an expression of astonishment and he seemed to be trying to dodge away even as he fired.

The bullet missed Wulff. His luck, if luck it was, continued to hold. He had another word for it though, not luck. He fired at the man's head. The top of the man's head came off like a dummy's and grey tears rolled down the surfaces. The man fell away.

Wulff held his position, waved the gun in front of him. He had seen only two in the car but that did not mean that there could not be a third or even a fourth taking up sentry duty. But nothing more happened. Protecting himself, bringing the gun in heavily against him, he grunted to a seated position in the passenger seat, then slid along toward the wheel and looked out.

The corpses, grotesquely, were piled against one another, almost embracing in the gutter. The black Thunderbird in which they had come was still open, engine running. Quick getaway planned, obviously. These were specialists. He got out of the car, still holding himself and checked out the street.

It appeared empty. Garbage flew in the brisk wind. Windows up and down the street were open or opening but even as Wulff checked them out, heads vanished, the windows slammed closed. This seemed to be a more public-spirited block, however. Even as he stood there, he heard the sirens. Someone had called the police.

Shit, Wulff said, putting the gun away, and measuring the situation. They were absolutely unreasonable. These people would not let him live.

He decided that this was amusing although he had not intended it quite that way.

Two bodies on the street, an idling Thunderbird. If he only had the time he would transfer the stuff from the trunk of the Continental to the Thunderbird; it would be a better car in a crisis situation. Hell, if anyone tried to take him off the road in this Continental he was done for. A bicycle could finish him off. But there was no time at all. The sirens were much closer.

For just an instant, Wulff found himself tempted. It was an unreasonable temptation but it was real. He found himself tempted to stay on the site and let the police take him. What, after all, could they do? There were witnesses around to this shooting who maybe would talk and exonerate Wulff, and in any event, once they got back to New York and got the full details on him, he would be clear. The San Francisco police might even wish him well. He had done more in a day to undercut their criminal element than these same police had done for years.

Oh yes, as the sirens came closer, it was very tempting. For just a moment he could see it all laid out before him. He had a wonderful future. The San Francisco police, would turn him loose eventually and he could go back to New York. Informers on the San Francisco department would tell the New York contacts his every move. He could do the furnished room bit in Manhattan again and he guessed that this time he might last all of three hours. There would be at least ten thousand men with his description and photograph in their wallets and all of them looking for him.

He could try to duck underground all together, of course. In Fargo, North Dakota or Poughkeepsie, New York he might last a week, slowness of communications being what they were.

He could not do it. The temptation was not even real. He was doomed. He was a doomed man. He could not go to the police, he could not go to the criminals, he could not even go underground anymore. There was no underground. *He* was his underground. For the rest of his life, however long it might be, he would have to live exactly this way, catching sleep on the rebound, catching small pockets of escape which could not possibly last, being driven, driven, driven, until his hopeless war either battered itself out or set the whole world aflame.

He was on his own. No one was going to help him, no one could even if they wanted to. The only man he could trust was three thousand miles away and there was nothing this man could do either. There was a girl some miles from here but she not only could not help him, any kind of involvement was going to get her killed. He had not thought of Tamara since she got into the taxi. He felt a brush of pain and realized, almost with futility, that the girl had reached him. He cared. He cared for her. The ascension to feeling was almost more than he could bear.

Sirens closer and closer, only a block away. In a moment a car would turn the corner, tires screaming, and police would bolt from it. He had to move now or be taken. He could not afford to be taken. He was the Wolf. He had a rendezvous to make.

Wulff got back into the Continental, kicked the corpses away, started and floored it. He turned the corner just as the police car came around it wailing, almost swerving the damned junker into it. The shotgun in the police car looked at him with amazement and shook his fist. But one call could not be exchanged for another. Police procedure. They would take the plates, maybe issue a call, but not follow.

Wulff, bad suspension and all, wheeled the worthless Continental down the ave at fifty-five perilous miles an hour, heading for the Golden Gate Bridge.

XV

The ship had come a long way and now it yawed at rest. A thick pool of oil like blood oozed from underneath its edges and puddled in the grey waters of the Bay. From a distance the ship seemed indistinguishable from the commercial freighters at anchor around it, or making their way to and from the ocean but the two men who stood on the foredeck had an inexplicable nervousness which a telescopic sight might have detected. No one, however, had a telescopic sight on the boat. The two men were counting on it.

"How long?" one of them said.

The other, an oriental, looked at his watch and said, "I don't know how long. I do know that it's six o'clock. How long it might be through is out of our hands. We—"

"That means three hours," the other man said. He had a beard and curiously dull eyes, ran his hand over a pistol in a pants pocket. "Three hours if everything's on schedule."

"We must assume that everything's on schedule."

"I don't know if I can hold out," the bearded man said.

The oriental raised his eyebrows. "I don't think that you have any choice," he said. He seemed to be a man who was accustomed to and functioned within larger circles of time than the other. There was, in fact, a hint of amusement in his carefully shaded eyes.

"I just don't like it. I don't like anything about it."

"What is there to like? It is not a question of *like,* my friend."

"I don't trust any of them. Godammit it, Lee, I've worked too hard—"

"Ah," the oriental said and walked to the rail, peered out through the mist to the Bay, "everyone in America works too hard. It is a fact of life. You should cultivate what we like to think of as a certain sense of resignation."

"That's easy to say," the bearded man said bitterly. "All of this philosophy sounds so good."

The oriental turned back to him. "You don't think I've worked hard? You don't think that this means as much or more to me than it does to you? Then you misunderstand everything, my friend."

"All right," the bearded man said, "all right, you've worked hard."

"But there is nothing to be done. In a way, the matter now is out of our hands."

"That's what I can't stand," the bearded man said, and turned abruptly from the rail, took a napkin from his pocket and began to tear and fling it, bit by bit, into the sea, "the waiting and the knowing that it's out of our hands."

"Hazards of duty, my friend."

"We bring it here and then we wait. We're at their mercy."

The oriental shrugged. "And they at ours. It is what you call reciprocal."

"They call the shots. They give the where or when. And we take the risks."

Lee said, "There are a lot of people taking risks. Their risks are great too."

"I have a feeling," the bearded man said abruptly, tossing out the last piece of napkin, "I just have a feeling that something is going to go wrong."

Lee risked a little smile. "With half a million dollars involved, there's a great deal to go wrong."

"They called it off once before. And they seem nervous about tonight."

The oriental said nothing. He seemed to be waiting for the other to go on.

"In fact," the bearded man said as if passing on a confidence, "I think that they wanted to call it off. To postpone it one day."

"That would be irretrievably disastrous."

"And that's what I told them. I told them we're sitting out in San Francisco Bay already too long for this stuff, and it's got to go tonight. How long can this go on? How long could we push our luck like this?"

"And what did they say?"

"You know what they said," the bearded man said and looked out the long frame at the Bay, ships scuttling like rats on the oily surfaces of the water, "they said okay. We're going ahead with it."

"Maybe we could have given them their day."

"And stay at anchor with this stuff? Don't be foolish, Lee. I told you, we're pressing our luck."

The oriental looked at his fingernails. "One day more or less might not have mattered," he said, "not in terms of the risks already involved."

"We don't know that."

"You people are too impatient. Impatience is built deeply into your culture. You should cultivate that sense of resignation I mentioned. In the long run even ten thousand years is as nothing. The sparrow's wing in the heart of flight."

The bearded man twitched nervously. "Don't give me that Confucian shit."

"It has nothing to do with Confucianism."

"I don't want to hear it. I just don't want to hear it anymore."

"All right."

"You work for *me*, do you hear that? On this ship *I'm* calling the shots."

"I think we shall terminate this discussion," the oriental said. He turned, walked briskly past the bearded man and toward the ramp leading below deck. "I will forgive that outburst because you are very nervous. Perhaps even understandably nervous although I am not sure."

"Thanks a lot."

"But," the oriental said, his eyes becoming cold and white, "I will not tolerate many more outbursts of this sort and I wish to remind you that the risks, equally great, are equally apportioned. I stand to lose as much or more than you do."

"I know that."

"Remember it," the oriental said in a level voice and went down the ramp.

Shading his eyes, the bearded man looked again out over the Bay. Now, from a great distance, he could see another ship heading dead on course toward them and with instincts he had long since learned to trust he knew that the ship was a tow and that it was directly involved with them.

The sons of bitches were going to bring them right up to port.

With a gesture of disgust, the bearded man left the deck to head toward the radio shack and pick up contact with this tow. Going into port was in a way crazy but on the other hand, as Lee had said, the matter was out of their hands. They had to go along. They had to presume that what the contact-point wanted was best.

At least, he thought, it would be over soon now.

XVI

Wulff got down to the bay long before sundown. The sun was still hanging high above the water, sneaking uneven rays through the fine mist; it looked clearer and brighter than it had all day. San Francisco in certain ways looked like the end of the world; as the sun got nearer to expiration it forced last little slivers of energy through the pollution and fog.

He got the Continental a distance away with a clear sighting of the wharf and there he could see it, his quarry, bobbing unevenly in the waters, at dock. As Severo had promised, they were bringing the ship all the way in, not risking the dangers of a transfer at sea. Then again there were concurrent dangers in bringing the ship all the way in, but he supposed that they did not have to worry about police interference, not with the kind of security they had, not with the preparations that had been made for the transfer. Besides, these things were generally taken care of in the overhead long before they got down to business.

Security they had. Wulff could see the little groups of men gathered in front of the wharf, all up and down the line there were singles who might have been longshoremen or sailors but were not, strolling with a kind of casual attention. He would not be surprised if they had a hundred men covering this operation and he had a feeling that at least fifty of them, seventy five perhaps, were there because of Wulff. Ordinarily twenty-five would have been all the lookout and security that one would need but Wulff had the strong suspicion that they were aware of his knowledge of the transfer and were waiting for him to come on in. Severo was a weak man. He could perceive the weakness. If he had squeezed information so easily out of him then people on the other side might have done the same.

They would be waiting for him.

For just a moment that strange disinclination he had felt when the police sirens were bearing down on him hit again and he had to get through it with a sheer effort of will. It was going to be difficult and the plan he had set for himself involved the most complex of all the actions he had taken. He had no doubt that with what he had in the trunk he could demolish the ship, take out the security, make the delivery impossible. He even had a small chance, tackling it that way, of getting out in one piece if he was lucky, had set the thing up right, and could take advantage of the surprise and panic that would surely come on the heels of that surprise no matter how professional this operation might be.

But it wasn't enough. It wasn't enough to sink the ship, rip off the delivery. He would like, if possible, to get his own hands on that shipment and there were some people he would very much like to take out of this scene alive. He wanted to talk to them.

He sat there for a moment, motor idling. He was a good distance back and there was a lot of traffic around the pier; they weren't going to notice him for a while. And the Continental was innocuous enough, it blended into the mist harmlessly. Sooner or later someone was going to get curious and wander out to take a look but he guessed that he could buy a little time.

He considered the situation. There was no time to attempt the kind of job he had perpetrated on Peter Vincent's New York townhouse; he had neither the cover nor the equipment, much less the secrecy to run lines down toward the pier. Rather he would have to come in there with full arsenal from the start; use the grenades to scatter and then hit with the heavy stuff, all of it launched by hand. The ship would break open if his aim were good and it would go down, but if he knew what he was doing he would have enough time in between the first hit and the sinking to get in there and do what he had to do. About four minutes, he calculated.

Against almost a hundred men.

Oh well, Wulff thought, it didn't matter. At least as between fifty and a hundred, a hundred and a thousand—it simply made no difference. The enemy did not understand that in terms of security, twenty-five men would have been as good as a hundred. On any reasonable basis, anything over a ten-man force really was overkill. But the enemy had not thought that way. They had, in fact, panicked. He allowed himself a distant smile at that. Panic could only work to his advantage.

Two men who were near the dock strolled out some yards and looked uprange. They seemed to have noticed the Continental. Even as he watched, one of them produced a pair of binoculars and focused on the car.

Under observation, behind the windshield, Wulff smiled. Posing for the pretty picture, looking nice. Underneath the dash his hands clenched and unclenched rhythmically as he allowed the tension to ease itself out along with the fear.

Then, very slowly and precisely, calculating his movements but using the slowness to waste not a motion, he got out of the car and went to the trunk.

He had clearance of a minute or so. That was all. He trusted that it would be enough.

In for a dime, in for a dollar.

It began.

XVII

Anthony had had no intention of going to the ship himself but at the last moment he decided that he had better. The orders came from nowhere but inside; within his territory Anthony was as supreme as Nicholas Severo had mistakenly thought himself to be. Anthony supervised, delivered orders, sat behind glass and sheet metal as his orders were carried out. The field was fifteen years behind him.

But for this one he decided that he had better show.

It was just too risky, that was all there was to it. There was too much at stake, too much had been invested in the shipment, and beyond that there was this lunatic Wulff wandering around. The man was incredibly dangerous and he was capable of anything. It was one thing to meet the executive committee and deliver the word to them, then leave the room taking it as a *fait accompli.* Most men of his rank would have left the job at that level.

But Anthony, not so very long ago that he could not remember, had been in the field. He had worked his way up from a field operative and he had known what it was like, at least in the old days, when things weren't as stratified as they were now. He felt that it was his obligation to be on the scene and at least supervise the job.

Then too, if something happened, which it could not possibly (could it?), there were people that he had to answer to. It was always a hierarchy, everything in rungs, little fish, big fish—and even at his position, Anthony could look up to another level and see, dimly inferred beyond, another level yet.

The captain's room in the ship had been hastily if clumsily fitted out as some kind of executive quarters. There was a bottle of good scotch on a crude night table, a scatter-rug thrown on the floor; dust, moulding, the stink of sea had been ineptly scrubbed out. Anthony sat in a lounging chair by the desk, drinking a very small glass of scotch, straight, and looked at the oriental named Lee who had just come in.

"Everything is all right, sir," Lee said deferentially. "The other parties have appeared."

"Is the transfer being made?"

Lee looked at him calmly. "There is a question of completing arrangements."

"Arrangements were completed on paper weeks ago," Anthony said tightly. "Get that stuff moving!"

"Ah yes," Lee said, "but it is not quite that simple. My men must be paid off, their own efforts must be compensated, we have our own expenses—"

"You want cash in advance?" Anthony said. "That was not in the arrangement."

"I do not know with whom you made these arrangements, sir," Lee said. "I can only speak for myself, and my policy has always been—"

"Son of a bitch," Anthony said and then caught himself. This was no time for lapses of control. "All right," he said, "have it taken care of."

Lee remained implacable. "It is not that simple," he said.

"Why not?"

"I have discussed this with some of your assistants and they appear unbelieving. I want fifty thousand dollars in cash," Lee said.

Anthony held the scotch in his hand, looked at the man impassively. It had been a long time since anything had fractured his public facade; this Chinese son of a bitch was not going to do it. But the temptation was strong to throw the drink into his face and begin cursing.

"Fifty thousand is crazy," he said.

"Overhead," the oriental said blandly.

"Fifty thousand dollars worth of overhead?"

"We sailed this ship from the port of Spain to the Gulf of Mexico and then north. With certain stops on the way and attendant risks."

"That was never provided for," Anthony said.

"I believe," Lee said smoothly, "that there is nothing in writing. It was understood that a fair price would be charged for fair services. The price is fifty thousand dollars."

"We don't have that kind of cash on hand," Anthony said. He would have the son of a bitch killed. All right: he had not wanted it to be this way but he was offered no choice. He would have to do it. The bastard deserved it. That was the trouble with turning yourself over to what in effect were individual sub-licensees. It occurred to him that it was about time that an old idea of his were adopted: complete control of all facets of the operation, from the harvesting straight through to the supply. It was coming.

It was definitely going in that direction. But unless matters were somehow hastened along, they would be held up time and again by people like Lee.

"I am sure we can wait while you get the cash," Lee said.

"You know we can't. This has got to go off on schedule."

"We would like it to go off on schedule too. Unfortunately my crew must be paid."

"You could have warned us about this," Anthony said bitterly. "You could have let us know—"

"We took it for granted," Lee said. He stood there impassively. Finally he seemed to bow. "I am sure that you will work out something," he said. "In the meantime, we will merely wait."

"We can't wait."

"Do you see any choice?"

"Yes," Anthony said, ponderously. "Yes, I see a choice." He was trembling with rage. Really, he could feel the rage pulsating within him, rattling away like a man pounding into a woman. *The rage had made a woman of him.* He had the gun in his hand before he even quite realized what he was doing.

He showed it to the oriental. "Complete the delivery," he said.

Lee looked at the gun unblinking. "That has no effect upon me," he said.

"It doesn't?"

"We have a different attitude toward death than you Americans do. We consider life to be a continuum of which death is merely another part. Believe me, I would welcome death."

Anthony held the gun steady. "I mean it," he said, "complete the delivery."

Lee did not move. But there was a hint of expression in his eyes. "Besides," he said, "it would not be worth your while to kill me. It would destroy all of your carefully-wrought plans."

Anthony picked up the glass of scotch, looked at the glisten, downed the remaining inch. He had not shot a man for many, many years. It had been a long time since he had not been able to use intermediaries. But the feeling, he decided, came back. Like sex or playing the violin, once you got it, you never lost the sensation.

He shot Lee in the hand. The gun had a good silencer; the noise was no greater than that of a dropped cigarette butt.

Blood sprang from the oriental's fist. It was the same color, Anthony noted absently, as his own. Underneath, they were all the same. Bags of blood. Lee held his hand and began to shake.

Anthony held the gun steady. "I don't have to kill you," he said. "I just can take you apart piece by little piece."

He levelled the gun again and very carefully shot the man in the right kneecap. Lee tumbled as if the room had been turned upside-down. He lay on the floor then, kicking like an infant in his cradle. There was just a faint ooze of blood appearing under the pants leg.

"You see what I mean?" Anthony said.

The oriental was in agony. His eyes rolled. He seemed to dwindle on the floor. Underneath the yellow, his face was ash.

"You're killing me," he said.

"No," said Anthony, "I'm not going to kill you. The wound is very slow bleeding and you'll find that you're able to crawl or even limp when you try to stand up. I'm just going to take you apart."

Lee gasped. He gagged and choked, a thin spew of saliva turning into vomit, dribbling from a corner of his mouth and into the rug. "I misjudged you," he said.

"That was your mistake. Nobody should misjudge me. Get out there and get the transfer arranged."

"I can't move."

"Yes you can. You can crawl and you can limp. The hand may keep you from holding a gun for a couple of years but you don't need a gun anyway. Get on out there."

Lee braced himself against the floor, managed a crouch. His face convulsed and then smoothed as if he were exerting will from within. "I congratulate you," he said.

"Not necessary."

"You are far more ruthless and determined than I would have thought."

"Necessary."

"Also you are more farsighted." Lee grunted with pain. Sweat that Anthony had never expected to see came out on his forehead. "You have hurt me very badly," he said.

"Not as badly as you think."

"I cannot move. You go out and tell them that our arrangements have been—ah—completed."

"No," Anthony said. "I'm not walking into anything. You're going to go out there. Right now."

"I can't move."

"Try. Grit your teeth."

The oriental reeled from the crouch to a standing position moaning and clutching his knee. Blood began to pool more rapidly at the spot where Anthony had seen it. The hand wound, however, was closed.

"See," he said, "it's not as bad as you thought, is it? You can move, Lee."

The door opened convulsively and the bearded man who had been on the deck with Lee came in, looking only momentarily at Anthony. "There's trouble down at the wharf," he said to Lee. "There's shooting—" and then he noticed what had happened. Understanding seemed to move into him in what were small stages. Anthony could see the surprise slowly, almost imperceptibly turn into comprehension and rage. The bearded man might be a slow thinker but he seemed to feel things deeply.

"You shot him," he said to Anthony.

Anthony held the gun in front of him so that the bearded man could see it. There must be no misunderstandings. "A disagreement," he said quietly.

"You son of a bitch, you shot him!"

"Stop it," Lee said to the man. "Stop it Harry. It is not necessary—"

"You're crazy," the man named Harry said, "this is our boat. You can't do something like this."

Anthony let him see the gun. The gun always stopped them, that was one of the basic things you could count on anyway. A gun would always take it out of them—even the angriest. "I said there was a disagreement," he said.

"Don't give me that, you smooth-talking son of a bitch!"

"Lee," Anthony said, "I want you to go on and do exactly what you planned to. Go up there and get things moving."

The oriental braced against a wall, little jabs of pain making his face move. "All right," he said, coming off the wall, then, "I'll try."

"Don't move, Lee," Harry said. "Don't listen to this bastard."

"This is quite pointless, Harry. He has the gun and he is prepared to shoot me again. We miscalculated."

"Yes you did," Anthony said. He looked at the bearded man again. His face was beginning to discolor, suffuse. "But the miscalculation need not be fatal."

"I'm going to kill you, you bastard," the bearded man said flatly.

Anthony held the gun on him. "We're wasting time," he said. "This is pointless."

"I don't give a fuck," the bearded man said. Step by step, slowly, he advanced on Anthony. "There's shooting down at the wharf," he repeated. "I don't give a shit if we lose the deal or not."

Anthony backed into the wall, the gun in front of him. "Don't make me shoot you," he said.

"You couldn't kill me with three of those," the bearded man said. He kept on coming.

Anthony felt the gun imperceptibly shaking in his hand. What was going on here? They always stopped when they saw the gun. Didn't they? The bearded man, however, was not stopping. Inexorably he came on.

"I want you to hurt, you treacherous bastard," he said. "Three months at sea for this. I want you to hurt. I'm going to hurt you bad."

The oriental, fascinated, slid into a corner watching this. Anthony felt the gun now beginning to waver out of control in his grasp. There was no more than six feet between them now, the man named Harry closing ground more steadily all the time. His march had given him assurance. His face broke open into a mad, wet smile. "I want you to be scared, you cocksucker," he said.

Anthony shot him.

The shot hit Harry in the lower belly. Little slivers of blood scattered in the room. Anthony waited for the man to go down. Stomach wound, deep in the plexus.

He didn't go down.

His eyes, momentarily blank, reassumed purpose. He closed the gap by a stride, reached outward.

"I don't care," Harry said with what seemed to be a giggle, "I told you, you can't kill me."

Anthony shot him in the neck. Harry gasped, his hand went to his windpipe, his face turned green. He staggered and then took another step forward. Unable to talk, all of the purpose was in his eyes. He lunged toward Anthony.

Anthony's control broke. He screamed, threw the gun and, running, slammed into the wall. Harry pinned him there.

He could feel the blood from the man raining down upon him and then the terrific pressure of Harry's hands digging, digging in. And behind that, mad laughter from Lee.

XVIII

Wulff had to work with almost no time margin. One instant the men were running toward him shouting, guns ready, the next he had the first grenade out and, pulling the pin, tossed it. God help him if it were a dud.

It was not a dud. The men and the ground in front of him vanished simultaneously. The impact sent him reeling, brought him to the ground. Instinctively he headed, rolling, for the cover afforded by the Continental. The big junker shook; he could feel heat coming off the frame.

But the balance held. He came up quickly, smelling the odor of explosion, mingling with the sharp penetrating odor of the sea which the grenade seemed to have lifted. The two men who had charged were ugly wet little heaps in front of him. They lay in a glaze of weaponry.

There was shouting on the dock. Men had appeared, what seemed to be hundreds of them shouting, jostling. Some of them were already heading toward him and others, brighter or with better reflexes were holding ground, trying to stop the charging men, or running in the opposite direction. In the opposite direction, however, lay only the sea.

There were men behind him too. Up to streetside there was a crowd charging him, screaming. *Cover the rear first,* he reminded himself through old infantry training. *What you can see comes behind what you can't. Protect yourself from the invisible.*

He had another grenade ready. He threw it toward the street, toward downtown. Little crackling sparks came off the grenade in flight, giving it a halo of death. It looked beautiful in an abstracted way.

It hit before it exploded and Wulff thought that this one had to be a dud but then it went off and everything vanished.

He was more prepared for the impact this time. He dived to the opposite side of the Continental, balling himself up, waiting out the waves and closing his eyes against the white, dreadful fire. It did not seem to last so long this time, or maybe he was becoming accustomed. How quickly you became accustomed to death. The junkies knew all about this. Waiting out the lashes of impact for only a few seconds, he came to his feet again, grabbed blindly for the machine gun which he had left on the front seat at ready. He found it, brought it to port arms, checked for the clip and the extra grenades wound around his waist and then he charged the ship.

He moved through haze, darkness, the rays of the sun splitting the landscape into little revolving spokes through which he alternately saw and did not see what confronted him. The grenade had set off waves, and the ship rolled in the water, bobbing unevenly, moving from starboard to port in that motion which indicated that she was in some distress. A junker, just like the Continental. A quarter of a million dollars' worth of pure Asian gold, Severo had babbled, and they took it in the hold of a ship which was falling apart. Wulff slipped and stumbled on the terrain, getting nearer the ship.

Corpses, or at least men who were on their way to being corpses, lay around him. Some of them worked feebly at his ankles as he went past them, not so much to hurt as to make some kind of contact, to retain him. They were looking for help. When you came right down to it, up the line of death it seemed that all differences were cancelled. They should have thought of that a while ago. At the ship itself there were screams, a rush of bodies. They were trying to get organized to gun him down it appeared, but the shock of the explosion had unmanned them.

"There he is!" someone shouted, and he heard gunfire, felt a substance like pebbles whisk by him. Close. That was close. He had the machine gun at ready and fired a short burst, crouching, sweeping the area, cleansing it. The gunfire stopped. Someone screamed from a high place, a yearning, lost scream, and a body plummeted in front of him. An expressionless man wearing a uniform. He might have been the captain.

Wulff put a clip into the man and went on.

The situation had collapsed. His perception was one of continuity absolutely fractured, the sequential nature of time being suspended by the assault. The landscape had broken open into slivers and shards of air, dirt, water, ship, pelting human forms. Someone less disoriented than most took a shot at him and this one Wulff felt as a direct hit into the bulletproof vest that he had taken out of the store. It worked. Everything so far worked. The owner sold good merchandise. He would have to give him a recommendation if he ever got out of this alive, but then again he better not. Word would get around further and the enemy would arm up with this excellent merchandise. The ship wavered in front of him.

He got onto the dock and moved in. No one stopped him. Behind, he had an impression of flight. The security forces, no matter how competent, only worked for money; money was not enough when opposed by absolute dedication. Wulff was dedicated. A man appeared at the end of a corridor holding a gun, unaware of Wulff. Wulff hit and killed the man before he knew what had happened. He went on in. He wanted the junk. He knew that he had the ship at his mercy. In fact, he had never doubted that he could sink it. Two more grenades lobbed casually from his protected position behind the Continental would have taken care of the ship and given him a clear escape route. But he didn't want it. Not simply an escape. It could not all end here. He was going to go on.

He stormed down the corridors, vaulted the stairs. He did not know exactly where he was heading yet, but he was operating on a profound set of instincts which he trusted. Little fires leapt out at him. Someone had torched the ship, either panicking or as a deliberate attempt to sink it with the evidence. *Dog in the manger,* Wolff thought. The fire was an added complication. He doubted if a hulk like this could hold out for more than fifteen minutes before water started to ooze through the bulkheads.

All right. Fifteen minutes was better than five. This thing had sailed six to ten thousand miles on its horrid business; perhaps it would hold out a little longer. There was a room with an open door at the end of the corridor in which he found himself. From the room came little evil strobes of light, drawing him in.

He headed that way. The room was an access which, like the magic caverns of fairy tales, might open up to all knowledge, a new life. He plunged down the corridor and into the room, holding the machine gun, taking charge of the terrain with his old combat training. It was all the same. Hue, Hamburger Hill, San Francisco Bay. That was what they had done. They had brought the war home to everyone. It all applied.

A Chinese lay in the corner of this room, holding his hand, legs crumped under him. His eyes were shocked and desolate. He was sprouting blood. Probably he had tried to move but had been unable to. Wulff did not even consider the man further or check out the room before he shot him. He put the Chinese out of his misery with three fast bolts in the head.

He turned fast, saw the two others. A bearded man and a thin businessman type dressed in what might have been elegant clothing before the bearded man had gotten to him. Now the clothing was torn open, scratches and deeper wounds were on his exposed arms and legs. He lay on the floor, the bearded man over him. His eyes searched the light, then turned to Wulff, hopelessly. He moaned. His internal organs appeared to have been ruptured.

The bearded man was dead. He had been bleeding from two huge wounds front and center, throat and stomach. Nevertheless, his dead weight pinned the man underneath him with the insistence of life. His hands were poised like talons on the thin man's wrists. The thin man was too weak to break the grasp.

Vultures. But unlike vultures, because in the absence of carrion they would eat their own. Vultures would never do this; they would rather starve. Nice, affectionate birds, vultures, performed a valuable scavenging function, they had been bum-rapped for years and years. Vultures had things like these on the floor beat all to hell. Wulff violently kicked the bearded corpse off the thin man and, oblivious of what further damage he might do, yanked the thin man by the collar to his feet.

The thin man screamed a despairing, soulless cry. Blood appeared at the corner of his mouth, trickled onto Wulff's hand. Wulff held the collar.

"Where is it?" he said, "where is the shit?"

The elegant man appeared to be trying to talk but he was not able. His mouth strained without sound, then he slumped against Wulff's hand. With his free hand, dangling the machine gun, Wulff hit him. The man convulsed, opened his mouth. Grey fluid poured out.

"Where is it?" Wulff said. He was willing to do this indefinitely. Instinctively he knew that this man now dying in his grasp was probably the highest placed he had found yet. You either knew these things or you didn't. He knew. This one outranked Severo. He hit the man again, almost lovingly. Let him suffer. Let him be beaten to death this way. Wulff half-hoped that he never got any information at all. He could take satisfaction this way.

If nothing else, the man's pain centers seemed to be working. Agony of the most inexpressible sort flowed in and out of his features. He opened his mouth again; this time blood mixed with the greyish spittle. His eyes bulged.

"Ah," he said, "ah God—"

That was distinct enough. If the son of a bitch could talk that well he could certainly think. Wulff hit him again, lightly this time. There was a science to it. Too hard a blow would only shut the man out of pain. But little taps, even caresses, were exquisitely agonizing. "You never thought of God," he said, "what did God ever mean to you? *Your God is death.* Where is the shit?"

The man hung in his grasp, swinging like a sheet. His arms fluttered. The central nervous system was gutted out, almost gone. Probably all of the internal hemorrhaging. Still, the pain held out. He extended a thumb and worked it into an eyeball. Felt the jelly. It strained his finger.

"Here," the man said, when Wulff released him. His voice had gone beyond pain and come out the other way. Now he seemed to be making an effort to speak in a controlled way as his only exit from agony. "It's right here," he said. He wept. He clung to Wulff. "Kill me," he said.

"Where? Where is it? Tell me and maybe I'll kill you."

"Room," the man said, "under—under the desk. Brought it with me. Treachery—"

Wulff flung him into the wall and charged toward the desk. The man hit with a wet sound, oozed down shrieking again. In and out of pain. Under the desk Wulff saw a heavy valise jammed at off-angles to the wall. He tugged on it, wedged it out, fumbled with the clips. He stripped down the clips and hoisting the valise onto the desk felt himself pausing again with that strange reluctance.

The man on the floor appeared to be in the last extremity of pain. He reached a hand toward Wulff. "Please," he said, again in that curiously distinct voice. Precision, control. He must have been something to deal with when he was alive. "Please kill me."

"In time," Wulff said.

Pausing no more he opened the valise and looked into that abscess.

And saw the pure, fine bricks piled upon one another as carefully, as immaculately as if they were ingots.

Half a million dollars worth of junk.

He could see it in that moment, could see the junk watered, cut, ameliorated, combined, passed out then through the fine tendrils of supply, passing into warehouses, furnished rooms, small perilous holds on street corners, cut and cut yet again by the dealers, passing through water and solids, ending up in hypodermics or clear, white powder. He could see it stroked, inhaled, shot, pumped, ingested and taken into all of the flapping nerves which extended from those points and then it would come out, pure gold again, always gold, extending its measure of death.

He had never seen anything like this in his life. A big cache on the narcotics squad might have been fifty thousand dollars gross. But the narks were small-timers, of course, everybody understood that. Big hauls, meaningful scores would never get to them. Narks would pick up only the droppings. It had all been prearranged.

At length, he could take it no more. He closed the valise and sealed the clips. He put his weight on top of it and pressed it into the desk. Then he turned once again to the man on the floor.

"Where next?" he said.

The man said nothing. He had fainted. No mercy for the fallen. Wulff walked over and kicked him in the ribs. The man's body gave under the pressure like a bag of water.

He revived, looked up at Wulff. Everything inside had been mashed, smashed, broken. Give him credit then. The spirit held on, imperishable yet in the framework of the man.

"Where next?" he said again.

The man's eyelids fluttered. There was comprehension in the eyes but little more. The dead oriental kicked a foot in a curiously animate way. Flexus. Wulff turned and put another bullet into the head, just to be sure. Blood came out of the corpse like a geyser.

He went to the door, looked out, listened. In the distance he heard rumblings, screams, the pounding of feet but nothing at the rim of the corridor. Everyone was getting out. He was alone in the room with two dead men and one who would have been a better corpse. Little seams of water bulged out at the bottom of the walls and spread thickly, like blood, along the floor. The ship was listing. Already it had probably taken

enough water into the holds to send it under. Time was limited—
unless, of course, he wanted to stay here. He would have the valise to
take down with him, though. That would be some comfort.

He went over to the fallen man and said yet again, very calmly,
"Where next?" Speak to the dying and the agonizing very slowly, use
simple words, repeat those words constantly. That was the only way to
get through to them. You learned a few things lurking around hospital
wards. Wulff had been there.

The man shook his head. "Kill me," he said distinctly.

Wulff showed him the gun. "I'll think about it," he said, "but first you
tell me where the stuff goes next."

The man said nothing. It could have been agony or a last, desperate
attempt to hold out. "That's a bad idea," Wulff said.

He shot the man in the forearm.

The man buckled on the floor. His eyes, far away from all of this looked
up at Wulff, empty, detached. "I'll tell you anything," he said, "if you'll
just kill me."

"Delivery is taken here. Then where does it go? Where does the valise
go next?"

"All broken up. It all—"

"No," Wulff said. He put a bullet into the wall. "See that?" he said as
the plaster sifted, "that could all be for you. The next one could have your
name on it. It isn't all broken up. It goes in a piece. Where?"

"All right," the man said. He tried to breathe. "It goes to Boston."

"Boston? Not New York?"

"Boston," the man said. "That's the major Northeast distribution
point now." A glint of humor, of all things, appeared in the tormented
eyes. "You don't think we'd go into New York, do you? Why that's the
most dangerous city in the world."

Wulff knelt over the man and showed him the gun again. "I'm not
going to kill you," he said. The man said nothing. "I won't do it," he said.
"I want you to suffer all the way as the ship goes down. I want you to
know what you are and where you're going. I wouldn't give you the
mercy."

He stood and hefted the briefcase. It was surprisingly light. All of the
evil things were light; it was only the avenger, the prophet, the saint,
who found their burdens heavy. He carried a half a million dollars' worth
of death to the door of the room, stumbling over the corpse of the
oriental and only at the door did he look back.

"I want you to think," he said, "think of all of it, think of what you are
and where you're going." He looked out; saw the water rising, spilling
into the hall. Things accelerate. There were now three inches. The ship

was perishing.

"And when it's all over," he said to the dying man, "I want you to look them up where you're going, about fifteen or twenty people, and I want you to send all of them my best regards."

Almost delicately, he closed the door behind him.

The water was over his shoes now, he could fell it grabbing him with fingers of ice almost up to the ankles. Pneumonia. Bronchitis. That was something to think of now, wasn't it? He went down the hall, carrying the suitcase. Taking it had been only an impulse but he knew he was committed to it now as he had been committed to a few things in his life.

At the landing he smelled smoke. Billows of it were drifting downward. He peered up, saw the fire. Fire was leaping at him. A dim explosion had rocked the ship or maybe it was a kind of last, desperate sabotage and the fuel had ignited. The ship was fragmenting. He could feel the heat assaulting him. The fire might get the ship before the water did. *Fire and water and ice and death.*

He struggled up the thin, metal stairs. He had to go on, he had to get out. The suitcase tugged against him, impeding his flight, but he did not relinquish it. The suitcase was his little piece of destiny now, as close to a realization of purpose as he might get. Hundreds of men had worked and died for this thing. He would be damned if he would allow the waters to get it.

He began to understand the passions of the men who moved this stuff. It meant too much in too small a space; it was so small that you could hold a hundred thousand dollars cut in a palm. It became a focus then for passions that could hammer themselves down in no other way. He sighed, grunted, screamed with a flare of pain and dragged the suitcase after him.

At the top he felt the heat of the fire working through layers of clothing, impaling him. The topdeck was blazing; sheets of fire moving toward him like ghosts. In the midst of this fire he thought that he could see forms waving, struggling. Men were dying on this topdeck and yet he had to get out.

He divested himself of the machine gun, of the clips. Excess weight could only destroy. He allowed the grenades to go as well. No more grenades would be needed tonight. God help him if the pins were not secure; if the fire tore through the binding and ignited these grenades— but again, as before, he would trust in the old man's integrity. The suitcase he would not relinquish. He held onto it desperately, grimly. He was the junkman. Half a million dollars' worth of junk. They might write songs about him someday. He plunged through the fire.

For an instant he thought he would not make it; that he miscalculated, and would join those other staggering forms on deck, devoid of breath, consciousness, everything except the factor of fear. But holding his breath and plunging through he decided that he had not. That if he only concentrated and kept his mind on the only necessary objective, which was getting off this ship and onto dry land, he would be safe. The trouble with the forms was that they had lost their sense of direction. They did not know water from land, safety from hazard, and so they were in the midst of the flames still trying to calculate the means of escape. But the fire had skewered their brains open after only a few seconds of disorientation, and now they did not know where they were anymore. They would all die. Survival of the fittest. Holding his breath against that one last instinctive gasp of air that could destroy him, Wulff headed toward the land.

He found it. He hurtled through the railing feeling splinters of wood parting for him; he plunged through space feeling the air cooling even as he fell, so that by the time he hit ground level some seven or eight feet below, he was less shaken by the impact than he was revived by the gasps of air he now permitted himself to take in slowly. The air was still burning hot, impossible for a man to breathe indefinitely, but compared to the atmosphere on the ship it was clear. He could feel sensibility drifting back to him. The suitcase was still in his hand, the reassuring thong of the handle solidly in his grip. He stumbled away from the ship wiping cinders from his weeping eyes, feeling his sight reconstitute itself.

From bow to stern the ship was ablaze, lighting up the whole wharf in the roaring, building fire. The fire was leaping from one dock to another, like an inflamed lover it drew fuel from its own energy and it was cutting huge, jagged holes in the dock, igniting pilings, leaping over the oily waters. It might bring the dock itself down, it might set the harbor ablaze.

Beyond him he could see the enforcers arriving. A thousand sirens were driving their way through the air, a hundred fire engines, patrol cars, emergency vehicles were tearing through the city. The first of them had already arrived. Yet few of the enforcers had moved beyond this established line. They were holding back, waiting for the engines to come. Smart enough, Wulff thought. It was too dangerous beyond that line and they had everyone bottled up here anyway.

Including a running man with a valise.

He swerved, picking up his speed, aware that it could all, ironically, terribly, end right here. If they stopped him he would be too weak to resist, could not outman a squad, and once they tore open this valise as surely they would, it would be all over for him. They would take him to be at the center of the operation. He could explain, he could put things to rights, one way or the other he would get out of custody tomorrow. But the valise would be impounded, forever, and his Boston rendezvous destroyed.

He realized that he badly wanted to go to Boston.

And he wanted to go to Boston with the junk. He wanted the damned valise, that was all. He had worked too hard to get it, it meant too much to him, he was not going to sacrifice it now. If that put him forever on the other side from the enforcers, so much the better, because the enforcers would do nothing with it. They would put it into a stash room and after twenty years someone or something would come to trial and in the meantime the contents of the valise would have painfully, inch by inch, been replaced by cane sugar or wadded up newspaper....

He kept on running. He could see the Continental now through the forms, through the confusion of men, miraculously it occupied a little space of its own and had not been covered. He put down his head and bulled his way toward it, the valise banging, dragging, hitting against his ankles. He realized that his physical reserves had almost vanished.

He had a chance. He had a chance to get out. Still some yards from the car he was observed for the first time by someone downrange, probably a patrolman. "Stop!" this one shouted. "Hey there!"

He did not respond but kept on moving. The valise was a dead lagging weight now. If he dropped it and concentrated on escape, his path to the car was clear—but he would not drop it. He had gone too far, worked too hard to get to this point. "Stop it!" the voice said again. He heard the crack of a pistol.

And another crack. They were shooting at him. *They would kill him.* But in the haze and fire the aim of the gunman was bad. The shot stirred up ground some distance from him.

Now his commitment to flight was absolute. They had turned him into a felon. He could no longer turn himself into the hands of the enforcers even if he wished; the valise had marked him irrevocably. It was no longer surrender with which he would have to deal but death. He felt himself collide, running, against the car. The roof came under his chin. He toppled to the ground.

Got up. Stood, wavering, still holding the damned valise, then yanked open a door. Left rear. He tossed the valise clumsily inside, slammed the door and, his eyes beginning to burn from the fumes, opened the driver's door and put himself inside, closing it.

The keys dangled from the ignition. At least he had shown that much foresight—he would never have been able to find them on his person. The engine turned, perilously, the battery weak, and then it caught. He raced it, dropped the car into reverse, spun away from there.

More gunshots. One impacted the windshield. The car stalled. Wulff ducked his head below the dash weeping from the fumes, struggled with the keys. The engine turned over slowly. Weak battery. Really, the owner of this Continental had been pressing his luck. But then he had probably not intended it as a getaway wheel. The engine turned over reluctantly just when he was about to abandon hope. He floored the accelerator, put it into drive that way and blasted the car in a circle, turning, heading toward the street. A spotlight caught him, the light blazing and digging into his eyes. He squinted, eyes burning, closed his eyes and headed out on instinct.

He was going to make it. He was going to make it now; for the first time he allowed himself a reasonable confidence. They were still shooting but the shots were coming blindly, without rhythm. They were already far behind him.

He heard a dull rumble, then, a tentative sound like a forest animal muttering to itself—and then the ship blew up.

He heard the explosion as a series of interrupted shocks, then the dull, whooping roar of ignition and the street underneath him shook. Risking a quick glance behind him, he could see the ship, prow up, blazing, sinking into the water. And there were no longer any forms on the docks. They had either run for cover or been completely devastated by the explosion.

He couldn't think of that now. Later, later, there would be time to think of this, time to deal with the fact of the explosion and the devastation it had wrought. He supposed that more than a few people had been killed or seriously injured, and he would have to deal with the responsibility for that, but right now the explosion was a complete benefit. It covered his escape. Behind him, under the roar, everything was very quiet. No one was in pursuit.

He wheeled the Continental through the streets of San Francisco. Left, right, up, down. In, out, around. The valise jiggled on the seat behind him: his only companion his escort, his friend. He was certainly alone now.

He had never been so alone in his life.

Half a million dollars' worth of junk to keep him warm, Wulff headed for a freeway to get the hell out of San Francisco, the Golden City, the Gateway to the West.

XIX

The girl was sleeping when her mother came into the room and said there was a call for her. She had been in and out of sleep all day like a boat bobbing in water, the dreams sluiced her but the waking periods seemed to be filled with dreams too, different and harsher dreams, and she could not separate the one from the other as she had been able to. She stretched on the bed and then slowly, reluctantly, came out of it.

"It's a man," her mother said with what seemed to be disapproval. Nevertheless, the woman had to be given some credit. She had led the girl into her bedroom, she had not asked questions, she had let her sleep. Her husband had wanted to make it a police matter. *She's been gone for months and now she just walks in? She's probably hiding from the law and we're harboring a fugitive.* But the woman had insisted that whatever the girl had done, she was not a criminal, she was not in flight, she needed them and eventually there would be time to talk. It was funny what stress did to people. The girl would have guessed it to go exactly the opposite way. But her mother, it seemed, could stand up under a crisis.

She took the call in her parents' bedroom. It was an elegantly furnished room; the phone was elaborate. These people lived well. They seemed to be dedicated to the proposition that no reality whatsoever should intrude into these rooms, or at least any reality of the type they thought unpleasant. Maybe they did not think of unpleasantness as being reality at all. It was something she would have to work out for herself later. Right now she was too tired; her last energies had been extended a day ago. She did not want to admit it but she was even glad to be home. "Hello," she said into the phone.

"Tamara?" a man's voice said.

"Hello," she said. "Hello, Avenger."

"Hello."

"My name isn't Tamara. I don't want you to think that it is. Tamara is the name they knew me as, but really my name is Betty. I wanted a glorious, exotic type name for my glorious, exotic type life. Do you feel the same way, Avenger?"

"Sometimes," the man said. He paused. "How are you?"

"I'm home. I'll be all right. How are you?"

"I've been busy."

"Where are you now?"

"I seem to be somewhere in the state of Nevada," the man said. "I haven't checked too closely. On route 80 everything looks the same. But

I'm pretty sure it's Nevada. It sure as hell isn't California."

"All right," she said. She held the phone more tightly against her ear, feeling her respiration increase. She could not have imagined that once away from him the man would affect her so deeply, but he still seemed to have that capacity. It was interesting. "When am I going to see you?" she said.

He paused. "I don't know," he said, "I just called to say goodbye. I'm heading east."

"Where?"

"It looks like Boston."

"You're going to avenge Boston?"

"Going to avenge *something*," the man said with what might have been a laugh. "Haven't quite figured out what yet."

"Will I ever see you again?"

"I don't know," he said. "Maybe."

"Are you going to get killed in Boston?"

"I hope not," he said. Behind him she could hear the sound of horns, tires skittering on pavement. He must have called from a roadside phone, not even pulling off to a rest area. That would be her avenger for you. He was a dedicated man. Still, he *had* called. That was something. It was definitely something. "Of course I could," he added, "but I'll try not to be."

"You weren't killed in San Francisco."

"No," he said, "I definitely was not."

There was another hanging pause. He seemed to be on the verge of saying something but the words were cut off. She looked around at the gleaming, porcelain surfaces of her parents' room, the late sunlight filtering in through the elegant curtains. People could do worse. People could do worse than this, she supposed. She had been one of them.

"I hope I'll see you again," she said.

"I hope so too. It all depends."

"On what?"

"On many things. Listen, Tamara—"

"My name is Betty."

"I'd rather call you Tamara."

"All right. If you want."

"Take care of yourself," he said. "I mean that. Please. Stay there. Stay where you are now."

"I thought I would for a while."

"A lot of people are looking for me," the man said over the rustle of tires, "and a lot more are going to join the list. If they hear that you were with me the trail may lead to you. I don't think it will but it might. It could get unpleasant for you. I'm sorry."

"That's all right."

"It's not all right."

"It is," she said, "it *is* all right. I'm glad I knew you."

She listened to his breathing. "I'm glad I knew you too," he said. "Stay away. Stay away from the places and people you were."

"I have no choice."

"And if I can do it I'll be in touch with you."

"Will you?"

"Yes," he said, "yes, I will. I want to see you again. But you have to understand—"

"I think I do," she said softly. "I really think that I do understand."

"That's all right then," he said. She expected him to hang up then, having completed whatever business was on his mind but he did not. She felt as if his light breath was down her neck all through the wires of the connection. "I want you to know that you've made me feel again," he said then.

"That's good."

"I didn't think that I ever would but you did. And that's not so good because you've increased the stakes, Tamara."

"Betty. Betty."

"Tamara. You've increased the stakes, because if you feel, you've got more to lose."

"But you'll also take better care of yourself."

"Yes," he said, "I'm going to try. It's a matter of what a lot of other people do, though. Goodbye, Tamara, Betty. You'll hear from me."

"Goodbye, Avenger," she said over the click of the departing phone.

She still did not know his name.

She got off the bed after a while and walked out of her parents' bedroom. She no longer resented it; it was just the way these people lived. There were all kinds of ways to come to terms with the world and her parents had merely chosen this one way as she had chosen hers. There was no one to blame. There was no evil in them, she saw now. Most people, most of the time, were victims.

She walked to her bedroom and sat on the bed. Her mother followed her nervously, stood at the open door of the room as the girl who had been named Tamara looked out the windows toward the hills.

"Are you going to be all right?" her mother said quietly. "Really, that's all I want to know."

She looked outside, at the fading light. Inside, for the first time in months, she was quiet. She looked up at her mother.

"Yes," she said, "I think I'm going to be all right."

EPILOGUE

Wulff drove. He drove through Nevada and he drove through Wyoming. He drove through Utah and then into the plains states. Night and day, dark and light chased their way across the windows, but he ignored them. When he was tired he pulled the car off to the side of the road and slept. When he was hungry he pulled off the road and ate. When the Continental needed gas he fed it. It had turned out to be a good car after all. Opened up to the eighty and ninety miles an hour of the highways, it had shaken off all of its debilities and roared as it must have in its youth. It was a road car.

He drove. The broken spokes of the wheel that was America spread out before him and he laid it down that pipe. The suitcase, locked and double-bolted into the trunk behind, now jiggled occasionally, bringing back memory but only in flashes. San Francisco was behind him. He blanked his mind.

San Francisco was done; it would never be the same again. Now it was back to the Northeast and Boston. He had his ticket; it lay in the trunk. He had his purposes, they had been assembled months before. And now, as never before, he knew his goal.

He drove and drove through the night of America, thinking every now and then of the girl—but whatever she was or could have been, the thoughts were only an aimless sea-lapping. She remained outside of him.

He drove on to Boston ...

The Ethic of Vigilantism

By Barry N. Malzberg

Vigilantism has always been at the core of jurisprudence in this damaged and damaging country; it could be argued that the foundation of law itself was to stand between the populace itself and the omnipresent, lurking vigilantism which was at the heart of the heart of the country. The lynch mob was never that far from the Tea Party off the shores of Boston nor from the Revolution itself, the concept of uprising outside the borders of the social contract was central to the Revolution itself. Mack Bolan may have been a more extreme manifestation of the rallies of the more contemporary, early third millennium tea partiers off that Boston Shore but they worked from the same presumption toward the same ending: blow up the system. The system, constituted by the half-hidden forces of repression, was your enemy, you were the victims. The lynch mob assembled out of fear, the fear that the anarchical State would obstruct the vengeance due the rapist, killer, suicide bomber and this would be simply intolerable.

Don Pendleton's Mack Bolan was the revisionist, the vigilante, the self-imposed instrument of vengeance who would clean up the corrupting forces, all of them, from the Mafioso to the drug dealers to the anarchical State itself which would tolerate them and the rapists and the serial killers too. Mack Bolan, conceived either by the author or perhaps—common in those days—an inventive, cynical executive editor in the bowels of mass-market publishing would see vigilantism not so much outside the law as the logical, the inevitable, the desperately necessary next step. The Anarchist one man convention as the executor of righteousness.

Like vigilantism itself, Mack Bolan was not the product of an immaculate conception, he came from the sprawling, violent continent of history itself, the Bataan Death March, that Trail of Tears, the mass round-ups of the veterans who stormed the White House lawn early in the Great Depression and demanded equity. The Holocaust was vigilantism in its most extreme form, the form that it would take if it had not only the allegiance but active encouragement of the State, and

Mack Bolan as portrayed was as sure of his circumstance and his righteousness as the Nazi guards portrayed in *Man's Quest For Meaning*, Viktor E. Frankl's guided tour of the concentration camp to which he was confined. "Even in the camps" Emmanuel wrote, "There were good guards and bad guards, merciful guards and cruel guards." Gradation. Mack Bolan was a good guard. He was Hamlet, doomed to set things aright in that rotten State not of Denmark but the riven, broken country which had fallen prey to evil.

It was a neat reversal, the lynch mob as collective or individual hero and it had been exploited in most of the John Wayne movies which became stereotypes of the emerging, revised social contract: cruelty wins. A cynical editor called the Mack Bolan series "Revenge Porn" and as a working application it would work as well in practice as it would as prescription. Pinnacle which inaugurated the series by paying Pendleton advances in the $2500 range quickly found itself accused by the hapless Pendleton when he came to the Scott Meredith Agency "of having me write a bestselling series and I have no money." Pinnacle claimed that it had invented the character, recruited the author to follow instructions, established a contract in the low four figures, assumed the copyright and made it work for hire. When the smoke around all of that half-cleared, when the Agency had done its work for the kind of writer and project which had always been at the center of Scott's desire, Pendleton was signing contracts for quarter of a million dollar advances and most of the paperback publishers in the Capitol of publishing were a kind of anti-lynch mob, yearning to free the prisoners and set them loose upon the population. This was in the early 70s. Nixon had been re-elected but the fumes of Watergate were well lofted in the air and Bolan's insistence that the system was rotten, rotten to the highest and lowest arc of possibility was beginning to resonate powerfully in the *Washington Post* and the subsequent Senatorial Committee.

Part of it too were the insane Rockefeller drug laws; the disappointed Presidential Candidate, now in his third term of Governor of New York State campaigned for, insisted upon, managed to convey parallel to *The Executioner* series a set of laws which essentially were carved to put everyone convicted of selling *or attempting to sell* hard drugs would be subject to lifetime imprisonment. This proposal, parallel to Bolan's mad excursion through the most brutal and immediate extension of punishment, whizzed through the Legislature and became law at just about the time that Rockefeller, one eye on Watergate, the other on his own riches and prospect, resigned in the middle of his final term in office to become a leader of some kind of National Commission, a Commission of Correction and Renewal, something like that, kind of vague on the details but as Nixon sunk, as Agnew sunk, it became likely or at least apparent that the Executive Branch might be needing some new furniture. Eye on the prize, Rockefeller positioned himself.

While Rockefeller was positioning, writers like William Martin Smith and I, writers in a stable newly cultivated by Pinnacle Books, Pendleton's pusher, were being signed to write—as quickly as possible—Bolan imitations, tales of vigilantism and revenge porn, tales from the darkest side now reconvened to light. Pinnacle took on a slew of them: *The Butcher* for instance, and other prizes of which the most prized must have been Warren Murphy...although William Martin Smith/aka Martin Cruz Smith was the writer among the recruits who went on to by far the most overwhelming career.

I was recruited by my editor at Berkley, George Ernsberger, recently recruited himself from Avon at which as science fiction editor he had taken on three of my novels, one of which, *Underlay*, remains half a century later, my most significant achievement (whether or not the world agrees). Ernsberger was asked by his publisher, Stephen Conlan, to enter the *Executioner* sweepstakes with a selection of his own and to Conlan's amazement to say nothing of my own, I was the nominee. Ten novels in ten months...as the Introduction here notes, my primary qualification was proof I could offer that I was capable of writing at that speed in the compression of time. Like all good or great editors, Ernsberger must have seen something in the writer that the writer had never seen in himself... I had never read, much less written, anything resembling a Mack Bolan novel.

But, entering with trepidation as I understandably did, I proved that I was capable of this. That the protagonist of a revenge porn novel, that the lead of a series of novels essentially validating vigilantism would have to be potentially and then, in careful or careless increments demonstrably insane, occurred to me immediately as it never had to Pendleton but I managed to keep this little deterministic epiphany to myself for a while. The project loomed before me in January of 1973 like a patient etherized upon a table and metaphoric scalpel, Smith Corona electric portable at hand, I entered the task. The advances bought us a new bookcase and a few months later a new Cadillac, the latter a mad indulgence inspired by a mad protagonist. I had plenty on my mind in that period and a poorly functioning impulse control.

— January 2022
New Jersey

Barry N. Malzberg Bibliography

FICTION (as either Barry or Barry N. Malzberg)

Oracle of the Thousand Hands (1968)
Screen (1968)
Confessions of Westchester County (1970)
The Spread (1971)
In My Parents' Bedroom (1971)
The Falling Astronauts (1971)
The Masochist (1972, reprinted as Everything Happened to Susan, 1975; as Cinema, 2020)
Horizontal Woman (1972; reprinted as The Social Worker, 1973)
Beyond Apollo (1972)
Overlay (1972)
Revelations (1972)
Herovit's World (1973)
In the Enclosure (1973)
The Men Inside (1973)
Phase IV (1973; novelization based on a story & screenplay by Mayo Simon)
The Day of the Burning (1974)
The Tactics of Conquest (1974)
Underlay (1974)
The Destruction of the Temple (1974)
Guernica Night (1974)
On a Planet Alien (1974)
Out from Ganymede (1974; stories)
The Sodom and Gomorrah Business (1974)
The Best of Barry N. Malzberg (1975; stories)
The Many Worlds of Barry Malzberg (1975; stories)
Galaxies (1975)
The Gamesman (1975)
Down Here in the Dream Quarter (1976; stories)
Scop (1976)
The Last Transaction (1977)

Chorale (1978)
Malzberg at Large (1979; stories)
The Man Who Loved the Midnight Lady (1980; stories)
The Cross of Fire (1982)
The Remaking of Sigmund Freud (1985)
In the Stone House (2000; stories)
Shiva and Other Stories (2001; stories)
The Passage of the Light: The Recursive Science Fiction of Barry N. Malzberg (2004; ed. by Tony Lewis & Mike Resnick; stories)
The Very Best of Barry N. Malzberg (2013; stories)

With Bill Pronzini

The Running of the Beasts (1976)
Acts of Mercy (1977)
Night Screams (1979)
Prose Bowl (1980)
Problems Solved (2003; stories)
On Account of Darkness and Other SF Stories (2004; stories)

As Mike Barry

Lone Wolf series:
Night Raider (1973)
Bay Prowler (1973)
Boston Avenger (1973)
Desert Stalker (1974)
Havana Hit (1974)
Chicago Slaughter (1974)
Peruvian Nightmare (1974)
Los Angeles Holocaust (1974)
Miami Marauder (1974)
Harlem Showdown (1975)
Detroit Massacre (1975)
Phoenix Inferno (1975)
The Killing Run (1975)
Philadelphia Blow-Up (1975)

As Francine di Natale

The Circle (1969)

As Claudine Dumas

The Confessions of a Parisian
Chambermaid (1969)

As Mel Johnson/M. L. Johnson

Love Doll (1967; with The Sex Pros
by Orrie Hitt)
I, Lesbian (1968; as M. L. Johnson)
Just Ask (1968; with Playgirl by Lou
Craig)
Instant Sex (1968)
Chained (1968; with Master of
Women by March Hastings & Love
Captive by Dallas Mayo)
Kiss and Run (1968; with Sex on the
Sand by Sheldon Lord & Odd Girl
by March Hastings)
Nympho Nurse (1969; with Young
and Eager by Jim Conroy &
Quickie by Gene Evans)
The Sadist (1969)
The Box (1969)
Do It To Me (1969; with Hot Blonde
by Jim Conroy)
Born to Give (1969; with Swap Club
by Greg Hamilton & Wild in Bed
by Dirk Malloy)
Campus Doll (1969; with High
School Stud by Robert Hadley)
A Way With All Maidens (1969)

As Howard Lee

Kung Fu #1: The Way of the Tiger,
the Sign of the Dragon (1973)

As Lee W. Mason

Lady of a Thousand Sorrows (1977)

As K. M. O'Donnell

Empty People (1969)
The Final War and Other Fantasies
(1969; stories)
Dwellers of the Deep (1970)
Gather at the Hall of the Planets
(1971)
In the Pocket and Other S-F Stories
(1971; stories)
Universe Day (1971; stories)

As Eliot B. Reston

The Womanizer (1972)

As Gerrold Watkins

Southern Comfort (1969)
A Bed of Money (1970)
A Satyr's Romance (1970)
Giving It Away (1970)
Art of the Fugue (1970)

NON-FICTION/ESSAYS

The Engines of the Night: Science
Fiction in the Eighties (1982;
essays)
Breakfast in the Ruins (2007;
essays: expansion of Engines of the
Night)
The Business of Science Fiction: Two
Insiders Discuss Writing and
Publishing (2010; with Mike
Resnick)
The Bend at the End of the Road
(2018; essays)

EDITED ANTHOLOGIES

Final Stage (1974; with Edward L.
Ferman)
Arena (1976; with Edward L.
Ferman)
Graven Images (1977; with Edward
L. Ferman)

Dark Sins, Dark Dreams (1978; with Bill Pronzini)

The End of Summer: SF in the Fifties (1979; with Bill Pronzini)

Shared Tomorrows: Science Fiction in Collaboration (1979; with Bill Pronzini)

Neglected Visions (1979; with Martin H. Greenberg & Joseph D. Olander)

Bug-Eyed Monsters (1980; with Bill Pronzini)

The Science Fiction of Mark Clifton (1980; with Martin H. Greenberg)

The Arbor House Treasury of Horror & the Supernatural (1981; with Bill Pronzini & Martin H. Greenberg)

The Science Fiction of Kris Neville (1984; with Martin H. Greenberg)

Mystery in the Mainstream (1986; with Bill Pronzini & Martin H. Greenberg)